THE PARADOX STATE

A collection of short stories

Neil D. Burton

CACTUS RAIN PUBLISHING

Arizona USA

THE PARADOX STATE

A collection of short stories

Neil D. Burton

THE PARADOX STATE

First Edition.

ISBN: 978-1-947646-21-6

Front Cover Design by Debra L. Burton
Certified Proofreader Anita Beery

Published 08 December 2025

Published by Cactus Rain Publishing, LLC
San Tan Valley, Arizona, USA
www.CactusRainPublishing.com

DEDICATION

To my wife and best friend Debra.
For all her dedication and love
in helping to bring these stories to life;
for saving mine in the process
and giving me a new LIFE.

Debra, I could write a book
on how much you mean to me,
another on what you do for me,
and still, one on your talents...

THE PARADOX STATE

This collection of short stories weaves together elements of mystery, nostalgia, supernatural intrigue, and human drama, exploring profound life-altering moments through the lens of everyday people's extraordinary circumstances. The stories are rich with themes of fate, time, redemption, and the unknown, often blending realism with speculative and eerie elements.

At its heart, the collection delves into the intersection of past and present, reality and illusion, with characters that face pivotal choices, encounters with the inexplicable, and journeys that challenge their understanding of the world. Whether through ghostly visitations, mysterious objects, unexplainable twists of fate, or the weight of memory, each tale offers a glimpse into the fragile, unpredictable nature of human existence. With a tone that shifts from reflective and melancholic to thrilling and unsettling, the stories seem to evoke a timeless appeal—blurring the line between the ordinary and the extraordinary, leaving readers with a lingering sense of wonder and contemplation.

1. HAPPY TRAILS TO YOU
Lucas Barnes is a second-generation farmer with an only son whom he expects to be the third generation to work the land. Uninvited guests challenge that expectation, which leaves Lucas at the end of his rope until he receives a lifeline from an unearthly source.

2. TIMELY MANNER
Since his retirement, Gerald Reynolds has noticed that time seems to move much faster by the year. While looking for an answer, Gerald uncovers a reality where time behaves in ways he never imagined possible.

3. MOONLIGHT SERENADE
How many times have you heard the phrase, things happen for a reason? Is this conveyed to us for comfort, or is it to

let us know that there are other forces that dictate our lives...or our deaths? For WWII veteran Charlie Maxwell, a haunting piece of vintage vinyl transports him down memory lane and beyond.

4. THE KEY

Dan Blake is a homicide detective. He's calm, collected, and rational, until the night he takes a shortcut through a cemetery and reopens an unsolved murder that will unlock a frightening reality.

5. RETIREMENT

The retirement of a person should be a joyous event, but there is no smile on the face of John Ainsworth. His last day of work seems more like his last day on earth. What John is about to find will be the treasure of his life.

6. THE HAPPY PLACE

Doug and Mary have a beautiful home, built on a solid foundation—unlike their marriage of thirteen years. You see, Doug is a man with a goal, self-destruction, and employs the gentle spirit of his wife to be the recipient of the violence he unleashes. But today is a day of change, and with Doug behind bars, Mary is heading to a place beyond Doug—or anyone else.

7. MEMORY BANK

Returning to your old neighbourhood to relive childhood memories with old friends carries a unique nostalgia. For Andy Tilman, however, those memories hide something far more profound—and potentially life-altering.

8. PAPER TRAIL

This isn't Chief Ed Brown's first clash with the government over land issues, but it promises to be the most devastating for his reservation. If he fails, will he retain the respect of his people?

9. RETOOLING

Along with testing people for drugs and alcohol, perhaps we should test what's in their hearts—things like greed and power. Carmin Gallo has lived his life wielding these attributes, but soon he will encounter a power he can't control.

10. YE OLDE BOOKSTORE

Simon Smith is a simple man with a simple name—uncreative, uninspired and unsuccessful. He lives his life through the fictitious characters in books. He has a chance meeting with an old man, in an old book store...where an empty book converges with an empty life.

11. THE LEGEND DISCONTINUES

Hockey is a national treasure. And so are some of its players. Lawrence Luster is one of them. He was traded three years ago for an obscene amount of money, and in that time, he has brought this team from the basement to the top of the league. He has money, fame, and the world at his feet. But soon...soon he will discover a world far removed from the reality of the one he embraces.

12. IN SPIRIT ONLY

We all need to love and be loved and have that special someone to share our life with. Some people find it at the beginning of their lives, some in the middle, and then there are those who, well, never find it. It's been said that timing is everything. So, what happens when you find it in the right place...but in a different time? Steven Page is in the right place.

13. POST MORTIMER

Mortimer used to be his best friend. He killed and buried him and that was the end of it...or was it?

14. WISER GUYS

Joe Pistoli has been reluctantly assigned a small and insignificant slice of the big pizza pie through the usual bloodline chain of command. For Joe, this is the opportunity of a lifetime—a long-awaited chance to prove to those in the upper echelons, the top bananas, that he has what it takes to be a leader. Soon, Joe will embark on a journey that will make him the unlikely and unsung hero of this small Italian community.

15. BRACELET

World-renowned archaeologist Philip Randolf Mackenzie had spent years exploring the Amazon, making countless trips and uncovering rare artifacts. His books on the subject became international best sellers, cementing his reputation as an authority. But now, sitting in his study, he begins writing a letter that reveals a truth hidden beneath years of deception, one that was never meant to see the light of day.

16. LAST TRAIN OUT

Those cold, bitter, short days and long, dark nights of winter can seem like a life sentence, and Malcolm knows that all too well. He works late every night and takes the train. It's Friday—the car is empty, but soon his mind will be filled with unexplainable terror.

17. THE ANGEL'S BOOK

Daniel works at the Royal Ontario Museum in Toronto. His job is to assist Professor Anton in the South American Department. He is in his early thirties and attractive, but most interesting are his eyes: bright and full of enthusiasm, ready to conquer the world. The sleeves of his white shirt rolled up, ready for any job at a moment's notice—confident and secure. Shortly a new exhibit will be on display—one that threatens not only his optimism, but the very core of who he is.

18. ERNIE

We usually pass in and out of many jobs as we're growing up. When reflected upon some may bring back thoughts of misery and drudgery, while others of fondness and laughter. The time is early December, 1964. Sixteen-year-old Thomas Riley has obtained part-time Christmas employment at a small downtown jewellery store. His job is to assist Ernie, an odd little Englishman who works in the damp, gloomy basement of the establishment. Thomas will soon discover that Ernie is more than he appears—leaving Thomas with a memory of Christmas that has been exclusively preserved and set aside for the imagination of small children.

19. ROY CORBETT IN REEL TIME

Roy Corbett, whose love and passion for film have endeared him and his theatre to the residents of his small town, like fine wine and old cheese. But he will come to the realization that even some of the best stories may fail to produce a happy ending—especially when it's his.

20. REHABILITATION CHAMBER

How does someone end up on death row as a serial killer? Was it fate, or a series of choices; and what about Ray Manning? He doesn't stand a chance of escaping his fate. But soon Ray will discover something that could change everything.

1

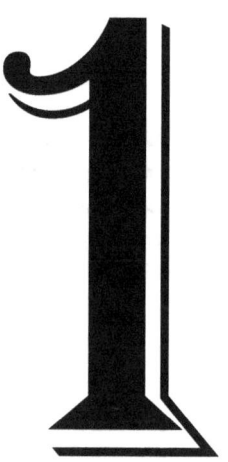

HAPPY TRAILS TO YOU

Lucas Barnes is a second-generation farmer. Content, and proud of his lot in life, but soon uninvited guests will change that. On the family farm, Lucas Barnes is finishing supper with his wife, April, and their forty-year-old-son Mark.

"That was a very nice roast, April," says Lucas.

"Thank you, dear. That was from the side of beef Gunter gave you for fixing his pump."

Lucas pats his stomach. "Yep, the barter system's alive and well."

"That's the way it should all be, an underground economy," says Mark.

"Mark, you can't have that," says April. "We all need to pay taxes. If we didn't, we wouldn't have a government."

Mark grins. "I rest my case."

Lucas gets up from the table. "Well, I think I'll go sit on the porch before you two start on religion."

"Why would you say that?" asks April.

"Because politics and religion go hand in hand if you want to start an argument."

Mark gets up. "I'll join you."

"First, I think you should clear the table after that nice meal your mother cooked for us."

Lucas steps out on the porch and settles into his rocker. He gazes out over his fields of corn, closes his eyes, takes in a deep breath through his nostrils, then raises his head and opens his eyes to the powder-blue sky. His eyes draw narrow as he makes contact with a white streak of smoke-like cloud that stretches from one end of the horizon to the other. He's mystified until he sees a jet appear so high it's barely visible. Behind it trails another streak of white, then crisscrosses with another jet leaving another streak.

"Now that ain't right," says Lucas.

Mark steps out on the porch and sits beside his father. "What are you staring at, Dad?"

Lucas points. "What do you make of that?"

"You mean those chemtrails?"

"What the hell's that?"

"They're spraying."

"Spraying? Spraying what?"

"Well, you know how you spray the crops to kill the bugs. We're the bugs."

"Don't be ridiculous! Why, that would kill everyone!"

"I know," says Mark.

"Son, I think you have internet fever. Everything's a conspiracy: JFK, 9/11, Bin Laden, and now this, what do you call them, hemp trails?"

"Chemtrails. They're all over the world and they're full of aluminum, barium, and other crap."

"Aw, hogwash. And who's doing it?"

"I think it's that New World Order."

"Well, if you ask me, it's 'New World *Disorder*.' I'll just add it to the list with UFOs, aliens, bigfoot, and vampires. Oh yeah, you can throw zombies in there too."

"Okay, Dad," says Mark, getting up from his chair, thinking he's given his dad enough to chew on.

"Now it's these chemtrails; any damn thing to try to scare the hell out of us. Next they'll be telling us terrorists are falling from the sky."

"I've seen them," jokes Mark.

"What?"

"Yeah, they're dressed in three-piece suits, like bankers."

"Smart ass."

Mark walks back into the house, leaving Lucas to stare out at the orange-grey, hazy sunset, and to wonder how much or any of what Mark said is true.

—

Lucas is in the barn tinkering on his tractor. The rooster let him know that all was right with the world. It's quiet, peaceful, and sets a positive tone to kick-start his long workday. At times a reflective moment may drift through: his wedding day, the birth of his son, or days farming alongside his father. These are priceless moments that Lucas can relive at the drop of a hat. He's always grateful to be alive and enjoy his good fortune.

A sharp voice cuts through the quiet.

"Mr. Barnes!"

Lucas whips around to the open barn door to see three silhouettes of men that appear to be dressed in suits.

"Who's there?"

"We're from Mountain Magic, Mr. Barnes."

His tranquil mood is now gone. They've awakened the bear from his winter hibernation. There's nothing that irks him more than salesmen. He leaves the tractor and calmly approaches them with intent his eyes.

"Mountain Magic? What the hell is that, some kind of circus show?"

They chuckle as one of them steps forward for a handshake, but Lucas's arm stays limp by his side.

"I'm John. And these are my associates."

"So what do you want? What are you selling?"

"Freedom, Mr. Barnes."

"Freedom? Freedom from what; salesmen?"

"No, sir. Agricultural freedom."

"If you're looking for me to buy a new tractor you're out of luck." He points to his tractor. "I've had that Deere for twenty-three years and she's good for another twenty-three before she's ready to give up the ghost."

"We wouldn't argue with that. We've done some test samples of the soil around your property, Mr. Barnes, and have found extremely high levels of chemicals that are very dangerous to your crops."

"You trying to tell me my crops are bad? Contaminated?"

"That's pretty much it, Mr. Barnes, and this is where we come in."

Lucas grabs his pitchfork leaning against a post.

"No sir. This is where you go out. My son works this farm. I work this farm, and my dad worked it since 1932. You step on my property, uninvited, look me straight in the eye, and give me the biggest insult you could give a farmer. My crops ain't good? Get the hell off my farm!"

"Mr. Barnes. You don't understand. We have special seeds that aren't affected by these toxins." The man takes a step forward with a brochure in his hand.

"Wait just a minute here. Are you the same guys spraying the skies with that crap—those chemtrailers?"

They look at each other, then back to Lucas.

"Chemtrailers?" says the man. "What are you talking about?"

"I'm sure you don't know! And now you want to sell me some of your magic beans. How did you get here? Climb down a bean stock or fly in on a broom?"

He raises his pitchfork to their faces. "Now, you get the hell out of here before I run you through."

As they head for the door, "You're making a big mistake, Mr. Barnes."

"And you'll be making a bigger one if you come back!"

Mark enters the barn, looking back at the men leaving. "What the hell was that all about? I could hear you from the house."

"Some damn salesmen! Trying to tell me my crops ain't good and wanting me to buy their magic beans!"

"Magic beans?"

"Yeah, some outfit called Magic Mountain or some damn thing. Sounds like a Disney movie. Did you happen to see if they left on broomsticks?"

"You mean Mountain Magic?"

"Whatever. They'd just better heed my warning."

"You don't want to get involved with them, Dad."

"I knew it. They're up to something."

"They're up to something all right. They'd have you bankrupt in a year. They want you to sign a contract to buy their seeds."

"Huh, fat chance of that. Well, I think I gave them enough of a scare so they won't set foot on this farm while I'm alive. But if they do," he holds up the pitchfork, "they'll be facing my weapon of mass destruction."

—

Lucas sits in front of the TV with a beer in one hand and the remote in the other. He pauses at each channel between clicks. "In Syria today thirteen people—Iran is about to—Gun control is an issue for—Bankruptcies are up for the—Unemployment hit an all-time—" He clicks the TV off.

"What the hell have they done to this world? Crisis after crisis; and they want to put people on other planets. They say there's intelligent life visiting us. Good God, what the hell for? Run, you little Martian buggers, run."

Mark walks into the room. "Dad, who are you talking to?"

"Your Martian friends. You know those little green guys. Say! Maybe that's what they mean by going green."

Mark shakes his head. "Another beer, Dad?"

"No thanks. I've had enough."

"No kidding."

—

Lucas and Mark are at the kitchen table eating lunch.

"Well, it's been two weeks now and no sign of those bean boys. Guess they got the message.

"Say, where's your mother?"

"She's doing laundry."

"Laundry? What about lunch?" Lucas asks.

"I guess she's not that hungry right now."

"Is she not feeling well?"

"She's fine, Dad. Actually, I have something to tell you, and she thought it would be best if she wasn't here."

"Sounds serious, did you have a break up with Cathy?"

"No."

"Is she...?"

"No, Dad, but we are getting married."

"Well that's great news! So why the long face? It'll be nice having another woman round the farm."

"Well, that's just it, Dad. We won't be living on the farm."

"Won't be liv—what do you mean?"

"We'll be moving into the city. Cathy got a job with the school board, and Terry asked me to partner up with him at his hardware store."

He just blew out his father's candle. "So, that's it then. I have to carry the farm on my own."

"I thought it would be a good time for you to retire and sell the farm. Start to enjoy life. You've earned it."

"That's right. I earned it. I worked side by side with your grandpa, working this farm year in and year out, through good and bad. When you earn something, you don't sell it, discard it like an old piece of furniture. You pass it to the next earner." He gets up from the table. “That’s you. Come here.” Mark follows him out to the front porch. “Look around. This was made from hard work. You can’t sell your soul. You can’t separate a man from his land. They’re one and the same. Your family’s blood and sweat are in that dirt. Leave this farm? No, this farm fed us, clothed us, and sheltered us. Your grandpa is buried on this land. And when I die, you can come back and bury me beside him.”

“Dad, I’m just thinking of the future.”

“That’s right; thinking of *your* future, because I ain’t got one.”

“That’s not what I’m saying, Dad.”

“My own son let me down.”

“But, Dad, I—”

"What did your mother say?”

“She worries about you with your heart problem.”

“She wants me to give up the ghost too, huh, traitors. Well, go in the house and tell her that you’ve done your duty. If she wants to leave too, that’s up to her. And when I’m dead, just plow me under and grow another crop of corn right over top of me.”

Lucas leaves the porch and heads for the cornfield. Mark watches him, sadly hangs his head and turns to enter the house. April is standing in the doorway.

“He didn’t listen, did he?”

“No. He didn’t give me much of a chance. He thinks you want to leave too.”

“Me? Why on earth would I want to leave?”

“He called us traitors. I think he’s losing it, Mom.”

“No. He’s just afraid of losing his farm.”

—

Lucas walks between the rows of tall cornstalks. He pulls an ear of corn from a stalk and shucks it.

“They don’t understand. This ain’t a job you leave. This is my life.”

“Mr. Barnes!”

He turns to see John from Mountain Magic. The way Lucas feels, if he had his shotgun he’d drop him where he stood.

“Didn’t I tell you to stay off my land? And where’s your friends? Too scared to show their faces?”

“They’re waiting in the car. I thought it’d be better just us.”

"Oh, you did, did you?"

"Perhaps, less intimidating."

"That's the word, intimidating."

"Mr. Barnes, just hear me out. This new type of corn will give you the best yield you've ever had, and it will be consistent every year. Nothing can penetrate this stuff. No more diseases. It grows like steel."

"Probably tastes like it too. You see this corn?" Lucas takes a bite of his corn. "Best damn corn in the county. Did you hear that? I got the best corn in the county. So you can take your bloody magic beans and sell them to China, 'cause Lucas Barnes is doing just fine. Now, for the last time—get the hell off my land!"

"Look, Mr. Barnes—"

"I've looked long enough. All I see is a snake charmer. Now git!" Lucas throws the ear of corn at him and picks up a rock. "This one's next!"

"You're making a big mistake, Barnes." He turns and walks away.

"And tell your friends in the sky to stop poisoning my farm."

Lucas walks over to the ear of corn, picks it up, wipes it clean and takes another bite.

"Yep," he says to himself. "Best corn in the county."

—

Lucas sits in his rocker on the front porch looking over his land. April steps out from the house and sits beside him.

"You hardly touched your supper."

He continues to stare out at the crops.

"Lucas, let me ask you something. You love this farm, don't you?"

"What kind of question is that? You know the answer."

"If there was a problem with the corn, you would do everything you could to save that crop, wouldn't you?"

"Of course. What are you getting at?"

"Why would you do that?"

"Why? That's a ridiculous question, because I love this farm. I put my whole life into it. It's a part of me. You know that."

"Look at me, Lucas."

He glances at her.

"No, look at me."

He looks into her eyes.

"You are my farm. I will never leave my farm. And like the corn having a problem, you have a heart problem. I want to save you too. I want to enjoy my farm for many years to come, and for you to keep going on your own will not save my farm."

"If Mark stayed, things would be good. Why is he doing this to me?"

"He's not doing anything to you. He's given forty years on this farm. After all that time, does he not have a right to have his own life, his own farm in the way that he chooses?"

He looks back into the fields, but reaches over and holds her hand.

—

Another early morning as Lucas fires up the tractor and begins his work of ploughing. There's a gentle breeze in the air that's calming and helps him to clear the clutter from his head. The breeze becomes a strong gust of wind that almost pulls Lucas from his seat. He looks up to see a ball of bluish, white light streak across the sky ahead of him. It disappears over the ridge in his cornfield.

"What the hell was that?"

He drives to the ridge to investigate. He stands on his tractor to get a better view. Looking over the field, in the distance he sees a glow of golden light. He climbs down from the tractor, and picks a path through the corn in the direction of the light.

"Best I can hope for is one of those hemp-trail jets landing on a car full of those magic bean boys."

He follows the light through the cornfield and searches the area to no avail. It's gone!

"That's strange. I wonder if the *Coast to Coast* show would be interested in this."

Before he takes a step, he hears movement behind him.

"My God! You guys don't give up, do you? Didn't I tell you?" He turns and sees a man wearing jeans and T-shirt.

"Oh! I'm sorry. I thought you were someone else."

"You mean the magic bean boys?"

"So you had a run in with them too?"

"No."

"Well then, how did you know—"

Lucas realizes there's something very strange about this conversation. This guy isn't moving his lips when he talks.

"How do you do that? You some kind of ventriloquist?"

"I'm speaking to you with my mind."

Lucas takes two steps back. "Wait a minute." He points to the sky. "That wasn't you flying around up there, was it?"

"Why not? You can also speak through your mind. Try it."

"How?"

"Think of something you want to say to me."

"All right, let me see." His face distorts as he concentrates.

"Not so hard. You'll hurt yourself."

The only thing that Lucas can think of is, "Do you come from Oz?"

Without speaking, the man answers. "Oz? Oz is the city in the fictional story of *The Wonderful Wizard of Oz.* It was a children's novel written by L. Frank Baum and illustrated by W. Denslow. It was originally published in Chicago on May 17, 1900. And therefore, being fictitious, I do not come from Oz."

"Jumping jelly beans! Did I ask you all that? Say, it does work. I'm talking with my mind."

"Lucas, I need your help."

"Oh, you know my name."

"I know all about you."

"Spies, huh?"

"No Lucas, just observers."

"Say, would you mind moving your mouth? It's more normal for me. Kind of spooks me out."

"Certainly, my name is Hadar. I come from Nanda. It is a planet that your people have no knowledge of."

"Now why would you need my help?"

Hadar grabs an ear of corn, strips it down and takes a bite. "It's delicious, absolutely wonderful corn."

"Wait a minute. You want my corn just like the bean boys."

"No, Lucas. The bean boys may think they are doing right, but they are ignoring the implications and repercussions. Nature fixes nature. We need you because you are one with the earth. We've observed you. You feel the plants and they respond. We have technology beyond your comprehension, but you have a special gift."

"A special gift?"

"You have an understanding of plants that we lack. We want to use your expertise. Have you show us how to connect to the plants like you do, so that our crops will perform at their best."

"You want me?"

"Yes. We won't keep you long. It's a small planet, but we like it. I think you will, too."

"When did you want me to go? I'd have to pack."

"No need for that. We will leave now."

"But I have to tell my family."

"That won't be necessary. Time is not an issue. They won't even know that you're gone. I want you to stand next to me. We are going to leave Earth now."

A bright golden glow surrounds them like a bubble. In a split second they shoot straight up into the sky and disappear in a flash!

—

April is preparing lunch as Mark walks in.

"Mark, is your father still ploughing?"

"I think so."

"Could you fetch him for lunch, please?"

"Sure. I don't know if he's still talking to me though."

"I think he'll be fine."

Mark sees the tractor on the ridge by the cornfield. The tractor is running, but no sign of Lucas. He shuts down the tractor, heads across the cornfield, and calls out, "Dad! Dad, where are you?"

Looking down between the rows he sees a figure lying on the ground, motionless. He rushes up. It's Lucas! "Dad!"

Lucas is standing on a hilltop with Hadar overlooking the richest farmland he has ever witnessed. Beautiful streams and cottage-like homes, as far as his eyes can see.

"It's magnificent! How much farmland do you have here?"

"Almost two-thirds of the planet is agriculture."

"What about cities and all your technology?"

"Underground. You can live above or below. We do not have a monetary system. Everyone does what interests them and all is shared. No need for greed or violence of any kind. We live in peace and harmony."

"Why, this is heaven."

"We think so."

"I wish we could have this on earth."

"You would have to eliminate your god."

"God? What do you mean?"

"Money. Your people worship it. Come, I'll show you where our problem lies."

—

Lucas is lying unconscious in a hospital bed. April is sitting beside him, holding his hand, while Mark and his fiancée, Cathy, look on.

"Mom," says Mark. "Cathy and I are going downstairs for coffee, can I bring you back one?"

"All right, thanks dear."

—

Mark and Cathy sit in the cafeteria nursing their coffees.

"I think this has been my fault," says Mark.

"Because your dad feels that you are abandoning him?"

"Yeah, me working the farm for all these years, I guess he was feeling pretty secure that I wouldn't leave. And if he pulls out of this, I doubt he'll have the strength to continue with the farm. That'll give him another reason to hate me. And I think his mind is going."

—

Lucas and Hadar are standing in an orchard sampling apples.

"Yep, I see what you mean," says Lucas. "The flavor ain't quite there and your yield is small. You're doing everything right. I would try cutting back on the water; that should bring out more of the sweetness. I think sometimes plants just need a little reassurance too. What kind of music do you listen to? You have music, don't you?"

"Of course."

"That's good."

"We have our own music. We also enjoy your classical composers."

"Perfect. I'd suggest you try flooding these fields with that music twenty-four hours a day," said Lucas.

"Twenty-eight."

"Twenty-eight? Wow. Wish we had that extra time on earth."

"The way things are there, Lucas, I don't think it would serve you well. More idle time to think of more ways to manipulate, extrapolate, and destroy, are not what you need."

"You're right. You have a wonderful planet and everyone's been so nice. If it weren't for my family and farm, I'd ask for permanent residence."

"Maybe you will. We could always use another good man."

"I'd appreciate it if I could go home now."

"Absolutely."

—

Mark and Cathy enter the room with a coffee for April.

"How is he?" asks Mark.

"He hasn't moved."

At that moment Lucas's whole body jerks.

"Oh my God!" yells April.

Lucas opens his eyes and smiles. "I'm back."

"How do you feel, dear?"

"I feel great." He looks around the room. "What am I doing in here?"

"You had a heart attack, Dad."

"I did? You won't believe where I've been."

"Was it hot?" asks Mark.

Lucas gives him a look and adds, "Not for me anyway. I was on another planet called Nanda and met this nice fella named Hadar. He needed some help with his crops. Well, let's go home, I'm hungry."

He starts to get up.

"Lucas! You can't!"

"Sure I can. I'm fine. Hand me my clothes."

They know better than to argue with him. "All right," says April. "Mark, get the nurse. I'll get his clothes."

April looks around the room. "Cathy, could you grab his jacket?"

"Better make it a strait one," says Mark under his breath.

—

Out on the porch Lucas sits in his rocker staring at the cornfield. April steps out of the house with two cups of coffee. She hands one to Lucas, then sits beside him.

"April, do you believe in God?"

"Now that's a silly question. You know I do."

He turns to her. "Something happened to me yesterday."

"Yes, you had a heart attack."

"No, there's something else. I went somewhere, and I think it was heaven. But God wasn't there."

"Now you were just dreaming. If you were in heaven God would be there."

"Just before I left, Hadar said that God was made in the image and likeness of man."

"Now you see, Lucas, that's all wrong. We were made in the image and likeness of God."

"No. Hadar was right. Don't you see? We made it all up. But there is a heaven, another world."

"Lucas, that's ridiculous! How could there be a heaven and no God?"

"I don't know."

—

Mark walks to the end of the long driveway to pick up the mail. He pulls out a magazine and some letters. One catches his interest—Mountain Magic. He tears open the letter and scans its content.

"Bastards!"

He races back to the house and up the front porch where Lucas and April are finishing their coffee.

"Can I get you a coffee, Mark?" April asks.

Lucas feels something's amiss. "What is it, son? What's wrong?"

He hands Lucas the letter.

Lucas squints. "Mountain Magic! Still trying to get me, huh?"

"No, Dad. They've got you."

"What? I don't have my glasses, what's it say?"

"It says that you have some of their corn on your property and they want payment for using their seeds."

"What the hell are they talking about? I've never used their stupid beans! So, what do they want?"

"Money," says Mark. "They say you owe them $350,000."

Lucas drops his coffee cup to the porch floor.

—

The family has gathered in their lawyer's office sitting on the edge of their seats after explaining their dilemma.

"I've heard of this before," says the lawyer. "Lucas, this is bad news. From what I understand they are in their rights if you have their corn on your property."

"But I didn't steal their damn beans! Didn't want those beans—told them to their faces—told them not to come back."

"I know you wouldn't steal their seeds."

"Then why is this happening?" asks April.

"I did a little investigating right after your phone call. Do you know Sam Cosgrove?"

"Sure, we know Sam," says Mark.

"Sam uses those seeds."

"Sam?" says Lucas. "Traitor! Well that's too bad for Sam. But what's that got to do with me?"

"Sam lives west of you, doesn't he?"

"About a mile and a half," says Lucas.

"The wind blows from west to east," says the lawyer.

"Are you trying to tell us his seeds blew into our crops?" asks Mark.

"Not the seeds, the pollen."

"But that ain't fair!" says Lucas. "We don't have control over that!"

"According to the law, they have a patent and it was violated."

"Theirs was violated! And what about them violating my crops? Don't I have any rights! Am I supposed to go out and pull every stalk of theirs out of my fields?"

"This may seem harsh, Lucas, but you'll either have to pay it, fight it, or sell your farm."

—

The mood around the kitchen table is sombre. Sandwiches sit on their plates, but no one is eating. They look comatose as they stare into space.

April picks up her sandwich. “Well, I think we should at least eat something. Nourishment might help us to clear our heads.”

“The only thing we’ll be clearing is the furniture,” says Lucas.

He turns to Mark. “I guess that saying is true. Be careful what you wish for. Looks like you win, son. I will be retiring.”

“Don’t talk like that, Dad. There must be something we can do?”

“Well,” says Lucas as he stands. “When you figure out what that is, let me know.”

“What about your lunch?” asks April.

“Guess I’ll have that for supper, if I’m even hungry then. I’m going out to see the only friends I have left.”

“What friends?”

“My corn.”

—

Lucas walks between the rows of corn and settles himself on a bale of hay at the end of the row.

“I don’t know how to fight this. Looks like it’ll be the last nail in the coffin. I don’t know what to do.” He looks at the ear of corn he plucked as he walked by it. “To tell you that you’ve served me well just don’t do it. You’ve given me so much in return, and for that I’m very grateful. We’ve had a wonderful friendship. If I could leave this world knowing that—”

“Dad!”

Lucas looks up to see an out of breath Mark running toward him.

“Dad, we just got a call from the lawyer!”

“What’s he want to tell me now? We’ve got a week to get off the farm?”

“No!” He said...maybe...the bean boys are bluffing.”

“Bluffing?”

“Yeah, he said that since they haven’t been able to get you to sign a contract, this is an easier way to get you to sign, by threatening you with prosecution.”

“You mean they’re lyin’?”

"He said it's been done before. If they can scare you enough to sign, it beats taking you to court. All we have to do is get two independent studies to show that we don't have their corn on our property. It's worth a try, Dad."

"Lyin' bean bags, let's do it."

—

The family sits quietly on the porch. Mark holds the phone in his hand as they wait for the most important call of their lives.

Lucas looks at Mark. "You sure they said they'd call today?"

"Yes, Dad. They said by two o'clock."

Lucas checks his watch. "It's five after. This is like waiting for your cancer results."

He gets up and heads into the house. "I'm going in for a shot of whisky."

Ring!

"Here it is!" says Mark. "Hello! Yes, this is his son. Yes." Mark's expression says it all. "Yes, I'll...I'll tell him. Thanks."

He looks up at Lucas standing over him. "We've got their corn."

Lucas continues into the house.

"Dad." Lucas turns back. "You might as well bring out the bottle."

—

Lucas is sound asleep on the porch. An empty whisky bottle and glass rests on a small table beside him. April peers out the door at him, then looks back into the house. She whispers to Mark, and he joins her at the door.

"Do you think we should leave him there?"

He looks to the sky.

"It's a nice night. I'm sure he'll be fine."

"I'll get a blanket. You rest his feet on the footstool."

The air is still. It's a peaceful night with only the crickets and a few cicadas breaking the silence. The porch light glows and Lucas is comfy-cozy with his blanket and footstool. The stillness is interrupted by a sudden breeze and the porch light flickers then sputters out. A large ball of light fills the porch. Both the light and the breeze then dissipate as the porch light resumes its normal glow. A familiar, gentle voice breaks the quiet.

"Lucas, Lucas."

Lucas stirs then takes his time opening his eyes. He looks up to see Hadar standing over him.

"Hadar?"

"Hello, Lucas."

Lucas sits up and grabs his head. "Oh, that hurts. Hadar, what are you doing here?"

"I sensed you had a problem."

"You must be login' a hell of a lot of air miles. Believe me, Hadar, there's nothing you can do."

"Is there something wrong with your corn? By the way, our crops are doing much better. You made a big difference for us."

"I'm glad. Wish I could make a difference for myself."

"Bean boys again?"

"Their pollen blew on my land and they want to sue me. I'm not just going to lose my corn, I'm going to lose my farm. And if that happens, well, there won't be much left, including me."

"I can fix that for you. The bean boys problem will be gone tomorrow morning at sunrise

"You can do that? But how—"

"Dad?"

Lucas turns to see Mark at the door.

"Dad, are you all right?"

"Yeah, I'm fine. Hadar here was just telling me," he turns to Hadar. "He's gone! Anyway, he's going to fix this problem with the bean boys tomorrow morning."

"Hadar? Tomorrow morning? Well, that's great, Dad. How about coming into the house now and getting some sleep?"

"Yep, I want to be up bright and early to see that."

Mark mutters to himself, "I can hardly wait."

—

April is at the stove making breakfast while Mark sits at the table waiting to be served. Lucas enters the kitchen pulling up his suspenders.

"You ready for breakfast?" she asks.

"Not right yet. I'm going out to see what Hadar's going to do."

He looks at Mark. "You coming?"

"No, Dad. You let me know when it all goes down."

"How 'bout you, April?"

"Lucas, I'm making breakfast."

"All right, suit yourself. I guess saving the farm ain't that important." Lucas walks out the door.

"Mark, I'm worried about your father."

"I am too, Mom. I think that heart attack changed him. I don't know if he's losing his mind or creating a new one."

Lucas leans on the railing of the porch, gazing at the sunrise over the cornfield.

"Okay, Hadar, make my day."

A gentle breeze begins to blow. A ball of golden light streaks across the sky and lands behind the cornfields and explodes without a sound, illuminating the sunrise with a gold mist that begins to spread over the fields.

"Yahoo! That a boy, Hadar!"

Mark and April rush out from the house.

"Dad, what is it?"

"What's wrong, Lucas?"

"What's wrong? Everything's right. Look," pointing to the mist.

"Dad, what are we looking at?"

"Can't you see it—the mist? It's Hadar. He's getting rid of the bean boys' corn."

April walks up behind Lucas and puts her arms around him.

"Lucas, that's just the morning mist," she says in a gentle voice. "You know. The dew that so often appears after a cool night."

He turns to her. "No, April. Not this time. Hadar brought it. He came and spread the mist over the fields to get rid of the bad corn."

She stares at him for a moment then bursts into tears. "Oh, my God! What's happened to you?"

—

Mark sips coffee as April places breakfast in front of Lucas.

"Boy, am I hungry now," he says. "All our worries are over."

April and Mark exchange a glance.

"Now, Mark," says Lucas biting into a sausage. "This is what I need you to do. Call up those guys to check the corn again."

"Dad, I can't do that. They'll think we don't trust their judgement. And, they'd think I was crazy."

"They won't think you're crazy when the results come back the corn is bean-boy free! Call them this morning. I'm going to nip this in the bud."

"For Christ's sake, Dad. This is ridiculous."

"Ridiculous, is it? Don't you want to save this farm? Maybe you don't. You won't be here anyway."

"Of course, I want to save the farm."

"Then act like it and call them up. Never mind, get me the phone. I'll call myself."

"Fine."

April is so distraught, she covers her mouth with her hands and rushes out of the room. Mark hands Lucas the phone.

"What's the number?" asks Lucas.

Mark hands him a business card.

Lucas takes his glasses out of his shirt pocket and dials the number.

"Good morning. This is Lucas Barnes. Yes, I did get the information, thank you. I would like you to come back and do another test. I know, but I believe the results will be different this time. Humour me. I'll pay you double if that's what it takes. Thanks." He hangs up. "Done." He looks at Mark. "Now, was that so hard?"

—

Lucas is in the barn standing at his workbench, tinkering and humming to himself.

"Dad!"

"In here," says Lucas.

Mark approaches with a stunned look on his face.

"Hear anything yet?" asks Lucas.

"Yeah, I did."

"Well, what they say?"

"They said, we're clean...We don't have their corn"

"Yes! I told you. What's the matter? You don't look very happy."

"No, I'm happy. I just don't understand it."

"It was all Hadar's doing. See, you do something nice for someone and they return the favour, even if they're on another planet."

"I don't know how this happened, but Dad, I've got to tell you, I still think this Hadar character just lives in your mind."

"You think I'm crazy, do you? And there you are giving me all those conspiracy theories and talk about aliens. So I actually meet one. Go to his planet and he takes time out of his twenty-eight-hour day to come here to save our farm. Now I'm the lunatic. Son, you just don't make any sense." Lucas walks away.

—

The family and Cathy are finishing dinner.

"Oh, my God, I'm so stuffed," says Mark. "That was such an excellent dinner, Mom."

"I do my best," she says with a smile.

"See what you'll be missing by living in the city," says Lucas.

Cathy and Mark give each other a look.

"Mom, Dad," says Mark. "We've got something to tell you."

"What now? You're moving to China?" asks Lucas.

Mark looks at Cathy and they both smile.

"No, we're staying here," says Mark.

"You're what?" says Lucas.

"Oh, that's wonderful!" says April.

"You mean no hardware store?" asks Lucas.

"Nope."

"Now what made you change your mind?"

"Well, I just realized how important this farm was to me by knowing how much it meant to you."

Upon hearing that Lucas pulls a handkerchief from his pocket and wipes moisture from his eyes.

"Between hearing that and getting rid of the bean boys, I'm the happiest man alive."

"Oh, there's one more thing," says Mark as he looks to Cathy. "Sweetheart?"

All eyes are on Cathy.

"We're going to have a baby," says Cathy with a pink face and the broadest of smiles.

"Oh my God! That's wonderful! I think I'm going to cry. No, I *am* going to cry," says April, as she gets up from the table and walks over to Cathy for a big hug.

There's a huge smile from Lucas.

"Another generation in the works, and life doesn't get much better than this. I can't wait to tell Hadar the news."

The others look at each other, then to Lucas with concern.

April shakes it off. "Well, by the time I clear the table, you just might have some room for my lemon meringue pie."

"I can't remember a time when there wasn't room for your pie, Mom. Now I think you and Dad should go and rest up on the porch, and let Cathy and me deal with kitchen duties."

"That sounds good to me," says Lucas. "Come on, April, before he changes his mind."

Lucas sits in his rocker with April beside him as they gaze on the sunset over the fields.

"Well, April, we made it through another disaster."

"Lucas, I don't think I've ever been so frightened in my life. I couldn't imagine losing our farm."

"Me either. And thanks to Hadar we don't have to worry anymore. Somehow, I think he'll always be there for us."

She turns to him and holds his hand.

"Lucas, where did this Hadar come from?"

"I told you, April. He came from another planet. He needed some help with his crops, took me to his planet, I helped him and then he paid me back by saving the farm."

"Lucas, if I were telling you this story, wouldn't you think it to be a little far-fetched?"

"Far-fetched?"

"Yes. Aliens flying down to earth, then taking you to their planet, and bringing you back. You were always against any notion of supernatural things or creatures from other worlds."

"But that's just it, April. Hadar looks and acts like us. Well, except for the part where he talks to me through his mind. But other than that, there's no difference between us. And his world is much better than ours. There's no stealing, fighting or wars. No money, credit cards, or taxes; just a peaceful, harmonious life."

"And no God."

"That's right. Why would you need one? There is nothing broken to fix."

She shakes her head. "Oh, Lucas."

"I'll ask Hadar to take us both back to his planet. You'll see what a beautiful place it is. I'm going to grab a beer. Can I get you anything?"

"No, it's okay, dear, you go ahead."

Mark and Cathy are putting the last of the dishes in the dishwasher as Lucas walks in.

"Looks like you two were made for kitchen duty. Got a little thirsty, so I came in for a beer."

"Getting dry from all that heavy conversation, are you, Dad?"

"Just telling your mother about Hadar."

Mark rolls his eyes. "Oh yeah, and how is the old boy? Still flying around?" Cathy gives him a prod.

Lucas reaches into the fridge and grabs a beer. "I can tell you one thing," he smiles. "He ain't no smart ass." And with that, he walks back out on the porch.

"I guess the only way anyone is going to believe there's a Hadar is for me to invite him over for supper. Your son thinks I'm full of beans too."

He turns to April, who has been staring out at the fields.

"So, when do you think I should ask him over for supper?" She doesn't respond. "April?"

He gently holds her hand and she slumps into his side. "No, April, no." He puts his arm around her and holds her tight, then with tears in his eyes, whispers to her. "April, my farm."

—

Cathy is in the kitchen making sandwiches for lunch. She has ballooned into her second trimester.

Mark walks in and asks, "Did you tell Dad lunch is ready?"

"Yeah, I did. He just wants to sit there on the porch, staring out at the cornfield, like he's waiting for something. You think it's Hadar?"

"Maybe, I don't know. He hasn't mentioned him. I think it's my mother, and I'm sure that will never go away. Did you know that they first met in grade school?"

"Wow. That's a long time to know someone, and to be in love with them all these years is even more remarkable today." She puts a sandwich on a plate. "Here, see if he'll eat this. He loves corned beef on rye."

Lucas sits comfortably with one hand on the armrest of April's vacant chair. Mark steps out with the sandwich in hand.

"Dad, Cathy made your favourite sandwich, corned beef on rye."

Lucas's eyes are fixed on the field.

"Dad?"

He turns to Mark. "Hm. What's that?"

"I said Cathy made your favourite sandwich."

"Oh. Oh that's nice. Tell her thanks. You can put it on the table."

Mark places it on the table and decides to sit beside him.

"Son, would you mind sitting on the other side of me. That's your mother's chair."

"Sure. Dad, is there anything I can do for you? I hate to see you like this."

"Like what?"

"You know, just sitting here all day, looking out like you're waiting for something, or someone."

"You mean, Hadar?"

"Well, are you?"

"You still don't believe he exists, do you?"

"I believe that you believe he does."

"That's the same thing. Well, I've got news for you. He told me that anytime I wanted to leave and live on his planet, I was welcome. So, I'm thinking of taking him up on that offer. There's no reason for me to hang around here anymore. You have a family now and I have nothing. The farm is yours, Mark."

"Dad, you said the farm was your life."

"I think what I really meant was, your mother was my farm."

A gentle breeze and the chirping of birds bring a moment of reflection.

"No, when Hadar shows up, I'm going back with him. It's a beautiful place, and so are the people. Who knows, son, maybe there'll be a time you'll believe it too and we can all live there."

"Yeah, okay, Dad." He gets up to leave. "Don't forget to eat your sandwich."

—

Mark and Cathy are cuddled up on the couch watching TV.

"I think I'll go and see how he's doing out there. It's been over an hour."

"Okay, sweetheart," says Cathy. "I'll start supper after this show."

Mark steps out on the porch. The rocking chair is empty, but the sandwich is still there. He looks to the cornfield to see Lucas just about to enter the rows of corn.

"Dad!"

Lucas turns and waves to him, then disappears into the field. Mark notices a glowing, gold ball of light hovering at the back of the field.

"Dad!"

Cathy steps out of the house. "What is it, Mark! Where's Dad?"

"He went into the cornfield. You wait here."

Mark follows the glowing light. He sees Lucas in the distance.

"Dad! Dad—where are you going?"

Lucas continues until he reaches a clearing where the glow is all-encompassing. Mark enters the area just in time to get a glimpse of Lucas and Hadar side by side.

"Dad! Hadar?"

Lucas smiles at him and waves, "Good-bye, son!"

With that they shoot straight up into the sky and vanish.

"Holy cow! Dad!"

He stares at the sky for a moment in disbelief. "How do I explain this?" As he turns away he's stunned to see Lucas lying motionless on the ground. Mark drops to his knees. "Dad!"

—

Lucas and Hadar stand on a hilltop overlooking farmland and orchards.

"Lucas," says Hadar, pointing. "You see that river down there and the farmhouse beside it?"

"It's beautiful."

"It's yours."

"Mine?"

"Yes." Hadar smiles. "Why don't you go down and have a closer look?"

A breeze pushes through a field of tall, luscious grass like ocean waves. The front door of the farmhouse opens and a figure steps out.

Lucas strains his eyes to focus.

"April? Oh, my God, it's April!"

April smiles. "Lucas!"

They run to each other and embrace with kisses and tears.

April says, "I have my farm back."

Lucas replies, "Me too."

2

TIMELY MANNER

Since his retirement, Gerald Reynolds has noticed that time seems to move much faster by the year. While looking for an answer, Gerald uncovers a reality where time behaves in ways he never imagined possible.

—

Every morning, at seven-thirty, Gerald Reynolds leaves the house and walks down the street for his breakfast of sausages and eggs at Auntie May's. When available, he would seat himself in the booth at the far back next to the kitchen. After years of deafening noise from the factory, he found the atmosphere of clattering dishes and conversations soothing to his ears. It also allowed him the privacy to read the morning paper undisturbed.

On this particular morning as he dipped his last piece of toast into the egg yolk, he overheard an elderly gentleman in the next booth exclaim to his friend, "The older I get, the faster time goes by. I'm being robbed!"

His friend added, "Time stands still for no man, especially seniors."

Gerald had removed the shackles of the workforce a year early and knew exactly what the man was talking about, and also wondered why that was.

Why does this illusion feel so real? he thought. You would think that after you exit your working life and have less to do and more time to do it, time would slow to a snail's pace. At that moment his memory immediately flashed back to his childhood. When I was a kid, I lived every waking minute with energy and gusto; my days were jam-packed with things to do. Sixteen-hour days back then seemed more like twenty.

The logic didn't add up for Gerald. There had to be a reason for this, he thought. If I could find out what that was, perhaps I might be able to slow my life down to the time clock of my youth. The words *time* and *clock* lingered in his mind. He began to ask himself if it was possible the earth had sped up its rotation and that was the reason for time passing more quickly. Could it be possible that time was actually slower back then? That thought brought another. If I had a watch that was, let's say, a hundred years old, wound it up to the correct time to the very second, and after a day or two, would there be a difference?

—

He decided to take a stroll into one of the antique shops in the area—Rudy's Antiques.

"May I help you?" asked the clerk.

Gerald's eyes did not make contact with the clerk, only surveyed the layout of the shop and then blurted out, "Old watches."

From that blunt answer the clerk had sized him up and pointed.

"There's a bin over there."

"How far back do they go?"

"Twenty-five years at the most," he said.

"I thought this was all about antiques? Twenty-five years isn't very old."

The clerk smirked, "That's because you have to be more specific. You said old, not antique. This way, please."

Gerald followed him to a glass display case near the back of the shop.

"Here we have our antique watches," he said with pride.

At that moment the front doorbell tinkled.

"I'll be back in a minute. If there is anything that catches your attention I'll take it out of the case to give you a better look."

Gerald's eyes scanned the orderly display of exquisite watches. He gave each one an allotted time of ten seconds. When he got to the end of the first of three rows, a gold watch in the second row captivated him. It was a pocket watch with a small protrusion in the shape of a human skull on the front.

"Wow, I like that," he said to himself.

"Well?" said the clerk on his return.

"That one with the skull, it seems to call me."

The watch hit the clerk's sweet spot and he let down his guard.

"I'm not surprised," said the clerk. "I've had many interested in that particular watch, but for some reason they shy away. I think it may look too sinister, especially when I mention the name of the original owner."

"Oh, and who would that have been?"

"Edgar Allan Poe."

"Edgar Allan Poe?"

"I can't verify it, but that seems to be the story that has followed it through the last century and a half."

"Do you know who owned it last?"

"I do. His name was Louis LeBlanc. But you won't find him. He died the day after I purchased the watch from him."

Gerald liked the sound of that.

"That's creepy. What happened to him?"

"It was a strange death. The police wouldn't elaborate; only to say that the death was natural causes, but the circumstances were not. They found him seated at the kitchen table with his eyes fixed on the wall clock. The wall clock hands were stopped at one minute to twelve."

Gerald's eyes widened. "That's very strange."

The clerk looked at Gerald for a negative reaction.

"Are you still interested?"

Suddenly a grin appeared on Gerald's face and a sparkle in his eyes.

"Yes. Yes, I—I must have it," Gerald said. "The only thing to sway me would be the price."

"Because of the strange circumstances of Mr. Le Blanc's death, I would part with it for the same price at which he sold it to me. I consider it a bargain at one hundred dollars."

"That's very generous."

"Generosity has nothing to do with it. I find the watch and all the circumstances surrounding it, unsettling."

That was all Gerald needed to hear. "I'll take it."

"Excellent. There is just one more item about the watch itself. It also contains a stopwatch."

"That's a nice bonus. Oh, I forgot to ask you, does the damn thing run?"

"Whenever a watch comes in, the first thing I do is to send it to a jeweller friend of mine, for cleaning and resetting."

"That's the one alright."

The clerk plucked the watch from the case, turned around and opened a drawer. He brought out a small wooden box and placed the watch inside, then stated, "If for some reason you aren't satisfied with your purchase, please, don't bring it back here. Take it to another antique shop."

Gerald paid him the hundred dollars and the clerk handed him the box. Immediately a gust of wind engulfed them. Gerald's face went limp.

The clerk chuckled, "Now that was timely. Our driver is unloading some furniture. Whenever the back door opens to the alley a force of air pushes its way in."

Gerald returned the chuckle with a smile. "Nice doing business with you. I'm Gerald."

"The name's Rudy, like the sign says."

"Oh, you're the owner."

"For over twenty years now."

As Gerald headed out the door, "Gerald!" hollered Rudy. "Hang on a second." He walked up to him with something in his hand.

"Here. It's a chain for the watch. I have a few extra hanging around."

"Well, thanks, Rudy. That will make it easier to hang onto." And with that he was out the door.

Gerald had been a fan of Poe's ever since his days in grade ten when his English teacher, Mr. Purdy, had the class study Poe's poem, "The Raven." After that he began to read other pieces of Poe's work, like *Tell-Tale Heart,* which scared the hell out of him. He was excited about his purchase, but Rudy's story seemed hard to swallow. How could a rare watch from such a giant in the history of writing end up at a local antique shop, not to mention the absurd story about the last owner's demise, and the suggestion that the watch may be cursed. Perhaps it was less about the story and more about Rudy's salesmanship.

—

On arriving home, Gerald took the pocket watch from the box and attached the chain. What a beautiful piece of workmanship, he thought. If it was true about Poe being its owner, I can only imagine the stories it must hold; and I hope Rudy was also right about it keeping perfect time. Then it hit him: "Time, my little experiment."

He looked at the watch and, seeing that it had stopped, took it to his computer, wound it up, and then set the time in both seconds and minutes to match the precise time on the computer.

"There," he said and clipped it to a belt loop on his jeans, then placed the watch into the watch pocket.

—

He hadn't read anything regarding Poe for a number of years and the excitement of the watch reignited his desire to go back and immerse himself in *The Unabridged Edgar Allan Poe.* It was a huge book to tackle, which was probably the reason it sat on his bookshelf as long as he had owned the house. He decided to make himself one of his favourite sandwiches, corned beef on rye, with a glass of beer. He placed it on the side table by his recliner, then took the book from the shelf—blew off the dust and carried the cumbersome eleven hundred pages back to the comfort of his recliner to begin his afternoon with Edgar.

—

His enthusiasm for the read was certainly there, but about a half hour in, the corned beef and beer rendered him inoperable. He slid effortlessly into the world of the unknown. He drifted through the day's events at the antique shop, and could hear the somewhat muffled voice of Rudy explaining the watch to him.

In an instant he was walking a city street of cobblestone, on a rainy, dismal day. Nothing looked familiar, though he found the people most interesting. They were all dressed in attire from the 1800s. He passed them with greetings, but there was not one response, as though he wasn't there. Soon he found himself at the gate entrance to a cemetery. A gust of brown leaves ushered him through the gate, and led him farther into the yard. As he walked a stone path he could hear footsteps approaching from behind. Before he could turn, a dark figure wearing a white scarf and a wide-brimmed black hat glided passed him with no acknowledgement. He carried a bottle of cognac and three red roses. The figure stopped at a gravestone.

Gerald's eyes focussed on the large stone. He was taken aback when he read the name, Edgar Allan Poe. The figure lowered his head for a moment as if in prayer, then sat down beside the monument, pulled a small glass from his coat pocket and poured in the cognac. He placed the roses and the bottle beside the gravestone then drank the glass of cognac, and proceeded to leave. Gerald caught a glimpse of his face, and it spawned terror in his soul.

Oh, my God! he thought. It can't be! "Mr. Poe?" he called out. The man stopped and, with a slow movement of his head, turned to Gerald. The first thing he noticed was Poe's eyes. They didn't look like the two black olives from the black-and-white photos; they were dark grey and gave Gerald the chill one feels on a cold winter's night looking up at the stars. Poe's glance fell short of interaction, but with one long-drawn whisper he spoke the word, "R-e-y-n-o-l-d-s."

Before Gerald could respond, the figure began to fade and vanished, like blowing out the flame from a candle. The cemetery also vanished abruptly, leaving Gerald to awaken back in his chair. He immediately understood why he had such a dream. The watch that belonged to Poe, the reading from Poe's book, and the memories of Poe from high school had already been choreographed in his subconscious. He also knew about the mysterious figure visiting Poe's grave, but was stumped to come up with an answer as to why the character in the dream was Poe himself visiting his own grave, and especially why he called out Gerald's last name.

He was intrigued and decided to look up Poe's biography on his computer. He had no idea how mysterious Poe's life was until he read about the circumstances in regards to his death. Poe was found semiconscious and dressed in another man's tattered clothes with old worn-out shoes. This lent some belief to the speculation that Poe's own clothing had been stolen. Poe never recovered well enough to tell how he had arrived in such a condition. Then, something leaped off the page.

"For no known reason he started calling out the name, Reynolds." It knocked Gerald back in his chair. No one knew who Reynolds was. This is more than mysterious, he thought. This is downright eerie. He reflected on Rudy's foreboding words, "I find the watch unsettling." Gerald had to do some serious thinking.

First, it was just a dream. Second, if my name was Smith, would Poe have said Smith? But then again, how do I know he was directing that at me? In reality he called out "Reynolds," and is it just coincidence that my name is the same? No, I don't buy it. Wait a minute. Could it be possible that I am related to the Reynolds he spoke of? Is that why I had the dream, because Poe wanted me to know and is asking me to solve this puzzle? Even if I was related to Reynolds, what good would it do Poe now? So many questions, Gerald wondered.

He could let it go. Leave it as a dream, but it wasn't that easy. It was now something he needed to know. He pulled the watch from his pocket and stared at it. Perhaps there is a curse on this watch, he thought. "Oh, my God, Louis LeBlanc—it seems more likely now his mysterious death was related to Poe and his watch!"

He quickly put the watch back into his pocket. Was he overreacting? But it's just a watch, he told himself. Then again, he didn't want to end up like LeBlanc.

—

Gerald was never much for family history, but decided this would be a good opportunity to explore it. His mother's old photo albums had been resting in his basement for years. It may shed some light on his family's past.

His mother's belongings were in cardboard boxes out of the way, in a corner of the basement which he purposely avoided. He knew at some point they would have to be sifted through, and items like Blue Mountain Pottery, figurines, jewellery and such, would have to be sent to a secondhand store.

He could sense his mother's spirit looking over his shoulder, ready to question the whole event as a lack of love for her.

—

In one box were four photo albums. He took the box upstairs and placed it on the floor beside his recliner. They seemed to be in chronological order. He sat down and took the first album out of the box. It contained photos of his parents' last few years. He dipped back into the box, pushing aside the next two and focused on the oldest album.

He placed the album in his lap. Going through his family history in pictures brought a tremendous amount of pleasure and pride in seeing how the family had evolved. There were photos that went back to the 1800s with most having small, handwritten, yellow pieces of paper taped below describing the scenes and the people involved. He smiled at the fact that his mother had been so diligent about preserving their heritage. A folded sheet of brown-edged paper dropped out when he shifted the book for better light. He carefully unfolded the delicate paper. It revealed his family tree going back to the 1700s.

He took the paper and the album to the computer. Poe's story was once again on his mind with the question of whether there had been any Reynolds in his family that might have had any association with Poe.

Gerald took on the project with fervor. He found there had been not one, but two Reynolds who had interaction with Poe. Jeremiah Reynolds, whose article Poe edited and who Poe owed money. The other was Henry R. Reynolds, a carpenter, serving at the Fourth Ward Polls as an election judge at the same polling station the day Poe was found there, delirious and incoherent. There was also a bankruptcy petition filed by Poe in 1842—a long list of creditors including a J.N. Reynolds. To Gerald, it seemed Poe's fictional stories were secondary to his reality.

Gerald returned to the photo album and came across a picture of a man sitting at an office desk with the caption, Henry Reynolds at work, 1847.

"That's got to be him—the carpenter! And 1847 was the year of Poe's death." There was also a slightly faded figure of a man standing beside a filing cabinet. "He looks like...Oh my god! It's Poe!"

Poe appeared to be looking down at something in his hand. No sooner had Gerald zoomed in on the screen the hairs on the back of his neck shot up like quills.

"It's the watch! The exact watch!" He began to giggle like a teenager on his first drunken stupor.

"Rudy was right. The story wasn't a piece of fiction to enhance its value. It's the real McCoy. I have the only proof that the watch was Edgar Allan Poe's! With this as proof I'll bet I could sell the watch for a substantial amount."

At that moment Gerald had another thought. He realized no matter what he could receive from selling the watch, the money would be spent in short order and the photo and the whole story connecting his family to Poe would be meaningless without it. Carrying a piece of not only his history, but of the world, would give him something to be proud of for the rest of his life.

His satisfaction with the purchase of the watch and the parting gift of the photo bequeathed by his mother was complete; there was nothing more. Although, that night as he slept, visions of Poe's mysterious end haunted him.

—

In the morning the dreams had been left on his pillow. He felt refreshed and was still riding the wave of his discovery when he picked up the Saturday paper and noticed an ad for the famous *Antiques RoadShow*. They were in his town—today.

"What luck!" he thought. "The perfect opportunity. I'll take it there with the photo just to see what it may be worth now. I could be sitting on a fortune," he stopped short and added, "not that I would sell it." He rushed to his printer and copied the photo showing a closer look at Poe and the watch, then placed it into a manila envelope and headed out the door.

—

The event was held in the high school gymnasium. The scene was organized bedlam as people frantically searched for the right line to enter with their particular treasure. Some were handheld objects, while other substantial pieces were hauled in on wagons or hand carts.

Gerald saw a sign that read Clocks and Watches and immediately reserved his spot in line. Patience was a must at these events, and after thirty-five minutes Gerald's line was starting to diminish, but so was his confidence. He had the picture to prove that the watch did belong to Poe...but was the one he purchased the one and the same?

What if there were hundreds of these made? he thought. The rumour of it being Poe's would have no credibility and most likely over-valued too—I'll bet I could pick one up at another shop for twenty-five dollars. He felt sick to his stomach. I should just go home before I make a fool of myself.

At that moment came the words, "You're next, sir. And what do we have today?" said the appraiser behind the desk.

Gerald looked behind him to allow the next person to go ahead, but there wasn't anyone else.

"Well," said Gerald with a lack of enthusiasm, "I just have this watch." He reluctantly held out his hand and opened his palm to reveal it.

"I see," said the appraiser. "Let's have a closer look, shall we."

The appraiser took the watch from Gerald's hand. He turned it every which way between his long, white, delicate fingers.

"Hmm, I've never seen anything like it. Where did you obtain this watch?" he asked.

Gerald thought if the appraiser hadn't seen it before, perhaps he was wrong about so many being made. "Antique shop," Gerald blurted out.

The appraiser picked up a magnifying glass to examine it further, and as he did so his hand seemed to acquire a slight tremor. He looked up at Gerald with a blend of concern and disbelief.

"Would you mind giving me a moment to discuss this with my colleagues?"

Gerald nodded.

The appraiser left with the watch and went into the crowd. A few minutes later he returned with the watch and two other appraisers.

"What is your name, sir?" asked the appraiser.

"Gerald Reynolds," he answered.

The three looked at each other with opened mouths.

A second appraiser jumped in. "Mr. Reynolds...do you know what you have here?"

"The rumour was that it originally belonged to Edgar Allan Poe. But that was just a rumour, right?"

The third appraiser threw his hat into the ring. "Mr. Poe had a watch especially made for him, a one of a kind with a gold skull, and this watch is that one and only."

Gerald's Adam's apple slowly rises, then drops. "So, you don't think it's a copy?"

"Here," said the first appraiser. He gave Gerald back the watch along with the magnifying glass. "Take a close look."

Gerald turned it over and looked through the magnifier. DEATH WATCH-E.A.P was inscribed on the back case.

"E.A.P, Edgar Allan Poe. You're right, it is Poe's."

"Now," said the appraiser. "We know a fair amount about Mr. Poe and the story that lead up to his demise: turning up at a pub in a delirious state and having been robbed of his clothes, shoes and also...his watch. And the name he repeated before he died was the name Reynolds. So, Mr. Reynolds, are you sure you purchased the watch at an antique shop, or were you the recipient of the watch being handed down to you from the original Reynolds that Poe spoke of?

"Your photo seems to confirm that the two had some interaction. On what level we will never know, but you must agree the evidence of the photo and the watch does lend a great deal of more than speculation that the cause of Poe's demise would have been at the hands of your ancestor."

Gerald didn't like the idea of them implicating that he was a liar and an ancestor of a thief, and especially a murderer.

"That's a very interesting theory. But the truth is, as I had said, I purchased the watch from a man named Rudy, the owner of the antique shop on Bellamy Ave."

"I'm acquainted with the owner of that shop," said the appraiser. "Let me verify that right now." He searched his bulging wallet filled with business cards. "Uh, here it is." He took his cell phone and called the number. "Hello, Jake. It's Michael. I'm at the *RoadShow*. Could you tell me if you had—just a minute." He turns to Gerald, "When was this transaction?"

"Yesterday," answered Gerald.

"Did you sell a pocket watch yesterday that was rumoured to belong to Edgar Allan Poe?—I see. Yes, I would think so too. Thank you."

He now looked at Gerald with more suspicion. "He never sold one pocket watch yesterday or all week for that matter, and he said if he had that watch it would have been a rare find and he would not sell such a valuable piece to anyone."

"But I purchased the watch from a man named Rudy and the sign hanging over the storefront read, Rudy's Antiques."

"Jake is the owner of that shop."

Gerald's mouth was agape with shock.

"If you pass by there again, you will see that the name on the sign reads Jake's Antiques."

Gerald stood motionless in disbelief. What's going on? he thought. Why is this happening? It doesn't make any sense.

"So, Mr. Reynolds, what do you have to say about it now?"

There was nothing Gerald could have said to counter the attack. He stood silently. But his mind was on overload with this new information.

The unease of the situation called for action. Gerald looked down at the watch, put it back into his pocket, and, without confrontation, but with all speed, walked away, melting into the crowd as the three men looked on in puzzled disbelief.

—

On his way home, Gerald's mind was filled with bits of conversation from the appraisers and Rudy. Then there was the inscription on the back of the watch, "DEATH WATCH," which he recalled from his reading of the book on Poe. It was used as a metaphor in *The Tell Tale Heart*. But there is something else going on here, he thought. Why would Poe have it inscribed next to his name? It must have more significance than any metaphor.

—

That night Gerald struggled to sleep. Too many questions crowded his mind and wormed their way into his sleep. Every fifteen minutes, he would roll over, open his eyes, and stare at the clock until the blurriness cleared enough to see the numbers, which now read 3:52 a.m. That was his last time check as exhaustion finely won out and dove right into REM sleep.

—

Gerald found himself back at the antique shop. Before entering the shop he looked up to see the sign above the door—Rudy's Antiques.

He smiled. I knew I wasn't crazy.

He entered the shop and called out to Rudy, but there was no response. On hearing some shuffling in a back room he decided to investigate. The door to the room was ajar. With the back of his hand he pushed it open and entered. The room seemed ten degrees colder, like stepping into a fruit cellar. The lighting was dismal. He heard a noise and moved toward it while calling out again for Rudy. Gerald had almost reached the far wall when a voice whispered, R-E-Y-N-O-L-D-S.

A crackling rush of fear mixed with adrenaline surged through his body. He stood frozen, almost paralyzed; not even a blink could he manage.

It was that same haunting tone that came from Poe in his first dream. Out of the shadows came a dark figure, not walking but floating, as if being pulled along on a trolley. It entered the dim light of the room and, as Gerald feared, it was POE.

He was larger than life, though in life he was a mere five foot-six in stature. There was no long dark overcoat and hat as Gerald had witnessed in the cemetery. His attire was the same as the few photos that were taken of him. The only difference, once again, were his eyes: They were more piercing, darker and sinister, which created an even greater contrast to his chalky, white complexion. All Gerald could do was watch—not a word, not a blink; looking more like a storefront mannequin.

Poe began to speak, but his lips did not move. He was speaking telepathically.

"Those who dream by day are cognizant of many things which escape those who dream only by night. All that we see or seem is but a dream within a dream."

"I don't understand. What is it that you want from me?" he asked.

"It is not what I want. My time of life has long passed. Life is a world of sweets and sours; mine of mystery and dreams. Never its mysteries exposed to the weak human eye unclosed. Focus your eyes—believe nothing you hear, and only one-half that you see." Poe paused and then added, "A watch's minute hand moves more quickly than did mine."

With that last haunting sentence Gerald realized that all these events took him off track from his original intent of finding out how to slow down time.

"Yes! That's it!" said Gerald. "But how does that work? How can I have time move more slowly?"

Poe begins to vanish, then pauses with some last parting words."I travel through time in a timely manner. My dreams are exposed, but my secrets remain hidden. The span of time lives more freely in dreams than in reality. Time is everything, yet, nothing."

Gerald tried to understand the meaning, but fell short. "What the hell does that mean?" he shouted.

Poe is gone and Gerald is left with more questions.

—

He woke the next morning after ten, which was a record sleep for a man that spent years on shift work. He sat up with his head spinning, trying to decipher his dream conversation with Poe. "Dreams! Time! Watches! What the hell are you trying to tell me?"

—

Gerald decided a more tranquil setting might benefit his sanity. He sat in a park, reading more about Poe in hopes of cracking the mystery of his death and possibly his theory about time. After a short while he noticed his focus was being compromised, so he put down the book, and for the first time decided to look at the other function on Poe's pocket watch. He took it out, flipped up the skull, pulled out the stem for the stopwatch, and it began to play out each second, and Gerald thought it was a nice added touch.

For some strange reason he could no longer hear the sound of the children in the nearby playground, the birds had stopped singing and the noise of traffic in the street had ceased, as if he were in a vacuum. He raised his eyes from the watch and witnessed an unbelievable sight—everything had stopped. The people and the vehicles; even the flock of Canada geese overhead with wings stretched out were suspended as if on wires. He looked down again at the watch and thought, No, this is ridiculous. It can't be the watch.

He pushed the stem back in, and in that exact moment the world was brought back to life. Nothing had changed. People did not seem to have any recollection of the event. Then Gerald remembered reading something about Poe's obsession—his obsession with time, watches, and clocks.

"But wait a minute," he said to himself. Then he thought, Poe wasn't obsessed; he had something the rest of us didn't. He had the watch. All he had to do was stop time, go on with writing his stories, and when he completed his writing, he would start the world again. This is why he was able to create such a large volume of work in his short life. And who would ever question it? It was brilliant. But with this knowledge, why did he live so low on the food chain? He could have been rich and lived the life of kings.

Gerald's wheels started spinning. Poe was brilliant, all right, but had made a misstep in his thinking. He had limited himself. I'm not going to end my life that way, he thought. Having such power in his hands was overwhelming, and what he could have achieved would have been mind boggling.

"I could be rich!" Then he chuckled, remembering the quote, "Time is money."

"Now ain't that the truth." He put the watch back into his pocket.

"So, where do I start? I could walk into any bank, pull out the stem on the stop watch and start hauling out the money, while the world stood still." He decided he should start with something small at first, just to make sure it worked out properly.

It was close to lunchtime, so he walked into a nice restaurant and had a very expensive meal.

"Would there be anything else, sir?" asked the waiter.

"No, thanks," he said.

The waiter then dropped the bill on the table and walked away.

"Well, that should come to a couple of weeks of groceries."

Gerald picked up the bill and checked the damage—$285.

That seems reasonable, he thought. He brought out Poe's watch and pulled out the stem of the stopwatch and looked about the room. The whole restaurant was in a state of suspended animation. For a moment he entertained himself with some of the whimsical images of the patrons. Then it was back to business. After such a large meal, he slowly raised himself from his chair and casually walked out without confrontation.

Outside, not a sound was heard; everyone and everything looked like a still life painting. It was quite interesting to Gerald walking along the street feeling as though he was in a 3D photo.

People were caught in their stride with a variety of facial expressions: happy, sad, angry, passive, or worried.

The restaurant was at least two blocks away now and it was time to ignite the world once more. He pushed in the stem of the stopwatch and the hustle of the city returned. Gerald walked down the street without any repercussions; no one ran up to apprehend him. Now, that was easy, he thought.

This simple trial run of deception sparked an almost immediate change in Gerald's brain. His emotional level seemed detached and the seed of narcissism and greed was planted. This puts me in the God seat. I can do and have anything I want... And so he did.

He stole large amounts of money which allowed him to purchase shares of stock in top companies, buy homes, cars, buildings and pushed his way into the hearts of other narcissists at the top of the wealth chain. His lack of people skills produced a ruthless business sense that elevated his status to be listed in Forbes as a financial wizard. He had his name on the side of an office building that he owned. The whole top floor was dedicated to his businesses. Reynolds was now a name to be reckoned with.

The one thing he couldn't seem to shake was his need for solitude. So much so that he refused get involved in board meetings, which didn't sit well with the members. His staff rarely saw him. He would be in his office before them and left long after their day ended. It was a blessing to them, for having a one-on-one conversation became vile. Employee turnover was second only to a dishwasher at the local steak and ribs.

Rarely seen in public, he became known as the Howard Hughes of Wall Street. His now non-relationship with the media also soured and ridiculous rumours and newspaper cartoons began to surface, depicting him as a pathetic tyrant. He was so elusive that at one point there were articles that he may not exist at all. It got to the point where no one wanted to deal with him. His decision-making came into question. Without interaction, his investors were worried, and one by one bowed out. This had no effect on Gerald. All he had to do was to stop the world and steal more money; but for the first time in his life, he was alienated.

One night as he slept, he was awakened by the sound of Poe's eerie voice repeating once again, "R-e-y-n-o-l-d-s."

He shot up in his bed to see Poe sitting in a chair across from him.

"What is it now?" he screamed at Poe. "Haven't you done enough to ruin my life?"

"I have ruined your life?" says Poe. "The watch is a curse only because you made it so. In truth, YOU are a curse to the watch. Time is everything, yet nothing."

"Nothing? Look what it did for you, it made you famous, but destitute. You didn't use it the way it was meant to be used and didn't live long enough to have what I have."

"The scariest monsters are the ones that lurk within our *souls*."

"Yeah, well you should know."

And with that Poe was gone.

Gerald took his words with less than a grain of salt. For narcissists never see anything that goes wrong as their fault, and so the watch makes everything right.

—

Gerald always kept Poe's watch nearby, in his left-side desk drawer in his office, just in case he needed to make adjustments to his lifestyle. On one particular day he needed more money for a business deal and removed the watch from the drawer. He proceeded to the door and tripped over a rug and the watch flew through the air and landed on the marble floor. Gerald's blood drained from his face. He picked up the watch and found that the face had cracked and the stem of the stopwatch had sprung open; the second hand had proceeded to tic. "Oh, my God!" he hollered.

He walked over to the light from the window to examine it further. He pushed on the stem, but it wouldn't budge. He looked out the window to see there was no activity on the street below. People and cars were visible, but no movement, no sounds. Now in panic mode, he rushed out the door and made his way down the hall to the main office. "No!" he screamed—all his staff were motionless. He tried in vain to push in the stem and finally lost the struggle when it broke off.

They always say be kind to the people on your way up, but in Gerald's case there wasn't anyone to meet on the way down.

—

He roamed for days with no one to talk to; no interaction. A strange feeling set in, one he had never had before—loneliness. This brought a deep-seated bout of depression. He couldn't even go to a park to settle himself because the birds had no song. Even a trip to the ocean saw the waves hanging like sand dunes.

He wandered around in a daze until he recognized a familiar sign above a shop, Rudy's Antiques. Full circle, he thought. It was fruitless to go inside, but he went in anyway; it wasn't like he was pressed for time.

The musty air inside seemed to hang like a fog. There were no customers, of course, and no one tending the shop. He went to the back where he was first introduced to Poe's watch. Looking into the glass display case there was still the empty space where the watch had been removed. Gerald walked around to the other side and pulled the now broken watch from his pocket. He rubbed it between his fingers and then gently placed it back in its rightful place.

In a blink of an eye his mind seemed to shut down; a blackout moment that found him back on the other side of the counter. A voice ripped through the silence—"Anything catch your eye?" He looked up to see...Rudy.

Seeing and hearing his voice sent him into a tailspin. All he could manage to do was scream. "*Ahhhh!*"

He raced out of the shop and faced moving traffic, car horns, and people walking by in conversation; the world was normal again!

—

Gerald arrived home feeling like Scrooge on Christmas Day; giddy, and in the happiest state he'd been in since childhood. Gerald didn't understand what happened to him, but he came to the realization: How fast or slow time goes by had no relevance; enjoying life to the fullest was time well spent.

3

MOONLIGHT SERENADE

How many times have you heard the phrase, things happen for a reason? Is this conveyed to us for comfort, or is it to let us know there are other forces that dictate our lives or our deaths? For WWII veteran Charlie Maxwell, a haunting piece of vintage vinyl transports him down memory lane...and beyond.

—

A funeral with a dozen mourners comes to a close at the gravesite of James's mother as he stands with his ninety-two-year-old dad, Charlie. The mourners slowly depart with some giving their final condolences. The two men are finally alone.

"I loved your mother so much," says Charlie. "She was the best thing that ever happened to me."

James puts an arm around his dad.

"I know, Dad."

"And you were the best thing that ever happened to us."

"Thanks, Dad."

Charlie looks at him with such pain.

"I told your mother that if she left before I did, I'd come looking for her. I miss her so much already. How am I supposed to keep going without her?"

"I'll help you, Dad."

"I love you, son."

They embrace.

—

The two sit at the table in Charlie's small, but comfortable kitchen. The sombre mood and the silence add to the unusually loud tick tock of the kitchen clock. James remembers other times when that clock had been the loudest sound in the house when he was growing up. It was when his father would sit him down for a man-to-man talk.

There's an obvious absence that makes James feel uneasy, and he begins tapping the fingers of one hand on the table. "Dad, can I get you something—a sandwich?"

"I'm not hungry."

He looks at the coffee pot. "How about some coffee? Looks like there's enough for a cup."

"Okay."

James fixes a cup and places it on the table.

"James," says Charlie, "I, I don't want you to worry about me. I'll be fine. I just need some time."

"Sure, Dad. I know that parents never stop worrying about their kids, but you know the same is true about the kids. I'll be in touch a lot more often now. Maybe we could start going to the movies again like we did when I was young. Remember that?"

Charlie sips his coffee. "Yeah, that was nice."

"Sure, and instead of going for hot chocolate afterwards, we'll go for a beer." He looks up at the kitchen clock. "Well, I've got to go now, Dad. Are you alright with that? Is there anything I can get you before I go?"

"You go ahead, son. I'll be fine."

"Okay, I'll call you tonight."

Charlie seems to be miles away.

"Dad?"

"Huh?"

"I said I'll call you tonight."

"Oh, yeah, sure. You call me tonight."

James gives him a hug. "Love you, Dad."

"Love you too."

—

Charlie sits for a moment, then moves to the living room and to his record collection. Shuffling through a few albums, he stops at one and pulls the record from its cover. He turns on the stereo, and places the record on the turntable. He carries the album cover to his recliner, sits, and waits for the music to start. The music plays Glenn Miller's "Moonlight Serenade"—their favourite. Charlie relaxes to the point where he drifts into thoughts of his wife Vera and then into a dream.

—

"Moonlight Serenade" continues inside the Sunnyside Night Club. It's 1942. The dance hall is filled to capacity. Glenn Miller and his orchestra are playing. Charlie sees himself on the dance floor as a handsome nineteen-year-old, dressed in a suit, and at his side, his beautiful eighteen-year-old Vera, wearing an elegant gown. She looks at Charlie with excitement in her eyes.

"Charlie, let's go out on the terrace and watch the sun set. It's such a beautiful evening."

"I can't think of a better picture; you and sunset."

They make their way through the crowd, up the stairs to the large open French doors, and out to the long terrace extending the width of the building along the lakefront. The sun is setting in all its glory over the water. Charlie and Vera hug the rail together as they admire the spectacle with the music from the dance floor in the background.

"Isn't it just the most beautiful picture, Charlie?"

He stares at her with such love as she takes in the sunset.

"I see another picture that's stealing its thunder," he says with a smile.

She turns to him. "What a wonderful thing to say. I love you so much."

They kiss while the sun begins to fade in the background, along with the music and the memory.

—

Charlie steps out of the dream and opens his eyes holding the album close to his chest. The record has ended and all that remains is the light scratching of the needle and the repetitive thud.

"Oh, my God, Vera, how I miss you, how I miss you."

He cries tears that would never be seen in public. Not even in front of James, for any display of emotion in his day was shunned. It was seen as a sign of weakness in a man.

—

James is nearing the end of English class with his students.

"And that's it for Shakespeare. Next week we will be looking at the works of an author that some of you have been waiting for, Stephen King."

"Yes!" yells one of the boys.

The bell rings to end the period. The students file out as Ron, the principal, enters.

"James, we just got a call from your dad."

"My dad?"

"Yeah, he sounded a little troubled. I told him I would have you call as soon as you finished your class."

"Okay, I'll call him right away. Thanks, Ron."

"You might as well use the staff room. It's quiet in there for the moment."

James is hoping this won't escalate to the point where Charlie is interrupting him every day. He loves his dad, but he has to work, and teaching has its restrictions.

Ron was right; no one was in the room. He pulls out his cell phone and calls Charlie.

"Hello," answers Charlie.

"Dad, are you all right?"

Charlie is sitting at the kitchen table. Old photo albums and pictures are strewn over the top.

"Did you know that your birthday is on the same day I got home from the army?"

"What did you say?"

Charlie holds up a newspaper clipping. "Yep, it's right here in *The Guardian*. I never noticed that before." He picks up another clipping. "Here's a picture of your mother and me on the front page."

"Dad I—"

"I looked pretty good back then. And look at your mother," he grins. "Boy, she was beautiful. Look at that smile. I was the luckiest guy in town."

"Dad."

"Hm?"

"Are you all right?"

"Yes. No. I miss Vera."

In frustration, James rubs the back of his neck.

"I know, Dad. I miss her too."

"Vera."

"Dad, have you had lunch? Have you eaten anything today?"

"No, I, I don't think so."

"Okay. Now listen to me. I have one more class to teach and then I'll be over. I'll take you out for dinner. In the meantime, would you please grab something to eat—cheese, crackers; something. Did you get that, Dad?"

Charlie thumbs through an album.

"Cheese, crackers."

"Good. I'll see you in a while."

"In a while."

Charlie hangs up and comes across a picture of the entrance to the Sunnyside Night Club. He picks it up. His memory goes back to the Club. "Moonlight Serenade" begins to play softly in his thoughts and he sees himself in his army uniform dancing with a young Vera.

"I love you, Vera. I got called. We're leaving Monday morning for England."

"Hold me tight," she says.

"When I get back, we'll get married."

Vera stops dancing and pulls away. "No. We're not getting married when you get back."

A stunned look appears on Charlie's face. "We're not?"

"If you're leaving Monday, I want to get married tomorrow."

"But what if I—"

She puts a finger to his lips.

"And when you get back, I'll be waiting and we'll never, ever, be separated again."

They kiss, and Charlie blinks back to reality.

"Oh, Vera, the Sunnyside; where we made all our plans, our hopes and dreams. Remember, Vera? We were there for the Christmas and New Year's dances."

He is overcome by the memories. His hand trembles as he turns the pages of the album. He stops at a picture of them sitting at a table in the Club on New Year's Eve, smiling with raised champagne glasses.

"Look at you, Vera! You look beautiful! Look at how beautiful you are! Beautiful!"

—

James decided that taking Charlie to his parents' favourite restaurant might just be what his dad needed. The restaurant is subdued with soft, ambient music—their conversation is thin at best.

Charlie points to another table. "Your mother and I used to sit at that table."

Realizing that the experience only reminds Charlie of Vera, James tries an upbeat approach.

"Well, Dad, how was that? I know you love the food here."

"Your mother loved the food. It was okay for me."

Like pulling teeth, thinks James. He tries again.

"Well, I think the food is very good, too."

"Your mother loved the hot and sour soup, and the chicken chow mein," says Charlie, breaking into a smile.

"She would get all excited when the fortune cookies came."

"Hey, perfect timing, Dad," as the waiter shows up with the bill and the cookies.

"Well, look at that. Shall we open them up and see what they have to say?"

"No, you go ahead," says Charlie with disinterest.

"Ah, come on, Dad. Just for fun. And if you don't like what you get, we'll switch. Come on."

Reluctantly Charlie picks up the cookie. They break them open.

James unravels his first. "Now, let's see what we have here. A new business venture is on the horizon. You see. I was going to buy a new briefcase tomorrow. Go ahead, Dad, open yours."

James feels like he's talking to a child, patronizing him, and thinks: My dad deserves more respect than I'm giving him, but it seems this is the only way to get through to him.

Charlie slowly pulls his apart. As he begins to read it his eyes widen. "It's Vera! She's sent me a message!"

"Dad, shhh. What are you talking about?"

"It's Vera! It's Vera!"

"Keep it down, Dad. Let me see."

James takes the message and reads, "Always meet at the sunny side. Dad, I've seen this one before. There's a spelling error in it. It should read, Always meet on the sunny side. Not *at* the sunny side."

"No! It's Vera! She wants me to meet her at the Club."

This whole incident terrifies James. He thought his father was handling everything fairly well, but this is something he wasn't expecting. Thankfully the ride home seems to calm him down.

James and Charlie are sitting in the kitchen having coffee.

"Dad, I still have grading to do," says James. "I have to leave. So, you understand about that fortune cookie? It was a mistake."

Charlie looks at him as though he were looking through him. "Mistake, I understand."

"Good. Okay, I'll let you go, and I will call you in the morning. You get some sleep now." James gives him a hug.

Charlie stares straight out. "Okay, son."

The front door shuts.

"No mistake. It was Vera. I know it's you, sweetheart." He rests his head on the table and the tick tock of the clock begins to lull him to sleep. At that moment "Moonlight Serenade" blasts through the kitchen. Charlie wakes in a panic.

"What's going on? Vera! Vera, where are you?"

He follows the sound into the living room. The record is playing on the turntable. He opens the dust cover, takes off the needle, and shuts it off. The incident leaves him panting.

"Now, how in the hell did that happen? Vera! She's calling me."

After nursing a couple of shots of brandy to calm him, Charlie goes to bed and it's lights out as his head touches the pillow.

—

Once again the dream of Vera begins at the Sunnyside Night Club. Charlie, in uniform, stands at the edge of the dance floor. People are dancing, the band is playing, but this time, there is no sound and no Vera.

"Vera!"

He moves through the crowd asking some of the dance couples, "Have you seen Vera? Vera, have you seen her?"

They are oblivious to him.

Then Vera's voice is heard above the crowd, "Charlie! Charlie!"

He frantically looks around the room and through the maze of people, he sees her on the terrace leaning her back against the railing. She looks radiant with a gentle breeze whispering through her hair. "Charlie, I'm here!"

The orchestra and the crowd disappear.

The room is empty, except for the sound of "Moonlight Serenade" begins to play softly in the background. Vera looks haunting as she opens her arms to him and calls out, "Charlie. I'm waiting, Charlie. I love you."

The music picks up steam. Charlie races to her, but the harder he tries, the farther away she looks and the louder the music.

He wakes with a start. "V-e-r-a!" His face covered in sweat.

—

It's morning and Charlie sits in his robe at the kitchen table with a coffee. The phone rings. Still feeling the effects of his restless sleep, he takes his time picking it up.

"Hello."

"Dad, how are you doing?"

"Rough night."

"You couldn't sleep?"

"Oh, I could sleep fine, but your mother wouldn't let me."

James is now concerned about his father's mental state.

"What do you mean, she wouldn't let you?"

"She keeps calling me to be with her at the Sunnyside Club. Just like the fortune cookie said."

James lowers his voice when he sees a couple of teachers coming into the Staff Room.

"Dad, I told you, that was a mistake."

"No, it's no mistake, son. I had a dream. She was out on the terrace calling me."

"But don't you see, Dad, that's all it was, just a dream."

He checks his watch. "Look Dad, I have to go. I'll see you after work. Just take it easy and make sure you eat something, okay?"

Charlie hangs up and heads for the front door. He picks up the morning paper and enters the living room. With the intention of reading the paper, he rests in his recliner, but the restless sleep from the previous night takes over. His eyes close and the newspaper drops in his lap.

Once again, "Moonlight Serenade" begins to play, setting the stage as Charlie picks up where he left off, in the middle of the dance floor.

The Club is empty and Vera is still on the terrace, but facing out to the lake.

He runs to her. "Vera!"

He reaches the bottom of the steps that lead to the terrace.

Vera turns to him with tears in her eyes.

"Oh, my Charlie. I've been waiting so long."

"I'm coming, Vera!" says Charlie as the French doors begin to close.

By the time he reaches them, they shut. He tries in vain to open them. He sees her through the glass doors and calls to her, "V-e-r-a!"

She just stands there with tears flowing and arms extended to him.

—

Charlie wakes exhausted. Putting his hands to his face he pleads, "Oh, my God. How much more? How much more, Vera? My heart is breaking."

He notices the folded newspaper in his lap and the headline —SUNNYSIDE NIGHT CLUB.

He unfolds the paper and reads, "SUNNYSIDE NIGHT CLUB —DEMOLITION TODAY."

He raises his head. "Demolition? No. They can't do that. I have to meet Vera."

He rushes to his bedroom and opens the cedar chest at the bottom of his bed. He paws through the items and finally he finds it: his old army uniform. He walks to the full-length mirror and tries on the jacket. He manages to put it on, but the buttons won't reach. Running his hands down the sides of the jacket he feels something in one of the pockets; his dog tag and chain. He puts it around his neck.

"There, now to see, Vera."

—

James walks through the school parking lot to his car. He turns and sees Ron walking toward him.

"James! How's your dad doing?"

"Well, to tell you the truth, I'm a little concerned. I was just on my way to see him now. He keeps having dreams of my mother and relates things to those dreams. I don't know if his mind is going or it's the loss of my mother."

"I know exactly how you feel. That happened to my mother after my father passed away last year."

"How did she get over it?"

"She didn't. She died six months later. They said it was natural causes, but I think it was a broken heart."

—

Charlie drives into the parking lot of the Sunnyside Night Club. He walks to the front of the building to find it surrounded by a snow fence with heavy machinery all set for the demolition.

The foreman approaches Charlie. "Coming to give the place a last look, are you?"

Charlie's eyes are fixed on the building. "Yes."

"I'm sure there are a lot of memories in that place." He glances at Charlie's attire. "Looks like you've invested a lot of memories here."

"We did. Any chance of going inside for one last look?" asks Charlie.

"I'm afraid not. We're scheduled to start in fifteen minutes. If you plan on watching, I'll have to ask you to step back."

Charlie steps back, but as the foreman moves to the machinery, he manoeuvres to the other side of the building where, to his surprise, a side door is ajar. Looking around for an opening in the fence, he spots two ends of fencing that are only tied together at the top. There's no one in sight, so he pulls himself through the bottom of the fence and reaches the open door.

—

James walks into Charlie's kitchen. It's quiet, except for the clock.

"Dad? Dad! Are you here?" He moves to the living room. "What the hell. Where could he be?"

The open newspaper rests on the recliner. James picks it up.

"Oh, Dad."

Looking into the empty garage confirms where he's gone.

The inside of the Club hasn't changed, but it has been in a neglected state for some time. There are old, tattered photos of the greats, like Frank and Bing. Most of the tables and chairs are gone. Cobwebs and dust are the main decor. Charlie stands in the centre of the dance floor and looks toward the terrace doors.

"Oh, Vera, I miss you so much," and drops himself into a chair. He leans forward, resting his head in his hands.

The silence in the room is short lived as the sound of the machinery is heard outside.

Then a voice, "Ladies and Gentlemen!"

Charlie bolts up.

"For your evening pleasure, the incomparable Glenn Miller and his orchestra!"

They play "Moonlight Serenade" and the place comes to life with a crowded dance floor and the orchestra.

Charlie looks to the terrace doors. No Vera. He calls her name softly. "Vera, my Vera."

Suddenly, a radiant Vera appears on the terrace and seems to float down the stairs to the dance floor. The crowd seems to open up to allow her room as she reaches the love of her life. They embrace and hold each other tight.

"I've missed you, Charlie."

"My dearest, Vera. How I've missed you, sweetheart."

They pull away to look into each other's eyes. Charlie is nineteen again. They begin dancing as the sound of machinery starts the demolition and walls begin to collapse around them. The room shakes, but Charlie, Vera, and the crowd keep on dancing to the music.

—

James pulls into the Club parking lot. He sees Charlie's car, looks at the Club being torn down, and rushes to the foreman.

"Say! You didn't happen to see an older fella here, did you?"

"What's that?"

"I said, did you see an old man here?"

"Okay, Tony! Tell them to start on the back now!"

"Yeah, there was an older guy here about twenty minutes ago. He seemed a little odd. He was wearing an army jacket that didn't fit and had dog tags from the war around his neck, like he thought it was still going on."

"Do you know if he went inside?"

"Do you think we'd be doing this if he was?"

"Well, did you see where he went?"

"Look buddy, I'm not a babysitter for seniors. I told him if he wanted to hang around, he'd have to step back. That was the last I saw of him."

James searches the park that surrounds the night club. In the distance an older gentleman is sitting on a bench.

"Dad! Dad!"

The old man takes notice and turns his head around, but it's not Charlie. Discouraged and baffled, he turns his attention back to the Club.

The demolition has stopped and the workers are leaving. The Sunnyside Night Club is now a pile of rubble and memories. James decides to sift through the ruins in hopes of finding some evidence that his father might have been there. Stumbling over the levelled pile of debris, he picks through some of the bricks and lumber. He decides it's fruitless and begins the trek out of the rubble. A shiny object in the distance catches his eye. He scrambles toward it and picks it up—It's Charlie's dog tag.

—

In the parking lot, there is a police car next to the cars of James and Charlie. A dump truck is loading up the last of the Club's remains. James is leaning against the hood of his car when a police officer walks up.

"Well, Mr. Maxwell, as you can see, there is nothing left. I don't know what to tell you. You can file a missing person's report. Other than that, I'm stumped."

"Thanks for your help."

James moves his eyes away from the barren site that once housed the memories of two people who were very much in love. Focussing on his father's dog tag, he rubs it with his thumb and puts it into his pocket.

He looks up into the blue of the sky and smiles. "Say hi to Mom for me."

He gets into his car and drives out of the parking lot. A tow truck follows carrying Charlie's car.

4

THE KEY

Dan Blake is a homicide detective. He's calm, collected, and rational, until the night he takes a shortcut through a cemetery and reopens an unsolved murder that will unlock a frightening reality.

—

Every hockey season, the Sudden Death Sports Bar comes alive with every sports expert in town. Dan and his three friends are no exception. They have season tickets to all the games and reserved seating at the bar. Being the first game of the season, optimism runs high—usually.

"I still say we should have had them. We were all over them, the whole game."

"It doesn't matter. It's just pre-season."

"Yeah, but you know, sometimes that sets the tone for the rest of the year."

"Maybe, maybe not," says Dan.

"Now that's typical Dan, the flip-flopper. I swear you could be two people—yes, no, maybe, sometimes."

"I think Dan has a point. You can't judge this stuff. We have nothing to go by. The slate is clean. It's a new season with a few new players."

"Well, it's that time again."

"Yeah, let's call it a night."

They stand and take care of the last of their beers and throw a few bucks on the table.

"What time do you go in, Detective Dan?"

"I hate to say it."

"Let me guess, another holiday."

"Just a week."

"You sure get a lot of holidays."

"I need a lot of holidays. The job sure isn't one."

"Homicide. Not something I'd want to be doing."

The group gathers outside.

"Where'd you park, Dan?"

"I didn't get so lucky tonight. I'm on the other side of the cemetery."

"You wouldn't catch me going through there at night."

"That's why he's homicide. He just can't stay away from those people."

They laugh and go their separate ways.

—

The sky is clear and the moon is full and bright; perfect night for a hike through the cemetery. The temperature is dropping, so Dan decides to up the pace by jogging and cutting across between rows of headstones. His foot catches a tree root. He stumbles, falls and hits his head on one of the gravestones, and he's out.

He dreams of a dark, wooded area with car headlights and indistinct shadows barely visible.

A woman's voice screams out from the car. The passenger door is kicked open. A young woman desperately struggles to get out.

"Somebody help me! Please help me!" She collapses to the ground and before she can get up, a hand grabs her by the hair and drags her along the ground. She screams and pleads for her life. The screams become too much for the assailant. He begins to punch her repeatedly in the face, but her screams continue. He grabs a rock and hits her hard on the side of the head. The screaming stops and the dream fades with a soft, eerie voice echoing in Dan's head, Help me...Help me...the key...the key.

—

The early morning sun has been warming Dan's body from the chill of the night. He wakes up feeling pain on the side of his forehead. His fingers pass over the area to find a cut with now dried, crusty blood. Getting to his feet, he reaches for his back, where more pain is felt.

"What a putz," he says to himself, as he looks down to see the large tree root that had stopped him in his tracks. His eyes then move to the headstone that put him out for the night.

MELANIE LYNN ABBOTT
Born June 18, 1979—Died April 21, 2010

"Melanie Abbott. Well, you didn't have much of a life, did you, sweetheart?"

Dan walks away, but the dream and those two words, the key, linger. What's that all about? he asks himself. "Are you trying to freak me out there, Melanie?"

—

Dan has always been calm, collected and rational. Murders, suicides; there isn't much he hasn't encountered in his twenty-three years on the force. He has never been one for the paranormal. When people died, they stayed dead. No ghosts, no haunting, no shit like that for Dan. He's never had an experience that aroused that curiosity until now. He delays his trip home and drops by the station to see if there is anything on this girl.

—

He enters the station to find it abnormally busy with uniforms and suits constantly interacting.

"Dan. What the hell are you doing here?" says Detective Mike Campbell. "Aren't you on holiday?"

"Yeah," says Dan, still focussing on the commotion in the room.

"You look like shit. What did you do, sleep in the park?"

Dan turns to Mike. "Ever think of becoming a detective? What's the story here?"

"Uh, they found some kid in the woods at the back of the university. The media's all over it, and, of course, we're never doing enough to solve it."

"Any suspects?"

"Nah, just checking the usual fare: students, family, friends, not something you should be concerned with. You're on holiday. So what's up? You drop by just to rub it in?"

"Was there a homicide in regards to a young woman by the name of Melanie Abbott?"

"Abbott, Abbott. I remember something. That name does stand out."

"Why don't I remember it?"

Mike chuckles, "Maybe you were on holiday. Yeah. That's it.

"You were on holiday. And I was just about to leave on mine. That's why the name rang a bell." He starts to reminisce. "Three weeks in Paris. Deb painted and I did the sightseeing; mostly the walking sights."

"Was that three years ago?"

"It sure was."

"Case closed?"

"Nope, it just sits there like a doormat. Have a look in the files, if you'd like. The leads went nowhere. So, why the interest?"

"Interest?"

"Hey, Mike," says another detective. "The chief's waiting to see you about the Keller case."

"Oh shit, gotta go. Yeah, she was a pretty thing. Anyway, enjoy the rest of your so-called holiday."

"Thanks," says Dan.

The second drawer of the filing cabinet reads UNSOLVED. Dan opens it and it doesn't take him long to get to ABBOTT, MELANIE. He pulls out the file, scans its content, then shoves the folder under his arm and walks out.

—

Dan plops on the sofa with a slice of day-old pizza and a coffee. He opens the file on the coffee table and thumbs through the evidence. He finds a picture of Melanie.

"Mike was right. What a beautiful girl."

She wears a chain around her neck that disappears into her blouse. Usually Dan has no interest in the subject other than solving the case, but as he looks more closely at the rest of the crime scene pictures, he realizes it was all in the dream at the cemetery.

He spent the rest of the day trying to shake off the unsettling similarities. With some yard work and the last thirty-two pages of a crime novel, he finally settles in at two beers and the last remaining slice of that now dry, bone-like pizza.

Throughout his life Dan has had a few relationships. Some were good and some went sour, but none went the distance. Other than the lack of companionship, Dan enjoys his personal time. His evening friend is the TV in the bedroom, which usually stays on all night to keep him company. The sound lulls him to sleep.

Tonight is no exception as he lays in his king size bed. He's always optimistic—you never know when you might have an unexpected guest, he says. He entertains his brain with old detective shows. "Everyone's a suspect until I say different," says the detective on the screen.

"Ain't that the truth," says Dan, and with that he rolls over and drifts to sleep.

—

At three in the morning Dan wakes to the annoying white noise of the TV, but there is another overriding sound, a voice that is unmistakable.

"The k-e-e-y." It's that whispering, eerie, soft tone of Melanie's voice.

"What's going on?" says Dan as he tries to clear his head and eyes.

"The k-e-e-y," the voice repeats.

He looks at the screen to see a cooking show.

"The key, the key ingredient is rosemary," says a plump little woman.

Dan drops his head back on the pillow and in his groggy state says, "Rosemary? I thought it was Melanie," then heads back to slumber land.

—

In the morning he can't shake Melanie or the subliminal message about a key. A coffee and two oatmeal cookies, and Dan heads back to the station.

"Dan," says Mike, "are you all right? You know you're going to have a hell of a time retiring if this is how you're going to be spending it."

"Yeah, I know."

Mike notices the dark circles around Dan's eyes.

"You still look like hell. Are you getting enough sleep?"

"Do you know anything about a key in regards to that Abbott case?"

"Like I told you, Dan. I was on holidays too. I have to work on this Keller case before the Chief sends me on a permanent holiday. Why don't you ask Pete? He was the main man in that case."

Pete is at his desk mulling through paperwork.

"Pete. Got a minute?"

Pete looks up. "Dan, aren't you on—"

"Yeah, I am. I just have a question for you."

"Sure, have a seat."

"The Abbott case."

Pete shakes his head. "Nice-looking girl. Damn shame."

"Yeah. Do you know anything about a key?"

"A key? What kind of key?"

"I don't know, maybe a special key."

"Where did this idea about a key come from?"

"I'm, I'm not sure about that either."

"There was no key."

"Nothing found at her residence?"

"The only keys were the ones to her apartment and her car. Look, Dan, I don't know what this sudden interest in Melanie Abbott is, but if I were you, I'd just go home and enjoy my time off. It's well deserved, and I really think you need it."

"You think I'm losing it?"

"Losing it? Dan, take it easy. The only thing I think you're losing is some sleep. You're the last person on my list for having a problem. Look, we all have to get away and recharge. That's part of the job, right?"

"Yeah, I'm sorry. Okay. Thanks, Pete."

"Say, isn't there a hockey game tonight?" Pete asks.

"Yeah, I've got to meet the guys for a cold one before the game."

"There you go. Get out and enjoy yourself."

"Thanks. I will."

Mike walks over to Pete and says, "Sounds like Dan got a little short with you."

"I don't know what's bugging him. I just told him to enjoy his holiday, and he accused me of saying he was nuts. And what's with this girl?"

"I don't know. I just don't get it."

—

Dan sits by the coffee table rehashing the evidence and the gruesome photos of Melanie as he dabs a grilled cheese sandwich into a mound of ketchup.

"This doesn't make any sense. There's nothing in this file about a damn key!"

He notices the name and address of Melanie's mother and thinks, mothers know everything.

—

Dan pulls up to a small house. The landscape of the home looks dismal. There are signs of caretaking in the past, but now it's in a state of severe neglect: starved of water and a nurturing hand.

Dan knocks. No answer. He tries again. The door opens enough to reveal the inside chain. One half of a grey-haired, old woman's face is seen through the gap. She has tended to herself as she has the garden.

"What do you want?" she says in a sharp tone.

"Mrs. Abbott?"

"What is it?"

"Detective Blake, Mrs. Abbott," he says, hoping the word detective carries some weight.

"Huh, a new one. It's been years. What have you got; more new evidence that leads nowhere?"

"I just wanted to ask you about a key."

She slams the door shut. There's a pause, then the sound of the chain being dismantled. This time the door is fully extended with a more cordial welcome.

"Come in," she says as she leaves him at the door.

Dan walks in with some apprehension.

She points to a couch. "Sit," she says as she settles into her well used, overstuffed chair. "What about the key?"

"So, you're aware of a key?" Dan asks.

"I don't like games. What do you know about the key?"

"I really don't know anything," Dan admits.

"Look. I'm Mrs. Abbott. Not Abbott and Costello. What do you know about the key?"

"Let's just say I was told about a key. That's why I'm here."

She picks up a framed picture of Melanie from the lamp table beside her.

"This is my daughter! And she's dead! You come in here and talk stupid to me! She was going to be a lawyer!"

Dan meets her intense stare.

"If she was still here she'd be prosecuting insensitive idiots like you!"

Dan looks at Melanie's picture. It's different from the one he had seen. It shows a key at the bottom of the chain. Bingo! He tries some detective strategy to calm Mrs. Abbott and hopefully gain her confidence.

"I know that key was something very dear to her."

At that, she opens like a rose on a summer morning. "It was. It was the key to her diary."

Dan's eyes light up. "And where's the key and the diary now?" His mouth begins to water.

"I don't know."

His detective balloon pops.

"It holds my daughter's life. The only thing left of hers that would have meant so much to me. She always carried it with her in her purse. When they found her, the key and the diary were missing."

"You didn't mention this to the police?"

"There was no point. The diary was gone. Even if I had the key, what good would it do me?"

Dan gets up. "Thank you, Mrs. Abbott. I'm sorry to have bothered you."

"So, you don't have any new information?"

"No. I'm sorry."

"Would you do me a favour?"

"Sure."

"Don't come back."

—

As the sun dips below the tree line, Dan's luck with parking remains at the cemetery.

"How early do you have to get here for a damn parking spot?"

Making his way through the graveyard, he is immediately drawn to Melanie's grave. He feels obligated to offer some words after meeting her mother.

"I'm sorry, Melanie. I tried. I talked to your mother. I tried."

He turns to walk away, "The k-e-e-y," whispers Melanie.

"I don't know where the damn key is!" he shouts in frustration.

"Help me, Dan."

To hear her use his name frightens Dan.

"I don't know where the key is! You're dead! It doesn't matter anymore!"

Like steam from a kettle, the spirit of Melanie rises from her grave. "The k-e-e-y, Dan."

Dan is terrified. He turns and runs as her voice follows him.

"The k-e-e-y."

Frantically stumbling between the gravestones he finally makes it back to his car. His hands shake as he struggles to get the keys out of his pocket. They slip between his fingers and drop to the ground. He whimpers as he bends down to pick them up. A hand grabs the collar of his jacket. Dan freezes and turns white.

"Hey, mister, you can't park here."

Dan gets up and tries to compose himself. He turns to see a traffic cop.

"Dan? How the hell are you? Sorry, I didn't recognize you. It's a little hard to see out here. I usually try to get down here when there's a game. It's good for the quota. Are you here for the game?"

"I was, but I'm not feeling very well. I was going to go home."

"You do look a little pale, even under the streetlights. Well, that's too bad. Should be a good game."

"I'll have to catch the highlights later."

"Okay, Dan. Hope you're feeling better. See you."

Dan gets into his car and takes a few deep breaths.

"All right, let's calm down." He quickly locks the doors. "This didn't happen. It's impossible. Ghosts—what am I, a kid? So what's going on? Okay, the bump on the head. That's what it is, a slight concussion."

—

In the morning he decides to have a long, hot shower. That has always helped in the past when he's had a difficult case. He decides his car could also use a wash and heads to the local car wash. A young, scruffy, ass-wipe by the name of Vince walks up to him.

"Hey, Detective Blake, how's it goin'?"

Dan has no patience for Vince. If Dan had his way, he would have him in a line-up every time there was some trouble.

"Just fine, Vince."

"Workin' on any big cases?"

"No, I'm on holiday."

"I didn't think you guys got holidays; thought you enjoyed dead people too much."

They exchange smiles, but their eyes say otherwise.

"Want the works today, boss?"

"Why not."

"Giving you the works would be an honour."

I'm sure it would, thinks Dan.

"Don't worry about a thing. It'll look like a million bucks inside and out."

Vince drives the car into the wash bay and Dan heads to the waiting room.

Dan finishes reading the latest car magazines from the previous year as Vince walks in.

"Okay, Dickey Dan, she's all set. I rubbed her down nice and easy, just like my women."

"I'm sure you did."

As Dan starts to walk out he hears Melanie's voice. "The key."

Dan turns back to Vince. "What did you say?"

"Hey, take it easy there, Blake. All I said was, here's your key." Vince throws him the keys.

"Sorry."

"Yeah sure, enjoy your holiday. Sounds like you need it."

Dan stops at a red light and reaches up to pull the visor down. His cell phone drops down and slides under the passenger seat. Fumbling around the floor with his fingers, he feels something other than the cell phone.

"Nice job of cleaning, Vince; asshole."

He pulls out the item. It's a necklace, with a key! Dan is stunned.

"What the hell?"

The traffic light turns green and the car behind him beeps. Dan pulls away in a panic. He turns down the next side street to pull off to the side of the road. He holds up the necklace and key for a close look.

"Where the hell did this come from? No one's been in this car except—Vince! That little slimeball!" He takes a second to think it out. Could this be Melanie's? Vince killed her? Why not? He must have taken it from her to hide the evidence. But why is it in my car? Is he that much of a psychopath that he would put it here to screw with me? Or is he that stupid? Maybe it fell out of his shirt pocket. "That's it! I've got the little bastard now!"

—

He enters the station and finds Pete enjoying a coffee and bagel. Pete sees him coming and shakes his head.

"Pete," says Dan.

"Dan, I've told you all I know."

"What do you know about Vince Rossi?"

"Rossi? Yeah, we checked him out, nothing. He was clean. The only connection he had was his residence. He lives in an apartment a block away from the crime scene."

"That's it!" says Dan.

"What's it?"

Dan sits in the chair beside him. Almost in a whisper, he says, "Pete, Rossi killed Melanie."

"And you came to this conclusion because..."

"Her mother said—"

"You went to see her mother, and she actually talked to you?"

"She said her daughter always carried her diary in her purse and the key was around her neck."

"Okay," says Pete.

Dan pulls the necklace and key from his pocket and dangles it in front of Pete. Pete sits straight as a pin.

"Where the hell did you get that?"

"Under the passenger seat of my car."

Pete sits back in his chair.

"Now listen, Dan—"

"No, you listen. I just came from the car wash and Vince worked on my car. It must have dropped out of his shirt pocket. Now all we have to do is find the diary, open it with this key, and I know something in there will point to Vince."

"That's great, Dan. And when you find that diary, we'll nail his ass to the wall."

"Are you patronizing me?"

Pete takes a deep breath, then exhales.

"Look, Dan, we're cops and this is what we do, but you're supposed to be on holiday. Plus, this isn't even your case—it's like you're obsessed with this girl."

Dan feels frustrated and deflated.

"Tell you what," says Pete. "Give me the key. I'll hold it as potential evidence. If you find the diary, bring it right down here." He holds out his hand.

Dan reluctantly gives him the key and walks away muttering, "The diary."

"Good thing you're not married. Be a hell of a holiday for your wife."

—

Dan decides to go back to Melanie's grave. He's not sure why, especially after the last episode, but he feels some kind of allegiance and wants to tell her that he's found the key and maybe she'll stop haunting him.

It's a beautiful sunny day. No eerie darkness, no long, black, looming shadows. He navigates through the cemetery and up the path to Melanie. He's feeling less threatened as he approaches her, not as a dead, decomposing remnant of what was, but the essence of Melanie that lives on.

At first, he has no words. He waits as though anticipating some sort of intervention, some direction. Then, he finds his voice.

"I'm doing everything I can to help you. I found your key. At least I believe it to be yours. I can't do any more without your diary. And right now, I don't know where it is or even if it exists. I'm not giving up. I just need more evidence. But believe me, I am doing the best I can."

He turns to walk away, feeling more at ease that she knows that he hasn't given up. As that thought settles in his mind, another occurs like a lightning bolt hitting a tree: Melanie's mother. "She always carried it with her." The phrase repeats over and over in his head. It was a message he wasn't getting until he repeated that one word. "Always," he whispers to himself. He turns back to the grave.

"It's with you, isn't it, Melanie?"

—

Dan once again enters the station to talk to Pete with a confident smile.

"What now?" says Pete.

"I know where it is, Pete."

"Okay, Dan. Where is it?"

"It's with Melanie. The diary is in the grave. Her mother said she always kept it with her."

"And who put it there, the Grim Reaper?"

"Well, it had to be Vince. He had the key, so he must have had the diary. Somehow he was at the funeral home and slipped it into the casket."

"Dan, I don't know about this. It's starting to sound a little—far-fetched. I think you're stretching on this one."

"I'm telling you, Pete, it's there."

"All right, let's suppose it's there. Do you know what's involved in reopening a grave, not to mention the cost? I'd have to get the okay and that won't be easy. And if you're wrong, you could be in for an unwanted extension to your holiday. And I know how you love those."

—

At the station the Chief is on the phone with Mrs. Abbott. "Yes, Mrs. Abbott. From what we understand there is a good chance it may have been put there. Yes, I will let you know right away. And thank you once again."

—

Dan is at home when he receives a call.

"Dan, it's Pete. Good news: They'll be opening the grave tomorrow."

"Great! That didn't take long."

"Well, the Chief was talking to Melanie's mother and she gave the nod. You must have made a good impression on her."

"I doubt that."

—

The backhoe has done its job. The grave is open. Dan and Pete and a few others hang back waiting for the results.

"Dan," says Pete, "If you were ever right about anything, please make it today."

A gentleman leaves the gravesite with something in his gloved hand and heads toward them.

"Is this what you're looking for?" He holds up the diary.

"That's it!" says Dan. "See, I told you it'd be there! We've got him now!"

They place the diary into a plastic bag.

"Okay," says Pete, "I'll take it from here." He looks to Dan. "Why don't you go home now? It's been a long day. I'll call you in the morning with the results."

"Okay," says Dan, feeling vindicated. "I'm glad it's over."

"Me too, you did a good job, Dan. Sorry I doubted you."

—

The next morning, for the first time since the whole episode started, the dreams and voices have stopped. Dan celebrates with a full breakfast of bacon and eggs. The phone rings as he wipes up the last of the yolk with toast.

"Hello."

"Dan, it's Pete, you better get down here. We've got more than we bargained for."

"Great, I'll be right there."

—

Dan walks into the station. It's strangely quiet. Pete is standing in front of the Chief's door.

"Come on in," he says.

The Chief looks subdued as he sits at his desk.

"Dan, how have you been?"

"Better now that the case is solved."

"I heard that you've been working on this case while on holiday. What made you take such an interest?" asks the Chief.

"Well," says Dan, "since the case has been solved, I guess I can let the cat out of the bag. I know this is going to sound crazy, but I was going through the cemetery one night and stumbled and hit my head. I was out cold. I had this dream of a girl being murdered and when I woke up I was lying on Melanie's grave. After that I kept hearing her voice telling me to find a key. You know I don't believe in that ghost stuff, but for some strange reason this seemed real, and she wouldn't leave me alone. I'm glad it's finally over. So, did you pick Vince up yet?"

"Not yet. I heard you went to see Mrs. Abbott," says the Chief.

"Yes, that's right. I thought she might have some information on the key and diary."

"And did she?"

"She showed me a picture of Melanie and I noticed the key around her neck, which confirmed what Melanie was telling me. We ended the conversation with her telling me not to come back."

Dan eyes the diary in the Chief's hand.

"So, was I right? Does it mention Vince in the diary?"

"It does mention Vince."

"I knew it!"

"It says that she went for a car wash and that he was coming on to her in a vulgar way. She also said that she stopped going there and had her car washed elsewhere."

"So the little slimeball started to trail her, abducted her, and then murdered her?"

"It's all here in the diary," says the Chief. "You'll find it on the last page."

He hands the diary to Dan.

"Finally, I get to nail his ass."

Dan takes the diary and begins to read...

"He's such a nice guy and so tall and handsome. We're going on our fourth date. I have goose bumps already. He won't tell me where we're going, but I'm sure it will be nice. It just seems to be a perfect fit; me becoming a lawyer and him a detective. It sounds so right, MRS. DAN BLAKE."

Dan's eyes begin to change along with his physical appearance, as if morphing into some other person or thing. He starts to laugh.

"See, this is all wrong. This is bullshit. Vince had the diary, so he wrote that in and left the key in my car to implicate me."

He laughs again. Only this time it's more like a lunatic in an asylum. "Oh, he's a smart little bastard. He thought you would fall for it. What an idiot!"

"Now that makes sense," says the Chief. "But there's one small question that still needs an answer. If he wrote that last entry, he had to do it in Melanie's handwriting and I don't think he's capable of that, do you?"

Dan's face distorts and his voice is different, like watching the *Three Faces of Eve.* "No one was going to find it. Not even Dan. I put that diary in the coffin myself. Dan sold me out! It was Dan! Why couldn't he have just taken his goddamn holiday like everyone else! Dan and that bitch Melanie! I told her it was a secret! But no, she had to tell Dan all about that stupid key!" Dan's eyes go wild. "It was the key! That damn key! That's all she kept saying! The key! The key! Women are like that. They just don't know when to shut up. You understand that, don't you? That bloody—damn—key!"

5

RETIREMENT

The retirement of a person should be a joyous event, but there is no smile on the face of John Ainsworth. His last day of work seems more like his last day on earth. What John is about to find will be the treasure of his life.

—

It's five-thirty in the morning; John Ainsworth is sleeping soundly in his bed. It will be two hours before the winter sun lightens the room. His loving wife, Edna, enters the room as she has done for the last forty-one years to wake him for work and a good breakfast.

"Good morning, John," she says cheerfully. "Wakey, wakey."

John makes little movement and groans.

"You should be so excited—it's your last day of work!"

She pats his rear. He groans again.

"Come on now. You get yourself up; breakfast will be waiting for you."

As she turns to leave the room, John mumbles, "It's not a big deal, Edna. People retire every day."

She turns back to him. "Yes, but this is your day. No more early rises unless you want to. Your time will be your own now."

He sits up. "My time? And what do I get for forty-one years of being on their time? A bloody watch to remind me of all the years I've wasted. Shuffling people around—and for what?"

She sits on the edge of the bed. "That's not true, and you know it. We have had a wonderful life."

John rubs his eyes. "Yes, we had a wonderful life."

She holds his hand. "Please, John, don't go there."

"Why shouldn't I? Because of some drunk, Danny loses his life, we lose our son and we all lose our futures. He had a great future, Edna. He was going to be a great surgeon."

"I know, dear."

"Damn it! All he was trying to do was get home for Christmas. It was only two hours from the university."

Edna gets up from the bed and turns to John. "John, you can't live the rest of your life in the past. Danny wouldn't have wanted you to feel this way."

As she begins to leave the room, he sits on the side of the bed. “What’s wrong with grieving for your son?”

She stops in the doorway. “Not for twenty years.” She turns to him. “Not for twenty years, John.” She pauses then adds, “Wash up and come for breakfast.”

John puts his head in his hands.

—

In the kitchen he settles himself at the table and sips the first of many coffees he will consume throughout the day.

Edna makes her way over with a steaming pot of porridge and pours him a bowl full. She takes a little for herself and sits down to keep him company, just as she does every morning.

“John?”

“Hm.”

She smiles and says, “How do you feel about going on a nice trip somewhere?”

He takes a sip of coffee. “I don’t know about a trip, Edna. A pension doesn’t mean that all of a sudden you go spend-crazy.”

“That’s not spend-crazy, you’re retiring. We should take a trip. You’ve always wanted to see Europe and they have some great package deals these days. And no one deserves it more than you.”

“And what did Danny deserve? How can I go halfway around the world and enjoy myself when our son didn’t even have the chance to finish school, let alone retire?”

The smile leaves Edna’s face and they eat their porridge in silence.

—

In the driver’s room of the bus garage the first shift of drivers has gathered. Some are seated at small tables, while others are standing around discussing their last accident or telling a funny story about a passenger. Three of the drivers are huddled in a corner having a conversation about John.

“Last day for John.”

“Wish it were me.”

“Don’t we all.”

“I’ll bet he doesn’t even have a smile on his face when he walks in.”

"Come on. Sure he's going to have a smile. It's his last day."

"Well, that'll be a first."

"Hey, give the guy a break, will yuh? When I started here John was the friendliest guy on the property. When his son died something died in him, and he just never recovered."

"You're right. I don't know how I could get on a bus every day with that over my head."

John walks slowly into the room with his lunch pail in hand.

"There he is. I told you, no smile."

Everyone applauds and wishes him well. Without emotion John says thanks as the supervisor comes in.

"John!" he bows. "Your chariot awaits you!"

They all chuckle.

"Your circle check's been done, the horses are running and it's all warmed up for you."

"Thanks."

The supervisor has known John for years and understands his inner battle over his son. He pats him on the back and rubs his shoulder to let him know that.

"And, as an added bonus, there's a nice hot coffee waiting on board for you."

"That's nice, thanks."

"Well, you don't get to retire every day. Have a good one and we'll see you when you get back."

There's always a little razing from drivers.

"Don't get lost on that country route!"

"Or fall asleep!"

John heads for the garage.

Under his breath the supervisor comments, "How's he going to handle retirement?"

—

John walks between two rows of buses until he gets to the top of the line. He boards the bus, sits in his seat and puts his lunch pail behind it. He makes the usual seat adjustments, looks around the dash with all its instrumentation and reflects on the years he's spent in that seat.

"Last time; then what?" He rubs his hands over the steering wheel. "Then what?"

Voices of other drivers blare over the radio.

"Don't need to listen to that on my last day."

He turns off the radio, takes a deep breath and slowly exhales. He closes the doors, puts the bus in gear, and gingerly moves out of the garage.

—

The sun is beginning to light up the morning sky. The countryside is covered in a fairyland of snow. John picks up his coffee from its holder and takes a sip. He feels very relaxed and is enjoying the drive. Snow begins to gently fall.

"Ah, come on. They didn't say snow today."

The snow intensifies. John throws on the wipers and shifts the engine into low gear. His vision becomes obscured. "I can't believe this."

He sees a figure by the side of the road and brings the bus to a stop then opens the doors. A woman in her thirties steps into the bus covered in snow.

"Wow! Out of nowhere!" She shakes the snow loose from her coat. "It's like a blizzard out there!"

She puts her ticket in the fare box and sits across from John. John quickly closes the doors and resumes driving.

"It sure is," says John. "They didn't forecast this on the radio this morning."

"No, they sure didn't," she says, taking her hat off and giving it a shake, then looks up at John. "How have you been, John?"

John glances at her. "Me? I'm fine. I'm sorry, do I know you?"

"Well, it has been many years. My name is Nancy, but I don't expect you to remember that. I'm so glad to see you again. You know, you actually changed my life."

"I changed your life? How could I have done that?"

"Let me rephrase that. You saved my life."

"I don't understand."

"Well, it was over fifteen years ago now. I was a know-it-all teenager, into drugs, hated school, teachers, friends, my parents and especially myself. Anyway, I was standing at a bus stop with my duffel bag stuffed with clothes. I was going to do what some teenagers do at that age. I was going to leave home and start a new life in a big city, where I could lose myself and my past.

"As the bus pulled up and the doors opened I hesitated and looked down the road at what I was leaving, then looked inside the bus and saw your wonderful smile and you said, 'Hey there, Sweet Pea! You going to stand there all day? Hop aboard and we'll take a trip to Paris and Rome!' For the first time in quite a while, I smiled. I couldn't resist your invitation. I sat in this very seat. Do you remember that?"

John tries to recall the event. "No, I— I don't."

"Well, I felt a warmth and trust from you that was always lacking in all my experiences with others. I began to tell you my life story. You sat there listening so patiently. When I was finished, you looked at me with such compassion and empathy. At first, you didn't respond. You looked like you were absorbing it all, and then you spoke. You talked to me in words that were so eloquent, yet simple. You explained things to me about myself and the world that I never understood or cared about. You gave my life meaning, purpose, and worth. You made me realize that I didn't have to change the world around me, just change the one inside of me."

John has a puzzled look on his face. "I said something eloquent? I gave meaning to your life? You're sure it was me?"

"Of course, and you talked briefly about your son."

He turns solemn. "Yes, that was me." Then snaps back. "So, what have you been doing since I gave you that none-of-my-business lecture?"

"Well, I got rid of everything on my dark side. Stayed in school, for what seemed to be forever, and now I'm a professor at the university."

John has an ear-to-ear smile. "My goodness!"

"Then I got married to a wonderful man, also a professor, and we have two fantastic kids. And life is so beautiful. Oh, I'll take the next stop, John, if we can see it."

John slows the bus down to a stop and opens the doors. "And you're a professor!"

She gets up from her seat and approaches him. "Yes. And I just came to say thank you and to wish you all the best on your retirement. You're a dear man and you deserve a wonderful life," she says, kisses him on the cheek, and exits the bus.

"But, how did you know I was retiring?"

Without another word, she disappears into the wall of white. John closes the doors and begins to pull away. Then suddenly, there's a repeated banging at the doors. John is startled and jerks the bus to a stop. He opens the doors to reveal a smartly dressed man in a business suit and overcoat.

"Hey! Hang on there!"

John's eyes squint to see who it is. The man enters the bus covered in snow.

"You weren't going to leave me out in that storm, were you, John?" He takes off his gloves and uses them to beat the snow from his clothes. John tilts his head from side to side trying to recognize the man.

"John!" He offers John his hand. "It's Paul. You don't remember me, do you?"

"No, can't say that I do." John shakes his hand anyway.

"I would have thought you'd remember someone who owes you money."

John is once again puzzled. "You owe me money?"

Paul sits down across from him in the same seat as Nancy had sat. John closes the doors and continues driving.

"Yes, twenty dollars."

John scratches his head. "Nope, doesn't ring a bell."

"Well, it was about five years ago now. I had an hour to get to the airport. I was one of two people vying for a job in New York. It was a huge opportunity for me. My car wouldn't start and I could see the job fading before my eyes. And then an angel appeared out of nowhere."

"An angel?"

"Yes, I would say an angel. A bus pulled up beside me and there you were and you said, 'Looks like you could use some help.' I described my predicament and you told me to hop on and you'd see what you could do. I told you I didn't have any cash." He smiles. "And you said, 'Did I ask for any?' I grabbed my luggage bag and boarded the bus. You looked at your watch and told me that there was an out-of-town bus that goes to the airport that should cross our path in about four minutes. You told me to hang on; you might have to break a couple of rules to make it."

"Boy, wasn't I the brave one."

"You sure were. I just stood there with a firm grip on that hand pole and watched you put that bus into overdrive. I couldn't believe that you would go out of your way, even risk your job for a stranger. When we arrived at the corner the bus was already waiting. I told you I was sorry about not having any cash and instead of leaving it like that, you reached into your pocket and said, "Here, you'll need this," and handed me a twenty. I tried to refuse, but you insisted and told me that I didn't have any choice. I told you I'd get it back to you as soon as I returned, but never got the chance. I felt bad about it."

"Never mind about that, how did the story end?"

"Well, I made it to the airport on time, caught that flight and got that job."

John waves his fist. "Good for you!"

"My life couldn't be better. I've done exceedingly well and I owe it all to you."

John shakes his head. "That's nonsense. I was just doing my job."

"It had nothing to do with your job. It had to do with you. The person you are. So, I would like to finally," he smiles, "pay you back what I owe you." He stands, reaches inside his overcoat, pulls out an envelope and hands it to John.

"Now that's not necessary."

"It never is for the man who has everything."

John takes the envelope. The thought of having everything brings his son to the surface.

"That's not true. I...I don't have everything."

"Believe me, John, you have more than you realize. By the way, you can let me out here."

John looks through the windshield. "But we're in the middle of nowhere."

"I'll be fine."

John stops the bus and opens the doors.

Paul steps off, and then turns back to John. "My chauffeur's right behind us."

"Chauffeur?"

"And John…"

"Yeah."

"Enjoy your retirement."

Paul walks away.

"Chauffeur? And how does he know I'm retiring?"

He closes the doors. Puts the envelope into his shirt pocket and then continues his drive through the snow. His face shows signs of contentment following the conversations with the two passengers.

Suddenly, he spots two deer in the middle of the road. He gently squeezes the brakes. It's not enough. He presses harder and hits the horn. The deer bound off, but for John, it's too late. The bus begins to slide and he loses all control. The bus goes off the road and into the brush and comes to a halt. John rests his head on the steering wheel.

"Not today." He sits back in the seat and takes a deep breath then lightly presses his foot on the accelerator pedal. Just as he thought, the tires begin to spin. He throws on the four-way flashers that are barely visible in the blowing snow, then turns on the radio and picks up the receiver. John's driving record is impeccable and there's no humiliation having to be towed in for a mechanical problem, but for being stuck in the snow, he wants to hide under the dash.

"Operator three to 505."

There's some static and then, "505. Is that you, John?"

"It's me."

"We've been trying to reach you for the last hour. You have to come in. The storm is too bad. We've told everyone else."

"Well, I'd love to come in, but I have a bit of a problem. I got stuck on the side of the road trying to avoid some deer."

"Not today!"

"My exact words."

"Okay, where are you?"

"Uh," he looks around as he tries to recognize the area. "I'm somewhere on the other side of Ninth Line."

"Okay. I'm sending out a tow truck. Hang in there and keep warm."

"Ten-four." John looks at his watch. He decides to eat lunch. He reaches behind the seat, grabs his lunch pail, and opens it.

On the inside of the top is taped a faded, worn picture of his son Danny: a handsome young man in his early twenties with a beautiful smile.

He becomes emotional and close to tears. “Danny. I miss you so much. You meant the world to me. There’s nothing left. I feel like today is the last day of my life.” Tears slowly trickle down his cheeks.

Then... “That’s not true.”

John is startled. He looks into the rearview mirror.

It’s Danny! He’s sitting in the first row of seats.

“Danny,” he says in a whisper. He turns to face Danny, but Danny’s not there. He turns back to the mirror and there he is.

“Hi, Dad,” he says with a warm smile.

“Oh, Danny, you don’t know how much I’ve missed you, son.”

“I do know, Dad. That’s why I’m here.”

“Danny, why did this happen? Why didn’t I just ask you to leave the next morning? I could have prevented it from happening. You would still be here, enjoying a wonderful life.”

“Believe me, Dad; it had nothing to do with you. It was my time.”

“But if I had of just…”

“We don’t understand these things in life. We understand them in death.”

“But what about all of your hopes and dreams and…”

“Earthly things are for the earth and that’s where they stay. Don’t think of my hopes and dreams. I’m not a part of it anymore. I have moved on to the next stage in a life that never ends. Think of your hopes and dreams for this world, Dad. Think of Mom and your happiness together.”

“Somehow I feel that I let you down.”

“No, Dad. You were a wonderful father to me. You gave me all the opportunities of life, and for that I am truly grateful. I would feel that I let you down if I allowed you to live the rest of your life in my shadow. You’ve helped so many people in your life, now it’s time to help yourself.”

Danny gets up and moves behind his father.

“Enjoy this life, Dad. There is more to come. And we will be together again.”

He rests his hand on John's shoulder.

John grabs his hand and kisses it. "I love you, Danny."

"And I love you, Dad, and always will."

Danny disappears and John is left with his own hand on his shoulder. He wipes tears from his eyes. He is overwhelmed with emotion.

Bang! Bang! John nearly jumps out of his seat. It's the tow truck driver.

"Come on, John! Or are you going to spend the rest of your life in there?"

"No," says John, and then he thinks to himself, I'm going to live the rest of my life.

—

The truck with the bus in tow pulls up to the open garage doors. Inside all the drivers and Edna are waiting for him. They all cheer. For the first time in a long time John has a huge smile for Edna and she smiles back.

"Is that a smile I see on John's face?" says the supervisor to Edna.

"It sure is!"

"Imagine that."

—

John sits at the kitchen table as Edna dishes out his supper. She kisses him on the cheek.

"What's that for?" he asks.

"I was so proud of you today. You looked so happy when everyone greeted you, and so handsome with that beautiful smile."

"Something happened today, Edna. And I've held off telling you because I, I haven't been able to believe it myself."

"Well," she says with excitement, "just hold off for another minute."

Edna walks into the bedroom and picks up a brochure on European vacations. As she is about to leave the room, she sees John's work shirt on the floor, grabs it and the envelope falls out. She examines it with curiosity.

"John. John, what's this?"

John enters the bedroom. "What's what?"

She holds up the envelope. "This envelope. It dropped out of your shirt."

He smiles. "That's part of what I wanted to tell you. You won't believe it. This guy got on my bus and said that he owed me some money and then went into this whole story of how it happened."

"How much money did he owe you?"

"Just twenty dollars, imagine that. It's been five years, and he still pays me back. I didn't even remember it."

"Well that was very nice of him, but this seems awfully thick for twenty dollars."

John takes the envelope and opens it. He pulls out a stack of one hundred dollar bills.

"Oh, my goodness!" says Edna.

"My goodness is right!" He counts the bills.

"Edna, there's, there's ten thousand and twenty dollars here!"

"Why on earth would someone give you that kind of money? John, you're going to have to give that back."

"Hold on, there's something else in here," he pulls out a piece of folded paper. "Looks like a note of some kind." He unfolds it and begins to read it to himself. "Oh, my God!" he says.

"What is it, John?"

He drops on the side of the bed like a lead weight.

Edna takes the note from his hand and begins to read it. "You gave me the opportunity to have a great life and I would also like to offer you an opportunity to enjoy yours in your retirement. Please accept this as a token of gratitude. All my best, Paul."

6

THE HAPPY PLACE

Doug and Mary have a beautiful home, built on a solid foundation —unlike their marriage of thirteen years. You see, Doug is a man with a goal, self-destruction, and employs the gentle spirit of his wife to be the recipient of the violence he unleashes. But today is a day of change, and Mary will be heading to a place beyond Doug—or anyone else.

—

The patio looks like a war zone of empty beer cans, pizza boxes and half-eaten chicken wings. Doug and his two buddies, Bob and Ralph, are gathered around the TV watching the afternoon basketball game.

"Okay, commercial!" Bob hollers. "Throw me another beer, Ralph!"

"Comin' up."

Ralph opens the cooler and sticks his hand into the icy water, fishes around, but comes up empty.

"We're out of the good stuff," he says.

Doug is sitting comfortably numb in his chair, gnawing on a wing.

"Don't worry about it. I had the woman go out to get some this morning. They should all be lined up like little soldiers in that fridge by the back door."

Ralph stumbles his way to the fridge, pulls open the door and the news isn't good.

"Hey Doug, I think you've been screwed by your wife, and not in a good way!"

"What are you talking about?"

"It's empty!"

Doug's face distorts into a side order of mean and gruesome.

"Did you say no beer?"

"Sorry Doug, just an echo in here."

"I'll kill her!" He pulls himself out of the chair, weaves, and trips his way into the house.

Mary, a wisp of a woman, is at the sink doing dishes, holding her cell phone between her chin and shoulder, whispering into the phone to her friend.

“He’s out on the patio with a couple of friends. They’ve been drinking since early this morning. I can’t take this anymore. And where do I go? I can’t hide, he’d find me.”

“Mary!”

He startles Mary and the cell phone drops into the soapy dishwater. Doug stands in the doorway holding up an empty beer can.

“Where’s the beer?” He moves toward her. His eyes are wild and intense, like a lion ready to pounce on its prey.

Mary begins to back away. She knows the look and the tone and what will follow. Her best defence is to go mute.

“You promised to get me beer! You’ve embarrassed me in front of my friends! How long do you think I’m going to put up with this bullshit?” He shoves her. “Huh! You think it’s easy living with a moron?” He shoves her again. She falls to the floor. He straddles her. She holds her hands up to her face, but to no avail as he begins his relentless assault. One hard blow finds its mark and renders her unconscious.

But today is a day of change. This day will hold no surprises for Doug. He will be moving directly into another home with bars, where he can self-destruct on his own—and Mary? She will also be moving.

—

“Mary...Mary, did you hear what I said?” comes a voice.

Mary stares into space as she sits in the office of Dr. Emily Ross, staff psychiatrist at Meadowvale Hospital. The once visible scars on her face have faded, but the emotional ones rest uncomfortably just below the surface.

“You can’t keep going back there.”

Mary turns her head to Dr. Ross.

“I’m sorry. What did you say, Dr. Ross?”

“I want you to look at me and listen.”

“Okay.”

“You’ve been here for quite some time and eventually you’ll have to leave, but right now we have to bring you back into society.”

“Why? Why can’t I stay here? I feel safe here. This is my home now.”

"No, Mary. This is not your home. It's an institution. You are an intelligent woman. We've been through this over and over. It's time for you to move on. Move past the past. I don't expect you to forget what happened, but you have to deal with the present and see that you *have* a future. A future that is wide open to so many possibilities. But *you* are the one who has to take that first step. I can't take it for you."

Mary's head tilts down. Her fingers begin fidgeting. "And what is that first step?"

"The first step is to focus on something other than you."

"Like what?"

"Like a job. It will help to build your confidence to get back into the real world."

"A job?" she says, squirming in her seat. "I don't understand. Doesn't that mean I would have to leave?"

Dr. Ross leans forward in her chair and smiles. "No, you can work here, as a volunteer. You can help other patients."

"Me? But what could I do?"

"Well, we have patients that are in what we call a comatose or vegetative state."

"Vegetative?"

"Yes. It's like being asleep, but they appear awake. It's a state of deep unconsciousness."

"Sounds creepy; how could I possibly help them?"

"By being a friend. Play music for them. Talk to them."

"But how would that help them if they don't even know what's going on?"

"That's just it, Mary, they *may* know what's going on, but can't reach out. Or, it may not help them at all, but it will help you."

—

The next morning Mary peers out the window of her room at the cold, rain-drenched street below. Water droplets trickle down the window, reminding her of all the tears she shed over the years living with that monster Doug. But it also makes her feel secure and comfortable in the warmth of her room, where the outside world can't get in. Without warning, she hears terrifying, escalating voices of her and Doug arguing inside her head.

"Leave me alone!"

"You're a useless excuse for a wife!"

"No! Don't!"

"You deserve what you get, you little bitch!"

"Stop it! Stop it!"

A cheery voice penetrates her wall of terror. "Good morning, Mary! It's volunteer time!"

Mary turns into the room to see a nurse who looks like Kathy Bates on acid. She holds a clipboard close to her large breasts.

"What was that?" asks Mary.

"It's time to go to work, remember? You're a volunteer now."

"Oh, yes, I remember. Is that now?"

"Yes, it is." She glances at her watch. "In about four minutes. Just enough time to get to the fifth floor to see your new patients. Just like a real doctor."

Mary hesitates.

"Come on, Mary. You don't want to be late on your first day."

Mary takes in a deep breath of stale hospital air and follows the nurse.

They stand by the elevator waiting for it to come up from the basement. Mary draws in a few more deep breaths. The doors open and an assortment of cafeteria smells push their way out: stale coffee, burnt toast, and boiled potatoes and cabbage.

The ride is a nightmare. Each floor creeps along with the squeaking sounds of the pulleys and cables stretching to their limits. Reaching the fifth floor is an experience of its own as the elevator box bounces to a halt like a bungee cord.

Stepping out into the hall is like entering the set from *The Snake Pit*. It's the wing of the forgotten, out-dated and unkempt. It houses the living carcasses of the once vibrant, exciting, and productive souls that are now mere shells of humanity.

Some of the lights along the hallway are either burned out or broken. Mary's hands and teeth are clenched as they walk down the darkened corridor passing the nurses' station. The nurse checks her clipboard.

"Mary, I have to go back and ask the head nurse something. You wait here, I'll be right back."

Mary begins to get edgy. The nurse is taking too long. Looking down the never-ending hallway that fades into a blurred haze of sinister shadows, she sucks in more oxygen. She turns back to the nurses' station and observes the nurse leaning over the counter in conversation.

"God, please hurry," she says to herself.

She turns back, but before she can take another breath, Doug appears out of nowhere. His face filled with anger and rage; grabbing her by the throat before she can squeak out a sound. He begins to strangle her, and pushes her hard against the wall. She struggles and tries to pull his hands away, but he's too strong. Finally she's able to scream out and shrinks down to the floor into a little ball.

The nurse hears her cries—Doug disappears.

"Mary!" The nurse rushes to Mary and squats down beside her. "Mary, Mary! It's all right, I'm here. No one's going to hurt you." She holds Mary. "It's okay. We'll try again tomorrow."

With the help of a sedative, Mary is able to sleep, but the nightmares are relentless.

—

In the morning Mary wakes with a relaxed body, but a tormented mind. She sits on the side of her bed and in the quiet of her room tries to concentrate on a book.

From the doorway a raspy voice, "Hello, Mary."

Mary jolts and looks up. There stands Lucy, a thin, old, prune-faced woman with long, white, matted hair, huge sunken eyes with dark brown circles, wearing a yellow stained and tattered nightgown.

"Lucy! I wish you wouldn't creep up on me like that."

"I heard that you're going to take care of the dead today."

"The dead? Oh, you mean the comatose patients."

"Well, comatose, dead, it's all the same." She takes up a position on the bed beside Mary.

"They're in a *special* place, you know," she says in an unsettling whisper.

"It's just in the day room on the fifth floor."

"That's not what I'm talking about."

Her skeletal hand reaches over and gently falls over Mary's hand. "That's where their bodies are, but not their minds, their souls."

Mary quickly pulls her hand away. "Okay, Lucy, that's enough. You're starting to freak me out. I want you to leave."

"Of course, my dear."

Lucy gets up and slowly moves to the doorway, more floating than walking. She turns back as Mary returns to her book.

"It's the happy place, Mary," says Lucy.

"What's the happy place?"

"Yes. That's where you'll find them, in the happy place. *Happy-Happy-Happy*," says Lucy with a crazed smile, then disappears along with her voice.

—

Once again Mary exits the elevator with the nurse and begins another walk down the long hallway to the day room.

"Now Mary, before we go in, I want to tell you that there is nothing to be nervous about. These people aren't threatening. They can't hurt you." She smiles. "And, who knows, maybe, by some miracle, you might be able to reach one of them. Now wouldn't that be nice?"

"Reach one of them?"

"You'll see."

The nurse opens the door that hasn't seen Three-in-One oil for some time. They enter the large brightly lit room. The wooden floorboards shift under their feet and squeak with each step. Drab, dusty curtains hang half-drawn from windows darkened by years of grime.

On one side of the room, lined up in a row like empty bottles, are five patients sitting in chairs, oblivious to the reality around them.

At this point Mary wishes the light had been dimmer. "Oh, my God," says Mary, just above a whisper. "Lucy was right. They do look like they're dead."

"Yes, I know," the nurse says with sympathy. "Sad, isn't it." There's a brief pause as the nurse seems to be contemplating their state. Then with an unexpected about-face she smiles and joyfully states, "Now, all you have to do is play them music, and sit and talk to them."

She points across the room beyond the patients.

"The CD player is on the table. I'll be back in an hour."

As the nurse moves to leave, Mary grabs her arm. "No! Please don't go."

"It's all right, Mary," she smiles. "You'll be perfectly safe here. I'll be back."

The door bangs shut with a dissipating echo, leaving an eerie silence. Mary begins her walk past the patients to the CD player. Each patient appears frozen like wax figures from Madame Tussauds. Their deep, dark eyes float in a sea of emptiness, void of time and space.

Mary makes it to the table. She picks up a CD and examines it briefly, then places it into the player. Soft classical music fills the room where the quiet had been. She gently runs her fingers over the player and closes her eyes to drink in the music. *This isn't so bad,* she thinks.

A loud bang shears through the tranquil setting. Mary's body reacts with a sharp jerk. She opens her eyes to see a can of soda rolling from the patients' area and stopping at her feet. She's terrified and looks at the patients only to find them still in their zombie-like state.

With her eyes focussed on the patients, she bends to pick up the can.

"What the hell is going on here?" she whispers to herself. "How did that can roll across the room?"

With trepidation she walks to the patients. "Did someone drop this?"

Even though the question was asked she prays no one will answer or jump out at her. Every face is as deadpan as the next. No response. She pulls up a chair and sits in front of them.

"Well..." she says. "I'll put it down here beside my chair and if anyone wants to claim it, here it is." *Someone doesn't belong here,* she thinks. *Either one of them is not comatose, or I'm really crazy.*

"Mary!"

"Uh!" Mary jumps out of the chair to see the nurse entering from the doorway.

"Mary, I just remembered. These new CDs just arrived. I thought you might like them."

The nurse looks beyond Mary to the patients and grins.

"How are you getting along?"

Mary looks back at patients. "I, I'm not sure."

"Well, if they get too chatty, you let me know. I'll see you shortly."

Mary wanted to tell her about the incident with the can, but thought otherwise. Mentioning anything out of the ordinary may work against her. She returns to her seat and glances at the can on the floor.

"Oh, my God!" she screams.

The can is on its side, open and empty.

"Alright! Somebody's playing a trick on me! One of you shouldn't be here! Who is it? Tell me!"

The patients sit expressionless. Mary has a meltdown. She cries uncontrollably and pulls at her hair. "I can't do this! I can't live like this anymore! I can't take it! I can't!"

Suddenly a calm and gentle voice is heard over her cries.

"Mary, Mary don't cry. Everything will be all right."

At first she thinks it's another voice in her head. "No! No, it won't! I'm crazy! I'll never get out of here!"

She realizes someone in the room is talking to her and quickly looks up to see one of the patients standing over her.

"It's you!" she points. "You're the one! The one that doesn't belong here! Why are you doing this to me?" Mary buries her face in her hands and continues crying.

"Mary, you're not crazy," says the patient. "You've been through a lot, but that will all change now."

He extends some comfort to her by stroking her head. The other patients come to life and stand in a circle around her.

"You have friends here, Mary."

She looks up to see the other patients. "See, we're all here to help you."

"Oh, my God! Now I know I'm crazy! There's nothing wrong with any of you!"

"Of course not. We have just chosen to live in a different world. A world that we are happy in."

"You don't want to stay here anymore, do you, Mary? Don't you want to be free and happy in a place of *your* choosing?" asks another patient.

"Yes, yes I do."

"Then, let us help you."

"Think back, Mary," says another. "Think back to the best time and place in your life when you were happy."

"When was that, Mary? When were you the happiest?"

Mary begins to think back. "Happy? Yes, I remember. I remember now. It was when I lived on the farm with my aunt and uncle."

"That's it, Mary."

"Remember that time."

"Think back."

"Close your eyes."

"See it. See it, Mary."

"Go to *your* Happy Place."

Mary closes her eyes. Like the sun appearing from behind a cloud, a smile stretches across her face.

"Happy place? Yes! I can see it!"

She begins to see herself at ten years old on the farm.

"I can see it! The farm where I lived. I would wake up early every morning and feed the animals. The sky was so blue, and the air so fresh, and fields of daisies, and the river, that beautiful river where I would swim and catch fish, and those wonderful Sunday dinners of ham and peach pie. We were all so happy then, so happy."

—

The nurse passes by the day room. She stops, looks at her watch and decides that Mary has been in there long enough. She walks into a quiet room, and observes each patient still in their vacant state. At the end of the row sits Mary, her eyes fixed on her dream in the far-off world of her happy place.

The nurse smiles. "It's so nice to see you getting along with the others, Mary. Dr. Ross knew exactly what you needed."

She squats down in front of Mary and holds her hand. "This is the beginning of a new and exciting life for you, Mary. I'll miss you, but I know that you'll be in a safe place. A happy place." She gives Mary a kiss on the forehead and then leaves the room.

—

Dr. Ross is in her office with a new patient.

"You've been sent here to be evaluated. During your stay we will put you to work. We have patients that are in a comatose or vegetative state. Did you hear what I said, Doug?"

Mary's husband, Doug, sits across from Dr. Ross with a faraway look.

"Sorry, what was that, Doc?"

"I said, you can work here. We have patients that..."

—

Doug is in his room, resting on his bed reading a magazine when Lucy floats in.

"You must be the new one, Doug. I'm Lucy."

Doug lowers his magazine.

"What do you want, old lady?"

"Me? I don't want anything. Just interested in your well-being, that's all."

"I don't need some moldy, old bag of bones interested in my well-being."

"Of course," says Lucy.

She moves close to Doug. "But you know, Doug; we can always use a friend in our corner."

Doug quickly sits up.

"Look, Lucy Goosey. I don't need a friend or a cadaver in my corner. So get back on your broom. Don't stop until you see a full moon."

She smiles, "Oh, I can go much farther than that."

Doug goes back to reading the magazine.

"Why doesn't that surprise me?"

He lowers the magazine to find her gone. "Well, that was easy."

"Good morning, Doug!"

Doug throws the magazine on the floor in frustration. The nurse stands by the door with a big smile.

"Holy shit! It's her younger sister. What the hell is it now?"

"It's time to see your new patients. Just like a real doctor."

"And don't you wish you were one?"

"Now, that's not very nice, Doug. We're all here to help you."

Doug stands up and gets right in her face.

"Then why don't you go and help somebody that needs it?"

For the first time the nurse shows her fangs. "Because that isn't how it works. Besides, you don't want to go back to that prison, now do you, *Doug?*"

"All right, Miss Ratchet, which way to the dum-dums?"

—

The nurse enters the day room with Doug in tow. The patients are in their usual positions.

"Look at the heads on those puppets."

"Yes. Sad, isn't it?"

"Sad?" Doug laughs, "It's hilarious. What do you want me to do with these cardboard cutouts?"

She points to the CD player. "The CD player is over there. You just play them music, sit and talk to them."

"Well, I hope they don't get too bored."

She smiles. "Yes. I'll be back in an hour." And with that she leaves the room.

Doug makes his way to the CD player, passing the patients as he goes.

"You guys remind me of my graduating class." He picks up a few of the CDs.

"What's this shit?"

He opens a small drawer under the table and finds some music to his liking.

"Striking gold! Here we go." He puts a disc into the player. Heavy metal music bounces off the walls. Doug starts to dance around the patients.

"This should wake up you assholes!"

The face of each patient remains cold and expressionless.

"Come on! Get up and dance! I've seen better heads on beer!"

—

The hour has passed. The room is quiet and still. The nurse enters, pushing the now comatose Mary in a wheelchair.

The patients are in their positions with one added feature, Doug.

The nurse wheels Mary beside Doug.

"Well, Doug, I see you've made yourself at home with the rest of the patients. And look who's come to join you."

She leans over, looking straight into Doug's blank eyes and smiles. "You remember Mary. Don't you, Doug?" She straightens up. "She's so happy to see you. Well, I'll leave you two alone to get reacquainted."

She leaves the room, and for the first time in years Mary and Doug sit side by side.

In his mind, Doug sits comfortably in his happy place of a baseball game on TV and drinking beer. Heavy, thick rope appears and begins to coil around him, binding his arms and torso around the chair.

"What the hell's going on?"

Mary becomes visible at his side.

"What are you doing in my happy place?" says Doug.

She has a baseball bat in her hands.

"You don't get to have a happy place."

Lucy appears on the other side of Doug.

"No, not for you, you bastard!" yells Mary.

"But we *are* going to play a little baseball."

Lucy has a hideous smile on her face. "You hit him first, Mary. Then let me have a whack."

Mary raises the bat and pulls it back behind her shoulder.

"Hit him hard, Mary!"

Doug screams, "No! I'll kill you!"

Mary laughs hysterically. "You'll kill me?"

"Go on! Hit him hard, Mary!" cackles Lucy. "Hit him real hard!"

Doug is terrified! Mary whirls the bat! Doug lets out a blood-curdling scream!

—

Mary is seated in Dr. Ross's office.

"Mary, Mary? Did you hear what I said?"

Mary looks straight ahead.

"You can't keep going back there."

"I'm sorry. What did you say, Dr. Ross?"

"I want you to look at me and listen to what I'm saying."

"Okay."

"Tell me, Mary, who is Lucy?"

"Lucy? Lucy's in Room 225."

"And the other patients, the comatose ones you talk about?"

"Oh, they're not comatose, Dr. Ross. They're my best friends."

"Can you tell me about that last day at home, when you killed Doug with the baseball bat. That must have been very traumatic for you, trying to defend yourself against him."

"Oh no, Dr. Ross, it was easy."

"Easy?"

"Yes. I didn't kill him by myself. Lucy and my friends all took a whack at him."

She looks at Dr. Ross and giggles. "I couldn't have done that on my own, Dr. Ross."

"Mary, there is no Room 225. There is no Lucy, and we don't have comatose patients here."

"Why would you say that, Dr. Ross?"

"Because, it's only in your mind, Mary."

Mary smiles and slowly shakes her head. "No, Dr. Ross. They're all in the happy place."

Beyond the vacant stare in Mary's eyes...

"Hit him hard, Mary! Hit him again!"

7

MEMORY BANK

Returning to one's old neighbourhood to relive childhood memories with old friends carries a unique nostalgia. For Andy Tilman, however, those memories hide something far more profound—and potentially life-altering.

—

A taxi pulls up to the top of Chestnut Street. Andy Tilman exits with a small luggage in tow. He looks at the street sign, smiles, and begins his walk down the quiet, lazy row of war-time houses.

He stops at the third house in, on the right-hand side. My God, he thinks to himself. The old house is still standing: new front porch, new windows. After forty-five years they should have seen some work, and it's probably been re-shingled three times by now. Boy, a lot of memories in that house.

He imagines himself at age ten, bursting through the front door, picking up his bike from the driveway and riding off down the street with a piece of cardboard clipped to the rear wheel that clatters along. He sees his mother opening the front door as he turns back to look at the house.

"Andy! I want you home by five for supper!"

"Okay, Mom!"

Andy takes in a deep breath and holds back tears. "Oh, Mom, I miss you so much."

He continues until he reaches the house of his oldest friend Russ, who has remained in the same house since the day he was created. He walks up to the door and immediately hears that oh-so-familiar '60s music. He smiles and thinks to himself, I'm home. He knocks politely. No answer. He knocks harder.

The music is turned down. The door opens and there is Russ wearing a Leon Redbone T-shirt. He stands at six feet tall with long, grey hair supported by a close-cropped beard and a belly, fuelled by liquid grain and nurtured by time.

"Andy, baby! How's it hangin', you old bugger!"

He gives Andy a bear hug, leaving no room for Andy's arms to respond other than staying limp at his side.

Andy responds with a warm smile. "I'm good."

"Well, you look good. I thought this big, bad world would have whittled you down to a pipe cleaner by now."

"They've been trying."

An Irish setter appears at the door and jumps up at Andy.

"That's Gus. He's a friendly old fart."

Andy ruffles Gus's face.

"I can see that. How you doin' there, Gus?"

"Well, come on in!"

They step from the front door right into the living room. Russ picks up the newspapers on the couch.

"I wasn't expecting you for another hour."

"I got through airport security in no time flat."

"Well, that doesn't happen very often. Sit down. Take a load off. How's a beer sound?"

"Sounds good."

Russ leaves for the kitchen with Gus at his heels. Andy looks around, and from what he can remember, it looks like Russ has moved his teenage bedroom to the living room. Memorabilia from the fifties and sixties are placed at will. There is no logical balance to the room. Record albums are the only items of order, lined up in old wooden milk crates beside an old Fisher stereo system and turntable. In one way it feels good to see remnants of his past, but also somewhat disturbing to know that Russ hasn't moved one iota, physically or mentally, his entire life.

Russ is back with two cold ones. "I'm so glad to see you. Just like old times." He hands Andy a beer, then sits across from him in a chair that Frasier's dad would turn down.

"Isn't that internet stuff something else? Nice connecting on email, and it doesn't cost you shit. No stamps, it's instantaneous. Man, can you imagine all the chicks we could have had back in the sixties with that."

The beer bottle doesn't touch the outside of his mouth. His throat just opens up and down it goes like a flush toilet.

"Did I tell you, you look good?"

Andy chuckles, "You did. And you haven't changed a bit. You're still alive and kicking. How did you manage that?"

"I could say it wasn't easy, but I'd be lying. I just stayed in my in my element. I never grew up," he laughs.

"I see that," says Andy.

"When my parents died—you remember them, right?"

"Of course. Frank and Audrey."

"Yeah, good people. They put up with a hell of a lot from me. Anyway, when they died the house was mine, and I knew damn well if I sold it and went my merry way, I'd blow it all and be homeless in a year. So, for the first time in my life, I did the right thing. You want to smoke some rope?"

"Uh, maybe later."

"It's legal now. Beautiful, isn't it? The government finally does something right. I think it'll go viral and we'll go full circle, back to the sixties, exactly where I am now. It's like you wear a shirt long enough and it comes back in style. And I'm the shirt." He laughs, "How sweet is that?" He takes another breath. "So, everything good with you?"

"Well, it's been a little lonely. I lost my wife three years ago."

"Shit. Sorry to hear that, man."

"Yeah, so I'm just hanging on for another six months, then retiring. I thought Ellen and I would be doing it together. We talked about our plans of taking trips to Europe and cruises and eating in fancy restaurants."

"Yeah, that's rough. Gets pretty lonely. I was engaged a few times. I never lost anyone that close though, other than my parents. Did you have any kids?"

"No."

"Me either. At least no one's ever left anything on my doorstep."

"We tried, but Ellen just couldn't have any. You know, with some people it drives a wedge between them. But for us, we actually grew closer."

"That's beautiful." Russ belches. "Another beer?"

"Absolutely."

"That's right, man! It's party time! And tonight I'm going to make us the biggest, juiciest steaks you've ever eaten!"

—

The wooden deck in the backyard is simply dressed with a barbecue, umbrella table and two chairs and, of course, the "never-ending" cooler of beer.

They have just finished their steaks and are sitting back inhaling beer and sunset. All is well.

"Boy," says Russ. "This sure takes me back. Remember all those summer nights we'd spend playing kick-the-can?"

"Yeah, simpler times."

"We had fun with nothing. You won't find one kid today doing any of the things that we did."

"They don't know how to have fun on the cheap," says Andy. "Yeah, they just don't know how to make kids anymore."

"Hey, remember those treks to the forest? I'd fly out the door at the crack of dawn with a bag full of mustard sandwiches. We'd grab our bikes and wouldn't be seen all day. Remember that?"

Russ laughs. "And nobody gave a shit! The only stipulation was that you had to be home by supper. You know, that forest we used to play in is full of box stores now."

"That sucks. So, is there anyone else still on the street?"

"Carolyn's still here."

"Carolyn Burrows? Oh, my God!"

"And Dewy."

"Dewy, too?"

"Yeah, but he's on the next street now. He moved into a house the same as his, another war-timer, but it had a finished rec room and above-ground pool. Get this: He said he was finally moving up in the world." They laugh.

"Hey!" says Russ. He leans over the side of his chair and grabs an old, beat-up photo album. "I dug this out of the ashes."

He hands it to Andy. The photo album has a faded title glued to the cover. "The Memory Bank?"

"Go ahead." says Russ. "Open it."

He opens the first page to reveal a large photo of the two of them at age ten, sitting with their arms around each other, with devilish grins on their faces.

"I remember this picture," says Andy. "We had just gotten back from stealing apples from old man Johnson's orchard."

"We looked like a couple of criminals."

"Compared to today, that was just clean fun," he says and turns the page. "Look at the pictures; all these memories; pictures of our street—there we are playing road hockey."

"Yeah, every night, out there freezing our asses off with numb fingers and toes, acting like we were in the NHL."

Andy laughs. "Remember that one year? We made a replica of the Stanley Cup out of aluminum foil and your mother was so pissed because we used two rolls."

"Yeah, who won that thing anyway?"

"I think it was Danny's team."

"I don't know how that little fart did it, but he always managed to be on the winning team."

"The whole street came out for those games." Andy points at a photograph. "There's Danny and Dewy, Frank, Tony, and the twins, John and Jerry."

"One wore a Toronto sweater and the other Montreal. They were always fighting. We couldn't have them on the same team."

"Man, I'd give anything to go back again."

"The best time of our lives, that's for sure. Carefree, no responsibilities. No taxes, mortgages, and no wars. And the only terrorism was from that redheaded, freckled-faced asshole that ran after us after school."

"What the hell was with those redheads? It was like they were possessed, and were all part of some alien organization."

"Those days are gone forever."

They sit for a moment reminiscing in their own heads.

"So," says Andy. "Carolyn's still here. She was a knockout. I had a crush on her for years."

"I'll take you over to see her tomorrow."

"How's she doing?"

"It ain't pretty. Best to wipe that memory of her out of your head, or you can wait and have her do it for you."

—

Andy and Russ arrive at Carolyn's front door. Russ taps on the wooden frame of the screen.

"Carolyn! Carolyn, you there?"

"Who is it?" she says in a gruff voice.

"It's Russ!"

"Come on in! I'll be right there! Just have to put my teeth in!"

He looks over at Andy. "I told you."

The living room is the same setup as Russ's, but in total disarray. TV on, ironing board out, newspapers and magazines strewn everywhere. They move some of the debris from the well-worn couch before they sit. Andy feels something under him and pulls out a bra that has also seen better days. He drops it on an end table beside him. Even though Russ is taller, his height is minimized by the lack of resistance in the springs under the cushion.

"Better look your best!" says Russ to Carolyn. "I have a surprise for you!"

"If it's George Clooney, sit on him until I get there!"

"It's not George, but pretty close!"

She waltzes into the living room. Her black, dyed hair pulled back in a ponytail. There's a problem with older people when they dye their hair in such contrast; they look like they're dead. She's about five foot two. She has Russ's wheat-belly, but in surround sound.

"Sorry for taking so long. I did say I was just brushing my teeth, right?"

They stand.

"Wow. There's a first. I don't ever remember anyone standing when I entered a room," she says, and looks at Andy. "Well, you're right, he ain't George, but he looks pretty damn good to me."

"Do you remember this guy?"

She squints. "You do look familiar."

"Let me help you," says Andy. "I lived at thirty-six."

"Thirty-six…that was...Andy. Holy shit! Andy!"

She walks up to him and throws her arms around him. She caught him on an exhale and he struggles to breathe.

"Andy! I can't believe it's you!"

I can't believe it's you either, thinks Andy.

"Well, sit down. Tell me all about yourself. Are you married?"

"Right to the jugular," says Russ.

"Stop it, Russ. It's every woman's prerogative to ask that question."

"That's okay," says Andy. "I'm widowed."

Sounding sincere she responds with... "Oh, I'm so sorry," then bounces back with, "Can I get you boys a drink? No beer, just vodka and orange juice, vodka and tomato juice, or vodka and cranberry juice. It's a good way to get some vitamins every day."

"I'll remember that," says Andy. "I'll go for the orange juice."

"Straight up for me there, princess," says Russ.

"Don't let him get away, Russ," she says, heading to the kitchen.

"We never leave before the drinks are poured!" he answers.

He looks at Andy. "So, how's your crush coming along?"

Andy whispers, "Crushed. I think name tags would have been a good idea."

"She hasn't had it easy. No one deserves a break more than this gal. It got so bad that suicide was on the doorstep."

Carolyn re-enters holding three coffee mugs. "Sorry about the mugs. All the glasses are dirty. I don't usually get visitors, except for Russ. He's been a lifesaver."

"Aw, just trying to be a good neighbour and friend."

"And full of shit, too," says Carolyn as she sits across from them on the old-style kitchen chair that has the two steps folding into it. Like a magic trick, it quickly disappears under her large bottom. She pulls out the steps and rests her feet. "Believe me, Andy, I could never repay this guy for all he's done for me. He's helped me with plumbing, roofing, windows; you name it."

"He was always there for me when we were growing up, weren't you, buddy?" says Andy.

"Okay you two. I'm going to need a shovel pretty soon."

"And humble too," says Carolyn.

"Hey! I just thought of a great idea," says Russ. "Let's throw a party in honour of Andy's return."

"I'm up for that," says Carolyn.

"A celebration of friendship and old times," says Andy. "Why don't we use the theme from your photo album, The Memory Bank?"

"That's a great idea! We can bring pictures and all the old family 8 mm reels. We'll make a night of it. I'll get hold of Dewy and we'll set this up for tomorrow night."

"I love it!" says Carolyn. "Where are we going to have it?"

"Dewy's place," says Russ. "He's always bragging about his great rec room."

"Is it?" asks Andy.

"What, great? I don't know. I've never seen it. He made some renovations on it, and ever since then he's been keeping it under wraps like some covert operation."

—

After a few mugs, Russ does a John Wayne walk back to his place with Andy doing his own rendition.

"I'll give Dewy a call."

"Are you sure he'll go for it?"

"I'm sure. He has to be dying to show that rec room to someone by now. What's the point of having a rec room, if you can't wreck it?" He picks up the phone. "Andy, can you grab that large tobacco tin on the top shelf of that cupboard and open it."

"Sure." Andy grabs the container and opens it. Inside are tightly packed, evenly rolled joints.

"Hey, Dewy, my boy!" says Russ. "How's it hangin'? Great!"

He signals Andy to light up a joint. "Guess who's sitting in my kitchen. I'll give you a hint, a blast from the past. No, he's gone, liver disease, no suicide, no overdose. No, this one's still kickin'. You sitting down? Andy Tilman! Yeah, no shit! I know, at least thirty. We are, that's why I'm calling."

Andy gets the joint going with a nice long drag.

"You don't have to go anywhere. We're coming over to your place."

Andy takes a couple more tokes.

"Tomorrow night. Yeah, your place. You know, your rec room. Yeah, yours. What do you think we're going to do—trash the place? We're not kids anymore, or haven't you looked in the mirror lately? Everyone's bringing pictures and reels from the past. You, me, Andy, and Carolyn. The old neighbourhood is back together again. See you then," he hangs up. "There, all done."

And so is Andy. He's ready for a trip on the Marrakesh Express.

"How's that stuff? Pretty good huh?"

Andy's eyes are half closed. "What?"

"Andy. You little pothead."

It's been years since Andy partook of the power of the flower.

"It sure has more of a kick than it did in the sixties," says Andy. "Maybe this could be the answer to all our woes as seniors. I think you're on to something here, Russ."

"Oh, I know I am. I've been on it for fifty years."

—

Andy's never had much of an appetite in the morning, but the smell of bacon, eggs, home fries, and coffee picks him up by the nostrils and guides him into the kitchen where Russ is dishing out breakfast.

"Man, that smells good," says Andy.

"Oh yeah, I challenge anyone to resist a breakfast like this."

"Aren't you worried about your cholesterol?"

"Cholesterol? It's a pharmaceutical wet dream and a senior's nightmare. Just like all the other drugs they're pushing. Home fries?"

"Perfect."

"The whole world is a piece of work, Andy. *Star Trek* had it wrong. It should have been 'Beam me back, Scotty; back to the fifties and sixties.'"

"That's true, but we lived it and no one can take that away. We can't go back physically, but we can go back in memory."

"Yes, sir. And that's what we're doing tonight, the big memory bank blast to the past."

—

All three show up at Dewy's front door loaded with bags of pictures, reels, booze, snacks, and a Bell and Howell projector in the original box that Russ carries. He taps the door a few times with his foot.

"Dewy! Open up!"

Dewy opens the door looking glum. "Hi guys. Come on in."

"Shit Dewy! Are you sure?" says Russ. "What's wrong? Not enough fibre in your diet?"

"No. I'm okay." They make their way in. Dewy looks at all the stuff they're carrying.

"You guys are just here for the evening, right?"

"No. We're moving in," says Carolyn.

Russ motions with his thumb. "Check out the guy in the back. Remember that kisser?"

"Hey, Andy. It's been a long time," says Dewy.

"How are you, Dewy?"

"Could be better, could be worse."

Russ pipes up, "Well, tonight it's going to be better: old friends, old memories, old Scotch, and some special brownies, compliments of Carolyn."

"Hey, I just baked them. You supplied the fibre."

Russ looks around. "So, we headed for your rec room?"

"Yeah, I guess so," says Dewy with some reluctance.

"Dewey, are you sure? You're not making us feel very welcome. What the hell's wrong? I thought you'd be excited to show us your masterpiece."

He suddenly has a change of heart and smiles. "Yeah, you're right. Come on down."

"All right!" says Carolyn. "That's the Dewy we love."

They are unprepared for what they see in his rec room. It's a miniature movie theatre. Two rows of three plush chairs that lean back. Rich, red carpeting, and a massive screen and top-quality surround sound. Plus a bar with a theatre-size popcorn machine. They put their items on the floor.

"Holy shit!"

"Oh, my God!"

"Dewy...this...this is incredible!"

Dewy looks down at the floor embarrassed. "Yeah, I know."

"You know?" says Andy. "You should be proud of this."

"Should be, but I can't."

"This must have cost you a fortune!" says Russ.

"That's the problem: I over-indulged and went way over my head with this. I'm starving just to pay for it. That's why I hesitated to have you over. I didn't want to get into it. I don't even come down here anymore. It hurts too much."

The room is silent. They look at each other, not knowing how to react.

He raises his eyes to them. "Sorry guys. I didn't want this to be a downer."

Carolyn jumps in holding a plastic container full of brownies. "That's why I made these suckers!"

"All right!" says Russ.

Dewy loosens the reins. "And that means party on!"

Russ sets up the projector while Dewy and Andy pull a white bed sheet over the TV screen. Carolyn grabs some bowls and fills them with snacks, then pops the lid on the brownies.

"Come and get 'em, boys!"

As soon as everyone settles in, the lights are doused and the room takes on a magical feel. Russ starts the projector. First the familiar clatter of the claws moving through the sprockets. Then the scratched frames with numbers pass by the white sheet and then an outdoor scene showing Carolyn as a child playing with a doll and carriage on the front steps of her house.

"Oh my god! My doll and carriage!"

"And look how cute you were."

"How old were you there?"

"I think I was seven or eight."

"Oh look! There's Russ on his bike!"

"I loved that bike. It took me everywhere."

"Yeah, back then the bike was the precursor to our cars."

"Boy, you were skinny back then."

"We all were. We burned more energy in one day than the kids do today in a month."

Fifteen minutes in and something happens. The room becomes silent. No dialogue, no background music; just the clatter of the old Bell and Howell. It is more than their eagerness to see the past brought back to life.

It's as if they are under a spell: totally mesmerized. They are surprised to see how young and vibrant their parents were, even though at the time they considered them to be old. They see the park, where they played baseball and touch football, and the hockey rink with the wooden boards; all gone years ago to make room for more houses. The trees on the street were only five or six feet tall, and now they tower the neighbourhood.

Hardly a word is spoken through the two hours of reels. The silence continues for a moment after the last film, and then Carolyn bursts into tears.

"I want to go back! I want to be a little girl again, and live with my parents! I want to go back and stay there, where it was safe! I don't want to end my life this way!"

Hearing that strikes a chord with all of them: hard to swallow, emotional lumps in every throat.

To see her pain demonstrated to such a degree is especially hard for Andy. The loss of his wife and his absence from the street for so many years, then coming back, also makes him homesick for another time.

He was the only one of them to leave the neighbourhood, and he did it two years after high school. He thought it was time to grow up. Break those apron strings and head for the bright lights and open his life to a new and exciting world.

New it was, but exciting? If toiling in the trenches to pay the next bill was exciting, he had plenty of that. When he finally got it together he lost the love of his life. No more thoughts of the future; no more wishes or dreams, just memories. The emotional stress Carolyn feels is not lost with Andy.

"I guess this wasn't such a good idea," says Russ.

"No. It was a wonderful idea," says Carolyn as she wipes tears and pulls herself together.

Andy puts his arm around her. "It's all bittersweet. But damn it, it was the best time of our lives."

Russ has a reflective moment. "Do you remember that little kid on Edgewater, Billy Galloway?"

"Sure," says Andy. "He had more flat tires on his bike. I don't know why his parents didn't buy him some new ones."

"You remember what happened to him?"

Carolyn lowers her head. "He died."

"That's right," says Russ. "He was run over. Now there's something to be thankful for."

"What do you mean?" says Carolyn.

"We made it through and have all those memories. Billy never got that chance."

He holds up one of the reels before he packs it away. "And thank God we had parents that cared enough to record it all. At least we have that."

A broad smile appears on Andy's face. "I've got an idea. What if I took all of these reels and transferred them to DVDs so that we could all have a copy."

"You can do that?" asks Carolyn.

"Sure. Just give me a couple of days."

Carolyn hugs and kisses him on the cheek.

Russ is all excited. "Man! That would be great! These old reels won't last much longer, and I don't know where I would get a new bulb when this one goes. What do you need?"

"First thing is for Dewy to allow me to come back and record the old films to my camera."

"You got it!" says Dewy.

"Then I'll need your desktop, Russ."

"Ditto."

"Ditto? Now there's a word from the attic."

All of Dewy's depression and anxiety has left and is replaced with the excitement of knowing that all the money that was spent on his rec room will now be justified by reconnecting with his friends and turning it all into a positive experience. And, of course, the booze and brownies didn't hurt.

"As soon as I get this done we should get back together and see how it looks on Dewy's mega screen."

"Fantastic!" says Dewy.

—

After copying the films to the camera Andy arrives back at Russ's place for the conversion. He sets everything up with the desktop and begins the process with Russ looking on.

"So how long will this take?"

"How much beer do you have?"

"Three bottles, I think."

"This needs a case."

A few beers and some smoke, and Russ passes out in his chair. Andy also settles in with one eye open, but even that one has its limitations. Andy eventually joins Russ.

Forty-five minutes later Andy is awakened by Russ shaking his shoulder.

"Hey man, I think it's finished."

Andy looks at the monitor, and sees it stopped transferring halfway through.

"What the hell is this? It stopped!"

"Yeah, that's weird. It stopped at a scene on our street with no one in the shot. I don't remember this."

"Neither do I."

"Can you fix it?"

"I'm sure I can, but not right now. I'm too tired. I'll look at it in the morning. I'm going to bed," says Andy.

"And I'm going to have another beer."

"I don't know how you do it. You must be close to being embalmed by now."

"It's easier this way when I pass on; I just go straight from the bottle to the box. No middle man."

—

As the sun rises there is no enticing aroma of breakfast in the air. Russ is still in the land of beer and weed. In the kitchen, Andy grabs a slice of cold pizza from the refrigerator and begins to gnaw on it like a piece of shoe leather, then he sits at the computer. Gus hears him and joins in by finding a comfortable spot on the rug.

"Morning, Gus." Andy pats him on the head. He turns on the computer and camera. The result is the same; the picture is still frozen on a scene from the old street.

"Shit. What's wrong with this damn thing?" While he ponders the problem, he glances up to see Russ's photo album on the shelf above. He pulls it down and a picture falls out. He picks it up from the floor. It's a picture of Gus.

"Now there's a handsome boy." He shows Gus, who wags his tail. At that moment the computer and camera start up. "Now that's strange, not that I'm complaining. Maybe I can get this done before Russ wakes up."

He watches the screen with the empty street scene. It begins to pan the area, a dog is now visible and looks similar to Gus.

"Hey, look, Gus! There's a dog that looks just like you. What do you think of that?" He looks down and Gus is gone. "Not that impressed, huh."

Once again the computer and camera stop, leaving the image of the dog on the screen.

"Come on!"

Russ enters the room. "How's it going?"

"It isn't. It started up and then quit again. All you see is this shot of a dog on the street."

Russ looks at the screen. "Hey, that looks like Gus! I've watched this reel over and over and I don't ever remember seeing a dog in it, especially one that looks like Gus."

"I know Gus didn't seem interested, he left."

"Where did he go?"

"I don't know."

"That's funny; he loves that spot on the rug. Gus! Gus! Come here boy!" No response. "Now that's weird. He always comes or answers with a bark.

They search the house and yard for Gus. He's gone without a trace.

"And you said he was with you by the computer?" asks Russ.

"Yeah, and then I looked down and he was gone."

"This isn't right. It's all screwed up like a dream. I want to look at that dog on the screen again."

Russ studies the scene. "I don't understand. Why is there a dog in this film that was never on the original reel, and why does it have the exact markings as Gus?"

"What's that in your hand?"

"Oh, it's a picture of Gus. It fell out of the album." He hands Russ the picture.

"Have you been into my can of pot?"

"What do you mean?"

"There's no picture on this."

"What?"

He grabs the picture back. It's blank!

"What the—I'm telling you, it was a picture of Gus."

"Well, let's check. I know exactly where that picture is in the album." Russ takes the album and looks through the pages.

"It's right here."

He turns to the page. There's a space where the picture should be.

"We had a picture that is now blank. A dog that looks exactly like Gus on the computer, and Gus is gone," says Andy.

"This is *Twilight Zone* shit!"

The camera and computer start up. Their heads snap to the screen.

"It is Gus," says Andy.

"That's him, alright!" Russ calls to him. "Gus! Gus! Is that you, boy!"

Gus looks straight at him from the screen and barks.

"Holy shit!"

"Okay, let's not panic," says Andy. "There's got to be some explanation for this."

"Oh yeah! Like what?"

Andy tries to come up with some logical explanation.

"Okay. Maybe, maybe the camera changed modes. You know how it was acting up. And maybe my elbow accidentally hit it...and it turned...and faced Gus...and filmed him."

"And Gus just happened to be on the street instead of here on the rug and barked back at us when I called him on the screen. What great timing that is. That's crazier than the real story! I need to smoke some shit."

"Are you nuts? That will just add more fuel to the insanity. Let's try it again. What if we take another photo from the album?"

"And do what? Wave it in front of the screen and say hocus-pocus."

"I don't know, but we don't have any other options."

Russ looks through the album and picks out a picture of his new barbecue.

"How about my barbecue?"

"Sure. You can mistake one dog from another, but a stainless steel gas barbecue back in the fifties, I don't think so. If that shows up, we'll know."

"Know what? That we should check ourselves into a rubber room?"

"Okay, turn over the photo so we can see it."

There's a look on Russ's face as if he has seen a ghost. "What's wrong?" asks Andy.

"That is the side with the picture."

The camera starts. They quickly look at the screen and the picture pans from Gus to...the stainless steel barbecue resting in the middle of the street.

"No way, this can't be. I'm going out on the back deck to see if it's still there."

Russ is back in a flash.

"Well?"

"It's gone!"

They look at each other.

"Are you thinking what I'm thinking?" asks Andy.

"You mean that we could go back too?"

"If we can, we have a dog and a barbecue waiting for us."

"Let's take some pictures of ourselves," says Russ. "I'll get the camera."

"Wait a minute!"

"What?"

"Those two pictures went into the computer and came out on the screen looking exactly as they look now. We don't want to go back to the fifties and be in our sixties. What the hell would be the point of that? What we need are pictures of ourselves back in the fifties, so we will be that age again."

"You're right, Andy! We can use that picture in the album of us together so we can jump ship at the same time."

"That's a great idea. I think we should ask Carolyn and Dewy if they want in on this."

"I'll call them and ask them to come over and then we'll tell them. They wouldn't believe it if we told them over the phone."

"I'm here and I don't believe it."

"Okay, I called them and they're coming over, but Carolyn seemed upset about something. Said she didn't want to talk about it, which is strange for her. She's always open about her feelings."

—

They assemble in the kitchen and Carolyn is definitely on a downer.

"So, what's the story?" asks Dewy.

"First," says Andy, "we all need to be on the same page. What seems to be troubling you, Carolyn?"

She bursts into tears. “I’m...losing my home!”

They all gasp.

“What?” says Russ.

“I haven’t paid my property taxes in three years and the fourth year is due.”

“Carolyn, why didn’t you tell me?” says Russ.

“I couldn’t ask you. You’ve done so much for me already.”

“I might have been able to help,” says Russ.

Andy puts his arms around her to give comfort. “It’s all right. Everything will be all right.”

“Anyone want a drink?” asks Russ.

“No,” says Andy. “No booze.”

“This sounds serious,” says Dewy.

“Well, I just think you should hear this sober.”

“Oh, my God!” says Carolyn. “Who got cancer?”

Andy smiles and hugs her tighter. “No one has cancer.”

He unfolds the story of the strange phenomena. They look at him with blank faces.

“You know how crazy that sounds?” says Dewy.

“I know, but Gus and the barbecue is proof in the pudding.”

“Let me see if I have this right,” says Carolyn. “You’re telling us that we can go back in time; back to when we were just kids.”

“That’s what I’m saying, exactly what you wanted,” says Andy.

“I won’t have to worry about my taxes anymore?” asks Carolyn.

“Nope,” says Russ.

“And I’ll see my parents again too?”

“It should be exactly how it was,” says Andy.

“What about my rec room?” asks Dewy.

“All gone, as well as the payments and the responsibilities,” says Andy. “You’ll just be a kid again.”

“I never stopped,” says Russ.

“I want to go first,” says Carolyn.

“Russ, you have pictures in that album of Carolyn and Dewy back then, right?”

“Sure do.”

“Then let’s get this show on the road.”

Andy sets up the camera and computer while Russ looks for the pictures.

"Got 'em."

"Okay, show us Carolyn's picture."

Russ shows the picture of Carolyn at eight years old.

"I don't feel anything happening," says Carolyn.

"The picture has to disappear first. There, it's gone. See how it works, Carolyn. Caro..."

"She's gone!" says Dewy.

All eyes are now on the screen as the camera starts up and pans the street.

"There! There she is!" says Andy.

On the street stands an eight-year-old Carolyn.

"Carolyn!" yells Russ. "Can you hear me? Are you all right?"

In a child's voice, "I am! I am! Hurry up so we can play! It's the most wonderful thing!"

They all have tears in their eyes.

"Okay, Dewy you're next."

Russ shows Dewy's photo. The image disappears and then Dewy is gone. He shows up on the screen the same age as Carolyn. He hugs her.

"This is fantastic!" he says in his child voice.

They both look to Andy and Russ.

"Come on! What are you waiting for?" says Carolyn.

Russ brings out the photo of the two of them with their arms around each other. They decide to pose the same as the photo. Poof! They're gone. On the screen they appear beside Carolyn and Dewy.

"What do you want to play first?" asks Carolyn.

"Let's play kick the can!" says Russ.

"Okay!" says Andy. "Dewy, go hide your eyes at the pole."

They all scatter out of view. In the background Andy's mother's voice sounds out.

"Andy! I want you home when the lights come on!"

"Okay, Mom!"

The screen goes black—the camera shuts off.

8

PAPER TRAIL

Rise with the sun to pray. Pray alone. Pray often. The Great Spirit will listen, if you only speak. (Native American Code of Ethics #1)

—

All the machinery and building supplies had sat idle for two months. The clashes and confrontations had been at a standstill. Each side waited for the big hand of government to wield the hammer of fate.

"Dad! They're back!" announced John.

His father, George, had finished his lunch and was resting comfortably with his second cup of coffee. "How many?" he asked, as if he had been expecting it.

"It looks like three from the company and two feds with four Mounties."

"We've lost the battle then."

"Maybe not," said John, trying to show some optimism. "Maybe they just want to talk."

"Again?"

His father took his time getting to his feet and patted his son on the back. "No, the talking's over, they're here to take. They wouldn't bring the Mounties, if we had won."

He stepped onto the front stoop of his small clapboard house with his son in tow. He saw the small group standing by their vehicles as Chief Ed Brown walked up to them with almost the entire population reserve behind him.

"Afternoon, Ed," said Terry Bolt, one of the two government representatives.

"Just say it, so I can get back to my work."

"Is there some place we can go to sit down and discuss this?"

"Would that change what you've come here to say?"

Terry looked at the ground. "No, I guess not."

"Then, that's all we have to say to each other."

"Ed, we really feel this is in your best interest. The paper mill is willing to give your people the first opportunity for jobs. It will make a big difference to everyone here."

George steps into the ring. "So, these are good-paying jobs?"

"Very good," says one of the company executives.

"Well that sounds great," says George. "So, once you've killed all the fish in our lake and river with your factory, we'll have enough money to go to one of those big-box stores and pay those big bucks for some overpriced, frostbitten, frozen fish. Am I right?"

"It won't be like that," says Terry. "We have the latest systems to prevent any of that from happening. Besides, the factory will be five miles from here."

George looks at Ed. "Does this sound familiar to you, Chief?"

"Same shit, different day," says Ed. "When is this rape of nature going to start?"

"This morning," said Terry.

"You couldn't have started any sooner? It's not hard to see how one hand washes the other," says George. "How is it that business and government always end up in bed together, but we are the ones that get fucked?"

Terry didn't like that one bit. "Don't start that, George. You know damn well we try to be honest and fair to both sides."

Ed ripped a necklace of beads from around his neck and threw them on the ground in front of Terry.

"There. Now the deal is complete, just like we did three hundred years ago."

Two of the Mounties look slightly nervous and begin to fidget. One actually raised his hand and slowly moved it to his gun, but decided to hook his thumb into his belt instead.

"We may seem powerless, but spiritually, in the end we will be triumphant. All roads lead back to nature."

With that the chief turned and walked away with his people behind him.

—

It took less than six months for the factory to be built and running. During that time not one person from the tribe handed in a request to the company for employment. Then three months later the reserve started to see some changes; subtle at first. The drinking water tasted different, and some of the children began to have health issues. And once in a while small fish would float by in the river.

Ed decided to gather everyone for a meeting.

Everyone was very concerned about the condition of their water despite the company's arrogance that it was all good. The Chief gave a short speech about the guardian spirits that are there to protect them. He told them all to pray and fast, to allow these spirits to intervene on their behalf and reset nature's path to harmony.

—

For one month they did exactly that and waited for things to change, but the drinking water became more bitter and then adults began to feel ill. As the Chief, Ed began to see some division in his people. This was not something new to him. The individual will follow as far as the strength of their faith will take them, and everyone has their limit or breaking point.

Ed decided that a powwow was needed. Before the event he spoke to the families about the importance of what they had already accomplished by praying and fasting, and that the powwow would be the second half of their journey to change the wrongs that have been committed.

While everyone danced and interacted in positive ways, five miles away their faith began to take hold. The factory was in full swing and tons of paper products were being stored in an old warehouse that had been dormant for ten years. During this period many insects had infiltrated the empty space. One of the insects was the scabies mite that quietly began to invade the paper.

Before the first order of paper products would be loaded on trucks, some of these products were brought into the factory and distributed to all the washrooms. This infestation was not a normal invasion of mites. They had been summoned by the transformers and tricksters on behalf of the tribe. These were Super Mites that burrowed into the unsuspecting employees' skin and fed on their cell fluids. They layed 10-25 eggs that hatched three to four days later. Then the larval mites traveled to other areas of the body and repeated the process. The situation at the factory quickly accelerated when a secretary had to stay home because of a rash she developed in an embarrassing location.

Itching began to occur on everyone's skin and was quickly transmitted to people visiting the facility.

Back on the reserve there was no change in the water and more fish floated on their backs. Ed decided to call in some environmentalists to see if it was a direct result from the factory. His assumption was verified.

Not long after came the domino effect. Workers couldn't fulfill their duties because of the unrelenting itching.

On Tuesday afternoon, just after lunch break there was a terrifying escalation of the infestation. One of the workers complained about an itchy throat and ears, and within minutes of the mention, thick, rust-coloured blood began to spew from all of his orifices. His shirt and pants were soaked with blood, front and back, and severe pain rushed through his veins. The man was screaming in agony. Then another took up the cause until everyone was infected except one young man in the office who quickly dialled 911.

Workers, driven mad by the relentless itching, frantically tore off their clothes. It resembled a scene from a horror movie. There were ambulance attendants, local police, and even the Mounties showed up as they scattered throughout the building trying to sort out the epidemic.

—

It took the workers six months to a year to recuperate. Not one person who worked in that factory went back, and because of the media attention, they couldn't get a soul to work there, so they had to shut the place down.

The atmosphere on the reserve returned to normal. The water was no longer bitter. The fish were swimming again. The spirit of the tribe was no longer an issue. The Chief smiled as he gazed up at the clear blue sky to see an eagle glide by. His counselling never came into question again.

9

RETOOLING

Along with testing people for drugs and alcohol, perhaps we should test what's in their hearts—things like greed and power. Carmin Gallo is all too familiar with these attributes, but soon he will encounter a power he can't control.

—

The business day has come to an end and the lit pool area of the mansion is inviting. Sidney Neville is stretched out on a lounge chair enjoying a well deserved drink. He's a distinguished English gentleman in his late sixties, and the president of an empire, Sid's Super Markets. He left the shores of the big island thirty-five years ago with a substantial amount of old money. Grocery stores were not the wishes of his predecessors, but he has magnified his wealth, which, in the end, is what matters.

His assistant appears, hands him the phone and whispers into his ear, "Carmin Gallo, sir."

Sid shows signs of concern. He takes the phone and pauses for a moment.

"Carmin, I assume you're calling because of the article."

Carmin Gallo is in his late fifties with a gangster persona: hammy, chiselled face, and just overweight enough to look intimidating.

"Sid, I think we should talk."

"There's nothing to talk about. You read it. We're retooling."

Carmin chuckles. "Come on, Sid. We all know retooling is just a fancy word to keep the wolves from the door. Look, just hear me out. Let me make an offer. If you don't like it, no harm done, we shake and go back to our corners."

"You're like a dog on a bone. I guess confronting you face to face is the only way to shake your shit from my shoes."

"That's pretty strong talk, Sid. I'm hurt."

"I didn't think that was possible. All right, I'll humour you. Tomorrow night in my office at seven. But I'm telling you, you don't have a chance in hell of buying me out."

"Don't be so optimistic."

—

Sid has a large, luxurious office with a bar.

He's pouring himself a drink as Carmin walks in.

"Nice office," says Carmin. "You've upgraded since I was here last."

"Ten years will do that."

"Has it been that long?"

"Ten years since you last tried this drink?"

"No thanks. Not when I'm discussing business. It distorts my focus. Maybe after we talk we can have a little celebration."

"You've always been delusional."

Sid takes a sip of his drink then leaves it on the bar, and moves to Carmin. They stand face to face.

"So, what's your proposal?"

"Thirty two point six—that's not just fair, that's generous."

"You're right. That is generous, if I were selling. But I'm not. My retooling includes four new super stores next year."

Carmin turns and walks to the floor-to-ceiling windows.

"And that's exactly what I'm talking about, Sid." He gently grabs the cord of the blinds and slowly closes them. "By that time, you'll be insolvent. Let me bail you out, so you don't have to go through the humiliation."

"Spare me your generosity. I know all about you and your ties to organized crime. You should be in jail with the rest of those slimeballs."

"That's not nice, Sid. You shouldn't speak before you think. You lose friends that way."

"I can't lose a friend I never had. I'll never sell, especially to you."

"So, the answer is no?"

"You must be deaf as well as corrupt. Of course it's no. You knew that the minute you walked in. You're wasting my time."

"That's really too bad. Then I'm afraid you'll just have to step aside."

"And what's that supposed to mean?"

"It means your negotiating needs some retooling. Nice doing business with you, Sid, but I guess I'll be celebrating on my own."

He turns to Sid and directs a gun with a silencer at him.

"Are you crazy?"

"Crazy? Maybe, but it's a crazy, fucked up world, isn't it?"

He lets Sid have it. POP! POP! Sid drops to the floor.

Carmin bends down to Sid's now lifeless body. He carefully pulls off Sid's wrist watch with a handkerchief and puts the time ahead, from 7:15 to 9:30. He smashes the face of watch with his fist and it stops. He gently puts it back on Sid's wrist and picks up the two spent shells. As he stands, he notices a small cut on his hand from the broken watch. He puts the wounded area in his mouth to suck away the blood, then wraps the handkerchief around it and heads out the door and down the stairwell.

—

Carmin is watching the news while having his morning coffee in his study.

"...The president had no further comments. In local news, prominent grocery magnate Sidney Neville was found dead in his office early this morning by a security guard. Police confirmed the death as a homicide. No further details are available. Mr. Neville was in the process of retooling Sid's Super Markets."

Click! "You see, Sid, we did come to a deal. I push the meat and vegetables, and you push up the daisies."

—

Carmin is so confident he's covered all the bases regarding the murder he throws a dinner party by the backyard pool.

"That was so tragic about Sid," says one guest. "Have you heard any more?"

Carmin plays it up. "No. Not a thing. It's so upsetting; such a tragedy and a loss for all of us in this industry. Even though we were competitors, we were still good friends."

His assistant, Jordan, approaches, waving a phone in the air.

"I'm with friends, can't you take a message?"

"I think this deserves your attention, sir."

Carmin takes the call in his study.

"Carmin here...Of course, yes, I've heard. Absolutely tragic...Questions?...The station?...Sure, I have time tomorrow. How 'bout eleven?...Okay, see you then." He smiles as he puts down the phone. "This should be interesting."

—

Lieutenant Hardy is well seasoned in homicide. He's going through Sid's case file when Carmin taps on the doorframe.

"Ah, Mr. Gallo."

He stands, reaching over the desk as Carmin extends his hand.

"Nice to meet you. Have a seat."

"Thanks."

"Now, I know you're a busy man, so I'm going to keep this brief."

Hardy looks down at the file, then to Carmin.

"How long would you say you've known Sidney Neville?"

"Oh, Sid and I go back about fifteen years."

"And would you say that you have had a pretty good relationship? I mean, considering you're in competition."

"We got along fine. We've always had a mutual respect."

"Now, from the information I have here from his assistant, you went to see Mr. Neville on the same night he was murdered. Video from the cameras in the building confirm you were there at seven."

"That's right; we had a meeting for seven. I'm never late."

"And may I ask the reason for that meeting?"

"Sure. Sid was in trouble and I was going to bail him out."

Hardy sits back in his chair.

"What kind of trouble? I read that he was actually expanding his company; adding a few more stores. That hardly sounds like he was in trouble."

Carmin sits back. "Well, there's always more to the story than what's on the surface or what the media tells you."

"How's that?"

"You'd have to know this business. He was going to bite off more than he could chew. Opening more stores than he could afford."

"That seems a little strange for a smart businessman like Mr. Neville."

"It's been done before. You want to give the illusion that everything's all right. So, when you go to sell, it all looks good on paper."

"And being the competitor, you just wanted to help him make that decision."

Carmin smiles. "I made him an offer."

"An offer he couldn't refuse?"

"I thought it was very generous. He wanted to think it over. I said sure and I left."

"I see in the video that you took the elevator to his office, but took the stairs when you left."

"Yeah, I often do that. I get to the meetings on time, but when they're over there's no rush. So, I take the stairs for exercise."

"Is there any reason why you didn't call us to let us know you were there that night?"

"I didn't see any point. I just did my business and left. Nothing unusual happened. I figured if you wanted my take, you'd call me. And here I am."

"Right...Okay, Mr. Gallo. Thanks for coming in."

"My pleasure. Sid was a good guy."

"Yes. That's the impression I've been getting."

—

In Sid's Super Markets boardroom, second-in-command Paul Woodman is trying to convince the board members to accept a takeover proposal by none other than Carmin Gallo.

"Well gentlemen. It certainly isn't the best time to be doing this, but it is necessary for all the stockholders. I've given you all a chance to look over Mr. Gallo's proposal. Now it's time to have your input."

"The problem I have is this," says one member. "We won't have a say in how our stores are going to be run."

"But we will still be under the banner of Sid's Super Markets," says Paul.

"I don't like Gallo. I don't like how he runs his chain!" says another member.

"I don't like him, period," adds another, "he's a snake with ties to organized crime."

Paul raises his arms in the air. "Okay, now we're getting off track. What we may think of him on a personal level has no bearing on the business. He is cutthroat; I'll say that for him. And I think that is what we need. With all due respect to Sid, he just didn't have that mindset and we are heading into a tailspin."

"Sid was honest and forthright. He didn't play games," says a member.

"You're right." Paul lays it on the line. "But what I think we have to keep in mind is the fact that we are still here, and if Sid were still here, even though he had a positive attitude, there would be a good chance that in six months, we wouldn't be here. So financially, and that is the bottom line, gentlemen, I propose that the board accepts the Gallo agreement. It's a generous one and the only chance we have to survive. All in favour?"

—

Carmin pulls his BMW up to the garage doors of his home as his cell phone goes off.

"Hello, Paul. What's the word? Well, I didn't expect an easy sell. Good. I'll be counting on you to keep your boys in line. Don't worry about your financial end. Like I said, I'll take care of you. You're in the big league now."

—

Lieutenant Hardy sits in his office discussing the murder with Detective Anderson.

"Gallo was the only one who showed up on camera between the hours of seven and Sid's watch stopping at nine-thirty."

"But we have him leaving at seven-sixteen," says Anderson. "So who killed him?" Hardy thinks for a moment.

"Gallo did."

"How the hell do you figure that?"

"He may be smart in the grocery business, but he's shitty at murder. He's used an old trick. The only way Gallo could get out of this would be to alter the time on Sid's watch. With any luck his prints should be on it. I found an old file on Gallo that goes back twenty years. I sent his prints to the lab for a match. I'm just waiting to hear back."

The secretary walks in. "Lab on two."

"This is it."

He taps the speaker. "Hardy, here."

"I've got good and bad," says the technician. "Take your pick."

"All right, give me the bad stuff."

"No legible prints on the watch."

"Damn it!"

"What I did find though was something that I didn't expect."

"I'm listening."

"It's minuscule, but it's there. Blood. We have DNA. And it's not Sid's."

"Fantastic!" says Anderson.

Hardy smiles, "All we need is a blood sample and I'm going to nail his ass to the wall."

—

Carmin enters his home with Jordan there to greet him with a message from Lieutenant Hardy.

"He said something about a blood test," says Jordan.

"Blood test? Why the hell would he want a—"

His thoughts roll back to Sid's office and smashing the watch with his fist, then sucking the blood from the wound. "That son of a bitch!"

Carmin quickly searches through his address book. "Here it is." He finds what he's looking for and makes a call.

"Good evening, Professor Palmer here."

"Professor, it's Carmin Gallo."

"Carmin Gallo. Well, this is a surprise. How have you been? I see your competition is dwindling. You must be happy about that?"

"Yeah, that's always good, but right now, I need you to do a little favour for me."

"If I can."

"How far did you get with your DNA research?"

"Good question. I have been working on different aspects of DNA."

"Can you change a person's DNA?"

"Well, let me put it to you this way. I have done it in a lab with very favourable results. We're talking only one cell here and that was from a mouse, certainly not a human being, if that's what you're asking. They've done some studies that say you can actually change your own DNA by changing your emotions and your diet."

"I haven't got time for that shit! Here's my favour. You say you've done tests and it works. I want you to try it on me."

"You? That's impossible. I'm eons away from anything like that."

"Well, just consider me your guinea pig."

"Carmin, I'm going to be quite honest here. I have no idea what the side effects would be. I could be sentencing you to death."

"I have to take that chance."

"I don't understand why you would want this."

"Never mind that. How would you like to have a $2,000,000 donation for your research?"

"That's a lot of money."

"It's yours. All you have to do is keep this to yourself. I need this done now."

"That's quite a carrot you're dangling. All right, but remember, I'm not responsible for the outcome. Meet me at the lab in an hour."

—

With apprehension, Professor Palmer gives Carmin an injection.

"So, this will do the trick?" asks Carmin.

"I told you, I don't know what it will do, but I'm sure it will do something, whatever that may be. But you should go home and stay there for twelve hours. If there are any side effects they should show up by then."

"Thanks, Professor." Carmin turns to leave.

"If it becomes something you can't handle, do me a favour."

"Sure, what's that?"

"Don't call me."

—

Carmin slept through the night like a baby. He wakes up feeling rather pleasant; looks at his hands and arms; everything seems normal. He goes into the bathroom and checks himself in the mirror.

"Looks good so far."

By the time he reaches his kitchen he is feeling more energetic with each step. At the breakfast table, Jordan fills his coffee cup.

"You must have had a good night's sleep. You look very calm and relaxed this morning."

"Yeah, I feel pretty good."

The phone rings. "I don't want to talk to anybody."

Jordan checks out the call display. He holds the phone out to Carmin. Carmin looks at him.

"Hardy?"

"Yes, sir."

Carmin takes the phone.

"Lieutenant, yeah, I got your message, but I was out late last night. Blood test? Sure. Why would I have a problem with that? I don't have anything to hide."

—

Hardy sits at his desk chuckling as he texts someone on his cell phone. Anderson walks in with a folder in his hand. He raises it in the air.

"I have the DNA results."

Hardy drops the cell on his desk.

"Now I'm excited."

"Don't be," he says and throws the folder on the desk.

"What do you mean?"

"No match. It's not Gallo."

"That's impossible! It can't be. I know it's him."

—

Carmin is celebrating yet another victory of dodging the murder along with the takeover of Sid's company by throwing a party for all the executives from both sides.

"I want to thank you all for coming out tonight. This is a momentous occasion. It's the marriage of two great companies."

Enthusiastic applause comes from Carmin's executives, but one from Sid's doesn't let that slide.

"He means takeover."

"I know that if Sid were here," says Carmin, "he'd be just as excited as I am."

"What a crock," says another of Sid's executives.

"Okay," says Carmin. "There's plenty of food and drink, so don't hold back. I won't be doing this every week."

There is, of course, some laughter from his cronies.

A beautiful woman approaches Carmin.

"Carmin, you look fabulous," says the woman. "How about us getting together for a little merger of our own."

Before he can respond Carmin notices Professor Palmer.

"Excuse me, sweetheart."

"I'll call you," she says.

"Professor," says Carmin. "Thanks for coming."

"Looks like the serum worked. No side effects?"

"Not a one! It worked like a charm! Come on over and join us. I'll have Jordan get you a drink."

"I'm really not here for the party."

"Oh yeah, the rest of the donation. Sure, come into my study and we'll fix that up for you."

Carmin sits behind his desk. "Have a seat, Professor. Now let me see. I gave you forty grand so far." Carmin brings out a check book. He fills out a check and hands it to the Professor.

"There. That should do it."

Professor Palmer takes the check and looks it over. He's dumbfounded!

"This is $10,000! Where's the rest of it?"

"Well, you see, Professor, with the financial burden of taking over another company, I just don't have the funds. You know how it is. So, I figured ten thousand, plus the forty, that's better than a poke in the eye with a sharp stick, right?"

"You bastard. I put my career on the line for you."

"And I appreciate that. But, I still have to use good business sense, and that's what I'm doing. It's nothing personal."

"I know you were there the night of the murder, and what I did got you off the hook."

"And I thank you."

"What's to stop me from going to the police?"

Carmin smiles, "Absolutely nothing, if you want implicated in a murder."

"You son of a bitch!"

—

After his morning coffee Carmin rests comfortably in his recliner without a care in the world.

"Mr. Gallo," says Jordan as he comes by to pick up the empty cup.

"May I ask a personal question?"

"What is it?"

"How old are you?"

"Fifty-eight, why?"

"Well, since I've been here, you've always looked, well, your age. But for some reason...you look younger than I do and I'm forty-seven."

"Well, thanks, Jordan. That's encouraging."

"Yes, sir."

After receiving Jordan's compliment, Carmin checks himself out in the mirror and is astonished by what he sees.

"How about that, I do look younger, even the grey is gone. Palmer should be bottling that stuff."

—

Carmin walks into his office past Ellen, his secretary. She looks up.

"I'm sorry, sir, Mr. Gallo isn't in yet."

He turns to her. "Thank you, Ellen."

"Mr. Gallo? Why you look—"

"Younger?"

"Yes. It's incredible. I mean, not that you looked old."

"I know what you mean. Thanks."

By the end of the day Carmin is flying high with all the compliments he received. He starts the car and moves his foot to the brake pedal. He can't reach it!

"That's strange," he says as he pulls the seat forward.

—

The next morning Carmin steps out of the shower and turns to the mirror and only sees as far down as his forehead.

"What the hell's going on? Jordan! Jordan, get in here!"

Jordan rushes in.

"What is it, sir?"

Carmin points to the mirror.

"Why did you move my mirror?"

"I, I haven't touched your mirror, sir."

"Then why is it up so high?"

He notices that Jordan is taller than he is.

"Aren't we the same height?"

"Actually you're slightly taller, at least, you were."

"What the hell is this? Get Palmer on the phone."

When he dresses, he discovers that his clothes are falling off.

Jordan has Palmer on the phone. Carmin has the look of a fifteen-year-old, with a voice to match.

"One moment, Professor," says Jordan.

Carmin grabs the phone.

"Listen to me, Palmer! Something's happening! You've got to reverse this shit!"

"And who might you be, young man?"

"It's Gallo, you asshole! My clock is going backwards! I'm getting younger and I'm shrinking!"

"Well, Mr. Gallo, I'm sorry to hear that, but I did warn you about side effects."

"You owe me, Palmer!"

"I owe you? You should have been a comedian."

"You're going to fix this, Palmer! I'm coming over!"

"I'm afraid I'm just on my way out."

"You wait right there, you bastard!"

—

Carmin starts his car. He pulls his seat up as far as it will go, but still has to stretch to reach the gas pedal. When the garage door opens, he squeals down the driveway and out to the street. Driving erratically, he tries to manoeuvre around traffic. He guns it through a red light and is broadsided. He's a little shaky, but manages to get out of the car and run. Passing store windows, his reflection shows a ten-year-old boy.

"No!" he screams. "This can't be happening!"

He bumps into a man and is knocked to the ground. The man looks down at him. Now he's five years old. He starts crying.

"Are you alright, little boy? Are you lost?"

Carmin screams and runs down an alley as fast as his little legs will carry him. Now a toddler, he can't run anymore.

"No! Please! Somebody help me!"

Now a baby, he starts crawling and making baby sounds. He can't move. He cries out as a newborn. A gust of wind picks up a discarded plastic bottle lifting it into the air as it passes Carmin, who is now a fetus. He's consumed by the turbulence and blown out of the alley and back to the main street, settling on the sidewalk. Oh, my God! No! Nooo! he thinks to himself. All he can see are massive feet passing by him as he lies there like a slug. Suddenly a foot is over him.

Uhhh!

Carmin is now embedded into the sidewalk like a discarded piece of stale gum. Above the gooey aftermath is a storefront sign that reads, Sid's Super Market.

10

YE OLDE BOOKSTORE

Simon Smith is a simple man with a simple name: uncreative, uninspired, and unsuccessful. He lives his life through the fictional characters in books. Then he has a chance meeting with an old man in an old bookstore where an empty book intersects with an empty life.

—

A cracked and weathered sign hangs above the door in old English script, YE OLDE BOOKSTORE. Inside the unpretentious shop are dusty, tattered books occupying the crowded shelves with an unmistakable musty fragrance, only intoxicating to a special breed of old-book lovers.

Gabe, the old man behind the counter, adds much to its charm and timeless visual aspect. He's dressed in a well-worn houndstooth sports jacket. His white hair is longish and connects flawlessly to his white beard, kept at a conservative trim. He sits on a stool with one elbow bent on the counter holding up his head as he reads a book through his round, wire-framed glasses while the other hand holds an unlit pipe that he gingerly chews on, beautifully framed for an artist's brush.

On this particular morning, the door of the shop bursts open, forcing the tiny bell hanging over the door to ring more of an alarm than its usual cheerful tune. Simon Smith enters and rushes to the counter, dragging with him an intensity that shears through the tranquil spirit of the little shop and hits Gabe like a cold winter wind.

Closing his book, he turns his attention to Simon.

"Good morning, sir. My name is Gabe. I am the proprietor of this establishment. And what would be your book today? Some humour perhaps. Maybe a little political satire, or—"

"Actually, I'm taking a two-hour train trip and I forgot my e-book, so I'm looking for a quick book replacement, something that will hold my interest, something adventurous."

"You crave adventure, do you?"

"I don't crave it, but this train trip is about as exciting as life gets for me. I don't have much time. What do you have?"

Gabe, in his calm manner, points toward a shelf of books.

"I would suggest that section over there. Yes, I do feel you'll find what you're looking for on that top shelf."

"You do, do you?" He makes his way over.

"I've been helping people find what they're searching for, for many years," says Gabe as he returns to reading from his book while keeping a vigilant eye on Simon.

Simon scans the titles and is drawn to a book that seems to lack a title. He pulls it from the shelf as Gabe looks on with amusement. Simon examines the cover. He opens the book to discover that the pages are blank and he becomes agitated.

"You have notebooks mixed in with your novels." He places the book back on the shelf atop the rest.

"I think you're mistaken," says Gabe. "That's not a notebook, and it is what you're looking for."

"What's this? There's nothing in it. The pages are blank. It's completely useless. It doesn't even have a title."

"It just appears that way."

"Appears that way?" says Simon. "Well, I think it appears to me that you're trying to sell me something of no value."

"Oh, you're wrong there, my good fellow. It is the most valuable book in the store."

"And you are a con. I don't have time for this. Where are your magazines? Or are they blank too?"

"Oh no, there are plenty of articles and pictures, as usual. Right over there, sir," pointing to a rack of magazines.

Simon walks over to the rack and plucks out one of the magazines and opens it to make sure it isn't blank and walks back to the counter.

"How much?" demands Simon.

Gabe smiles. "We have a special on magazines today. No charge."

"Hmm. Feeling guilty, are you?"

Gabe ignores the remark. "Allow me," he says.

He takes the magazine from Simon and places it into a brown paper bag.

"There you are, sir, and have yourself a wonderful and exciting trip."

"No need for sarcasm," says Simon, as he rushes to exit.

"None intended. I'll look forward to seeing you on your return."

"Like that's going to happen," says Simon. And with that, he slams the door shut.

Gabe chuckles to himself and goes back to his reading and pipe sucking.

—

Between the confrontation with Gabe and almost missing the train, Simon's anxiety level escalates as he makes his way down the aisle of the half-filled train car with his traveling bag in tow. Taking a window seat, he places the bag on the aisle seat to discourage unwanted conversation. He settles in and looks out the window, observing people milling around the station. The whistle blows, and the train begins to pull away.

Looking down the aisle he sees the conductor at the far end of the car, checking tickets. Unzipping his traveling bag, he grabs the paper bag that holds the magazine.

"Blank pages," he mutters to himself. "The most valuable book in the store. Well at least I got a free magazine out of it. So, who conned who? Silly old man."

He slides the magazine out of the bag and is shocked to see it's not the magazine, but the blank book.

"What the hell. He did screw me, that old bugger!"

He then notices something different about the book. It now has a title.

"Wait a minute. What's this? Maybe it's not the same book." He reads the title, "THE ADVENTURES OF SIMON SMITH." Simon's face is now a picture of confusion.

"Ticket, sir?" says the conductor, sporting his British accent.

Simon looks up to see the conductor towering over him.

"Ticket? Yes."

Simon fumbles through his jacket pocket. He finally retrieves the ticket and nervously hands it over to the conductor, who in turn punches it and hands it back to Simon.

After years on the train the conductor can quickly detect trouble in advance.

"Everything all right, sir?"

"What? Sure. Everything's fine." But his face says otherwise.

Not to deliberate further, the conductor replies, "Excellent."

"Say, any chance of getting a drink?" says Simon.

The conductor turns back. "Soft or hard?"

"What?"

"Soft drink or something stronger?"

"Stronger. Scotch."

The conductor's second thought is the Scotch may be something he may have to contend with in the near future. He looks at his watch.

"I will be by with the trolley momentarily, sir," and then carries on.

Simon throws his attention back to the book.

"How the hell did he do that? Probably some cheap magic trick he picked up from reading one of those moldy books. Wait a minute. I didn't give him my name."

—

The train roars along the tracks.

Simon stares at the book's cover, pondering the old man's trickery. He finally opens the book expecting the clean, white pages. But no, to his shock and amazement, they are filled with typed paragraphs.

With apprehension he reads, *Simon enters Ye Olde Bookstore. He approaches Gabe, the proprietor. He tells Gabe he is looking for a book of adventure.*

Simon looks up from the book terrified, then resumes reading. *Simon thumbs through the book. The pages are blank. He announces to Gabe that the pages are blank. "There's nothing to read. It doesn't even have a title."*

He slams the book shut, puts it down and sits there thunder-struck with the absurdity of it all. His mind and heart begin to race.

The conductor approaches with the trolley. "Your Scotch, sir."

Simon stares straight out. His face is pale. Beads of sweat dot his forehead.

"Sir?"

"Huh? Sorry, what was that?"

"Your Scotch."

"Scotch? Yes, thank you." Just in time, thinks Simon.

He takes the drink like a child on a hot summer's day, downs it like lemonade and then places the glass on the trolley.

The conductor raises an eyebrow. "Will that be all, sir?" Below the surface he's thinking—Please say yes.

Simon pauses briefly before answering, allowing the warmth of the liquor to spread through his system. He quickly comes to the conclusion that one Scotch isn't enough to distort the reality of the situation. "Another, please."

The process is repeated once more. The conductor raises both eyebrows. Simon pays him and the conductor continues down the aisle wondering if this event will curtail or foretell any further activity.

Simon stares at the book, as though it were an evil entity. He finally gives in and once again picks it up.

He opens it to read, *"Will that be all, sir?" Simon pauses briefly before answering, allowing the burn of the liquor to spread through his system. He quickly comes to the conclusion that—*

He stops reading and begins to question his mental state. His anger has been replaced by fear. He gently rests the book on top of his bag. His breathing becomes erratic and labored as dots of sweat gather together and begin to trickle down the sides of his face. He looks back to see if the conductor is still there and sees he is just finishing with the last passenger at the end of the car.

Simon waves an arm frantically in the air. "Excuse me. Another drink."

The conductor immediately sees Simon's arm waving like a red flag and replies with measured authority.

"I'm not a bartender, sir. I can't just turn this cart around. You'll have to wait until I pass again."

"All right, all right. Wait right there." Simon manages to get to his feet and grabbing each aisle seat for balance he heads for the conductor. He is becoming desperate to escape whatever reality has possessed him.

"I'd like a double please."

The conductor looks Simon over and leans into him. "You're not going to be a problem, are you, sir?"

Simon teeters on the edge of no return. "Just give me the Scotch or we will have a problem. I'm just having a bad day."

"I understand, sir," says the conductor and whispers into Simon's ear. "But please, don't let it spill into mine." He reluctantly pours Simon a double. Simon disposes of it in short order.

"Well," says the conductor. "That should put any bad day out to pasture. I know it would mine."

Simon says nothing, but pays him and rides the wave of Scotch back to his seat. He glances at the book and then decides to ignore it by looking out the window. The alcohol presses down on his eyelids, and the added humming of the train renders his conscious mind obsolete; he sleeps.

—

As the train races along, Simon begins to stir with the sound of the train's whistle. His eyes open. He gazes out at the lush farmland rushing passed.

"There you are!" comes the exuberant words in a Scottish accent.

Simon is startled as he turns from the window to see an elderly, distinguished gentleman seated opposite him. He is dressed in a finely made, chocolate, double-breasted tweed suit and sporting a grey, walrus-style moustache.

"You're a sound sleeper, I was wondering when you would wake."

"Only when under the influence."

"I had deduced that already. And what be your preference?"

"Scotch."

"And a wise choice indeed. I see you're a writer."

Simon acknowledges the book. "Me? No."

"Well, I beg to differ. Is your name not Simon Smith?"

"That is the name on the book, but why would you think I was the author?"

"A simple deduction. The label on your bag carries the initials S.S."

"Yes. Well, I have considered being a writer, but—"

"Considered? Good God, man. There's nothing to consider. Either you are or you aren't. I hope you don't mind, I took the liberty of browsing the first few pages of your book while you were—elsewhere. It's a good beginning. It has merit. Now, you just have to change merit into gift. Then develop that gift."

The train whistle blows.

"And, I'm afraid, that signals my stop. I must leave you now, Simon Smith. You have the potential to be a good writer. You must be observant and diligent. The world is filled with stories waiting to be told." He extends his hand. "Nice to have met you, Simon."

"Thank you. And you are?"

"Arthur."

The train begins to slow.

"I must hurry. Good-bye."

He makes his way to the end of the car and begins to disembark.

Simon looks over and sees an open leather billfold on the seat.

"Oh, no."

He grabs the billfold and reads the name inside.

"Arthur Conan Doyle? Oh, my God!" Simon races to the end of the car. "Arthur! Mr. Doyle! Sir Arthur!" Arthur is nowhere to be seen.

—

The train starts to pull away. In desperation Simon leaps and falls to the ground hard and rolls. Dust explodes up into his eyes and mouth. He gets to his feet rubbing his eyes and coughing. As the dust settles and he regains his sight and composure, he begins to take in the surroundings and observes a busy train station and a sign that reads, RICHMOND. "Richmond? What Richmond? This train doesn't go to any Richmond."

"Is you'd aw right, Mista?"

Simon looks to his side to see a black man dressed in simple, well-worn attire. The man dusts Simon off.

"What Richmond is this?"

"Virginia."

Simon is dumbfounded. "Virginia?"

"Das right, Richmond, Virginia."

He takes in the scenery and realizes that the people and the station seem to be from a different era.

"Are they filming a movie here?"

"Movie? Waz dat?"

"What year is this?"

"Has you bumped you head? It's 1845."

"1845?" says Simon. "Did you see a gentleman leave the train? He was dressed in a suit and had this huge moustache."

"I's only sees you."

Simon looks down to the billfold in his hand. It's gone and has been replaced by the book that he left on the train.

"My book, but—"

"Albert."

They both turn to see a tall, well dressed, older man. He looks at Albert with piercing, ice-blue eyes.

"Does that man own you?"

Albert lowers his big, dark eyes and turns his head to the side, like a dog in submission.

"No, Masta Maxwell."

"Does he feed and clothe you?"

"No, Masta Maxwell."

"Then get the hell over here and pick up these bags."

Albert rushes over and picks up the bags, puts them into a horse-drawn carriage, then runs around to the other side to help Maxwell up. Then back again to the other side, climbs in and grabs the reins.

Maxwell looks at Simon with disdain. "You may have cost this boy a whipping."

Albert puts his head down and looks at Simon from the corner of his eye. The anguish is evident.

Simon tries to explain, "But I just—"

"Proceed, Albert."

Albert gives a short jerk of the reins and off they go.

Simon looks for shade and refreshment. His eyes zoom in on a sign down the street, hanging in front of a plain, long, two-story frame building that reads, Swan Tavern.

He wets his lips and approaches the front door of the establishment with caution, thinking, if the reality of the situation is 1845, I could get shot just opening the door. Of course, it could be worth it to try a Scotch in 1845.

The tavern is dimly lit. It is quiet, with only a few patrons. Simon feels uneasy, but his thirst for liquor nudges him to a small table. He places his book on the table as a waiter appears.

"Yes, sir."

"Scotch, please."

With hesitation, "I'm sorry sir, we just ran out of Scotch."

The waiter glances to one side. Simon's gaze follows to a dark corner of the room, where a shadowed figure sits and a bottle of Scotch rests on the table.

"How 'bout a rye?"

"Rye will be fine."

An eloquent voice is heard from the dark. "Nonsense. If a man's taste is for Scotch, he should have it. I will share my good fortune. Please find yourself at my table."

Ah, kindred spirits, thinks Simon. He grabs his book and heads for the darkness of the corner.

Infiltrating the shadows, he sees a somewhat distinguished-looking gentleman who has a familiar presence. The man has a high forehead with a dark moustache.

Simon reaches for his hand. "Simon Smith. Thank you for the invitation."

"You'll have to excuse me for not standing. I've been here for the better part of an hour, so trying to stand at this point may be futile. Edgar Poe. Please sit down."

Simon can't believe what he just heard.

"The Edgar Allan Poe?"

"The? I fail to understand the emphasis of *the*, but yes, Edgar Allan Poe. I have tried to drop the Allan, but as you have just confirmed, to no avail. I see you carry with you a book. Are you a writer or a reader?"

Remembering what Arthur had told him, he answers with conviction. "I'm a writer."

"Excellent. And what do you write?"

"Oh, just stories." Hearing his words echo in his mind, he has just opened a fresh can of criticism.

"Just stories?"

Here it comes, thinks Simon. "What I mean is, the stories aren't very exciting. I live a boring life, always have."

The waiter drops off an empty glass. Poe fills the glass for Simon.

"Would you say my life is boring?"

"No sir, just mine."

Simon takes a small sip of the Scotch, and is thankful he did. It is twice the strength that he's used to.

"If there is one thing life isn't, it's boring," says Poe. "There is love, death, and everything in between. Since you seem to know something about me, how would you describe my life?" Poe consumes his drink like water.

"I would think that your life is unbelievably exciting. Your stories are insanely creative," says Simon.

"Insane? Possibly; but my life is no more exciting or boring than yours. I have little control over my life, but total control of my mind, that is where we find the excitement. Allow the life to follow the mind, not the mind to follow the life. The only limitations of the mind are the ones you give it."

Poe fills their glasses. "Now, raise your glass that I may make a toast. To Simon Smith, a man with a wearisome life, but a damn exciting mind!"

They down the Scotch. It makes its way past Simon's tonsils like a ghost pepper on a mission. His eyes begin to water. He lowers his glass to find Poe and his glass have disappeared. The half bottle of Scotch still adorns the table.

The waiter walks past, and Simon stops him in his tracks.

"The other gentleman that was sitting with me, did you happen to see where he went?"

"Other gentleman? I'm sorry, sir; there has been no other gentleman. You came in, sat down, ordered a bottle of Scotch and there you remained."

"I ordered this bottle of Scotch?"

"Yes, sir," says the waiter.

Suddenly Simon feels extremely drunk. He looks at the now empty bottle and slurs out, "Who would order an empty bottle of Scotch?"

"I assure you, sir; it was full when I placed it on the table."

"You know," says Simon, "this is getting far too strange."

"Would there be anything else, Mr. Poe?"

Simon does a double take. "Mr.—" Simon surrenders his sanity and drops his head to the table.

"Mr. Poe? Mr. Poe," says the waiter.

Simon lifts his head from the table. "The name is Smith."

"Yesterday, it was Evans. May I once again offer you a room and once again, assist you to that room, sir?"

Simon's sense of reality dismantles. The waiter slides his head under Simon's arm and helps him to his feet.

"I conclude the answer to be yes on both counts," says the waiter.

He picks up Simon's book from the table and hands it to him. "Your book, Mr. Poe."

Simon takes the book and stares at the cover through glazed eyes: THE RAVEN BY EDGAR ALLAN POE. Simon giggles, "Of course. Of course it is."

The waiter escorts him to a room and unravels him on to the bed. Simon clutches the book and passes out.

—

A vivid dream unfolds. Simon finds himself standing under an iron archway with the name, ST. JOHN'S CHURCH 1741.

Without warning, Poe appears. His attire is completely in black. Dark circles surround his sunken, bloodshot eyes. His black moustache hides all signs of expression, while his coal-black hair swirls in the breeze; constantly in motion, like the head of Medusa. He points beyond the entrance into the cemetery.

"It is through death, you will find life," says Poe with piercing eyes bulging from their sockets, like two poached eggs.

Simon is transfixed and riveted to the ground. In a blink, they are standing by a grave. The wind picks up and the sky becomes a backdrop of ominous black clouds folding within themselves like kneaded dough.

Poe towers over him. "This is my beloved mother, Elizabeth. I knew her not. I only knew of her. Her only possession bequeathed to me was this."

Out of thin air, he presents a picture of his mother. "I have carried it close to my heart all these years." He looks directly into Simon's eyes. "Can you understand the anguish of a child who bears this cross?"

Simon can't speak. He can only nod.

"Through the grave, we feel our loved ones: mother, sister, brother, wife. We learn of love, of yearning, of desire, and above all, acceptance. And what service does this render the living?"

Simon shrugs his shoulders.

"It connects the soul to the mind."

A large raven, the size of an eagle, descends on Poe, resting on his shoulder.

"Do you have a soul, Mr. Smith?"

With one hand Poe grabs Simon by the throat. "Can you dig deep enough into your soul to uncover and release the words of power to elevate your convictions? Can you? Can you, Simon Smith!"

Lightning streaks across the sky like fingernails across a blackboard. The ground on the grave begins to sink then pushes upwards and cracks open, like the top of a muffin baking in a pan. A clay-like grey hand forces its way to the surface, then another. Simon tries desperately to pull away from Poe who transforms into a fleshless figure. The hand that holds Simon is now mere bone.

The raven flies atop Simon's head and begins to unleash an intense barrage of pecking that dislodges chunks of hair and flesh. Simon screams and is finally able to run. A stream of blood trickles down his face. He trips and becomes airborne. Soaring through the air, he sails headfirst into a pitch-black, open grave.

—

Simon hears the welcome clatter of the train. A ray of light from the sun gently aligns itself with his right eye, provoking it to open. His head still leans against the train car window. He raises his head, looking about the car to see the same passengers as before.

"You've had quite a nap, sir," says the conductor. "I trust the demons have departed?"

"Demons? Yes, yes they have."

"I often find that a couple of shots and a snooze can do wonders, though the dreams can be more vivid than one needs."

"I'm with you on that."

"Your stop is next, sir."

"Thank you."

Simon prepares himself to leave the train. He sees the paper bag from the bookstore resting on top of his luggage bag. He picks it up, reaches inside and pulls out the magazine that Gabe had originally put inside the bag. Simon shakes his head. He places the magazine back in the bag, then puts it into his luggage. The train whistle blows for the next stop.

—

It has been a long week of meetings and conferences that Simon couldn't keep his mind on because, for the first time in his life, he's excited. He now sees his future, his destiny. He can't wait to get home and start his new life as a writer. But first he must take a trip back to the bookstore to see Gabe.

—

He enters the store and there's Gabe, exactly where Simon had left him. He looks up from his reading and pipe chewing.

"Well," says Gabe, "how was your trip?"

A different Simon makes his way to the counter. "It was quite an adventure."

"Excellent. Now is there a specific book you are interested in today?"

"No. I've decided that my life isn't as boring as I thought."

"Well, that's always an eye opener, isn't it?"

"And for some strange reason, I feel you had a lot to do with it."

"You do, do you?" says Gabe with a smile.

"I do, and I'm changing the direction of my life. I'm going to be a writer."

"A writer? Well, isn't that interesting and exciting. Now what brought this sudden change of events?"

"I met a couple of...old friends. They passed along some very valuable information."

"Yes, there's nothing like old friends to set you straight."

"I wanted to apologize for my past behavior and thank you for somehow showing me the way."

Just then, the tiny bell chimes and a woman enters.

"Excuse me. I'm looking for a book; something romantic and adventurous. Could you suggest something? I'm in a hurry."

Gabe and Simon look at each other and smile.

"Certainly," says Gabe and points. "There's a book on that shelf that I think will serve your purpose."

"Thanks for everything, Gabe," says Simon.

"Like I told you, I've been helping people find what they're searching for, for many years."

As Simon walks out the door he hears the woman exclaim, "But these pages are blank!"

Simon smiles.

11

THE LEGEND DISCONTINUES

Hockey is more than a game; it's a national treasure. Some of its players are national treasures, too. Lawrence Luster is one of those rare players who transcend the game. He has money, fame, and seemingly limitless power. But soon, he will discover a world completely unlike the one he knows.

—

The parking lot is well lit as a cold, blustery wind swirls through the dark of the evening. The snowfall from the morning has been ploughed and tucked away into the farthest extremities of the lot. A Porsche crawls into a reserved space near a back door to the arena. Larry Luster steps out of the car. He's tall, smartly dressed and handsome. He walks up to the door and is met by one lowly, short gentleman with pop-bottle glasses.

"What do you think, Mr. Luster? Are we going to win this one?"

Willie's hands shake from the cold as he holds his pen and paper anxiously awaiting a comment.

"We? I didn't know you were playing. Who the hell are you?"

"Willie Wodsworth. I'm a reporter, Mr. Luster."

"I gathered that. Look, Willie. Just piss off and don't bother me before the game, would you?"

"I'm sorry, Mr. Luster. All I wanted was a little something I could put in the paper, so I could stand out from the other guys."

"Does every asshole in this world have to make money off me?"

"I'm just trying to earn a living," says Willie as he opens the door for Larry.

"Yeah, well so am I."

The door slams shut. Willie is left standing in the cold with the wind howling around his ears.

"Evening, Mr. Luster," says the security guard. "Have a great game. The whole country will be cheering for you. I've got a pitcher of beer riding on this one."

"Wow, you bet the farm."

The guard responds under his breath with two words that are inaudible, but his facial expression was clear.

At the door to the players' dressing room, a crowd of reporters has assembled waiting for their hockey hero. They see Larry and the frenzy begins. Like a ham in a pool of piranha, they quickly surround him with cameras and microphones shoved into his face.

"Luster! You guys haven't been to the finals in forty-five years!"

"I wasn't here forty-five years ago," says Larry.

"You need one more point to clinch first place and only two games left. How do you—"

"What do you think, Larry? Can you win these next two?"

Larry opens the dressing room door.

"Hey, I'm not the expert. Go ask Cherry."

"But what about—"

Larry slams the door behind him. The reporters leave their post disgruntled and shaking their heads.

—

The arena is at its capacity with screaming fans. Two young women, Maddy, Larry's girlfriend, and her friend Tracy take their seats.

"Maddy, this is too exciting! Larry must be going crazy by now!"

"He calls it pumped," says Maddy.

"That reminds me, when are you two going to pump it up a notch and get married or at least engaged?"

"I've been wondering about that myself."

—

The game comes to an end and the result is obvious by the sombre mood in the dressing room. The only voices that can be heard are those of the reporters as they huddle around Larry like a flame in an igloo. He tries to dress as they bombard him with questions. Each reporter's face pressing against the side of the other's, trying desperately to get answers, while cameras and lights fill the background.

Larry is in no mood.

"What happened, Luster? You were up two goals!"

"What were you thinking when you missed that breakaway?"

"Do you think you can come back? Do yuh? Do yuh?"

They show no mercy. The Gatling gunfire of overlapping questions becomes too much for the hero. Finally, the egg cracks.

"Shut the hell up!"

Dead silence.

"There's twenty other guys in this room that were on that ice! Go ask them why we lost!"

He grabs his coat and makes a hasty departure from the dressing room. Walking briskly down the hallway he passes the security guard at the door.

"Tough loss, Larry."

Larry bolts through the door.

"Yeah," says the security guard. "Fine for you, you still get paid. I'm down a pitcher of beer."

Larry walks right into Willie shivering in the cold.

"Are you still here? Get the hell out of my way!"

Willie steps aside, but becomes his shadow.

"I'm really sorry about the game, Mr. Luster. But you were great."

"I sucked! We lost! How would you know anyway? You weren't even there."

"I watched on the TV from the donut shop across the street, until they kicked me out, and then I listened on my car radio. The game ended just as my battery started to lose power."

"Shit, you've got some great perks with that job."

Larry reaches his car. "Okay. What the hell do you want, Willie?"

"Maybe the question should be, what do you want, Mr. Luster?"

Larry opens his car door. "What do I want?"

"Yes. What do you really want out of life, Mr. Luster?"

"You know what I want, Willie? I want you to leave me alone. That's what I want. Why are you out here, anyway? Why aren't you in there, nice and warm with the rest of the jokers?"

"I'm not considered press. I'm just a small town reporter for a small, and perhaps to most, meaningless community paper."

Larry gets into his car and starts the engine. He lowers his window.

"If it's meaningless, then why bother?"

"I've been doing this for a lifetime."

"A lifetime? Guess you should have made a career change years ago, because you sure ain't making any money at this job."

"My reward is the pleasure I get from doing my job. It's all about choices, Mr. Luster."

"Choices? Well, you choose poor and I choose rich. Gotta go, Willie. And if I were you, I'd choose to get the hell out of the cold before you catch one."

Larry puts up the window and pulls out of the lot. Willie stands there abandoned once again with no story.

—

Maddy and Tracy are seated at a table in the local bar having drinks and nachos awaiting Larry's arrival.

"I guess Larry won't be in a very good mood tonight?" says Tracy.

"Nope. I'm really not looking forward to this. He doesn't take losing well. And now it's down to the last game. If they lose the next one, they won't end in first place, and I wouldn't want to be in the same town with him, let alone the same room."

She calls the waitress over. "Could we have two more, please?" She turns to Tracy, "I think we'll need them."

"He's not going to take it out on you, is he?"

"We'll see, it wouldn't be the first time. Here he comes now."

Larry makes his way to the table wearing a tight face.

"You all right, honey?" asks Maddy.

"You're kidding me, right? Why would you even ask?"

Maddy and Tracy glance at each other.

"And what's she doing here," asks Larry.

"Support," says Maddy.

"Mine or yours?"

Tracy feels uncomfortable already. "Maybe I should leave."

Maddy grabs her arm. "No, you won't." Turning to Larry, "I want you to apologize, right now."

"If she wants to be here, then she's going to be in the line of fire."

"Let me tell you something," says Maddy. "Tracy is my best friend and she came along to support you."

The waitress returns with their drinks.

"Excuse me, Mr. Luster. Can I get you something?"

"Yeah, a new hockey team."

"I'm sorry about the game, but you were fantastic."

"If I was, we wouldn't be having this conversation. I'll start off with a double rum and Coke, and a beer."

"Yes, sir."

Maddy and Tracy glance at each other once more. Larry catches it.

"What? I'm not allowed?"

Patrons are now taking notice.

"Of course. You can do whatever you want," says Maddy. "But there are repercussions to adding fuel to the fire."

"Oh, there are, are they?"

Tracy tries to smooth things out.

"Larry, I think—"

"You think?" says Larry. "Who the hell are you to open that big mouth? I don't want to hear what you think!"

Maddy's had enough. She's fuming, but keeps it under control.

"All right. You want to be an asshole, do it on your own time. We're leaving."

"So what else is new?" says Larry.

She calmly walks back. "Larry. I'm telling you. Don't push it."

"Or what? Are you going to leave me? You'll be missing out on a lot of money."

"No. You'll be missing out on a lot...Honey," she says and walks out with Tracy in tow.

"Ah, who needs you," he says to himself.

The waitress comes with the drinks.

"Your drinks, Mr. Luster," she says with a sexy look.

"Call me, Larry."

"Okay, Larry."

"Have you ever had a ride in a Porsche?"

—

Larry's coach scheduled a light practice the next morning; just a little tweaking. The team is on the ice, and from the bench the coach hollers out his instructions. Larry enters the bench dressed to go. The coach acknowledges him from the corner of his eye.

"You know this practice wasn't optional."

"I thought you said it was a light practice."

"Light doesn't mean fifteen minutes late!"

"Yeah, I know."

"No. You don't know. The reporters in the stands don't know either. They're wondering if you're one of three things: sick, injured, or an asshole."

"Hey, I'm here aren't I?"

"So, it's three. You know what that 'C' on your sweater stands for. Don't make everyone think otherwise. Maybe I should change it to an 'A.'"

—

The big game is about to begin. The arena is full of excitement and booze. Maddy and Tracy are in their seats nursing cups of beer while discussing the events of the night before.

"I tried calling him a few times, even left messages," says Maddy.

"Nothing?"

"No. He doesn't want to deal with me right now."

Tracy tries to downplay it. "Well, I guess it's understandable, considering the circumstances. I mean, we're talking the Stanley Cup here." She looks at her cup of beer, then takes a sip.

"Of course it's understandable. But you know what? It's always understandable under his circumstances. I know the hockey world revolves around him, but when that becomes his only world—"

"Ladies and gentlemen, please rise for the singing of..." The echoed voice of the announcer tries to overcome the booming sound of the fans as the anthem is played.

"All right!" says Tracy. "Here we go!"

—

It's the nail-biter of the year, with just over two minutes left in regulation time. The fans are pulling out their hair. The score is tied at two and neither side wants to take that trip to overtime.

The game is being lost in Larry's end.

Larry is on the bench taking a much-needed rest. The crowd screams for their saviour to get back on the ice. The coach sees an opportunity, gives a short jerk with his head. Larry responds, jumping the boards onto the ice. At that moment, the puck makes its way to the other side of the blue line as Larry skates by. He scoops it up and tears up the ice on a breakaway with one of the opposing defensemen in hot pursuit. The crowd is on their feet.

Maddy and Tracy are jumping up and down, holding each other. Larry closes in on the goalie. The defence man makes a last ditch effort by reaching out with his stick—it trips Larry. He heads one way as the puck goes the other and enters the net. Larry hits the boards, head first.

"Nooo!" screams Maddy.

"Oh, my God!" yells Tracy.

The crowd goes insane over the goal, but when they see that Larry hasn't moved, the noise shuts off like a tap. Now it's the silence that becomes deafening. From a fan a few rows behind Maddy and Tracy, they hear, "I think he broke his neck."

Maddy collapses into her seat.

—

Larry lies motionless in a hospital bed. His eyes slow to open. He's alone. It's quiet. A complete contrast to the last sounds he remembers in the arena. He moves his eyes from one side to the other and can distinguish metal rods. He now knows what happened. He's wearing a halo, but not the one he expected after winning the game. His eyes lower to see his right hand. His face distorts as he tries to move it, but to no avail. The door of his room partially opens. Maddy peeks in.

"You're awake." She enters and moves to the bed. "How are you feeling?"

"I wouldn't know. Physically, I'm just a piece of furniture. Emotionally, not much better. I'm dead."

"Far from it, sweetheart. The doctors said with time—"

"Time? Yeah, I'm so grateful I have time, time and money. Look at all the wonderful things I can do now."

Maddy tries her best to console him. "I know you're angry, but try to remember that there are other things to consider," she says as she holds his hand. "Hope and love."

"Hope and love. My only hope is to die before I shrivel up and decompose. And love? Does that include sex? I can't wait. Bring in the porn, so I can torture myself."

"Please, Larry. Things don't have to remain this way. With therapy anything is possible. I'll be here with you all the way."

"And how long will that last? Two weeks, a month. Then what? You're off with some other guy with money who will be parking his car in your garage."

"Money and sex? Is that what you think of me? I'm here for your money and a roll in the hay. How dare you? Do you think I put up with all of your cheating because of money? I cry every night hoping you will change, and see how much I love you."

"Well, now there's nothing to love, except my money."

"No. There's everything to love in spite of your money. And with time you'll be able to see and understand that."

"Maddy, the only thing I'm going to see are four walls and a bed. My life is fucking over. I'm the not walking dead. So you might as well get used to it."

She realizes he's too angry and upset. He needs time to sort everything out, including how he feels about her.

"Maybe you should just rest right now," she kisses his hand.

"Yeah, rest. Rest is exactly what I need."

She heads for the door.

"I'm not getting much of that, am I Maddy, am I?"

Her walk quickens as she leaves the room discouraged and emotionally drained with tears streaming down her face. As the door closes...

"At least you can run away!"

—

Three months can feel like three years, and the only positive note for Larry has been the removal of the halo and his ability to manipulate his head. Maddy is now far removed. She thought she could pull it off and hang in there, but she just couldn't compete with Larry's relentless attacks.

—

The hospital grounds are filled with gardens and pathways with a nice assortment of birds and squirrels. The atmosphere is tranquil as Larry, to some degree, enjoys the sun sitting in his wheelchair. His attendant is nearby on a bench reading a book. A familiar voice breaks through the calm.

"Larry!" It's Larry's coach.

"I didn't realize what a beautiful place they have here."

"You want to trade places?"

"You know, Larry, I can't begin to imagine what you're going through."

"No, you can't."

"Hey, take it easy, I just came to see how you're coming along."

"Oh, I thought you came here to tell me I missed practice or that maybe I've been traded. There must be somebody that could use an extra pylon."

"I thought you might have been a little different by now. You know, softened."

"Yeah. I should be happy and glad that I'm not dead. Do you think this is any better than being dead?"

"Some people would look at their situation and say that there must be some good that comes out of this."

"Well, if anybody knows what the hell that is, they're sure not telling me."

"Look, I just came to tell you that I'm your friend and I care about you, and if there is anything I can do for you."

"All you do is remind me of what I had and who I was. Now, I'm just a cadaver in a chair."

"That's an awful thing to say. You're still Larry Luster who played the best game of hockey anyone had ever seen. How's your girlfriend Maddy?"

"I wouldn't know."

"What do you mean?"

"I'm going to tell you the same thing I told her. You want to help? Don't come back."

Larry calls the attendant. "I want to go inside now."

His coach shakes his head as he watches Larry being wheeled away.

Larry is in bed coming out of his afternoon nap. His out-of-focus eyes see someone sitting in a chair, staring at him from across the room.

"What the hell, Willie?"

"Yes, Mr. Luster. It's me."

"How did you get in here?"

"I see you haven't been having much success with your new lot in life."

"I think you mean plot. What do you want, a story, now that you have my undivided attention?"

"Perhaps."

"The story ended the day I did."

"My main objective is to help you, Mr. Luster."

Larry chuckles for the first time since the accident.

"Help me? Willie, you should be doing stand-up. From what I've seen of you, you can't even stay out of the cold."

"Nevertheless, I shall do my best. You see, Mr. Luster, life is like a contract. And, as in any contract, you must live up to your obligations."

"My obligations? You're in the wrong place, Willie. The psychiatric ward's on the fourth floor."

"Choices must be made, Mr. Luster. Choices must be made."

"Okay, get the hell out. I've had enough of your bullshit."

And with that, Willie disappears.

"How did he do that? Must be the meds; gotta love 'em. Choices must be made. I sure as hell didn't choose this one."

—

The nurse finishes feeding Larry his dinner and wipes his mouth. "There you are, Larry. How was that?"

"The same as every other day, boring."

"Well let's knock it up a notch. Would you like to watch TV?"

"Sure. Let's see how the living are doing."

She swings the TV over to him and turns it on. "What would you like, news, sports?"

"No. No sports. You can leave the news on."

He hears the words of the newscaster.

"The Mayor is asking taxpayers once again to tighten their belts in response to the..." Larry begins to fade. His eyes are heavy, but he catches something on the screen: a commercial showing a tropical beach with a beautiful woman in a bikini walking toward the camera.

In a very sexy voice she delivers her pitch. "Is life getting you down? Do you find yourself looking to escape the boredom? Hi, my name's Crystal. Come join me, where you can be pampered beyond your wildest dreams, where the skies are always blue with white, sandy beaches and cool, clear water."

Larry is captivated by the girl.

"Come with me and enjoy it all. Come with me now...Larry."

"What? Did she say, Larry? Huh, meds." He falls asleep.

—

Larry dreams that he is on that beach. He's not paralyzed. He walks along the beach looking for that girl, Crystal. He spots a grass hut farther up the beach. Getting closer, he sees Crystal, looking just like she did in the commercial, standing in front of an easel, painting on a canvas. Larry approaches and she turns to him with a beautiful smile.

"Larry!" She puts down the paintbrush and runs to him, throwing her arms around him like a long-lost friend.

"I knew you'd come!"

She kisses him like he's never been kissed before.

"You're so beautiful." His eyes drink her in. "I can't believe I'm here. I can't believe I'm walking, and with the most beautiful girl I've ever seen."

She looks up at him with the sexiest smile.

"Then, you'll stay with me?"

"I'd be out of my mind not to."

"Oh, Larry, we'll have such a good life together."

Faintly in the background Larry hears a familiar voice calling.

"Mr. Luster! Mr. Luster!"

They look to see Willie running along the beach toward them.

"Willie?" says Larry. "Shit! What the hell is he doing here?"

Crystal becomes panicky. "Come on, Larry! We have to get out of here!"

"Why? It's just that idiot Willie."

She grabs his hand and starts to pull him away.

"No! You don't understand. He's a wicked man!"

"Willie Wodsworth? He's harmless, but he is a pain in the ass."

"Mr. Luster! Wait!" He closes in on them.

Crystal is desperate now. "You don't know him! He doesn't want us to be together! He hates me! Please Larry, run!"

He chuckles. "I can handle Willie."

Crystal screams with Willie just seconds away. She breaks from Larry and runs into the forest.

"Crystal, wait!"

Willie arrives, catching his breath. "Mr. Luster, I'm so glad...I thought...I would be too late."

"Too late? What the hell are you doing here? You're ruining my life."

"No, Mr. Luster. I'm trying to save it."

"By chasing away the girl of my dreams?"

"But that's just it. She's in your dreams."

"Well, if she's in my dreams, then what's the big deal? So are you. Now get the hell out of it!"

Larry turns to go after Crystal.

Willie grabs him by the arm. "No! You can't! She'll destroy you!"

"You're destroying me, you little bastard!"

Larry pushes him to the ground and Willie disappears.

Larry wakes exhausted and breathing heavily and yearning for Crystal.

"Man that was so damn real."

—

Larry is taking in fresh air in the garden as his attendant quietly sits reading. He feels upbeat after his exciting dream of Crystal. So much so, that he feels the need of a conversation with his attendant.

"Must be a good book."

The attendant, who has never had any interaction with Larry, looks up from his book.

"You talking to me?"

"Well, you're the only one around here that's reading a book."

The attendant goes back to reading.

"What's your problem?"

He looks back at Larry. "My problem? I've been taking you out here every day for three months and all you've said to me is, take me out, take me in. Now you want to be my best friend?"

Larry ignores the comment and decides he'd rather sleep than confront him. He shuts his eyes and listens to the sound of the birds singing in the background. He sleeps.

—

Larry finds himself where he left off, searching for Crystal in the tropical forest.

"Crystal! Crystal!" He hears her faint, urgent cries calling back to him.

"Larry! Larry! Help!"

He runs, following her voice to a clearing that leads back to the beach. Willie has his arms wrapped tightly around her.

"Willie! Get away from her!"

"He's crazy, Larry! Help me!"

"You don't understand, Mr. Luster. I'm trying to save you."

"Will you stop with that bullshit? Save me from what—a better life than this?"

"This is not life, Mr. Luster. Do you understand what I'm saying?"

"Okay. It's just a dream, I get it, but I don't give a rat's ass. I'm happy. And I'm walking again."

"It's more than a dream, Mr. Luster. I once told you that you have choices to make. This has to be your choice. Not hers or mine."

"I don't want to go back."

There's a pause in the conversation, then Willie asks him in a calm voice, "That's your choice, Mr. Luster? To stay here?"

"Yes. That's my choice."

Willie releases her. She runs into Larry's arms.

"Very well. Good-bye, Mr. Luster," says Willie.

"Is that for good?" asks Larry.

"Most definitely."

Larry looks at Crystal in his arms and kisses her. Willie starts to walk away then turns back.

"Oh, Mr. Luster. I forgot to mention that life contract. There is a slight debt that you owe."

Larry's puzzled. "A slight debt?"

Crystal pipes up. "Don't listen to him, Larry! It's just a trick!"

Willie pinches his two fingers together and smiles.

"Just a small one, Mr. Luster; just a small one." As those words leave his lips, he disappears.

"Stupid old man," says Crystal. She looks at Larry with loving eyes.

"Oh, Larry, I finally have you all to myself."

"Let's take a walk along the beach," says Larry.

They walk along the shoreline, holding hands and splashing each other. Larry grabs her and brings her in tight.

"I love you, Crystal. I've never felt this way before."

She looks into his eyes. "You'll never leave me?"

"I'd be a fool to leave you."

"Good," she says. "Kiss me, Larry."

He kisses her with all the passion he can muster. Larry's eyes are still closed as they break from the kiss.

"I'll be with you forever, Larry," comes in a strange, raspy voice.

Larry opens his eyes to discover that Crystal has turned into a hideous and grotesque old hag.

"Forever, Larry. Forever."

She tries to kiss him again with drool streaming from her open mouth full of decayed teeth, and breath like rotting fish.

Larry screams in horror, "Noooo!" his voice echoing down the beach.

—

The attendant looks up from his book.

"Hey! Lack Luster! I think we should go in now. That sun's starting to bore a hole through the top of my head."

No response from Larry. The attendant gets up and moves to the front of the wheelchair.

"Okay, I'm sorry. I apologize. Hey, I said—"

Larry stares straight out. His mouth hangs open.

"Ah, no man!" He places two fingers on Larry's neck. "Shit! They better not blame this one on me. I hope you're in a better place there, Luster, 'cause you sure as hell didn't like this one."

12

IN SPIRIT ONLY

Some people find it at the beginning of their lives, some in the middle, and then there are those who, well, never find it. It's been said that timing is everything. So, what happens when you find it in the right place...but in a different time? Steven Page is in the right place.

—

A blanket of snow covers an empty lot that rests between two huge office buildings. A car pulls up alongside the curb. The driver's door opens and out steps Matt Macauly. His age is reflected in a sprinkle of grey around his temples. He's a good man, with a good family, and works as a reporter for one of two city newspapers.

A thin layer of brittle snow crunches under his shoes as he walks through the empty lot. He abruptly stops at midpoint and begins to survey the area as if searching for something. Reaching into the inside pocket of his overcoat, he pulls out a small, long, white box that has a handwritten message scribbled on the lid. He opens it and smiles, then pulls out a cigar, lights it, takes a few puffs, and reflects upon the past two weeks.

—

Matt is in his office punching the keyboard of his computer as fast as his two fingers will allow while his eyes follow the words on the screen. A man quietly enters the office and leans against the wall behind him.

"I hope that's you, Steven, and not my editor?"

"It's me."

Steven Page is a portrait photographer in his thirty-ninth year and not looking forward to seeing that next number roll up. Steven notices a cigar in the ashtray.

"I thought you were giving up those cigars?" he asks. "You're not even supposed to smoke in here."

"Steven, did it ever occur to you why no one else is on this floor?"

"No one likes you, I guess?"

"Good guess. This area is for storage. I made a deal. I could continue to smoke as long as I stayed here. The room's bad, but the cigars are great. And as far as quitting, not now Steven, I've got way too much pressure right now. You know, deadlines, Christmas, parties, the kids."

"Sure," he says. "I know all about that."

Matt turns to him. "Are you all right? You sound a little down."

"I'm okay."

Matt smiles. "How 'bout a cigar? That'll pick you up."

"Yeah, right."

"Ah, you just need a couple of beers. There, I'm done. Let's get the hell out of here. I'm thirsty."

He gets up from his chair, grabs his coat from the rack, and begins to walk out of the office.

"Oh!" he says and turns back, opens a desk drawer and scoops up a few cigars.

Steven shakes his head.

He grabs Steven by the arm. "Come on! We've got a few beer heads to decapitate."

—

In the summer, the three blocks to Bailey's would seem a short dance away, but even walking briskly in the bitter winter cold of early evening seems like crawling on hands and knees, which may be the case when leaving the bar.

The place is filled with patrons and decorated for the season. Matt and Steven sit at a small table nursing their beers.

"Well, how did your day go? Lots of whining kids, I suppose. Trying to keep them still and quiet and take their picture at the same time. I'll tell you, Steven, you deserve a medal. I think I would have lost my mind by now," he says, downing the last of his beer.

"It's not that bad. I love the kids."

"Well, I sure know how you feel about mine. You treat them better than I do."

"That's not true, Matt. You're a great dad. It's easier for me; I don't have the responsibility of taking care of them." He finishes his beer and picks at the label on the bottle.

"All right, what's wrong, Steven? I've never seen you so down."

"I don't know. Must be my age or stage of life, something."

He looks into Matt's eyes. "I'm lonely, Matt. I'm tired of watching the world go by. I want to be a participant, not an observer. The only family I have is yours, which I love dearly, but I'd like to have my own and a wonderful woman to share it with."

"There are so many women out there looking for a guy like—"

"Me? I don't mean to be negative, Matt, but I've heard this all before. It's just worse at Christmas. I'll get over it. I always do."

"Sure. We all have our ups and downs at Christmas. Now don't forget, tomorrow is Christmas Eve, and as usual, we expect you over Christmas Day. Wait 'til you see the size of the turkey this year! Hey, we'll have a great time, just like we always do, right?"

Steven forces a smile, "Right."

—

Christmas Eve: The sign above the door reads, STEVEN PAGE PHOTOGRAPHY STUDIO. The snow is gently falling as Steven locks the door, but before he can turn around—

"Mr. Page! Yoo whoo! Mr. Page!"

A well-dressed woman quickly shuffles toward him.

"Oh, Mr. Page! Have you forgotten me? I told you I would be picking up my pictures at six o'clock!"

Steven looks at his watch and in a calm voice, "It's twenty after six, Mrs. Turner."

"Oh my, I'm so sorry. I didn't realize how late it was. Would it be too much to ask you to go back in to get my pictures?"

"That won't be necessary." He pulls a large envelope from inside his overcoat.

"Here you are, Mrs. Turner. I was on my way to your house to drop them off."

"Oh, how thoughtful." She takes the envelope. "Now I really am embarrassed. You are such a sweet man. You deserve a wonderful woman in your life."

"Yes."

"You know, I have a cousin who would be perfect for you."

Steven quickly looks at his watch again. "Oh, I'm so sorry, Mrs. Turner, but I have an appointment."

"Well I don't want to keep you. Merry Christmas, Steven."

She gives him a hug and then pulls away.

"Oh, I'm sorry! It's just that Christmas spirit."

"Of course."

"And I called you Steven too!"

"Nothing wrong with that either. Have a Merry Christmas, Mrs. Turner."

"You're just a dear," she says and rushes off.

—

The streets are empty of shoppers and traffic as Steven casually walks down the street, glancing into the decorated windows of the closed shops along the way. He finds himself back at Bailey's. He pauses for a moment and ponders the thought of going in. It's not like I have any place to go, he thinks to himself and decides to go in.

It's a stark contrast to the evening before with only a couple of patrons sitting at the bar, discussing sports with the bartender. Looking like he's carrying the weight of the world, Steven plunks himself down at a table. Marsha, a long-time waitress and friend, says, "Steven. Two nights in a row, I'm impressed. What's your pleasure, beer?"

"Uh, no, I'll have bourbon, Marsha."

"Things that bad, huh?"

Steven doesn't respond.

She sits down beside him. "Hey, honey. What have you got? The Christmas blues? I get them myself once in a while. There's never that comfortable middle ground this time of year. Either you're the happiest or the saddest."

"It would be easier if it was just this season, but we have four of them."

"I know. There are a lot of us out there who have to deal with the loneliness twenty-four-seven."

"It's funny. All you need in life is the other half of you; that one person that can make you whole."

"Yeah, it's like we're all walking around as one-half of a puzzle looking for the other piece that is the perfect fit."

She rubs his shoulder. "I'll get your drink."

He looks around the room and his eyes become fixed on the large flat screen where the opening credits to *It's A Wonderful Life* start to roll…

"Every time a bell rings, an angel gets his wings." Steven carries the bar on his own now, clutching his latest drink as if it were holding him up.

"Steven...Steven."

He looks up at Marsha with eyes that drift from one side to the other like a slow-moving tennis match.

"It's ten o'clock, Steven, and it is Christmas Eve. I think you've allowed yourself enough of the Christmas spirit for one night. Listen, I get off in fifteen minutes. I'm grabbing a cab. You could spend the night at my place. No strings attached."

"You're a good person, Marsha," he says with a slur. "But I think I have to be alone tonight. I need to clear my head of those Christmas blues."

"I think you drowned them."

Steven swallows the last few drops of his drink, and slowly gets to his feet. "Merry Christmas, Marsha," and gives her a kiss on the cheek.

"Steven. Are you sure about this?"

"Sure as rain, or snow. I'll be fine. I've had a few years of practice. Just need a good walk in the fresh air. Which way is the door?"

Steven stumbles his way down a dark street surrounded by tall office buildings. Under a lamppost he sees the street sign, Elm Street. He straddles the road and the curb. Behind him, in the distance, a speeding car moves erratically up the street. Steven is too drunk to acknowledge the impending danger. The car races by and clips him, knocking him to the ground, then speeds away with voices hollering from inside.

"Keep going, man!"

"It's just some drunken loser!"

Steven lies stunned on the side of the road. He looks up at the clear, black sky. He hears footsteps coming toward him—then passes out.

—

Light begins to filter through Steven's distorted vision. Two images become one and begin to capture a picture of a young woman's face. She's breathtakingly beautiful with long, soft, auburn hair and chestnut eyes. The ones that can pierce through steel or be so inviting and deep, that you could fall into them and never touch bottom. He blinks a few times, not believing what he sees. His first thought is that he died in the street, froze to death and has gone to heaven.

"Are you an angel?"

Her mouth smiles and simultaneously engages her amazing, exotic eyes, with a twinkle.

"No. I'm Emma."

"Nice to meet you, Emma. I'm Steven."

"Nice to meet you too, Steven."

He tries to look around and realizes he's horizontal.

"Where am I, in the hospital?"

"No. You're in my home."

"How did I get here?"

"Well, it wasn't easy. I helped you up and had you lean on me. How are you feeling?"

"Actually, I feel pretty good for being drunk and hit by a car. At least I think it was a car."

A white cat jumps up on Steven and sniffs his face.

"Looks like you've made a friend. That's Missy. Okay, Missy, get down. Do you like cats?"

"I like any animal that likes me."

"I made coffee. May I offer you a cup?"

"Coffee would be wonderful."

"Good. I'll be right back," she says, while giving Steven an opportunity to check out the surroundings.

He sits up, winces in pain and grabs his side. He looks about the large living room that is lavishly put together, but everything is antique, even down to the decorations on the Christmas tree.

Emma returns with a tray of coffee, sugar and cream. Steven notices that her attire adheres to the theme of the room.

"Cream and sugar?"

"Normally, but I think at this stage I should have it black."

She bends down to pour the coffee and Steven notices a beautiful gold locket at the end of a chain around her neck. He looks away, so as not to imply anything else.

"That's a beautiful tree. Is it real?"

She laughs, "Of course it's real. Is there any other kind?"

"No, I guess not."

She passes the coffee cup to him, and then sits in the chair beside him.

"Thank you. I really appreciate what you did for me. I might have frozen solid if you hadn't come to my rescue. That's quite unusual, helping a total stranger, bringing them into your home and placing yourself in harm's way."

"My father told me that a man's true wealth lies in his charity."

"Is he a minister?"

"No, he was a doctor."

"Oh, I'm sorry."

"Sorry?"

"Well, you talk about him in past tense, so I assume he—"

"Yes. My parents were killed two years ago in a car accident."

"How awful for you."

"I miss them dearly." She stands and walks to the mantel above the fireplace and picks up a beautiful, gold-framed picture and hands it to him, then sits beside him. Steven loves the fact that she moved closer.

"Here is a picture of them three months before the accident."

He looks at the picture and studies it for a moment. Her parents are dressed in clothes from the 1930s and are standing in front of a car from that same period. Steven is puzzled.

"You said they died two years ago?"

"Yes, why?"

"It's just that the car looks—a little older."

"Oh, no, that was a brand-new 1934 Packard Victoria." Emma appears amused. "I gather you're not a car enthusiast?"

Steven tries to grasp what is happening.

"That car was my father's pride and joy. I guess in a way it was befitting that he died in it."

Steven once again notices the locket. "That's a beautiful locket."

"Yes." She opens it to reveal a portrait of herself.

"That's a stunning picture of you."

"Thank you. I'm always a little embarrassed to show it because it is a picture of me, but it belonged to my mother and I cherish it."

The grandfather clock in the hallway begins to strike twelve.

Bong!...Bong!...

Emma becomes nervous. "You'll have to leave now. I hope you're feeling better, Steven."

"Why yes, I—"

She abruptly takes the picture from him. "Good. I'm so glad." She gets to her feet. Steven feels like he has no alternative, but to do the same. Ushering him to the front door, she opens it, turns to Steven and in an anxious but sincere moment says, "It was so nice to meet you, Steven."

Steven gets close.

"I, can I see you again?"

With a soft and loving response she answers, "Yes. Please."

The clock strikes twelve. She gives him a quick, unexpected kiss on the cheek.

"Goodnight, Steven!" She shuts the door.

Steven stands there completely at a loss, but he knows one thing for sure as he touches the cheek that she kissed; he has just met the girl of his dreams; the other half of his puzzle.

He runs down the steps of the porch, passing the white picket fence that surrounds the home, then out to the sidewalk. He looks back to see that the house is a wonderful Victorian home.

"Yes!" He raises his arms in jubilation and feels a sharp pain in his side from the accident, but still manages a smile and fades away into the darkness cheerfully singing...I wish me a Merry Christmas, I wish me a Merry Christmas, I...

—

Matt thought that if he kept the kids up late watching *It's a Wonderful Life* they would give him a break and sleep in for Christmas morning, but no such luck. The boys blew the reveille call at 5:45 a.m.

It is now noon and the living room is quiet and comfy-cozy. Matt's two boys are lying half asleep in front of the TV. Their early morning Santa call finally hit them. Angela, Matt's wife, is in the kitchen preparing the twenty-nine pounder for the feast while Matt sits in his easy chair reading the article he wrote in yesterday's paper.

"For crying out loud!"

From the kitchen, Angela asks what's wrong.

Can they not get anything I write, right? How do they misspell, misquote, and mislead an article that was perfectly written?"

Ding! Dong!

"Okay boys! Sounds like Uncle Steven's here!"

"All right!" they holler.

The words Uncle Steven means presents. Matt chuckles watching the boys scramble to their feet and head for the front door. When they open it, Steven is standing there with two identically wrapped gifts.

"Merry Christmas, guys!"

Their eyes pop when they see the gifts. "Wow! What is it?"

"Well," says Steven. "You won't find out standing there with your mouths open."

They each grab a present, then head for the living room. Matt greets Steven at the door and gives him a manly bear hug.

"Merry Christmas, my friend."

"Merry Christmas, Matt."

"Now, what did you get these kids that they don't deserve?"

The boys waste no time stripping off the paper.

"Dad! Laptops!"

"Ho-ly!"

"Well, do you spoiled kids have anything to say?"

They run over to Steven and put their arms around him.

"Thank you, Uncle Steven!"

"Thank you so much!"

"This is the best Christmas ever!"

"And you are the best uncle ever!"

"Let's show Mom!"

They run into the kitchen as Matt and Steven look on. Angela's voice can be heard through the kitchen door.

"What?"

"Steven, you shouldn't have," says Matt.

"No, Matt, like I told you. This is the only family I know. I'm happy to do it," he smiles.

"That's it!" says Matt.

"What's it?"

"I knew there was something different. You're happy. What's going on?"

Steven chuckles, "You won't believe what happened. I'll tell you all about it after dinner."

Angela enters from the kitchen with the kids. "Steven, that's too, too much!"

"Well, I just figured high school is just around the corner."

"They're such wonderful gifts. You're so thoughtful, as usual. I see two desserts for someone tonight."

"Hey, aren't you forgetting someone else?"

"Oh yes, of course, as soon as those cigars take a nosedive into the trash bin."

Matt shakes his head then puts an arm around Steven's shoulders. "Can you smell that turkey?"

"Only the last two blocks."

—

The dinner and the boys have now been cleared from the table. Matt pours Steven and himself a glass of wine.

"Okay, Steven, let's have the short of it because I'll be going out on the back patio to have a cigar."

"Why don't you make that your New Year's resolution?"

"Going out on the back patio?"

"You know what I mean. Anyway, last night after I closed up the studio, I decided to go back to Bailey's to lift my spirits."

"You mean some spirits."

"Matt."

"Sorry, I couldn't resist, go ahead."

"I left the bar feeling no pain. I found myself stumbling down this street and this car came racing up behind me and side-swiped me to the ground."

"Geez, Steven, are you all right?"

"I am now. Next thing I knew, I was in a house, laying on a couch in a living room. I was groggy, of course, but when my eyes began to focus, there, standing over me was the most beautiful woman I had ever seen."

"Sure that wasn't the booze?"

"Her voice was so soft, and she was so kind and loving. But there was something different about her."

"She had three legs?"

Steven gives him another look.

"Okay. Sorry, no more. I think it's the wine."

"I couldn't help but notice that she was dressed in clothes from the 1930s, right down to her hairstyle. And the room was totally from that period, like I had stepped back in time."

"Well, there are some people that like a certain look and they try to duplicate it."

"There's something else, Matt. She told me her father was a doctor and her parents died two years ago."

"Nothing strange about that, people die."

"Yes, but then she showed me a picture of them. They were dressed in the same period and they were standing next to a 1934 Packard."

"Boy, that's got to be worth a few bucks!"

"Matt...They died in that car three months after that picture was taken."

Matt mulls it over with another sip of wine.

"Too bad about the Packard. Well, either you heard wrong or she meant her grandparents."

"No, it was her parents."

Matt puts his hand on Steven's forearm.

"All right. Now don't go on the defensive, but is there any chance she may be a little...loopy?"

"Crazy?"

Matt gently shrugs his shoulders.

"No. She's not crazy. She's just the most exciting thing that's ever happened to me. If she's crazy, crazy is where I want to be. I've got to see her again."

"Of course you do." He picks up the bottle of wine and smiles. "More wine?"

—

BOXING DAY SPECIAL—FRAMES 50% OFF.

Steven pulls the sign from his store front window.

He disappears with the sign only to reappear seconds later outside locking the door and heads for home.

Steven's home is a typical two-bed apartment. Two because the extra one he uses as a darkroom.

It's comfortable, but nothing like the dream he has of having a house like Matt, with a wife and kids. He sits in front of the TV, but his mind is already a few days ahead, waiting for the other shoe to drop: New Year's Eve.

Loneliness can be a killer on that night. Just in case he's forgotten, a news report hammers it home. "So, what are your plans for New Year's Eve?" says the reporter.

He shuts off the TV.

"I'm not spending another New Years alone." He leaves the security of his apartment and heads out for some fresh air.

Seeing store windows advertising New Year's Eve sure doesn't help the situation, but maybe Bailey's will. He grabs the handle of the entrance door and realizes that it's only a quick fix that will fan the flames of despair. Better judgement prevails as he declines and carries on down the street.

He suddenly stops. "What's wrong with me? Am I losing my mind? I was with the most wonderful woman I've ever met and I'm walking the streets alone. I have to find her."

He takes the same route that almost killed him the week before. There it is, Elm Street. A broad smile stretches across his face and from his lips, "Emma. How could I have forgotten so soon?"

My life has to change, and without a doubt, Emma is that change. He quickens his pace. In no time the Victorian home is in sight. His confidence and conviction that she is the one for him heightens as he runs up the front porch steps, barely touching every second step. He rings the doorbell. There's a moment of nervous silence as he waits. Suddenly the thought occurs to him: Will Emma's image be the same one I encountered when I was under the influence, or will she be like Matt said, have three legs?

Before that thought settles in, the door opens and there stands Emma. She's all that he remembers and more. Her smile is bright, warm and inviting, just as he remembered it.

"Hello, Steven. I was so hoping to see you again."

"Me too," says Steven.

They sit side by side on the sofa in the living room, having a wonderful conversation as the light from the fireplace glows and flickers throughout the room. Steven takes her hand and there isn't a glow from any fire that could ever emulate the ones in their eyes.

—

Emma brings out cake and coffee.

"This cake is delicious. Did you say you made it?"

"Yes, but I really owe the recipe to my grandmother."

"A wonderful woman, I'm sure."

There's a pause as Steven puts his thoughts together.

"Emma. Would you like to go out sometime, maybe to the movies?"

"I love movies. I also enjoy ice skating. Do you skate?"

"When I was a kid."

"Excellent. The park is just a couple of blocks away; High Hill Park. They have a beautiful ice rink there with lights all around. It's very ro—it's very nice under the stars."

"That's for me."

Bong! The grandfather clock begins the countdown to midnight, and once again Emma becomes restless.

"Oh, I don't know where the time has gone," she says as she gets to her feet. "You'll have to leave now, Steven."

Steven stands but this time he's looking for answers.

"What's wrong, Emma? What makes you so nervous when twelve o'clock arrives? And why do I have to leave you?"

She moves in close and looks at him with her big brown eyes.

"Please, Steven. Don't ask me any questions."

She gently holds his face with her hands and brings her lips to his and kisses him with the passion of a woman seeing her soldier off to war.

The last bong sounds from the clock.

"Hurry, Steven!"

As they reach the front door Emma looks into his eyes, gives him a quick kiss and pushes him out the door.

He turns back. "Skating!" he says.

"When?" she asks.

"Thursday, I work till nine."

"I'll be ready." As she closes the door, "Steven, I love you."

Before Steven can respond, the door is shut.

Steven stands there for a moment, stunned, then smiles, and in a whisper, "She said...she loves me."

—

The next day Steven takes a lunch break and heads to the small sporting goods store a block from Matt's office. After purchasing skates he decides to drop in to see Matt to tell him the good news about Emma.

Matt sits at his desk chomping a cigar when Steven enters with all the excitement of a school boy. "Matt! You are not going to believe this!"

Matt swirls around in his chair. "What the hell's gotten into you now?"

"I'm in love, Matt! And the best part is, she loves me!"

Matt runs his hands through his hair. "Isn't this a little sudden or premature? Are we talking about this same apparition?"

"Yes! I mean no! She's not an apparition! But she is an angel. Her name is Emma. You're going to love her. I want you to meet her, Matt!"

"Sure." He turns back to the computer and starts hitting the keys. "But not today, I have to finish this great idea they threw into my lap. They want me to write a story about a robbery last week and hook it with, why people steal at Christmas. And you wonder why I smoke and drink."

Steven is oblivious to what Matt is saying. "I'm taking her out tonight."

"That's great. I'm glad to see you so happy. Where are you taking her?"

"We're going skating." He raises the skates.

"Skating? Wow. You'll break the bank on that one. That should impress any woman. I guess you'll be going to the arena."

"No, to the park. High Hill Park."

"Well, have yourself a great time. How long has it been since you were on skates?"

"Twelve."

"Got a helmet?"

"See you later, Matt. I'll let you know how I make out."

"On or off the ice?"

After Steven leaves, Matt thinks back, "High Hill? They haven't had a rink in that park for years."

—

Steven stands at Emma's front door with his skates tied together around his neck. He glances at his watch; perfect, he thinks, and then rings the doorbell. The door opens and there's Emma, looking absolutely stunning. Wearing a beret tilted just right, scarf, and a long wool coat and a beautiful smile.

"Come in, Steven. I'll just grab my skates."

He steps in. She returns with the skates around her neck. Steven can't control himself. He looks passionately into her eyes. "I've never seen a more beautiful sight."

He initiates a kiss, but their skates get in the way. Holding the moment, they drop the skates to the floor and bring themselves together for a long, passionate kiss.

"My," she says with dreamy eyes. "What were we doing?"

"Skating, I think?"

—

The park is just as she described with floodlights filling the trees that turn the park into a fantasy land. People abound; some skating, some sitting on benches, while others are just watching, and all dressed in the same vintage attire. Steven jokes to himself, I have a feeling I'm not in Kansas anymore.

"I can't believe this," he says.

She smiles at him and he holds her tight.

"As beautiful as a dream," she says.

He looks at her. "Not as beautiful as the dream I'm holding."

She looks up at him with a smile and eyes that sparkle.

They sit on a bench and exchange their boots for skates, then onto the rink. Emma glides smoothly while Steven gingerly tries to coax his body to remember the days of adolescence. He timidly pushes off.

They skate, swirl, laugh, and bump into each other and once in a while, into other skaters. Steven tries a little more than his twelve-year-old memory recalls and slips and falls to the ice.

Emma skates to him and helps him to his feet. "Are you all right, Steven?"

"I'm fine. Just a bruised ego," he laughs.

He looks at his watch. "But I can't say the same for my watch."

"Oh, no."

"Yep, time for a new one."

They skate back to the bench.

"Steven, you sit down. I'll be right back."

"Okay. I could use the rest; I mean break."

Emma goes to a small shack-like structure where they sell coffee and hot chocolate, while Steven looks up at the clear, black sky, admiring the moon and stars. He sees his life through new eyes, something that wouldn't have been possible a few days ago.

"Whatever this is..." he says to himself, "please, don't let it end."

Emma returns with two cups of steaming hot chocolate.

"Well, what do we have here?" he asks.

"I hope you like hot chocolate?"

"Love it. I haven't had that in years."

Emma hands him a cup and sits beside him. She looks down at Steven's skates.

"Steven, your skates; they're very unusual."

"They are? The guy at the store said they were the latest design. As I have demonstrated, it doesn't improve my skating. Just as bad as I ever was."

"You're adorable."

They cuddle, sipping their hot chocolate.

"Steven, this is so wonderful. I haven't laughed and enjoyed myself so much in quite some time."

"Because of your parents?"

"That and life. I miss all the good things. Like skating, hot chocolate and," she looks into his eyes. "Falling...in love."

"I like that one," he says with a smile. "How 'bout a movie next?"

"Yes. Oh, yes, Steven. I want to see a movie. We could see *Modern Times* or *My Man Godfrey* or *Camille!"*

"Or all three."

"Oh, Steven, I don't ever want this to end."

"And why should it?"

There are now only a few people left in the park. A man skates by with his wife trailing.

"Come on, Mildred. We better go, it's almost midnight."

Emma catches the word midnight.

"Midnight?" She breaks from Steven as the panic sets in.

"Steven, we have to go! I have to get back!"

He doesn't question her. Whatever it is, it must be serious. She practically rips the skates from her feet. Steven follows suit.

"Please, Steven, take me now!"

They grab their boots from under the bench and put them on with all speed. She stands and grabs his hand and pulls him up, leaving their cups of hot chocolate. They race out of the park and down the street. In the distance the first bong from a church steeple sounds the beginning of the midnight countdown.

Tears run down her face. "Please, Steven! Hurry! Hurry!"

He feels her desperation.

Bong!

Finally up Elm Street they go. Now, just a few steps from the house as the last bong sounds! Emma runs up the front porch with Steven trailing! She opens the door!

Steven blurts out, "I'll see you—"

The door slams shut! Steven stands there out of breath and totally bewildered.

—

Matt saunters into the newspaper building, but before he can get to the elevator, "Matt, can I see you for a minute?" says John, his editor, as he peers out from his office.

This can't be good, thinks Matt.

He walks into the office with a clenched mind. "Okay, so you didn't like the article. You didn't give me much to work with."

"The article? Oh, that was fine. Everything you do is fine," he says with a grin. "As a matter of fact, it's always top-notch."

Matt is taken off guard by the compliment. "It is?"

"Matt, I'm like you. I enjoy a little confrontation. That's why having you on a floor by yourself doesn't feel right. I miss those great conversational scraps we used to have."

"If you're that lonely, I could email you once in a while. Now I know you didn't call me in to hand me a raise, so what's up?"

"I want to show you something."

He walks past Matt and out of the office. Matt follows him into a large office next door.

"Here's my dilemma," says John. "First, let me tell you that I have no choice in this matter. The floor you're on has been rented out. I'm offering you this office and the title of co-editor. It does come with a raise. And now the hard part, not for me, but for you. The cigars have to go."

Matt takes in a deep breath and slowly exhales. "And when is this taking place?"

"You have a week. If you can rationalize this offer, it's a no-lose situation for you. You move up, get a raise, and you improve your health, because I want you to be here for a long time."

Matt is speechless.

John puts his hand on Matt's shoulder. "I know the cigars will be hard for you. I want you to take the time to really consider what is important to you. I know you'll make the right decision."

Matt feels like he's just been hit by a truck. He sits in his chair with his feet on the desk nursing a cigar, gazing out the window and contemplating his future.

"Matt," says Steven in a soft voice.

He turns. "Steven, you sound pretty sombre. What's wrong? Did you fall on your head at the rink?"

"I wish it was that easy," he says and sits down. "Matt, Emma is the most beautiful, wondrous person I have ever met in my entire life."

"Then what's the problem?"

"Whenever we're together something always happens at midnight."

"You've been watching too many vampire movies."

"I'm serious, Matt."

"Steven, I don't know how else to put this, but are you sure you're not chasing a dream?"

"There is only one way to convince you. I'm taking you to see her now."

"Now?" Steven glances at the clock on the wall.

"Look, it's 4:15. You finish at 4:30. What's fifteen minutes?"

Matt takes a deep breath then exhales.

"All right, Steven. I'm not sure if keeping you in a positive frame of mind is good for my health. I'm telling you, if this doesn't turn out the way you want, please, don't bring it up again."

"Deal."

—

Matt is driving as Steven navigates.

"Are you sure this is the street, Steven? I don't ever remember a house on this street."

"Yes, Elm Street. It's just up here on the right."

The car slows to a stop beside an empty lot.

"Is this the house, an empty lot?"

Steven looks around, visibly upset. He's confused. Anxiety sets in.

"No! This is where the house should be! Something's not right!"

"For the first time, I totally agree with you."

Steven climbs out of the car in a panic. He stomps around the area, looking every which way for an answer.

Matt fears a meltdown. He wastes no time getting out of the car and makes his way to Steven. He grabs Steven by the shoulders. At this point Steven is shaking and his eyes are full of tears.

"Steven! It was the booze! You were drunk! You were hit by a car! Maybe you had a concussion!"

"There's no concussion and I wasn't drunk last night or the time before that! I had the most romantic evenings I've ever had! She made cake. We drank coffee, we went skating! She loves me, Matt! And I love her! And I don't understand! I don't! The only thing that makes sense is Emma!"

"Okay. Let's calm down and go over this rationally." Matt pulls out a cigar and lights it. He takes a few puffs and contemplates his next move.

"Now, stay with me on this. You're absolutely sure this was the street?"

"I'm absolutely sure this *is* the street!"

"Okay, okay. Calm down." Matt takes another puff. "All right, the house was here. It was an old Victorian house. Her father was a doctor. They died in a car accident." He takes another puff from his cigar. "I've got it." In a calm voice he adds, "Let's go back to my office. You can look up the old newspapers on my computer. Maybe, maybe there's something there."

"Yes! That's right, Matt! There has to be something! Some article about their death! He was a doctor! They would have had some coverage!"

"Exactly."

—

Steven is sitting at Matt's desk clicking away on the computer. Matt looks on then glances at his watch. "Damn! I'm late! I have to let you go now, Steven."

"Aren't you even curious about what I might find?"

"Steven, aren't you curious about why I can't stay?"

Steven stops and turns to Matt. "What do you mean?"

"How about this? It's New Year's Eve, Steven."

"It's New Year's Eve?"

"And it's costing me a second mortgage for a babysitter and triple that to take Angela to this big party!"

"Oh, I'm sorry, Matt. You better hurry."

"You're not kidding!"

Matt opens a side drawer in his desk and grabs the last of the cigars from the box. He places one down on the desk.

"Here, Steven, Happy New Year, and if you get lonely, there's Scotch in the second drawer," he says as he heads for the door.

Steven picks up the cigar and holds it up.

"Why don't you make this one your last?"

"Not now; too much pressure."

"How did I know you were going to say that? Happy New Year, Matt."

"Let's hope so. See you next year. And, good luck with that."

Steven notices a small, white, empty pen box in the drawer. He places the cigar inside and writes MY LAST CIGAR on the lid and drops it into his coat pocket thinking he will present it to Matt at a more appropriate time. He decides to take Matt up on his offer of Scotch to give him some courage before he delves into the question of whether Emma is real or something that he has contrived in his mind, as Matt believes.

One drink slides into two before he begins to feel relaxed. He pours himself a third, gets up and looks out the window into the street. He realizes that this will affect his whole life.

"If she doesn't exist...what's left?" And with that he finishes his third shot of Scotch and plunks himself back in the chair. After mulling that thought around he realizes he is being sucked into the New Year's Eve prophesy of doom.

"No. I'm not going out that way."

He turns his attention to the screen and types in, 1934 car accident kills doctor and wife. A page appears on the screen, Prominent Doctor and Wife Perish in Car.

He begins to read the article. "The well respected Dr. Edgar Camden and his wife Anna, who have occupied their stately home on Elm Street for a quarter of a century, were killed instantly this morning. Witnesses say their car hit a tree after the doctor tried to avoid a stray dog. They are survived by their only daughter, Emma."

His eyes look up from the screen. "It is true," he says in a soft voice. "She is real. And she does live in another time."

Looking back at the screen—RELATED STORY. Steven opens the page to reveal a large picture of Emma, the one from her locket. He stares at the picture with great affection. "Emma." His eyes move to the headline below.

"Fatal fire takes young life. No! No!"

His eyes race through the column. "The community is in shock with the tragic death of Emma Camden, the beautiful young daughter of Dr. and Mrs. Edgar Camden, who passed away two years ago in a car accident. Miss Camden died in her home sometime after midnight, New Year's Eve, when her home was engulfed in flames."

He looks up from the screen. "Oh, my God, that's it! That's why she wouldn't let me stay! She couldn't!"

He continues, "She was found in a second-floor bedroom. A lit candle on the main floor may have been disturbed by the family cat that somehow escaped the tragedy." In a whisper he says, "Missy, New Year's Eve." He looks up at the wall clock: 11:15. His adrenaline hits the roof and now he's completely sober.

He doesn't bother with the elevator. He runs down the three flights of stairs and out the front doors of the building. He tries hailing down a cab, to no avail. Finally, he waves down a bus. He boards and sits near the back door and can barely sit still. He is the only one on the bus. He glances out the window and after a brief pause he yells up to the driver, "Say, when do we get to Elm Street?"

The driver shakes his head. "Elm Street? I don't go anywhere near Elm."

Steven rushes to the front of the bus in a panic. "Well, how far do you go?"

"Three more blocks and I'm done. End of the line. That's where I leave you, buddy."

Steven reaches into his pocket and pulls out some bills. "Look. Can't you make an exception? I'll pay you."

"Any other night would be fine, but come on, man, it's New Year's Eve. I'd like to be able to give the missus that big kiss at midnight. You know how women are; she's counting on me."

Steven exits the bus. Looks at his broken watch and then turns back to the driver. "What time is it?"

"Eleven-forty; times a wastin'," says the driver. "Happy New Year!"

The bus pulls away and leaves Steven on a empty street. He pulls his coat collar up and starts running through the icy slush. In the distance he hears the church bell countdown begin.

"Damn it!"

He reaches Elm Street when the church bell hits its final ring for the New Year. He races down the street with everything he has left. The house is all aglow. He dashes up the front porch and tries the door. It won't open. He kicks it in. Missy, the cat, screeches and darts out. Flames are everywhere. He sees the staircase through the flames and fights his way up to the second floor.

"EMMA! EMMA!"

Steven makes it to the doorway. Emma's in her bedroom, backed into a corner of the room crying, as the flames move in. He sees her through the flames.

"Emma!"

"Steven! Steven, go back!"

"Not without you!"

"You can't. It's too late!"

"It can't be too late!"

A wall of fire separates them. Steven backs up then leaps forward through the flames to Emma. He grabs her and holds her tight in his arms.

"I love you, Steven."

"And I love you, my precious Emma."

The heat crackles as the flames engulf the room.

—

Matt enters his office as his phone rings. "What the hell? It's New Year's Day. Nobody knows I'm here." He winces in pain. "Oh, my head." He gently picks up the phone and speaks softly. "Happy New Year. Who the hell is this?"

"Matt? It's George Walsh."

"George. For the love of God, it's New Year's morning."

"Sorry, Matt, Angela told me you'd be there."

"Don't detectives get a day off either?"

"This would have been a good day to have off. I need you down at the morgue."

"The morgue? Oh, my God, who is it?"

"I'm afraid it's...Steven."

"What! He was just here last night! I left him right here in my office! It can't be! Are you sure it's Steven?"

"Yeah, I'm sure."

"Did you say anything to Angela?"

"No, of course not. Can you meet me here in twenty?"

"Be right there."

Matt looks at the black screen and gives it a click. He sees the page that Steven had left open and sees Emma's picture. "My God, she is real and beautiful too." He begins to read the article. "No. This is impossible. I can't believe it."

—

George is in the room as Matt enters. There's a table with a sheet covering Steven's body.

"How did it happen?" asks Matt.

"Well, now comes the strange part."

"You found him in an empty lot on Elm Street." says Matt.

"How did you—"

"Don't ask."

"The strangest thing is that he died of smoke inhalation. But there are no signs of fire, smoke or even burn marks on his clothes. It's really weird."

"You don't know the half of it. Give me a few minutes, will you, George?"

"Sure," says George and pats him on the back.

Matt pulls down the sheet and looks at Steven with great affection. He notices a bit of a smile on his face. "Steven, Steven. What have you done? I miss you already." He picks up Steven's hand and holds it.

"What a great friend you've been to me and my family."

He feels Steven's hand clutching something. He gently unfolds it; Emma's locket. A chill shoots up his spine as he opens it. There's the picture of Emma and on the other side—it's Steven. He quickly puts it into his pocket as George comes back.

"I found this in his coat pocket," says George. "It seems a little odd too."

He hands Matt the white box with MY LAST CIGAR written on top.

Matt grins. "No, this I understand," and puts it into his coat pocket.

—

Matt drags himself back to his office. With his head down and emotionally drained he flops into his chair and grabs the bottle of scotch and the glass that Steven had left. He pours himself a good one then rests his feet on the desk. He gazes out the window and ponders how he's going to tell his family. Still in disbelief his eyes drift to the page on the screen. Something catches his attention. He puts his feet down and closes in.

"Wait a minute!" His eyes are drawn to the end of the article: "She was found in an upstairs bedroom along with her husband, Steven Page, local photographer."

—

Matt looks once more around the empty lot then takes another draw from his cigar.

"Take good care of him, Emma. He's a special guy. And I've never known a man to love a woman more." He stares at the remainder of his cigar, then with reluctance, throws it into the snow and puts the little white box into his pocket.

"Well, co-editor, welcome to the first floor."

13

POST MORTIMER

I hear him again, as I have for the last two weeks—scratching and clawing at the lid of the wooden box that I painstakingly assembled months earlier. He is relentless. I couldn't allow him to continue: to stand idly by as he drained every aspect of my life. Why in the hell won't he STOP? I should have put him farther from the cottage. That was my mistake. Five acres of land and I settled on a hundred feet away. What was I thinking? And now I'm paying the price.

Mortimer was my best friend, but even so, friendships can become cumbersome and wane after a while. I do think twenty-eight years is a sufficient length of time. I imagine I could have severed the relationship years ago, but I had a conscience back then. In addition to the financial disappointments, and the embarrassment I endured, he was intolerable. He'll change, I kept telling myself, but he was beyond redemption.

What I did for Mortimer was more than I would have done for my own child, if I had one. Sure, we had our differences, but to accuse me of forcing my ideas and my way of thinking onto him was ludicrous. He was who he was and I, me. I may at times have placed obstacles in his path, but they were for his own good. I wanted him to be stronger, and more resilient: I wanted him to grow into the person I knew he could be. Was I really asking too much of him?

But the writing was on the wall. He knew it as well. The time had come and he was more prepared than I was. He savaged my good nature like a beast mauling its prey. Defenceless, I failed to respond with any strength or dignity. He had me and he knew it. I begged for mercy, but he gave me none. I just lay there in silence, licking my wounds.

He's a nasty one, all right; continuing with that infernal noise and moaning. I could dig him up and replant him in the forest.

The ground I buried him in bakes under the full glare of the August sun. I hope it bakes his little balls off; that's if he had any. I could take a walk along the shore, let the northern breeze soothe me into thinking it was all a bad dream or nightmare—but it would only last until I walked back into the cottage. I could turn the tables and make him infuriatingly jealous by finding a new friend, but that would mean starting all over, and at my age, the whole process just seems insane. Damn you, Mortimer! Our lives were perfect—the prestige, the fame, and of course, the money. There was no stopping us. We were on top of our game, top of the world! And look where you have taken us: to the abyss, to the end of the road.

I keep asking myself, why. Sure, I could have helped you, given you more—perhaps an opportunity to develop yourself further. But I was afraid. Afraid they would all turn against us; turn their backs and walk away in disgust. I couldn't allow you to fail. If you didn't meet expectations, I would live out my final days as a failure and in the end—that's what happened. But we did have some good times, didn't we, old friend? We rode the wave of success as far as we could take it. We laughed and dined, and travelled the world. How many get to do that?

For some strange reason, I'm starting to miss you. Could it be that I really can't live without you? Is it possible that we could reconcile our differences, start over? Give it one more kick at the can? We were such a great team.

The ground has settled after the rain from last week, and now with this stifling heat, the patch has the texture of concrete. I'd need the pickaxe. For one brief moment, I reverted back to feeling anger for having to go through this ordeal just to save his life. I hope I sealed the wooden box tightly enough to keep out the rain, so it didn't soak in and start rotting everything.

Even with my sunglasses and hat, the sun is whittling my energy down to a slug's pace. I need a break before I go on. A nice, tall glass of rum and Coke with ice should do it.

—

I sit comfortably on the porch watching a few sailboats glide through the water on the lake. The rum mixes well with the light breeze and the allure of the heaving motion of waves unfurling and gently kissing the shoreline, all of which lull me to sleep.

I wake with a jolt. The sun is now a memory, replaced with a quarter moon floating over the crest of the lake. It's too late to go back to digging. I'll resume in the morning.

—

Mortimer was quiet all night. Perhaps he has anticipated my plan of reuniting. Whatever his thoughts, I was happy to get in one full night's sleep. I delay the inevitable by having breakfast.

My palms are sore from yesterday's dig so I grab my garden gloves and head out the door. As I approach the dig site, a chilling sight grips my soul. The hole has been completely unearthed; pushed out from within.

On closer inspection, I notice the lid to the box is open and there are deep-cut grooves leading away from the hole. I follow them as they lead down to the lake. My hands clench and my heart pounds as I see Mortimer face down by the water's edge.

"You fool!" I shout. "Why would you try to end it all when I've decided to give you another chance? It's always been about you, you selfish, narcissistic, ego-driven bastard!"

I brush the sand from his back and turn him over. His face could use a little attention, but his spine seems to be intact. I gently lift him up and carry him into the cottage and set him on my desk beside my laptop.

"I'll do things right this time, I promise you. You'll be more brilliant than Holmes ever was. We can do it, Mortimer! We'll be on top again. You'll be the most genius detective—and I'll be the author the world has been waiting for! You just wait and see, Mortimer ...you just wait."

I gently pick him up and place him on the bookshelf in his rightful place. I sit back at my desk and begin punching the keys. It was a dark and stormy...

14

WISER GUYS

Joe Pistoli has been reluctantly assigned a small and insignificant slice of the big pizza through the bloodline chain of command. For Joe, this is the opportunity of a lifetime—a long-awaited chance to prove himself. Soon, Joe will embark on a journey that will make him the unlikely and unsung hero of this small Italian community.

—

Tony Biscotti is a heavyset man wearing a dark suit as he walks along a city street carrying a bulging brown canvas bag that nonchalantly swings from his side. He stops from time to time, browsing store windows and having brief conversations, then turns down an alley and enters the side door of a building. He continues along a grungy-looking hallway into a small office. The space is occupied by Joe Pistoli.

Tony drops the bag on the desk.

Joe eyes the bag. "Where the hell you been?"

"South side," says Tony.

"How much?"

"Fifteen."

Joe grabs a slice of pizza from a box on the desk and takes a bite. "Fifteen hundred, that's a pretty good start. Maybe this territory they gave us is better than we thought."

"I don't think so."

"What do you mean?"

"That's fifteen bucks."

Joe chuckles. "Hey, if you're going to try and rip me off, don't make it so obvious."

"I'm serious, Joe, that's it. There's something going on."

"Yeah, there's something going on all right. You're trying to screw me."

"Hey, I'm your brother-in-law, for Christ's sake." Tony points to the pizza. "Cosmo's?"

"Yeah."

"Ah, they make the best." He sticks his hand in the box for a slice.

Joe smacks his hand.

"What do you mean, there's something going on?"

"It's weird. They're telling me they ain't got the dough."

Joe tries to talk through a mouthful of pizza. "What the hell's wrong with you? They always say that."

"No, no. They really ain't got it; something about the banks putting the squeeze on them."

"The banks? I thought they only did that to homeowners? Must be something new, hitting the little business guys."

"Maybe we should call Leo."

"Are you out of your mind? They just gave us this territory and already you want me to call Leo? You don't call Leo and tell him you got problems unless you want problems."

"Yeah, you're right."

"We've got to straighten this out ourselves. We have to prove we deserve to be here."

Joe grabs another slice of pizza.

Tony tries his luck for another slice.

Joe raises a finger.

"Just one."

"Anchovies?"

"Yeah."

Tony smiles. "Nice."

"First thing we've gotta do is check the other areas. You take the east side. I'll do the west, then we'll both go to the north end." He points to the bag. "That looks pretty full for only fifteen bucks."

Tony shrugs his shoulders. "Coinage."

Joe winces as he shakes his head.

—

Joe walks into a bakery store where he finds the owner, Gino, standing behind a glass counter tending to Mrs. Petroni.

"...and maybe some nice pane today Mrs. Petroni, to go with your mama mia gnocchi."

She feels flattered, but embarrassed. "Uh, Gino, maybe uno."

Gino looks up to see Joe, and that means trouble. He hollers to the back of the store. "Anthony!"

Anthony reaches the counter.

"Anthony will take care of you, Mrs. Petroni. I gotta some business here. Mi scusi, Mrs. Petroni."

She turns, studies Joe for a moment, and senses the mood change. She turns back to Gino. "Si, Gino. Do you business."

Gino walks around to the other side of the counter. They speak with their eyes. Gino heads for the back of the store. Joe follows close behind. They walk into a small office. Gino sits behind his desk and points to a chair. Joe takes a seat and wastes no time on small talk.

"I guess I don't have to tell you what day it is?" says Joe.

Gino's emotions immediately surface. "No. Let me tell you what day it is. It's the day the money stops: finito."

"What do you mean, finito?"

Gino leans forward in his chair. "You don't come back here no more."

Joe tries a little toughness, but remains steady. "Oh, you think so? And why would that be?"

"Because I can't feed the two-headed dog anymore."

"What are you talking about?"

"I talk about you and the bank."

"What's this thing with the bank?"

Gino sits back in the chair and raises his arms and folds his hands over his forehead.

"They want to close my shop."

"Bastards. How much?"

"Five thousand!"

"That's not good."

"Sure, no good! They give me one week!"

"One week?"

Gino grabs an empty coffee cup from the desk and flings it across the room.

"Si. One fuckina week! My father make this business for fifty years! He never have trouble! Now looka me!" He looks up as if to heaven. "He cry now!"

Joe wants to get to the bottom of this as soon as possible. "Which bank?"

Gino picks up a stack of business cards and thumbs through them. He picks one out and deals it across the desk. Joe glances at it and then shoves it into his jacket pocket.

"Okay. I'll be in touch." He starts to leave.

"Tell Anthony to give you some pane, a nice baguette."
"Sure."

—

Tony enters a butcher shop. The place looks deserted. A small bell rests on the counter. He taps it.

Ding! Silence. He hits it again.

A frail old man, Angelo, wearing a not-so-white butcher's apron, slowly plods his way from the back. He doesn't bother going behind the counter, but meets Tony face to face and reaches out for his hand.

"Tony Biscotti. Come stai?"

Tony takes Angelo's hand in one hand and covers it with the other.

"Sta bene. How's business?"

"No good, Tony, and the bank, she no care; they want money too. Maybe time to retire. Hang upa the prosciutto."

"What bank is that?"

Angelo reaches into his apron and pulls out a card from his pocket. "Questo," he hands it to Tony.

"They know I have good month/bad month. Never change, but these porcos, they no capisce. They need the cementa shoes. Puta the son uh bitch in the trunko."

"Ah, we don't do too much of that anymore. Leave it with me. I'll talk to Joe."

"That's a good. Maybe Joe fix. Come, I give you nice hotta salam."

—

Joe walks into a grocery store carrying the baguette under his arm. He listens intently to the store owner as he repeats the same story in regards to the bank. A business card is handed to Joe. They shake hands and Joe exits with a bag of oranges.

—

Tony, with the salami tucked under his arm, enters a flower shop. After a brief conversation he receives a card and a bouquet of flowers which he reluctantly accepts.

By this time Joe walks out of a shoe store with a boxed pair of fine Italian-made shoes.

Tony receives a nice bottle of wine.

They meet on the street, both loaded down with their good gestures.

"Mannagia!" says Joe. "You too? This isn't good."

"What do you mean? It's like Halloween. You knock on the door and they give you a treat."

"And you've got the face for it. All right, we'll take this stuff home, and then I'll meet you at the office at six."

"What about the north side?"

"I don't have a shopping cart for the north side."

"But the north side has that nice Panini Cafe. I was hoping to grab a free lunch."

Joe takes his baguette and shoves it between Tony's legs.

"There. Mannagia," then walks away, leaving Tony looking awkward and embarrassed as people walk by staring at his baguette.

—

Joe sits at his desk trying to wrap his head around the problem with the banks. He spreads out all the business cards he received. He's surprised to see that every card reads, PYRAMID BANK OF AMERICA.

"What have these guys got, a hard-on for Italians?"

Tony walks in and Joe looks at his watch. "I told you six. You're an hour late."

"Angela said I had to cut the grass first."

"Bravo. Meanwhile, somebody's cutting ours. Let me see those business cards."

Tony pulls out the cards and hands them to Joe. He quickly goes through them.

"Same damn bank! The Pyramid Bank of America. And what's this?" His eyes narrow to read the fine print. "Where all your investments go to the top. No kidding. Who are these assholes?"

Tony chuckles. "Sounds like the Mafia."

Joe gives him a look. "I'll remember to tell that to Leo. If we don't straighten this out soon, he'll be paying us a visit."

"Hello, boys."

They look up to see Leo standing in the doorway.

"Leo," Joe with a smiles. "We were just talking about you."

"I heard."

"You did?" says Tony.

Leo takes his time walking over to them.

"And I also heard you've got problems, already."

"Boy, that didn't take long," says Tony.

Joe gives him a look.

"Not when you watch two idiots parading around town like an old married couple doing grocery shopping. What gives?"

"We have a slight problem with one of the banks," says Joe.

"Banks ain't your problem. People are. And if people can't straighten out their problems, we give them another, capisce?"

"Sure, Leo." Leo looks at the empty pizza box on the desk.

"You guys should be eating better than that."

Joe and Tony look at the empty box.

"But it's Italian," says Tony.

"So's your mother. And she's just as wide as she is tall. Is that how you want to be? You're off to a good start."

Tony lowers his head.

"So, we're going to fix this little problem, right?"

"Sure we are," says Joe. "We were just about to do that."

"Good. Don't make me come back." He turns to walk out, and then turns back. "You're good boys, but you're stupid." And with that he leaves, sucking all the energy out of the room with him. For a moment the room is dead quiet.

"That was awful," says Tony.

"Yeah, I hate when he lumps me in with stupid."

"I meant about my mother. She's not that big."

"She is that big. Now get the hell out of here, so I can think."

"All right. I'm going to my mother's for supper, if you need me. She's making salad and soup."

"Who do you think you're kidding, yourself? I know damn well every Tuesday she has you over for ravioli."

"Okay, but I'm not putting any cheese on it."

Joe gives him a look. "Quit while you're behind."

—

Joe is alone with his thoughts, and they're not happy ones. "Somehow I've got to fix this. What the hell am I supposed to do? It's a bloody bank. I can't walk in there and say, you can't steal from these people because we are. And I can't go back to the stores. It would be like trying to squeeze Tony into a 40 regular." He cuddles up to the desk, lays his head down and drifts off.

—

There's shuffling in the room. Joe wakes to the disturbance.

"What's going on?"

A deep voice replies, "So, what's the problem?"

Joe raises his head. "What?"

There, across the room is a gentleman, impeccably dressed from head to toe, in a chocolate pin-striped 1930s-style suit with a red handkerchief in his breast pocket. He clutches a matching fedora. Even though Joe has no idea who he is, he obviously demands respect.

"You've got a problem, right?" Joe's first thought is Leo.

"Leo sent you?"

"Leo? Leo's small potatoes. I'm here on your behalf. Do you know who I am?"

"I know I should, but no. No, sir."

"Call me Lucky. You look hungry. Let's get something to eat. Is there a good pizza joint around here?"

"Pizza?"

"You got something against pizza? It's Italian. What's the matter with you?"

As they walk the few doors down to Cosmo's, Joe begins to wonder, who is this guy and why would he want to help me? Maybe he's going to steer me down an alley and do me in. The thought disappears once they enter the restaurant. There are a few scattered patrons. Joe picks a table in the middle of the restaurant.

"Hey," says Lucky. "Easy target. Go to the back."

They settle into a darker area in the back.

"What can I get you gentlemen?" says the waiter.

Joe looks at Lucky.

"A nice big pizza with mushrooms, sausage, and hot peppers. Anything you want to add to that?" asks Lucky.

"Sounds good to me," says Joe.

"And drinks?" asks the waiter.

"What'll you have, kid?"

"Beer?"

"That a boy. Two beers," says Lucky as his eyes rest on Joe. "Okay. Let me have it."

"Well, a bank wants to shut down all the businesses we insure."

Lucky looks across the room and sees a pretty girl sitting with her man. He smiles at her, she smiles back, and then he turns his attention back to Joe. "A bank, that's it?"

"Well, yeah. Isn't that enough?"

"So, what's your plan?"

"That's the problem. I have none."

The waiter drops the beers at the table.

Lucky takes a sip. "All right, here's what you do." He leans in towards Joe. "I want you to look for the best computer hack you can find. Tell him that you'll pay him well, but make sure you let him know that if things don't go as planned, his mother will be getting a call from the florist. That's always a good motivator."

"A computer hack? I don't understand."

"Listen closely," says Lucky in a whisper. "When you find this guy, I want you to..."

—

The phone rings loud into Joe's ear. He wakes with a jerk, lifts his head from the desk and looks around for the phone. It rings again and he scrambles to find it under the pizza box.

"Yeah, what time is it?...I've got a plan...yeah me, smart ass. I want you here in twenty minutes...Tell her to do it herself." He hangs up. "Now, where do I find a hack?"

His eyes light up. He picks up the phone and makes a call. "Hey, Jimmy. It's Pistoli. Listen. Do you still keep a record of prison releases?...Good. Have you got any hackers on that list?...Not whackers, hackers. You know, computers. One, okay, give me his name and number. Yeah, yeah, I owe you one." He writes down the information. "Benjamin Rosenberg. He wasn't a banker, was he?...He ripped them off…Perfect."

—

Inside the Rosenberg residence, Benjamin is at the dining room table on his notebook while his mother yells at him from the kitchen.

"...and if your father was here, God rest his soul, he'd take a two by four to the side of your head!"

"Can you not see? I'm looking for a job. It's not easy when you've got a criminal record," says Benjamin.

"What's the matter with going out and knocking on doors? It was good enough for your father!"

"I told you. People don't do that anymore!"

Benjamin's cell phone rings.

"Oh, my God!" says his mother. "I hope that's not the police!"

"Give it a rest, will you!" He picks up the phone and in a soft, pleasant voice, "Hello, Rosenberg residence."

"Is this Rosenberg?"

"Yes, it is."

"I hear you're a hacker?"

"And, who am I speaking with?"

"Joe Pistoli. I work for Leo Bruto."

"Yeah, I've heard of him."

"Okay. I've got a job for you."

"How much?"

"I know you don't have anything going, so let's just be happy this came along. Now, this is what I want you to do..."

—

A limo pulls up to the curb in front of the Pyramid Bank of America. Joe gets out dressed like he owns the place. He carries a fine leather briefcase and has added a little face fungus for identity purposes. He comments to the driver, "About fifteen minutes, Sam."

"Joe?"

"Yeah, I know. I owe you one."

Inside the bank Joe approaches the receptionist sitting behind the information desk.

"Good afternoon. May I help you?"

"Yes. Mario Mafiano. I have an appointment with Mr. Leach."

She looks in her book. "Oh, yes, Mr. Mafiano. I'll let him know you're here."

She picks up the phone and presses a button.

"Yes, Mr. Leach, Mr. Mafiano is here to see you...yes, sir. You can go right in, Mr. Mafiano, second office on your right."

"Thank you so very much. You wouldn't be interested in working for me, would you?"

"Oh, that's very nice of you," she says with a smile. "But I'm quite happy here."

"Yes, of course. I'm always in the market for a good woman," he winks.

"Yes, sir," she says with a smile and a blush.

Joe walks in through the open door and Leach stands and walks around the desk to greet him. Joe reads him like a book. He looks at Joe with a huge smile that says, how much can I screw this guy for?

"Come in."

Joe shakes his hand.

"It's nice to meet you, Mr. Mafiano. Have a seat." He walks behind his desk and sits.

"And what can we do for you today?"

"Well, Mr. Leach, I'm a man of few words and can't afford to waste time. I'm building a housing complex on the west side and need an additional million dollars."

"Well, that's a substantial amount of money."

"For some people, that's why I came to you. Pyramid seems to be a company that moves forward and doesn't flinch when it comes to investing in this cutthroat world of business. And I agree with your motto, where all your investments go to the top."

"Well, it's nice to see someone who thinks like we do."

"Now, to show good faith I have deposited two big ones into your bank."

"Big ones?"

"Yeah, two million bucks. And I'm going to leave that in the account until the project is done. So, you lend me one and I lend you two, and everybody's happy."

"That's very nice of you, Mr. Mafiano, but there's one thing I don't understand. Why borrow a million dollars when you already have it?"

"Well, Mr. Leach, my father and my grandfather were both businessmen. I had great respect for them, as I do you." He can tell by the smile on Leach's face that he's starting to reel him in.

"One of the first rules they told me was, never use your own money...and remember that the banks are your best friends." Joe wants to throw up on that one.

Leach is starting to have a financial erection. "Well, that's very nice of you to say that. I'm sure your family is held in the highest regard. That does show a lot of trust in what we do here at Pyramid. You don't mind if I...check those figures, do you?"

You schmuck, thinks Joe as he smiles. "Of course. I would expect nothing less."

Leach goes to his laptop. Joe waits patiently.

"Yes. There it is; Mario Mafiano. Deposit $2,000,000. Well, Mr. Mafiano, it will be a pleasure doing business with you. However," Joe tightens up on that word. "There will be some paperwork, of course."

"Paperwork, of course. Where would we be without the paperwork? I'll uh, have my lawyer pick it up. Like I said, I don't like to waste time. I need to see that money in the account by noon tomorrow."

"Noon tomorrow; why, yes, I'm sure we can do that for you."

"Excellent." Joe shakes his hand. "My respect and money go with you."

"Thank you. Thank you so much. May I call you Mario?"

"Mr. Mafiano."

"Yes, of course."

—

Joe and Tony are in the office eating pizza and huddled around Benjamin on his notebook. They stare at the screen waiting for the two big ones in the account to turn to three.

"I hope this works," says a shaky Benjamin.

"If it doesn't," says Joe, "I know a good florist."

The wait is killing them.

"Come on! Come on!" yells an impatient Tony.

$2,000,000.00 appears on the screen then instantly changes to $3,000,000.

"There it is! Look at those beautiful zeros!" says Joe.

They cheer! "Way to go, Benji!"

"It's not over yet. Now, transfer that into the Swiss account," Joe tells Benjamin.

"The million, right?" says Benjamin.

"No, all of it."

"Holy shit!" says Benjamin as he punches away at the keys, then stops.

There's total silence. Their eyes stuck to the screen.

Joe tries to coax it along. "Come on. Let's go."

"Okay," says Benjamin. "Here it comes."

The words blast onto the screen.

TRANSFER COMPLETE!

They jump around like school kids.

—

The first thing Joe does is pay off the mortgages of all the small businesses with the bank's own money. He feels like three million bucks as he strolls down the street with Leo following behind. He drops into the florist who wastes no time hurrying over to Joe.

"Joe! I thank you so much! I'd never think somebody pay my mortgage! Now I free! Nobody bother me no more. And I make sure I pay you every month. Best investment."

"Just make sure when I come in for some flowers, I get the very best."

"I start now." He rushes over to the cooler and grabs a few bunches of flowers, makes them into a beautiful bouquet and hands them to Joe.

"Bello, grazie!" says Joe as he smells the flowers.

Joe turns and hands the flowers to Leo. "Here, make yourself useful."

Leo looks as dejected as a man could look after having to give up his position to Joe.

After a morning of visiting and gift collecting, Joe remarks to Leo, who has his arms full of appreciation, "This could be a long day, Leo. You might want to bring the car around." Leo gives him a smirk.

—

Joe locks the side door of the building and heads to the front. The only illumination is from a lamppost. A BMW with tinted windows pulls up to the curb. The back door window lowers. The occupant is in the shadows, but Joe knows, it's the BIG GUY.

"Pistoli."

"Yes, sir."

"You did me proud."

"Thank you, sir."

"I would like to invite you to dinner at my house at seven."

"Yes, sir. Thank you."

The window begins to go up, then reverses. "And uh, I made a slight alteration to that bank account."

"You did?"

"You were going to do that anyway, weren't you, Pistoli. After all, you do work for me, right?"

"Yeah, I mean, yes, sir, of course."

"See you tomorrow. We'll discuss your future. Ciao." The window goes up. The car pulls away.

"Shit! Damn it!"

"Pistoli."

He turns back to see Lucky under the lamppost.

"What are you so upset about? You proved yourself, and with that comes respect. Now you're on top. All you have to do is stay there."

"But the money! All that money!"

"Money comes and goes. Respect, that's not an easy thing to get, and once you have it, you don't want to lose it. It's all about honour. Just consider it an investment into your future."

"If I had that money I wouldn't need to invest in my future."

"And if you kept it, you wouldn't have a future."

"That's true."

"And believe me, it wouldn't be pretty. You played it right, kid." Lucky turns and walks away.

"Lucky! What's your real name?"

"Luciano," he says, and then disappears into the darkness.

15

BRACELET

Famed archaeologist Philip Randolf Mackenzie spent decades exploring the Amazon, embarking on numerous expeditions and uncovering rare artifacts. His books on the subject became international bestsellers, establishing him as a leading voice in Amazonian archaeology. But now, sitting in his study, he begins writing a letter to unveil a truth buried beneath years of lies, a secret never intended to surface.

—

Philip enters the study of his elegant country residence. Quiet and empty, exactly as it has been for most of his adult life. No children, no wife. Not even the companionship of a dog. Settling into his chair, he pours himself a shot of cognac and downs it in one gulp, which he usually sips. He opens his laptop, and for the better part of an hour he struggles to find the words he is about to write. Then, as if nudged, he takes in a deep breath and slowly exhales; places his fingers on the keyboard and he begins to write, well past midnight.

—

The next morning, publisher David Fryer rings the doorbell. He waits without response, which he finds unusual, for Philip has always been an early riser. He punches a code of numbers into the small box by the door. Entering, he calls out to Philip. No answer. This he finds somewhat disturbing since he had made an arrangement the day before to see Phillip at this precise time. Seldom has David experienced any form of anxiety unless it was a deadline. He heads to Philip's study at the back of the house. Perhaps he's on the phone or listening to music through headphones.

He taps on the door, but to no avail, and decides to enter. He finds the room empty. On Philip's desk rests the open laptop. He sits himself down and begins to read...

I am writing to my publisher and best friend David, and to my colleagues and all the wonderful people who have supported me in my work. At this time in my life I feel it necessary to confess a truth, a dark secret that has been kept in a vault deep within my memory for many years. All the events that are forthcoming are real. I am not mad nor do I have some mental deficiency or disease.

In order for you to understand the verity of what I am about to disclose, I must go back and through my adolescent eyes revisit a time period as a twelve-year-old boy. Please bear with me as I recall to memory all my experiences and thoughts that have contributed to this, my final chapter...

—

It was in the fall of 1953. My seventh grade class was taking in what most of us considered a tiresome day at the museum. We had just finished seeing the highlight of the trip, the dinosaur exhibit, and were on our way upstairs to the Egyptian display, when a little troublemaker by the name of Jack decided he had had enough. I had never talked much to Jack, so it was somewhat of a surprise when he quietly approached me, and whispered in my ear, "Hey, you want to go exploring?"

Not knowing exactly what his intention was, it sounded more exciting than anything that could possibly be upstairs. As the class began to round the top of the stairs, we held back and made our move in the opposite direction. We moved swiftly downward, not knowing where we were going, and not really caring. We were free. That seemed to be the theme as we moved past other groups on their way up. It felt as though we were escaping from prison in plain sight of everyone. Funny, how easy it was. No one seemed to pay much attention. I did, however, catch a quick glance from one teacher, who was knee-deep with her own little ducklings and had no time or energy to stop and question us.

As we continued our descent, we reached the main floor and stopped short at a sign that hung from a chain stretched across some stairs. It read, BASEMENT—DO NOT ENTER. Jack looked at me as though he was possessed.

"Come on. Let's go!" he said with great zeal.

I turned to leave hoping, no, praying, that that was what he meant.

"Hey, where are you going?"

I was wrong. Jack was now on the other side of the chain.

"Come on!" he said once more.

Only this time his words echoed down the stairs and into what seemed to be the bowels of the earth. Taking a deep breath and moving forward, everything seemed to move in slow motion as my sweaty hands gently lifted the chain.

It felt so wrong, leaving my class and now, disobeying the direct order of the bold, blunt sign. It was completely out of character for me. But something was pushing me on. It was more than Jack. The stairwell was dimly lit as I followed him down. When we reached the bottom we stopped dead in our tracks. The museum has always been for me a cold, foreboding place. The deafening silence, the damp, musty smell and that dark macabre-looking tunnel that lay before us seemed to shoot through my veins like ice.

"Looks kinda spooky, don't it?" he said with the emphasis on kinda.

He used that word to buffer his own fear. It wasn't very reassuring for me, but what came out of my mouth in return sure didn't help Jack any.

"I wonder what's down there." It was an invitation, a dare. He knew he couldn't back out now, for anything less than, let's find out, would be a sign of weakness.

"Let's find out." He said it, sealing our fate. No backing out now. We slowly moved forward—step for step. So close to each other it looked as if we were stitched together.

My heart was pounding so hard that I'm sure I heard it echo. The tunnel began to turn to the right, and as we turned with it, the walls took on an orange glow. We hesitated for a moment, glanced at each other and realized we had gone beyond the point of no return. It wasn't a curiosity any longer. We had to know where this would lead us. We continued on. The curve in the walls began to straighten. Then we saw it. Not an ominous creature looming in the shadows, just a light bulb hanging over an old wooden door.

In the imagination of a young boy all seems possible, and I thought the light was more than for illumination. It was there as a sentinel, guarding the secrets beyond. My first impression was that the door seemed much thicker and heavier than an average house door. An antique-looking knob extended out so far that it seemed to be reaching out to me. My eyes fixed on it and I had to turn it. I could feel Jack's eyes fixed on me. After wiping my sweaty hands on my pants, I reached out to grasp the knob and it pulled my hand toward it like a magnet. My fingers wrapped tightly around it. The knob was extremely cold, and I felt a surge of energy that ran its course through my entire body. But something else was happening.

It was immediately followed by another surge. One of power that seized control of my emotional self and brought to the surface every feeling that I ever had: laughing, crying, jealousy, rage, compassion, love. It seemed to be realigning my inner workings; like clicking "reboot" or "update" on a computer. Invading the privacy of my very soul—my very existence. What bothered me the most was how it was done, swiftly, easily and with absolutely no resistance from me. It took all my strength and will to rip my hand from that knob.

When I did, I was overcome by such a feeling of peace and calmness of euphoric proportion, I could barely contain myself. Jack was in a state of shock. Not knowing what he saw me go through, whatever it was, it was too much for him. "Jack, are you all right?"

There was no response, just an absent stare. Was it possible that he too experienced the same phenomenon? I repeated the words, only this time with more urgency. Jack snapped back to reality like a rubber band.

"Well, what are you waiting for, are you going to open it?"

Amazingly, he had no recollection of me holding onto the door knob or any awareness of what I had been subjected to, and there was no point in explaining it. And for the second time, with great reluctance, I grabbed the knob. To my surprise, nothing happened. Now the question was, would it be locked?

I'm sure Jack was probably wondering the same. The knob followed my hand as I turned it. It could still be locked. It was almost humourous watching Jack watching my hand while biting his lower lip.

The knob stopped turning and now the moment of truth. All that was needed now was to push against the door. It should be an easy task, but I was so drained emotionally that the honour was passed to Jack. The only word I could manage to squeeze out was, "GO."

The pressure was all on him now. Could he do it? He decided to use a conservative approach. He placed his right foot against the door, putting all of his weight there. That way, if there were any surprises he would be able to push off and be gone. Placing his left hand on the door and tentatively pressing against it, the door moved slightly. That now familiar overpowering feeling of wanting to continue on grabbed hold. I felt that I had to regain some of my own power back. Pressing the weight of my body firmly against the heavy door, I began to push with all that I had. It invaded me, and now I was going to invade it.

The door began to move an inch at a time. There was no creaking sound like you'd expect in an old door, especially in a place like this.

Finally, it was open. A blast of cool air, with a strong and somewhat sweet odour, blew out from the room, as if it had held its breath for a lifetime and was finally able to exhale. A chilling tingle pushed its way up my spine, bringing every hair on the back of my neck to attention. Jack looked white, even under the glow of the orange light. The door was now fully extended on its hinges and only allowed the brightness of the orange light to expose the interior of the room about three feet beyond its frame. We stood there in silence peering in, trying to make sense of the shapes contained within.

I could make out a large, long table with objects of different shapes and sizes that rested upon it. Then, the whole room lit up like an atomic explosion without the earth-shattering sound. I thought I had gone blind.

Then came, "Geez, that's bright!" I turned to Jack and tried to open my eyes. I could only make him out in a blur. Gradually my eyes began to focus and I saw that Jack was leaning against the doorframe with his right arm extended along the inside wall. He had switched on the light. I glanced back down the tunnel just to make sure we were still alone before entering the room. Jack was already ahead of me.

I went straight to the table covered with very old artifacts. The room itself was a fair size with a few pictures and more artifacts displayed on the walls. There was a stool by the table for the poor soul who had to sit in that crypt for hours at a time piecing together his findings. Also on the table was a book that seized my attention. Jack, in the meantime, was picking up some of the items and trying to guess what they were.

"Hey, what do you think this is?" he said.

The book was all I saw or cared about. It was an old, well used book, covered with dust. It sat there closed, yet seemingly ready to burst with secrets long hidden through the ages. It had a faded title, and after brushing off the dust with my hand the letters emerged, *Lost Cities of the Amazon.*

For some strange reason it struck a chord. Why it did, I had no idea. I knew nothing of the Amazon or any part of South America, except where it was on the map. Even that bit of knowledge came about from a rare moment during a geography class when I had raised my head from my desk to check the time on the clock and inadvertently focussed on the map.

I proceeded to put my hand on the book to open it, but it opened itself to a page with writing on one side and a drawing of a bracelet with detailed engravings on the other. Below the drawing were the words, Gold Bracelet worn by Ancient Warrior. Just then my eyes were pulled from the book to a shiny object on the table that wasn't there moments before. To my amazement, it was the same bracelet in the drawing. Once again, a strange sense of urgency took over and drew me toward it. I reached over to pick it up and, without a lie, the bracelet seemed to leap from the table and affixed itself to my wrist. At that moment I could hear Jack's voice echoing in my head, "You find something?" Then everything went black.

—

Immediately I found myself transported into a jungle. I was now running; running fast. My heart was pounding and it was hard to breathe. Leaping over fallen trees, ducking under huge leaves of tropical plants, I thought to myself, I could never move this fast. Then I came to the immediate conclusion that it wasn't me. I was in someone else's body, but whose?

I began to feel the emotions of this other person. He was running for his life. Then there was the sound of a high-pitched whistle that seemed to whisk by my left ear and another and another. Now they were coming from both sides. My eyes caught a glimpse of what they were—arrows. This person was being hunted. Suddenly, I felt a sharp pain in the middle of my back. My eyes began to fill with water as I looked to the sky and dropped to the ground. An arm extended in front of me and on the wrist was—the gold bracelet. The picture quickly became blurry and faded away to darkness once more.

—

My eyes opened and I was back in the room. Tears were trickling down my face, my clothes drenched with sweat. Jack was no longer in the room. I could hear his faint footsteps echoing as he ran back down the tunnel. This time, I did see something. On the table was the gold bracelet once more. The urge to pick it up and take it with me was short lived. I didn't want to take that chance of going through the same ordeal or something worse. Another gust of wind blew through the room, giving me a chill as it swirled around my wet clothes. I felt the room telling me to leave and that what I had witnessed was enough. I walked up to the light switch, gave the room a final look and clicked to black. I grabbed the knob with both hands and shut the heavy door behind me.

On the way back through the tunnel, I proceeded to replay the events in my head, trying to answer one question: Was this mystical experience real or was it—was it what? A dream? It would have been a hell of a dream starting from my waking moments that morning until now. My conclusion was that, yes, it did happen. But answering that question only raised more. What did it all mean? Should I tell someone? That said, I would have to disclose the fact that I disobeyed, left my class and entered a place that was forbidden.

My mind formed a picture of movies about people who saw strange things or thought they did and they ended up in a cell wearing a straitjacket. Sometimes they'd have electricity shot through their body, or even worse, they would have their head split open and checked out by some half-wit doctor. Could that happen to me? Would I find myself locked up for the rest of my life, only to see my parents on weekends? Even if I kept quiet, what about Jack? He's probably told the teacher by now and the museum security guards are probably out looking for me. Funny what goes through your head at that age.

—

Wet, cold, exhausted and now shivering, I climbed the winding stairs. It seemed to take forever to reach the Egyptian exhibit as I moved through each room looking for my class. Every statue, every picture, even the mummies seemed to be staring at me. I began to hear strange voices. They were speaking in another language, and there was no echo like you'd expect in the museum. That made me realize that they were in my head. It was terrifying. The faster my legs moved, the louder the voices. Finally, passing under an archway I collided with my teacher and the voices immediately stopped.

"Oh my! Are you all right?" she blurted. "Did you find it okay?"

Find it? What was she talking about? Find the tunnel, the room, the bracelet? Did Jack spill his guts?

She leaned over and spoke softly into my ear, "The washroom. Did you find the washroom?"

I was dumbfounded. What was going on? I already came to the conclusion that this wasn't a dream, and now she's gone and blown that idea out of the water for me.

"Yeah, I found it." What else could I answer?

She directed me into the next room where my class was sitting on the floor, most of them talking or horsing around. Not one took any notice of me. Jack was in his usual position of boredom, lying on his back with his hands behind his head.

He looked up at me and said, "What do you want?" as though nothing had happened.

I had to test him. "It was pretty scary down there, wasn't it?"

He blinked his eyes. "What, the washroom? How would I know? I haven't been there."

I thought for sure he'd say something about our escapade, but there was nothing. Then out of his mouth came words that chilled me to the core and made me doubt my sanity.

He said, "Do you want to go exploring?"

The words kept repeating in my mind. I was losing it. I backed away from him as if he was the one responsible for this madness. My body began to shake. Once again tears filled my eyes and dribbled down my cheeks. I felt extremely cold, yet, once again my body started to sweat. The room began to spin; first one way, then the other. Then I felt my body dropping to the cold, hard floor.

Muffled voices of concerned classmates filled my head. I saw a blurred vision of my teacher's face and then, no sound, no picture; in and out of consciousness. A flash of the ceiling in the main corridor of the museum zoomed by, then briefly opening my eyes in the ambulance.

In the hospital, my parents, God bless them, were right there by my side. They were the only reality I knew for sure. They asked me what happened. What could I tell them? I didn't know myself. The only answer I could give them was the simplest one. I felt sick. I didn't lie. I was sick; mentally sick.

The doctor told my parents it was stress related. I had either seen or done something that was very disturbing to me. That was an understatement. If they were uneasy with the doctor's diagnosis, I sure wasn't going to elaborate. Doing that would only mean a short walk to another wing of the hospital, where they would greet me with open arms, while mine would be strapped into a white jacket.

—

The next day they sent me home. Over the following months my parents, as good parents of an only child are, kept all eyes on me, just to make sure there was no recurrence of this strange illness.

Things were different at school. I was considered somewhat of a freak. Each student in their own way began to distance themselves from me as if I had some contagious disease. At that point any form of teasing would have been welcomed, but there was none. I was invisible; even my teacher seemed aloof.

—

The next year seemed to pass with all speed. This I considered a blessing, but there was still a reluctance to associate with me on most levels. I had to keep telling myself that I would be having two months of summer holidays to myself. No more Jack. No more alienation, and no more museum.

In the fall I would turn fourteen and start a new life in high school. But then again, high school was something that I feared. I would be at the bottom of the food chain. Another fear arose. The thought of having my previous years follow me and escalate with distorted rumours that would put me in the front line of the odd and peculiar. When that happens, the bullying starts. I certainly didn't want to spend four years being that one odd sock in the dryer.

For some reason though, I felt better prepared having gone through the museum incident. It made me feel stronger, more confident; at least I felt that way. What impact that would actually have when facing those difficulties of higher learning would remain to be seen.

—

Summers were always a wondrous, fun-filled time for me. It was during this last fling before high school that I came to the realization that I was getting older. I remembered my parents and others of their generation reminiscing about their childhood, agreeing that summer holidays seemed to last forever. Now, it was just a fleeting moment. That frightened me, because I knew once I stepped into that huge high school fortress for the first time and the door shut behind me, it was over; the end of adolescence.

I would then be responsible for everything I did. At that moment I started to have disturbing thoughts about my future. I alone would be in control of my homework and passing from one grade to the next. No excuses. Oh, my God! My graduation! That's four years down the road, and that's if I don't fail. I can see it all now. Left behind and watching my friends moving up that chain, and I'm left to wallow in the stench of inadequacy and shame. With great effort I shook those thoughts out of my mind. What the hell am I doing? Why am I making up these ridiculous scenarios?

It wasn't that I was a bad kid like Jack and ignored rules or the advice of adults; I guess I just didn't want to grow up yet. I was smart enough to know what I had for the last thirteen years. I had been free to be me, and I wasn't ready to give that up. So what was I going to do about that? I now had only two weeks left before high school started. Two weeks before my life as a free-spirited individual ended. I knew I couldn't stop it or even slow it down, but I could take these final days and make them the best ones I've ever had.

"Yes!" I said. "That's what I'll do!"

Okay, where do I begin? Finances! I'll need money. My piggy bank was actually an empty peanut butter jar.

I knew that I had a small treasure stuffed into that jar because I had been saving for a new bike. I rushed to my room, grabbed the jar that was sitting on my dresser and raised it to eye level. It was a wondrous spectacle of shimmering coins and a few tightly rolled bills that came my way through birthdays and holidays from seldom-seen aunts and uncles. I opened the jar and spread the wealth over my bed. What took months to accumulate flowed out in a flash, and now the task of counting it all. Math wasn't my forte, so I used the practical method of nickels here, dimes there, quarters, etc. and thankfully, no copper. The end result was $43.25, a small fortune.

Now comes the hard part of rationalizing how I could spend it on a good time instead of saving for a bike. In high school some of the older kids would be using their parents' cars to get to school, or they would have their own earned through summer jobs. Now, did I really want to show up on a bicycle looking like a mama's boy or a geek? There is my answer. Now, to have the best remaining two weeks of my kid life.

Always looming in the background, though, was the museum incident. It was something that entered my thoughts more often than I wished. I couldn't shake that deep-rooted feeling that it wasn't over. I knew what I saw and went through, and couldn't deny it, but couldn't reveal it either. It was all tied to that bracelet.

—

For the next two weeks I did everything possible that $43.25 would allow. I was hoping to distance myself from that horrifying, yet extraordinary, museum event. I went to the movies, rode the subway downtown; ate the freshest fruit, cheese, and salami at the Farmer's Market. I took a trip through Chinatown, and witnessed a culture that seemed far removed from the Golden Dragon Restaurant that my parents took me to.

I was having a great time all by myself. No accountability; total freedom. Then it happened and I sure wasn't expecting it or prepared—blindsided.

There was a vendor selling bags of oily popcorn and rich, red, rosy taffy apples that I couldn't resist. I took a bite and happened to glance up and there it was. Unknowingly, I found myself standing in front of the dreaded museum. A chill ran through me and then an energy force that was all too familiar. It was drawing me in, like waving coke in front of an addict.

But how? How could it have that kind of power when I was standing outside of the building? I wasn't in that room where the energy was so intense. Because of my distance from it, I thought I could fight it and the fact that I had another year under my belt. But I was wrong. Once again it had ahold of me. There was no strength in my body to resist. The highly prized apple slipped from my grip and fell to the pavement and wobbled its way to the curb. I could hear the vendor saying something in a muffled voice about dropping the apple, but I just followed my feet up the many steps to the main doors; more gliding than walking, as if on some track or escalator. One of the main doors started to open so I hesitated to give way to the person exiting, but there was no one; it opened for me.

—

Walking into the main corridor immediately brought back the memories so vividly it felt like I had never left. Looking down the hallway, in the distance, I could see that damn stairwell that led to the basement. That warning sign is still dangling from the chain. Was this going to be The Forbidden Basement, Part Two? I had no urge to investigate it a second time, and I was compelled to move on from the stairwell to seek something out, like an itch that had to be scratched. I was being pulled up the stairs until I reached the room titled Rain Forests of the Amazon.

Passing the entrance, my eyes were immediately directed to one corner of the room with a table of artifacts encased in glass. Like a magnet—the negative being drawn to the positive. I was forced to look at one specific item on the table. I was terrified that I was once again confronted with that infernal bracelet. The very one that sent me into a tailspin and terminated two years of my life—the last thing I ever wanted to see again.

It began to glow a bright, fluorescent green. I wanted to run, but couldn't move. Trying to talk or scream was futile. Then the glow disappeared along with the bracelet. Feeling a tingling sensation on my left wrist I looked down, and there it was. If that first episode was any indication as to what would follow, that bracelet had to come off.

There was no one else in the room. There was no break in the bracelet to bend it open; any amount of twisting or pulling was useless. Anxiety immediately set in. Would it take me on another mind-blowing hell ride?

Then another thought: It didn't matter how that bracelet arrived on my wrist, there was absolutely no way to explain it. I would now be considered a thief, a criminal. Why was this happening to me? That question would have to take a back seat. The main objective was to get out of the museum without being noticed. If I had worn a long-sleeve shirt I could have hidden it under the cuff. The only feasible solution was to cover it with my right hand; holding my hands in front of me at crotch level and walk out like a monk.

It was working perfectly until...

"Hey, there!"

I stopped cold. Turning and looking up, there stood a tall, heavyset man with a badge that identified him as a security guard. My stomach felt sick and it must have showed.

"Are you alright? You look a little pale. Looking for the washroom?"

Good, I thought. I'll do a little squirming. "Yes, sir."

"Go straight down that hall and to your left."

"Thank you."

Walking briskly added to the authenticity. A glimpse back and he's walking in the opposite direction. The washroom sign was straight ahead, but what really interested me was the sign beyond it—Exit! I slowed my pace and nonchalantly walked out the door.

Under the circumstances, my outing for the day was over. It was too risky to walk around a large city with a solid piece of gold wrapped around my wrist that would be visible to every criminal element, not to mention the possibility of leaving this world for another Jungle Jim experience.

—

My father was still at work and my mother was doing laundry. I went straight to my room, laid on my bed and stared at the bracelet. What was this extraordinary power? And why did it still have this attachment to me after so long? I turned to face my open bedroom window. The sun was beaming through and the warmth of it settled on my face. A gentle breeze followed, and with all these questions and thoughts mulling around in my head, sleep seemed to be the best antidote.

It was a deep sleep. No thoughts or dreams, just drifting along in a boat on a slow-moving river. Then a gentle voice called to me. I woke to see my mother standing over me, telling me supper was ready, which meant that I had been out for some time. My first thought was the bracelet. Did she notice it on my wrist? Would she question me about it? I raised my left arm, and to my surprise it had conveniently left my wrist. Where did it go? Why did it go? Asking these questions made me feel that perhaps because of my negativity toward it, I wasn't worthy to have it. I was trying to escape it. But then again, I did have in my possession something extraordinary. Was it a gift? A gift that should have been embraced, and because it wasn't, it was taken away.

—

Time passed and education became my focus. Thoughts of the bracelet melted away to the point where it never entered my mind again. My thoughts about being left behind in high school kept me going and pushed me to my graduation. My parents were proud, and for the first time in my life I was excited to continue my education. I leaned toward teaching and thought to myself, Yes, this is it. I'm going to be fine.

—

While packing my belongings to leave home for university, I found in the back of my closet, tucked away, an old shoe box that held my childhood memories. It hadn't been opened since my days before the bracelet. Now at nineteen, they would have more meaning for me. It was amusing to see what I cherished back then. The box was so full that I decided to empty it out. As I picked through the sentimental gems, the thought occurred to me that they should be put back into the box and saved like a time capsule for my future offspring. As I grabbed the box I felt a shift of weight. Peering in, at the bottom was...the infamous bracelet. At first I felt sick. No, not now, I thought. Everything is going so well. Then like a long-lost friend, I became excited. Perhaps I was worthy. I picked it up, and added it to my luggage.

—

Coming to the end of my first year at university things were good, as far as my marks were concerned. Then I realized, as many do, that teaching wasn't what I wanted. It lacked excitement. So what was it that I wanted to do? I needed to take some time to consider my options. But time was not on my side, and frustration turned to desperation.

—

It was Friday night. My roommate convinced me to tag along with him and a few other students to the local pub: a couple of beers to take the edge off the workload. University students in their first year can seem sub-human. You get caught up and lose your ability to use better judgement. Drinking too many beers is one thing, but mixing that with everything under the sun is incredibly toxic. Stumbling back to my dorm room early, leaving my roommate to his own demise, I landed on my bed, miscalculating my lower limbs by about two feet. I felt myself drifting away. My head dropped to one side and there on my wrist was the bracelet. Within seconds I was out, sawing a forest of logs.

—

Out of that darkness, a sudden burst of bright, white light appeared. I was filled with thoughts of death as I waited for the inevitable tunnel that people see before they are finally taken home. But then I was transported back to the jungle that had terrified me so many years before. This time I wasn't running and I wasn't in someone else's body. I was calmly walking. What my destination was, I had no idea. The heat and humidity was well above anything I had been accustomed to.

Raising my hand to wipe the beads of sweat from my brow, there was the bracelet, clinging to my wrist, and as before, its power took over.

After a few minutes of walking I heard voices and the laughter of children and the fragrant smell of wood burning and smoke rising above the trees in the distance. There was a clearing and beyond it was a sight so extraordinary, so beautiful. Situated right in the middle of the dense jungle was a city. I wanted to stop from going any farther, not knowing what the repercussions might be, like more arrows. But the bracelet pushed me on.

I saw magnificent gardens, fountains and pyramids. Indigenous people were going about their daily lives as they would in any modern city. People began to acknowledge my presence with a smile as if they knew me. One, who was dressed differently than the rest, approached me and introduced himself. He spoke in his native tongue, but for some reason we were able to understand each other. It was truly amazing. He said he was a shaman. At the time I had no idea what a shaman was. He took me inside one of the pyramids and into a small room.

We sat on the floor and he began to tell me of his people. He was the most compelling and sincere man. When he had finished speaking I asked him about the bracelet and why I was there. He told me that this knowledge and much more would be revealed to me after I drank a tea-like beverage that he had brewed. He called it Ayahuasca and said it would open my spiritual eyes and give me the knowledge I needed.

Trusting in him, I consumed the liquid which was so bitter and foul that within a short time I began to feel violently ill, vomiting everything in my stomach. At that point doubt began to surface as to his credibility, but then a miraculous transition took place. Euphoria like nothing I had ever experienced filled my mind. Cleansed of all inhibitions, I was a free spirit.

Visions took over reality. I saw trees, plants, and flowers of enormous size, so vivid, so intense, all in a range of glorious colours that would overload an artist's palette. There were reptiles, animals, and insects of all design and size.

As quickly as it appeared, it vanished, leaving me with a tremendous sound, like an ocean wave crashing into a harbour break wall. I was thrust back in time to witness the indescribable birth of the Amazon; an explosion of enlightenment crackled through my brain. I understood with complete clarity the significance and value, not just of the indigenous people and the Amazon, but of all mankind.

Whisked forward into the future I encountered a different Amazon: one with modern cities, manufacturing, pollution and all the evils that we bestow upon ourselves in the name of progress. The indigenous people had all but perished; those who survived were absorbed into the mainstream of society and lived in poverty and despair. The scene fractured and dissolved, leaving a memory that waxed strong in my own reality.

—

My eyes opened and I was back in my room, staring at the foot of my bed. The bracelet was no longer on my wrist. I sat up with no ill effects from my alcoholic stupor, but the euphoric enlightenment remained all the next day.

—

It was mid-fall. I dressed for the weather and left my room to take in the cold air and colours of the maples. I sat on a bench at the park sipping coffee and reflected on the previous night's journey. The shaman said I would understand the purpose of this. Replaying the hallucinations and time-travel experience was more than an eye-opener. Seeing the magnificent evolution of the Amazon in its entire splendour laid out before me was like a gift from the heavens. The tragic and uncompromisingly destructive end in the future was so troubling that it became more and more devastating for me—a whole civilization wiped out. At the time it seemed unfathomable that this would happen.

Was I supposed to do something with this newfound insight and knowledge? The only thing that did not come to light was the bracelet, and the warrior who owned it. Reflecting on this led me to the conclusion that these events had to be true, for I had never, over the course of my twenty-young years seen or heard anything remotely tied into these hallucinations. I concluded that they came from outside my realm of thinking; not from within.

Realizing this truth, the brightest light clicked on when I glanced at a book that my roommate left on his dresser. It was titled *Archaeology*. My purpose in all of this had now been inadvertently unravelled and revealed to me. I recalled the words from Charles Dickens' *A Christmas Carol*—"If these shadows remain unaltered by the Future, the child will die." I could make a difference by knowing exactly what I had to do; what direction my life should take. My course of action would be to study anthropology and archaeology, zooming in on South America.

It didn't take long to find that I had a natural ability for it and loved every moment. I sucked up information like a Hoover. Throughout that period I had no further contact with the bracelet.

—

Three years later I graduated and moved back home. Great, I thought, now what? Finding out that jobs in that field weren't easy to come by, I became discouraged, until one day, as I was writing another resume, the bracelet entered my mind.

I opened my dresser drawer and reached into the back past my socks and underwear and pulled out the bracelet. This could be my time machine! I'll use the bracelet to explore the Amazon and its people without leaving home. But would it still work after three years of neglect? Perhaps after giving me insight, its job had been completed.

If it does work, I should prepare myself for my first expedition before putting it on. Pens, pencils and paper went into my leather backpack. I dressed in light shorts and a short-sleeved shirt. I took off my watch and placed it on my dresser and slung the backpack over my shoulder then held the bracelet in my hand and waited patiently. Nothing happened. It was over. The great gift was gone.

I became frustrated, then furious. After putting me through this ordeal for years, it was going to abandon me now? Now, just when I needed it! My knee-jerk reaction was to throw it across the room. It hit the wall with a ping and dropped behind my bed. I sat on the edge of my bed with my head in my hands. My life was back to having no meaning. Without the bracelet how could I do a damn thing without actually being in the Amazon? All my funds had been absorbed into the school system, and with no chance of employment, I saw no way of moving forward.

At that moment the area beside my feet began to give off a green, fluorescent light. Falling to my knees I looked under the bed, and there was the bracelet, all aglow. I felt that familiar surge of energy. No sooner off my knees, the bracelet affixed itself to my wrist.

—

It was back and I was off and no longer in the reality of my room, but walking through the forest of the amazing Amazon once more, and once again with the indigenous people. This time I spent a few days there, talking to the shaman and learning more.

—

There were times when I would spend months in this world that was becoming more my own than the one I was born into. I wrote book after book. None of it being fictitious, as some critics would claim. Every word came by way of the shaman or the people themselves. All the artifacts that I obtained on my many journeys were given to me by these people in friendship and love.

—

It has now become clear to me that I have written and preached all I can on this subject and that the people of my world should now embrace this land and the wonderful people who dwell side by side with all living things. We should all appreciate this land as well as our own. We can't be passive. We must find the will to be diligent in preserving the earth. I pray that through this, my last article, my readers feel that they were never deceived; that as I leave the world of today for the final time and go back to the people that I now see as my own, I may feel vindicated. The shaman explained to me that some people ask to come back after their lives are over so that they may continue some unfinished work. We call it reincarnation. I eventually found out who that warrior was.

Forever yours, Philip Randolf Mackenzie.

David lifts his eyes in shock.

"All these years without a word?"

He sees the bottle of cognac and an empty glass. “How could he have kept this from me? Has he just lost his mind? Is it possible he has been consumed by alcohol all these years?”

He pours a shot to settle himself and as he raises the glass to his lips his eyes catch a fluorescent, green glow emanating from a small table in the corner of the room—the bracelet. He reaches to pick it up...it disappears.

16

LAST TRAIN OUT

Those cold, bitter, short days and long, dark nights of winter can seem like a life sentence, and Malcolm knows that all too well. He boards the last train and enjoys the leisurely ride; a time to unwind. Usually only a few passengers, but tonight, the car is empty, and soon his mind will be filled with unexplainable terror.

—

He places his briefcase on the seat beside him—the one his lovely wife gave him for his 50th birthday last August. Staring at it for a moment he decides to open it and retrieve the crime novel he's been reading. He opens to the bookmark.

"Here we are," he says to himself.

It didn't take long for his tired eyes to blur and invite a rush from the sandman. In the background he hears the fading sound of the train whistle as he drifts away like the snowflakes that blow by his window.

—

Not long after, the train slows to a stop in the middle of nowhere. The absence of movement awakens him. He gazes out the window into the white-covered forest and notices a pair of headlights moving in and out of the trees. In a clearing the lights reveal a car. It stops and four men get out. One is forced out from the back seat. His hands are bound behind him. Malcolm can't hear them, but it's obvious a few words are being exchanged between the men. One of them pulls a gun, shooting the bound man. He drops like a stone. One of the three looks to the train and notices Malcolm watching from the window.

He tries to pretend he didn't see anything by picking up his book and holding it close to his face, but keeping an eye to the window. The men re-enter their vehicle and slowly pull away from the scene as the headlights capture the fallen man and red splattered on the snowdrift beside him.

Malcolm is horrified. He's all alone. The train jolts forward, picking up momentum. He thinks to himself, I have to tell someone, but it would be too dangerous to attempt a walk through each icy car. All he would need is to slip once on one of the gangway connectors and that would be the end of him.

Then he thinks, What if they decide to follow the train to see where I get off and nab me? All they would have to do is stick a gun into my ribs and walk me off the platform to some secluded area and I'm toast—just like that other guy.

He realizes it would be easy pickings for them; being the only one in the last car would make it easy for them to spot him getting off the train. There is the chance, he thinks, that I was too far a distance for them to actually make me out. Especially with the headlights directed my way, I certainly have no idea what they look like.

He throws around scenarios like tossing a Caesar salad, convincing himself that they wouldn't be able to identify him. Once he gets home, he'll call the police. Coming to this conclusion allows Malcolm to lean against the window and re-enter sleep and once more the sound of the train whistle fades.

—

"Malcolm!" Malcolm stirs in his seat. "Malc! Wake up!"

Who's calling me? he thinks to himself. He opens his eyes to discover that he is no longer on the train. He's in the front passenger seat of a car.

"Malcolm. Get your head on straight. We're here."

He looks at the driver. "We're here?" he asks.

"I told you to stay awake!"

Then from the back seat, "Ah, Malcolm's all right."

Malcolm turns around to see a man with a bluish bruise on his cheek and a cut over one eyebrow. Further inspection shows a gun he is holding is pointed at another man beside him with his hands behind his back.

"He's just not used to this, that's all."

"Well, you better get used to it right now," says the driver. "Let's get it over with."

"No, please, no! I've got a family!" says the man being held.

"Not anymore you don't!" says the one with the gun.

"All right," says the driver. "Everybody out."

The one with the gun begins to pull the poor soul out.

"Please! I'll give you all the money I have!" cries the bound man.

The driver walks up to him and grabs him by the neck.

"You still don't get it! It has nothing to do with money. It's about betrayal. You came in knowing what the rules were and you broke them."

Malcolm is speechless. He doesn't understand what he's doing there and why this is all too familiar.

"Let him have it," says the driver.

The one with the gun points it at the back of the bound man's head and fires. He drops into a snow drift.

Malcolm looks across the clearing and sees a stopped train with only one passenger in the last car watching them—for some reason he looks very familiar.

"Let's get the hell out of here!" says the driver.

Malcolm blurts out, "Are you just going to leave him here?"

"If you don't like it, we can have you cuddle up beside him."

They get back into the car and speed away.

"What about the guy on the train?" asks the shooter.

Now realizing the passenger on the train is him, Malcolm tries to save himself and pipes up. "He couldn't recognize us. We were too far away and the headlights were in his eyes."

"You have a point. That's enough damage for one night. It's a long way back. You might as well go back to napping," says the driver to Malcolm.

Not wanting to be involved any longer, Malcolm decides to lean his head against the door and closes his eyes, hoping it will all go away. The sound of the car engine lulls him to sleep until...

"Wake up!" yells the driver.

He opens his eyes to discover he is now in the back seat of the car.

"Get your head on straight. We're here," says the driver to the man now in the passenger seat.

Oh, my god! thinks Malcolm. It's the guy they shot! He's alive!

"I told you to stay awake."

"Ah, he's all right," says the shooter, who is now beside Malcolm in the back seat.

Malcolm discovers that his hands are bound behind him with the shooter's gun pressed into his side.

"What the hell is happening?" asks Malcolm.

"He's just not used to this, that's all."

"Well, you better get used to it right now," says the driver. "Let's get it over with."

"No, please, no! I've got a family!" says Malcolm.

"Not anymore you don't!" says the one with the gun.

"Alright, everybody out," says the driver.

The one with the gun begins to pull Malcolm from the car.

"There's been a big mistake! Please! I'll give you all the money I have!" cries Malcolm.

"Let him have it," says the driver.

The shooter puts the gun to the back of Malcolm's head.

Malcolm screams at the top of his lungs, "No!"

A shot rings out!

The train whistle is heard and Malcolm awakes to find himself back on the train.

Over the speaker the conductor announces "Last stop coming up...Last stop."

—

Monday night arrives and Malcolm asks his co-worker if he could get a ride home. He also changed his book selection —Alice Munro.

17

THE ANGEL'S BOOK

The Grosso Region of the Amazon jungle—August 1925. The scorching heat of the sun beats mercilessly down on the treetops. The enormous trees blanket the jungle floor with cool, but unbearable humidity.

The faint sound of chopping and native voices can be heard echoing through the dense forest. In the distance, three natives can be seen hacking their way through an endless wall of green. A few yards behind them are three white men, and bringing up the rear are more natives overloaded with supplies. The backs of the natives are drenched in sweat as they slowly, but steadily, work their way through the brush.

The front-runner is Colonel Sims. His face is darkened and weathered from his countless expeditions. His hair and long moustache are white and age him considerably more than his fifty-six years, but he is an Englishman of action and great determination. Behind him is his son, John, a young man in his early twenties who believes in his father and his work, and would follow him to the ends of the earth. Following close behind is John's best friend Peter, who, at times, can be as irritating as the mosquitoes that swarm about his head.

Suddenly, a sharp high-pitched sound echoes loudly enough to stop everyone in their tracks. The jungle is filled with an eerie silence. A native pushes away some of the tall grass that hides the object that was struck. By this time the other two natives had joined him. In their native tongue, the level and tone of their conversation begins to escalate.

The Colonel hurries his way to them, having no patience for their jibber-jabber.

"What is it, damn it? What have you found?"

The three natives move quickly toward him. He is expecting an answer, but the three run right past him, screaming something over and over again as they vanish into the forest with the rest of the natives in hot pursuit.

"What the hell was that all about?" asks Peter.

The three men walk up to the object in question. Reaching the spot, their eyes slowly rise to see a stone pillar with a height of more than ten feet, partially hidden in vines. At the top of the pillar is the crystal head of a serpent.

Peter turns to the Colonel. “Colonel, what—”

“Quiet,” says John. If there is one thing he has learned about his father, it’s not to say anything until the Colonel has made his observations; even that may be a mistake.

The Colonel moves in on the object. He kneels down and rubs his fingers along the base of the stone, where a strange inscription is carved. Excitedly, he reaches into his shirt pocket and pulls out a worn folded paper. Quickly, but carefully he opens it to show a document that is written in Spanish and reveals the date 1753 and also contains the same markings on the stone.

The Colonel is overjoyed. “This is it!”

That’s the signal John was waiting for. “What is it, Father?”

He turns to them with a huge smile and eyes as large as saucers. “The gateway! Finally, finally I’ve found it! The gateway to the Lost City of Gold!”

Under his breath John whispers, “Gold?”

—

As night approaches the trio stand on a high ridge overlooking the jungle and a beautiful sunset.

“We’ll stop here for the night,” says the Colonel.

With relief they remove their backpacks.

“Father, I don’t want to sound pessimistic, but what do we do for provisions?”

“Yes, Colonel, they've left us virtually naked,” says Peter.

“I’m quite aware of our situation, Peter.”

“What do we do for a tent, Father?”

“We don’t. We’ll clear the surrounding area. Build a fair-size fire, stay close to it, and most importantly, keep it going all night. Three-hour shifts should do it. Now, who wants to take first watch?”

John and Peter exchange glances until John volunteers, knowing that is what his father would expect from him.

“Now, that’s a good lad,” says Peter.

“At least,” says John, “I know my sleep won’t be interrupted.

—

After a period of time the fire diminishes, as does John's will to stay awake, and sleep finally overtakes him. For a moment all is quiet and for the most part, the jungle sleeps.

A crack of a branch and John wakes abruptly. He looks around and sees the condition of the fire and scrounges the area for more wood, picking up pieces as he goes. Bending down to pick up another piece, he notices something in the distance that sets his face aglow. He straightens up. "Father—Father!"

Peter and the Colonel's sudden awakening have them confused and dazed, as they struggle to get to their feet. Some commotion ensues as they collide with one another.

The Colonel cries out, "John! Where are you? What's wrong?

"Over here, Father!"

They reach John and the area over the ridge and are astonished by what they see: a huge glow about two miles away above the trees, with a trail of lights, like a runway leading up to it.

"It's unbelievable!" says Peter.

Even the Colonel is awe stricken. "The eyes of modern man have never seen such a sight until now."

"What gives it light, Father?"

"It's something I've heard about, but never seen: a combination of quartz crystal and phosphorus. It absorbs the light from the sun during the day and releases it at night."

"It is truly something to behold," says John.

The Colonel points to the huge glow. "And it leads right to the Lost City."

Peter moistens his lips and smiles. "The Lost City of Gold."

"Gold? Yes...but much more," says the Colonel in a more serious tone.

"What could be more important than gold?" Peter asks.

The Colonel turns to Peter. "Right now it's sleep. And I believe it's your turn to keep watch."

John yawns with a smile.

—

The jungle awakes with the sounds of all manner of birds. The coolness from the night air is still hanging over the jungle floor, which aids the Colonel as he hacks his way through the low brush, wielding his machete as though he was possessed. John and Peter follow at a much slower pace cutting a wider path.

Then, without any warning, the jungle comes to an abrupt halt as though every living thing took a deep breath and held it. The Colonel immediately ceases his attack. John and Peter stop in their tracks.

"Father, what's happening?"

No response.

The two look at each other and then race toward the Colonel. He stands with a transfixed smile, looking into a clearing. The young men follow his eyes. At the end of the clearing is a high stone wall, with a huge archway sculpted into two large serpents. The Colonel's face no longer reflects the excitement of the discovery, but of something sinister and foreboding.

"We've arrived. From this moment on, we must be very cautious. There are curses, traps, and evil spirits that are here to protect everything that lies beyond these walls."

"Colonel, surely you don't believe that tripe," says Peter.

John holds his breath, knowing that a statement like that to the Colonel is foolhardy.

The Colonel turns to Peter with visible anger.

"And before today, Mr. Kent, this site was also tripe! Am I correct?"

Peter cowers, "Sorry, sir."

"Apologies won't do you any good if you're dead."

They enter the city through the archway. The site is of enormous proportions. The buildings and the streets look more modern than ancient. Beautiful gardens are everywhere. There is no sign of the passing of time. No huge growth of vegetation that would exist over the centuries.

"Father," says John, "there doesn't seem to be any sign of time passing. It's as if the people just got up and left right before we arrived."

The Colonel's eyes cautiously move from side to side. "Yes, very strange indeed."

They continue down the main thoroughfare. Suddenly, there's a strange sound. They stand for a moment.

Vibrations are felt under their feet. They look for the source. Under the archway the earth starts cracking and separating, as thin vines push their way to the surface and rise quickly up the walls, thickening as they grow. They quietly become part of the jungle and hide any trace of the entrance, sealing it off from the rest of the world.

"How will we get out?" asks Peter.

The Colonel shakes his head. "Why in hell's name would you want to get out? We've only arrived."

"Yes, but when the time comes—"

"That's right; when the time comes."

John knows exactly what his father is thinking. Why did I allow my son to talk me into bringing this half-wit along?

With that aside they can now take in and marvel at the beauty around them, but Peter takes it upon himself to break away unnoticed and enters one of the buildings.

The inside of the building is colourful and lavishly decorated, with four pillars that stand at each corner of the room. In the centre, of the room is a large sunken pool. On the back wall, a huge sculptured head of a hideous-looking serpent. A steady stream of water flows from its gaping mouth. Peter laughs and throws himself into the cool water clothes and all, then swims around enjoying the luxury of a bath.

The Colonel and John continue, unaware of Peter's absence.

"Father, last night you said there was something other than the gold, something much more. What did you mean?"

The Colonel stops dead and points toward the end of the street. "That's what I meant."

John looks in the direction his father is pointing. He raises his eyes. What he sees is unmistakable. At the end of the street is a massive pyramid that rises hundreds of feet in the air.

"It's breathtaking! But, Father," he chuckles, "that's certainly not something we could take back."

The Colonel looks intensely into his son's eyes. "It is what's inside that holds my interest—a book; a gold book."

John realizes his levity. "Pardon my stupidity, Father, but I thought it was something other than gold."

"You are absolutely correct. It is what's in the book that I'm after."

"And what might that—"

The Colonel's eyes look beyond John. "Where's Peter?"

Peter is still enjoying his bath. “Well, at least I won’t be suffering from the heat.” He turns away from the back wall with the serpent’s head looming and begins to exit the pool. The water in the pool below the serpent’s head begins to turn black and moves toward him. A closer observation reveals a horde of long black snakes.

Unaware of the impending danger Peter slowly steps out of the pool just as the snakes arrive at his heels. He leaves the building unscathed and unaware. He enters the street only to succumb to the Colonel’s wrath.

“What in heaven’s name is wrong with you, boy?”

John looks at his clothing. “Peter, you’re soaking wet.”

“It’s a bathhouse, a beautiful, cool, running water bathhouse.”

The Colonel moves in on Peter. “You could be dead right now!”

“It’s only bloody water.”

The Colonel slaps him hard across the face and knocks him to the ground.

“You stupid bastard! It could have been your bloody water!”

John tries to calm the waves. “He’s just a little over-zealous, Father. He’ll be fine now, won’t you Peter?”

Peter slowly gets to his feet, still feeling the impact of the blow. “Fine? Yes...” He feels the side of his face with his hand. “I’ll be fine.”

“Well, see that you are. We can’t afford any more mistakes. Now, with the utmost caution, let’s move toward the temple. John, you lead the way.”

They begin their climb up the temple steps. Reaching the top they are totally exhausted and discover that the entrance is sealed with a huge smooth sheet of rock. John looks a little deflated. “Well, this should be interesting. What do we do now, Father?”

“We rest,” says the Colonel as he reaches for his canteen then sits with his back to the entrance and sips water from his canteen.

John and Peter look at each other then proceed to do the same.

“Father, tell me more about this gold book. Why is it so important, other than the fact that it’s gold?”

Peter's ears perk up.

"Because, it wasn't written by a human being," says the Colonel.

"You mean some gorilla wrote?" says Peter, sarcastically.

The Colonel finds no humour in Peter's statement and lets him know with a piercing glare.

"Peter, shut up. Go on, Father."

"It was written by...an angel."

Peter stands up. "I still like the gorilla better."

John knows Peter is walking on thin ice and has no idea what his father is capable of, especially in this remote area, where there are no other eyes to pass judgement.

"It's a long way down the side of this pyramid if you happen to accidentally fall," says the Colonel.

John tries to bring his father back on topic. "What would these writings contain?"

"I don't know. Legend has it that the book is sealed. No one had ever been able to open it."

Peter clears his throat loud enough to get John's attention. He then taps his head with a finger to indicate that he thinks the Colonel has lost his mind, and then quickly turns to the temple.

"If we could open it, it could be the most important book since the Bible, maybe greater."

"Colonel!" shouts Peter.

The Colonel and John rise quickly to their feet and turn to Peter. The temple entrance is now completely open.

"What the hell is going on?" asks Peter.

"Hell indeed, sir...hell indeed," says the Colonel.

"We are going in, aren't we, Father?"

"The opportunity has presented itself. But, as I have said, with all caution and care. Understand, Peter. He knows we are here."

"And who might he be?" asks Peter.

The Colonel takes a sip from his canteen then grins. "Why, the devil, of course."

Peter and John look at each other with concern.

Slowly they walk along the dark, narrow corridor of the temple and find that it is lit by the same type of illumination they had witnessed the night before.

"Something's amiss," says the Colonel.

"What do you mean, Father?"

"The light."

"It's the same light we saw last night," says Peter.

"Think again," says the Colonel.

"What do you mean?"

"That's right!" says John. "There's no sunlight in here to illuminate these stones."

"Which means only one thing," says the Colonel. "This is for our benefit."

He pulls out his revolver, then the boys follow suit. The faint sound of a drumbeat and satanic chanting echoes through the tunnel. They finally stop at an archway that is intricately carved with symbols. At the keystone of the archway hangs the now too-familiar serpent's head. The music and chanting escalates to the point of insufferable pain to their ears.

The Colonel screams out to be heard. "What lies beyond this entrance has never been seen before."

A strong gust of wind blows from within the archway with a deathly howl. The drumming and chanting is intolerable. A crazed grin appears on the Colonel's face. He raises his revolver to the side of his head and cocks the hammer. "Gentlemen...I give you...LUCIFER!" With that the Colonel charges through the archway like a madman, yelling and screaming into the darkness.

John and Peter become so paranoid that they too abandon all sense of reason and caution and follow the Colonel's charge.

"Ahhhhh!"screams the Colonel.

Their figures and voices fade quickly into the darkness.

Gunshots ring out and echo through the passageway along with flashes of light and screams of confusion and terror.

The sounds of drumming and chanting stop. A small river of blood begins to flow along the ground from the archway.

—

ROYAL ONTARIO MUSEUM, TORONTO, APRIL 2019

—

Meticulously dusting the bust of an ancient emperor, young, heavyset Harold appears content as he goes about his work while chewing on a granola bar. To everyone at the museum he has a mundane, custodial job. But if you talked to Harold, it is one of the most important jobs—he identifies himself as part of the restoration team.

A voice rings out, "Harold!"

It's Daniel. He's in his early thirties and attractive, but more interesting are his eyes: bright and full of enthusiasm—ready to conquer the world. The sleeves of his white shirt rolled up, ready for any job at a moment's notice—confident and secure, but not to the point of arrogance. He works in the South American Department under Professor Anton.

Harold stops. "Is it lunchtime already?" he asks jokingly.

"Dr. Roberts wants everyone in the rotunda immediately," says Daniel.

Harold looks at his watch. "Holy snappers, it's eight-thirty. We open at nine. What's he thinking? I still have an hour's work with the Egyptians."

"It must be about our new South American exhibit coming in next week," says Daniel.

Harold chomps away on his granola. "Is it my imagination, or didn't we go through this already?"

"I know, but don't forget he's only been the head curator for three weeks, and my guess is that he wants to make a good impression and he's probably a little nervous about it."

"Nervous? You could have fooled me. I think he's just an arrogant—"

"Harold," says Daniel. "Let's not be too judgemental and give the guy a break."

"Which arm?" says Harold with a mouth full of granola.

—

The rotunda is filled with people from all areas of the museum; from security guards and tour guides to curators of each department. Conversations abound as Dr. Perry Roberts, Head Curator, enters. He is well groomed, right down to his flawless goatee, and tops it off with a smart three-piece suit.

He quickly acknowledges a wave in the crowd from Professor Anton, a short, balding man, who never seems to be without his leather apron. He slowly moves through the crowd of confusion toward Dr. Roberts.

Their conversation is loud as to be heard over the multitude.

"Dr. Roberts, did we not go through this same procedure precisely one week ago?" asks Anton.

"Ah, you remember, Professor Anton," says Roberts. "Then the procedure is working quite well."

"But I'm very busy, Dr. Roberts."

Roberts looks into the crowd and claps his hands to get everyone's attention.

"As we all are, Professor. Attention, please! May I have your undivided attention?"

Daniel and Harold show themselves on the second floor balcony overlooking the rotunda as the crowd is hushed.

"It has been brought to my attention by the keen observation of my distinguished colleague, Professor Anton..."

Harold rolls his eyes at Daniel. "Not again."

"...that this is the second such gathering of the minds in a week."

"Why is he always calling out Anton?" asks Harold.

"People have their own agenda," says Daniel. "Some are right in your face and others are hidden."

"And for that we should give him a break?" says Harold.

Roberts continues. "Today is Friday. In three days, that makes that Monday for those without calendars or toes, the artifacts for the Amazon exhibit will begin to arrive."

"What do you mean, he has an agenda?" asks Harold.

"Dr. Roberts feels threatened."

"By little Anton?"

"I want this whole event from arrival to departure to run as smoothly as a Rolls-Royce," says Roberts.

"It's not his physical presence, Harold," says Daniel.

He gently pokes Harold in the stomach then turns around and begins to walk into the Egyptian room.

Harold follows him in. "You mean his mind?"

Daniel runs his fingers over some Egyptian engravings then looks at Harold. "Do you know what this says?"

Harold stares at the stone. "Sure, burritos, two for one."

"It says, He that causes strife comes himself to sorrow."

"Is that like, what goes around comes around?"

"Precisely."

Daniel walks away.

"Or, you reap what you sow?" says Harold.

Daniel continues with his back to Harold. "That's good, too."

"How 'bout, you pay your money and you take your chances?"

"No."

"Okay, what about—you prepare the bodies, I'll get the ice?"

As Daniel leaves the room, "Stop while you're behind."

"I always liked that one."

—

In a booth at the local pizzeria three young women are in joking conversation, and the waiter drops the bill on the table then continues to the next booth.

"...and he said, but I can't get her off the toilet. Imagine someone calling 911 for that?" says Sara.

They all laugh.

"Shit!" says Melanie. "I've got tons of work on my desk. I hate Fridays."

"So, Debs, what's going on?" asks Sara.

Debra is still smiling from the joke. She pulls the straw in her drink from her lips. "Going on?"

"Yeah," says Melanie. "You and Danny boy. Is he in or out?"

"It's Daniel, and what are you talking about, in or out?"

"I know what I'd be talking about if he were in or out," says Sara, laughing along with Melanie.

Debra shakes her head. "You two are just disgusting. Why do you have to pull everything down to the gutter? Daniel is a wonderful man. He treats me the way I should be treated. The way every woman should be treated."

"And that is?" asks Sara.

"With respect, for one."

"I would think a year without sex is way over the top as far as respect goes. Doesn't this guy have needs? Don't you have needs?" asks Melanie.

"You know, Deb," says Sara, "you're right. I wish I got that kind of respect."

"What are you talking about," says Melanie. "Jerry shows you respect. He buys you all kinds of things."

"That's for services rendered."

Debra has no use for this type of conversation. She stands and reaches inside her purse and pulls out a twenty and places it on the table. "If you want respect, show some to yourselves for once."

Sara and Melanie give each other a sober look as Debra walks away.

—

In a basement room of the museum, artifacts are hung on walls and rest on tables. Uneven rows of books clutter the shelves. Daniel and Professor Anton are discussing an artifact on a table.

"It's very different, Daniel," says Anton. "But it does have similarities to the piece that was found in Peru."

He picks up his magnifying glass for a closer look at the stone tablet.

"Here, look at these symbols." He passes the magnifying glass to Daniel. "What do you make of them?"

Daniel examines the tablet. Then, with total confidence announces, "It talks about a hunting expedition that brought a large quantity of food back to the tribe and celebrated for many days."

Professor Anton looks puzzled at first, then laughs. "Daniel, you couldn't possibly know what that means. I know you've been very good in the past at identifying artifacts, but to decipher this would be like looking at a blank page. These people went extinct 3,000 years ago. The only record of their existence other than this tablet are a few pieces of pottery and bones."

"I'm sorry, Professor," says Daniel and then adds with conviction, "but that is what it says. I don't know how I know this, but I do. And sometimes it gives me the creeps."

The Professor pats him on the back. "Daniel, you look tired. You've put in a long day. Perhaps the weekend will give you a chance to recharge before Monday's shipment arrives. We'll need to be on our toes."

"That's an understatement," says Daniel. "Dr. Roberts is very particular."

Professor Anton looks over the top of his glasses. "I think the appropriate word would be...Peculiar."

Before Daniel makes a motion to leave, Anton grabs his arm. "Daniel, one more thing about Dr. Roberts." Anton's face turns deadpan. "Try to avoid him as much as possible. Even though he hasn't been here that long, I have been at odds with him on a number of issues, and I know if he could, he'd fire me at a moment's notice."

"But why would he want to get rid of you? You've been here for years. You know this place inside out. You would think that he would see you as quite an asset."

"You would think that, but some people like to clean house when they move in. They have their own ideas and want things done their way. If they get pushback they start wheeling the axe and heads roll. So, just to be on the safe side, keep your distance. It will work out better for you in the long run."

—

Finally, the end of a long week for Daniel and he can't wait to see Debra. He walks out of the museum and parks himself on the stairs and makes a phone call.

"Hello, sweetheart. I just finished up...Of course we're still on for dinner. I'll pick you up at six. See you then...Love you, too."

"Sounds like you have a nice evening planned."

Daniel is somewhat startled and looks up to see Dr. Roberts towering over him.

"Yes, I'm taking my girlfriend out for dinner. It's been a long week without her."

"I'm sure it has. I'm sure it has," says Dr. Roberts. He begins to walk away then turns back. "Oh, and watch yourself on the road tonight. Traffic is always bad on Friday nights."

"Yes, thank you."

—

Toronto is a vast city, and traffic is the number one killer for time. Your lifesaver is the subway system of which Daniel is a frequent passenger. He grabs the train north and then switches to the westbound train that takes him to High Park. He gets off at Keele Street and strolls down Parkside Drive, turns left onto Grenadier Road. A few houses down and he's home. He rents the upper floor of a two-and-a-half-storey house. For him it's perfect, but for a couple, not so much.

Daniel grabs a quick shower, a fresh change of clothes, then heads back to the subway to continue his journey west to Royal York Road where he grabs a bus south. Five minutes later he steps off the bus and walks to an apartment building. He doesn't have to go far.

Debra is waiting in the lobby. She throws her arms around him. "I think you beat your record by five minutes."

Daniel smiles. "Someone said, never keep a woman waiting."

Debra returns with, "He must have been a very smart man."

"I think he was under duress at the time," says Daniel.

"Is that how you feel?"

Daniel kisses her then pulls back. "Only if I couldn't beat my record."

—

In the back parking lot Debra hands over her car keys to Daniel and he opens the passenger door for her. "You still trust me, do you?"

"No," says Debra and then adds with a smile, "I'm just lazy."

"That works for me. I like your car better."

—

They pull into a parking spot in front of their favourite restaurant.

"Wow," says Debra. "How lucky is that, right by the front door."

"It's all about skill and technique," says Daniel.

"Oh, I thought it was the car ahead pulling out and you pulling in."

"That's when my psychic ability kicked in."

Debra smiles. "I know what else should be kicked."

"On that note," Daniel leans across the seat and kisses her, "let's eat."

—

The dinner is winding down to coffee. Daniel's demeanour is unusually quiet.

"Daniel, you're out of words?"

"No, just trying to find the right ones."

Now Debra turns serious. "What is it, sweetheart?"

"I'm not sure. The last couple of days I've been feeling a little strange."

"Strange? In what way?"

"I'm feeling anxious, but have no idea why. As if there is something coming that could be disturbing."

Like a premonition? Is it visual? Do you see something happening?"

"No. It's just a feeling of...dread."

"Dread?" Debra tries to disengage his anxiety. "Perhaps you think I'm after your fortune," she says with a smile.

"You mean the $236 in my bank account?" Daniel smiles back. "That is something to consider. A woman could go a long way with that amount of cash."

Laughter replaces the feeling of doom, and the thought disappears.

—

Monday morning at the museum starts early, and before Daniel enters the building he takes a deep breath and slowly exhales. He has assisted in a number of shows in the past and anticipates a long and gruelling workday.

Upon entering the rotunda, Daniel catches sight of Professor Anton sitting on the stairs with a coffee in hand.

The Professor gives Daniel a slight wave of his hand. "Come and have a coffee with me, my boy." He reaches over to his far side and grabs another coffee next to him. "Here, you're going to need this. I was hoping you would get here before it got cold."

"I had one before I left my apartment."

"Never look a free coffee in the mouth. No, that's not quite right. Anyway, you know as well as I, you can never have too much caffeine working here."

Daniel takes the coffee and sits beside him. "Thank you, Professor."

"How long have we known each other now, Daniel?"

"I would say, too long for the job, but not long enough for the friendship."

"Nicely put. So I would think this is well overdue. Why don't you just call me Karl?"

"I'd like that. It has a nice ring to it."

"My mother thought so, too."

They raise their coffee cups and toast to their friendship.

At that moment Dr. Roberts walks down the steps behind them. "Well, gentlemen." He takes out his pocket watch and gives it a glance, "You have precisely three minutes to disengage your coffee pleasantries and join the rest of our enthusiastic staff in accommodating this new exhibition."

Karl raises his eyes to him. "With all due respect, I have been working here for thirty-two years. Do you honestly think your words and tone will have any effect on my coffee habits?"

"Whatever works to get the job done."

"What about: Gentlemen, when you have finished your coffee, would you direct yourselves to the City of Gold exhibition...please?"

"That's exactly what I said," says Dr. Roberts, and turns his attention to Daniel.

Daniel, not knowing how to respond, gives him a half smile.

"You find this amusing, Daniel. I could extend your day by a couple of hours. I'm sure your girlfriend would appreciate that. Absence does make the heart grow fonder. By the way, how was your dinner engagement?"

"It was very nice, thank you."

And with that Dr. Roberts continues on his way.

"Perfect," says Karl. "Don't engage him and keep your nose to the grindstone." Karl takes one more sip of coffee. "Shall we remove ourselves from these intolerable seats before my ass becomes numb?"

—

Inside the exhibit room the first item they encounter is an impressively large archway with a serpent's head jutting out from the keystone. Daniel stares up at it and seems transfixed.

"What is it, Daniel?" asks Karl.

"I'm not sure. For some reason this looks familiar to me, but I don't know why."

"Perhaps a picture from the newspaper or magazine, advertising its debut," says Karl.

"No, and that's another thing—being such a large and interesting item, how could it go unnoticed by the press and media? No, I have never seen this before, but something keeps telling me I have."

Karl places his hand on Daniel's back. "Mysteries—where would we be without the mysteries of life."

They continue with their first look at the special treasures.

Karl stops at a glass enclosure with a single gold book resting on a pedestal. "Daniel, look at this. There is a legend that goes along with this book."

"What kind of legend?"

"I'm not sure; something about God and angels—actually, one angel. That's why the name, *The Angel's Book*."

Daniel stares at the book.

"Daniel. Daniel, are you all right?"

"Yes, why?"

"I had asked you something."

"Oh, I'm sorry, Karl. What was it?"

"I just said it would be tremendously exciting to be able to open the book and read it."

"Yes, it would. Hasn't anyone done that? Just open the book and decipher it?"

"I'm afraid it can't be done."

Daniel looks puzzled. "Because they can't identify the language?"

"No. The book can't be opened because it's sealed." He opens the door of the glass enclosure and picks it up. "See, it almost looks like it was welded shut."

"What would be the purpose of having a sealed book? Why even write it if no one is able to even open it, let alone decipher it?"

"Perhaps it's waiting for the right person."

"Sounds like the Sword in the Stone."

He hands Daniel the book, but Daniel has an eerie feeling wash over him and declines. "No, it's okay. I can see that it's sealed."

"It makes for an interesting draw to the museum," says Karl. "Some say if it can't be opened it doesn't bear much credibility to any tale you wish to give it. I've always felt that any tale that left you with hope that someday it would come to pass kept the story alive, and everyone needs something to believe in."

They continue their walk through the exhibit while Daniel's anxiety keeps pace.

"Daniel, are you sure you're all right? You look a little pale. It's going to be a long day. Let's grab a second coffee in the cafeteria and hopefully that will keep us going until lunch."

"Professor...sorry, Karl. This may seem odd, but have you ever looked through an old photo album of your family and had a yearning to go back and possibly relive some of those memories?"

Karl looks at Daniel with the most sincere eyes. "Yes, of course. I think we have all done that, and the older I get the more I seem to be in tuned with the past and less with the present. It always ends up to be a mixed bag of gratitude and regret. Do you have some regret about something from your childhood that haunts you?"

"The funny thing is...I don't remember my childhood. It's as if it was completely erased from my memory or that I never had one. Yet, I have always been drawn to the South American exhibit."

"You do seem to have some insight into the languages and culture that at times astounds me."

"Yes, you see what I mean: I have no idea where it comes from."

Karl smiles. "Wherever it comes from, please keep it coming."

—

Karl was right: It was a long day that left Daniel quite fatigued.

Karl's eyes scan in the exhibit. "Well, Daniel, I think this exhibit is taking shape. Two more days and we should be able to open it for visitors." He looks at his watch. "Time to go home."

"You go ahead, Karl," says Daniel resting on a bench. "I'm going to sit here for a few minutes to get my second wind before I tackle the subway crowd."

"Yes, fighting the mob for a seat is always a concern. For me, it's only a fifteen-minute walk to my apartment. Good luck and I'll see you in the morning."

Daniel looks about the exhibit and after a few moments decides to head out head for the subway.

"No point in prolonging it any further," he says to himself. "The sooner I get home, the sooner to bed." He stands and his eyes catch sight of *The Angel's Book*. Now curiosity rises above his fear and he can't resist another look. This time he decides to open the glass door and pick it up, but notices something has changed—the book no longer has the welded look that sealed it.

"What's going on?"

He is able to pull back the cover, and before he even begins to focus on its content he becomes dizzy. The room swirls around him like a merry-go-round where the racing horses and the speed accelerate to a whirlwind pace. There is no controlling it. The force is so incredible that he feels his body separate from his mind. Then, like a high-speed car chase that ends with a crash, the whole event stops.

Daniel tries to engage his disoriented brain and eyes. Finally, he sees he is now standing in a place filled with beautiful landscapes, waterfalls, spectacular gardens of brilliant colours and the bluest sky he's ever seen. But there is more. Another picture fades in with the landscape becoming filled with spirits. Hundreds of them that extend back into the thousands as far as the eye can see. He marvels at the sight—as quickly as the vision appeared, it vanishes.

Daniel finds himself back on the bench still holding the book which is sealed once more. He tries to wrap his head around the experience. "What was that?" I know that there have been strange things that have happened in the past—stories of devils and demons and all manner of witchcraft. Is this one of those? Does this book carry some kind of curse? And what were those spirits? I know I haven't been getting much sleep and I have been drinking far too much coffee. I'll have to tone down the coffee and try to up the amount of sleep."

—

For the next few days he is sleeping longer, but nightmares about *The Angel's Book* are leaving him exhausted. They become relentless—spirits and demons taunting him to the point where he has great anxiety and apprehension about stepping into the exhibit.

Finally, the exhibit comes together, and without delay Daniel takes no time in removing himself from the museum.

—

Debra hasn't seen him all week and is looking forward to an evening of dining to celebrate their return to normality. As usual,

Daniel is at the wheel. He drives into a tunnel and midway through..."That's strange," says Daniel. "Where are the cars that were ahead of me?"

Debra has been preoccupied with texting a friend and looks up. "Maybe they were just going faster. You aren't a speedster."

"I can go faster," he says. Daniel accelerates. "How's that?"

"Don't overdo it," she says. "Daniel!"

"What the—"

Straight ahead is a brick wall! Daniel SLAMS on the brakes! Debra screams! The tires squeal and smoke! The car turns sideways and comes to an abrupt stop. Behind them are more screeching tires and honking horns.

A heavyset man in the car behind gets out of his car and marches quickly to their car and angrily punches the window. "Are you out of your goddamn mind?"

"It's a wall!" shouts Daniel.

"Wall?" screams the man. "What the hell are you talking about?"

Daniel looks over and there is nothing there, but a clear view of the exit.

"Damn drug addicts!" says the man. "Get the hell out of here before I drag you out of there and rip your bloody head off!"

Daniel looks at Debra. "Are you all right?"

"I'm fine, Daniel. Hurry, let's get out of here."

Daniel wheels the car around and exits the tunnel.

For one brief moment they sit silent.

"What just happened?' asks Debra. "There was a wall there, wasn't there?"

"Looked as solid as any wall I've seen," says Daniel.

"But it disappeared," says Debra. "Which means it wasn't real, yet we both saw it."

"I had no option, but to stop. We could have been killed if that guy hadn't been sharp enough to keep his distance and stop as fast as he did."

Debra looks at him with a new concern. "What would have happened if we had kept going? Would the wall have vanished?"

"Good question."

The experience has left them understandably shaken.

—

While eating dinner the conversation couldn't deflect from the thought they could have been killed.

"Daniel, I feel hollow inside, as though I'm unable to distinguish reality from fantasy."

"I feel the same way. Like finding out you've got some incurable disease and your life doesn't exist anymore."

"But we should be grateful we weren't killed."

"I am, but I just don't understand the whole thing. It's not like I made it up in my mind—you saw it. Wait a minute. I wonder if this had something to do with what happened to me at the museum."

"The museum? What happened?"

"I didn't mention it because I just thought I was overtired and overworked and had some sort of dream while I was awake."

"I think you're talking about a lucid dream. Are you sure you didn't fall asleep?"

"No. I was opening a book, one of the artifacts on display, and suddenly everything started to swirl around me at a terrific speed and I felt like I was separating from my body."

"That must have been terrifying."

"It was, until it stopped and I found myself in the most tranquil and beautiful place imaginable. Then...and this is where I might lose you...spirits seemed to rise out of nowhere—thousands of them. And just as fast as it all happened, it vanished and I was back in the museum."

"Daniel, that is very creepy."

"That's not the strangest part. The book was sealed; no one had ever been able to open it, and when I picked it up and sat down to examine it...it was no longer sealed."

Debra rubs her arms. "I've got goose bumps and not in a good way. What do you think it all means?"

"The only sense I can make out of it is the book is called *The Angel's Book* and that's what I think the spirits were—angels. One other thing that was really mind-blowing was the feeling I had that it all looked familiar to me, as if I had been there before, and it actually felt comfortable in the strangest way."

Debra reaches over the table and holds Daniel's hand. "Do you think it was some kind of spiritual intervention?"

"From everything I've researched, I think it was more like a type of spell or curse; you know, like voodoo or witchcraft."

"I don't know, Daniel. Usually those would leave you with a bad feeling, but you said it was a good feeling, familiar and comfortable."

"That's true," he says, and now he just wants to deflect from that and settle in on being with her. "You still up for a movie?"

"Depends, what is it?"

"They said it's something like *The Omen."*

"Oh! How about a walk in the park?"

—

Even though going for a walk ended up being a far better choice, and discussing their summer holidays was a good distraction, the tunnel event was always resting below the surface. For Daniel, the experience raised its ugly head as he tried to sleep that night. Strange and macabre dreams kept him restless and filled with anxiety.

—

The next morning at the museum, it was obvious to Karl from the dark circles around Daniel's eyes that he had been battling insomnia.

"Daniel, what the hell have you been going through? In layman's terms, you look like shit."

"Have we got some time?" asks Daniel. "I'd like to discuss some issues with you."

"Certainly, let's get a coffee in the cafeteria."

They grab their coffees and find a table in a quiet corner.

"Now, what seems to be the problem? It's not Debra, is it?"

"No."

"I didn't think so. She's a lovely girl."

"Do you remember that night when you left me in the Amazon exhibit?"

"Of course."

"Well, I know that what I'm about to tell you will sound strange, but believe me, it wasn't a result of sleep deprivation or too much caffeine."

"All right, my mind is open and I'm all ears."

"That book—*The Angel's Book*—you said it has never been opened."

"That's right, perfectly sealed from man's eyes. You saw that yourself."

"Yes, well...it opened."

Karl takes a sip of coffee. Chokes slightly. "Daniel, I promised I wouldn't recant on believing you, but I am getting close."

"I understand, but let me tell you the whole story. I sat down on a bench with the book and it opened on its own as if it had a need to reveal what was inside."

"And what was inside?"

"I don't know."

"All right, Daniel, I have to get to work."

"I'm not finished. As soon as it opened..."

As Daniel continues, Karl's eyes begin to widen and his scepticism fades. The curator's mind begins to open up.

"Well," said Daniel. "What do you make of that?"

"Extraordinary!"

"Good; now the second part in this story. I wasn't sure if they were related, but now I am concerned that they were."

He goes on about the tunnel and Karl's interest heightens as he leans forward in his chair. Daniel finishes, and Karl now falls back into the chair and contemplates the events.

"First," says Karl, "I believe every word of it. And I will tell you why. Back in 1925 a Colonel, who was obsessed not only with finding a certain Lost City of Gold in the Grosso Region of the Amazon jungle, but he had heard about a legend that was handed down through one of the tribes in the area that there was a book hidden in that city that contained the writings of an angel. If it could be opened and translated, it could be the most valuable treasure in all of history. It could either verify the stories in the Bible or debunk them."

"So what happened to the Colonel?"

Once again Karl leans forward. "He never came back."

"Did they ever find out what happened to him?"

"Six years ago a group of archaeologists and part-time explorers found the city, and in time they found the remains of the Colonel, his son, and a friend in a cave. What was strange about the discovery was that their clothes were intact, looking exactly like they had just put them on, yet their bodies appeared to have been scorched."

"That sounds like those stories of spontaneous human combustion."

"Yes."

"You believe that?"

"I'm not sure, but there have been more than 200 cases of spontaneous human combustion around the world."

"That's enough to give it some credence."

"Getting back to the Colonel: His skeletal hand was clutching a book."

Daniel suddenly has chills. "Are you saying that the book I opened is that book?"

"Precisely."

"But Karl, why did it open to me? Who am I?"

"There's always a reason, and perhaps in time you'll find the answer. But right now I am more concerned with the incident in the tunnel."

"Yes, as if some force was trying to discourage me from having anything to do with it."

"A dreadful encounter that could have rendered Debra obsolete," says Karl.

Daniel found that statement somewhat strange. Why did he only mention that Debra could have died? I was just as vulnerable, he thought.

"Karl, what did you mean by Debra being obsolete? What about me?"

"Oh, well...I just meant that she is so petite and fragile." There's a pause and Karl seems to change gears. "Daniel, I want you to understand something. This is all speculation and most likely these events could be explained. The legend that is tied to that book is exactly that—a story that was handed down perhaps to scare other tribes away because of the gold."

Daniel looks for some solace in Karl's eyes. "You believe that?"

"I believe that in the end, you will have nothing to worry about. I don't want this to consume you." Another strange pause before Karl adds, "And don't mention any of this to Dr. Roberts."

What's he mean, in the end? And why would I even think of discussing it with Dr. Roberts? Daniel finds that part of the conversation somewhat vague and decides to drop it.

Another day at the museum comes to an end. The lights are dimmed. The building is quiet and Daniel just wants to get home. In order to leave the building, he has to go through the Amazon exhibit. He takes a deep breath, slowly exhales then proceeds into the room. So far so good, he thinks. The next obstacle is walking through the archway with the serpent head at the cornerstone. Good. Another challenge met, he thinks to himself, and in the distance he sees the glass enclosure that holds *The Angel's Book*. Then something changes. Everything becomes a blur and dizziness sets in. The room spins like a top. Daniel feels a force so strong he can't move, yet he sees himself being lifted into the air and through the ceiling and out through the roof of the museum. The speed by which he is elevated accelerates and he soars into space like a rocket.

Looking down, the earth is the size of a tennis ball, then a marble and it's gone. He can't breathe, but finds he doesn't have to, and all the while there is a calm feeling that takes over him. Even if he could fight it, he doesn't want to. Planets and stars flash by. Then straight ahead is a wall of mist. He sails through the mist and finds himself in that same beautiful paradise. But this time he is there alone, no angels or spirits. In the distance he sees a huge tree that glows as bright as the sun. Beneath it is a white bench. He is drawn to it, and there on the bench rests *The Angel's Book*.

Once again he sits down, picks up the book and opens it. At first the language is foreign to him, but in the blink of an eye he is able to read it. His comprehension seems to increase with every word and a visual picture appears. He witnesses angels in a fierce verbal battle. There are two factions, and Daniel sees himself amongst the smaller group. Suddenly he realizes he, too, is an angel.

The experience is so familiar to him. One angel is standing high on a hill looking down on the group and speaking in sharp tones. Daniel identifies with the voice, but the angel is too far away for any facial recognition. The discussion is heated, in regards to some plan about how the world should evolve, and this smaller group is not in favour of it. It all looks so familiar to Daniel. At that moment the skies open with the sound of thunder and lightning and all the angels that are opposed begin to drop like stones from the sky, including Daniel, and they plummet toward the earth. Reaching the earth in spirit form, they scatter like rats.

Daniel is terrified, and before reaching the earth he pleads for forgiveness. A voice calls out to him announcing that he will be spared and will be given a human body and live amongst people of the world. If he lives a worthy life he will be spared death until the earth is no more.

The scene turns black and once again Daniel is standing in the exhibit room. His breathing is labored, and the event has left him with weak knees.

"I'm an angel?" he whispers. "But that would mean I've been here since the beginning of the world. I can't be an angel. This makes no sense. If I've been here since the beginning why can't I remember any of it?"

A voice is heard through the room. "I can help you with that, Daniel."

I know that voice, thinks Daniel. That's the voice of that angel on the hill—but also one that's even more familiar. He looks around the room.

"Up here, Daniel." Daniel looks up and sees a figure sitting atop the archway with the serpent's head.

Daniel steps closer.

"Dr. Roberts?"

"I knew you'd be surprised."

"But I don't understand."

"Yes you do. I know it's been, shall we say, eons—but let me refresh your memory."

He floats down to the floor and rests a few feet from Daniel. "Let's change this environment to something more relaxing."

In a blink of an eye the scene is now a lounge bar and they are seated at a table with two glasses and a bottle of Scotch—soft jazz plays in the background.

Daniel tries to keep his wits about him. "What the hell is going on?"

"Hell? That's such an old, biblical term. We don't use that anymore; only those diehard fans on earth." He pours two drinks. "Better indulge yourself, Daniel...it will help."

Daniel takes a sip.

"There, that will allow you to absorb what I'm about to say." Dr. Roberts downs his drink. "You see, Daniel, we had a plan: you, me and thousands of others. We wanted to make this world a great place for all of us, but the committee in charge had other ideas."

"You mean God?"

"Another word that's finally falling by the wayside." He leans in to Daniel. "So the end result was that we lost." His face turns solemn. "It was tragic and we were expelled from there. Thrown out and discarded like a worn-out pair of shoes." He pours another drink and raises the bottle to Daniel. "I do think you'll need at least one more."

Daniel nods.

"We all made a pact that we would stay together and work toward proving that their ideas weren't working. So, since the beginning, which has seemed to be an endless amount of time, we have tried our best to reverse it, and eventually persuade the others that took the opposite position that we were right and to have them follow us in initiating our plan to save the souls of this planet."

"Can you refresh my memory further and tell me what that plan was?" asks Daniel.

He smiles again. "Very simple. We give them everything they want, and in doing so we eliminate greed, lust, thievery, coveting, murder, and wars, and all the disgusting things that make them human. Oh yes, and get rid of the main culprit."

"Which is?"

"Religion, of course."

Daniel ponders that for a moment. "But if they have everything handed to them, what are they learning or achieving? There's no growth for anything; they would become stagnant as if they were just zombies."

"That was their argument. But Daniel, don't you feel for these human spirits? Suffering day in and day out—year after year. They can't survive on scraps of bread and fish, and dreams that never happen because the phone is always off the hook. At least we listen. We hear their cries, but don't have the power to change it. They should have those rewards now." On the verge of tears he pours another round. "Surely you can see that, can't you, Daniel?"

"So why are you telling me this?"

"Because, Daniel, YOU are the missing piece in our future. When you decided to betray—I mean leave us, it just took the wind out of our sails. We were looking to you for leadership." He downs another shot. "And we've been lost without your leadership. But now we have a chance of getting you back. They have given us until midnight to convince you, of your own free will, of course, to return to the fold and lead us into a bright future for all."

Daniel rubs the side of his glass, but doesn't take a drink. "Dr. Roberts—"

"Let's dispense with that title. Just call me Luc."

Daniel pulls back. "You mean Lucifer?"

"There's another shameful thing they bestowed upon me. I was the highest-ranking angel and my name was synonymous with goodness." He drops his head and tears start to roll down his cheeks. "They took my name and ground it into the dirt and turned this whole world against me." He looks up at Daniel as he wipes tears from his eyes. "But I'm not a quitter. Even though you went against me, I am still willing to show good faith and return you to the fold. My love and compassion for you runs deep, Daniel." Looking at Daniel with soft eyes he says, "This is your hour of reckoning."

"Reckoning— I don't understand. What kind of reckoning are we talking about?"

"They have decided that your time on earth will expire at midnight." He points to a clock on the wall that reads 11:50.

"No!" says Daniel. "I have a life here. I have Debra. I refuse to go back!"

"Exactly how I feel, my brother. It's not fair and I want to help you with that."

"How?"

"Just one simple thing and you will be able to have the life you want."

"Is this some kind of trick?"

"No trick. You see, they don't want to admit to their mistake. They should have allowed you to be with us. We have free reign over this world, and you could too and still have your loving Debra—such a lovely girl."

"Daniel!" a voice rings out. It's Karl.

Luc and the bar scene disappear.

"I'm in here, Karl!"

Karl rushes into the room. "Daniel, what are you doing in here? I received a call from Debra, she's been worried sick."

"Karl! I know what's in that book."

"That's nice, Daniel, but you shouldn't be here at this hour. I'm surprised Security didn't kick you out."

"Listen, Karl, *The Angel's Book*; I know who wrote it."

"Yes you do, Daniel."

"You know it was me?"

"Yes. You see, I was there when you wrote it. And I know you have been talking to Dr. Roberts."

"You mean Luc?"

"Oh, he's told you that. And did he give you his sob story along with it? The reality is this, Daniel—he wants you back for betraying him. He wants you to suffer alongside of him and all the others that were lead astray. He was the one that made you see that wall in the tunnel. You can't die, but he was hoping that an accident would terminate Debra, and that would eliminate your need to stay here. This would make it much easier to sway you over."

Daniel is more confused than ever. "He said that my time will be up at midnight and I'll have to go back. He said he could help me so that I could stay."

Karl smiles. "It's not your time that is up at midnight, it's his. He has till then to persuade you to rejoin the wicked and live on this earth until it has run its course."

"But how do you know all this, Karl?"

Karl smiles. "Because I represent the other side. Let me explain something to you." Karl points to a bench. "Sit down, Daniel."

They sit on the bench together.

"From the moment you realized what you were doing was wrong and asked to be forgiven, this plan was in the making. If you could live all these lives through time and prove that you can be the best person you could be, you would be able to return to us."

"But that's what Dr. Roberts, Luc, said, and I don't want to go back. I want to stay here with Debra—I love her."

"And that is exactly what we want for you. He wants you to be here until the end, long after Debra has passed and help him continue to torment the people here. Is that what you want?"

"No. I want to live a normal life and have children and grow old with Debra and leave this world the same as everyone else."

Karl smiles and pats him on the back. "And we want that, too."

Dr. Roberts reappears in the middle of the room just as Debra enters and sees Daniel. She runs to him and throws her arms around him.

"Oh, Daniel! I've been so worried. What are you doing here?"

Before Daniel can get one word out, Dr. Roberts's body begins to enlarge and his clothes seem to melt off his body. He grows to a height that is inches from the 30-foot ceiling. His back shows the sprouting of wings, but not white—they are blood-red. Horns push through each side of his head. Both Daniel and Debra shake with fear.

Karl smiles once again. "I must say your theatrics have much improved in the last thousand years, Luc." He points to a clock on the wall that reads 12:00. "But I'm afraid your time has run out. Next time try *America's Got Talent."*

In a puff of smoke, Luc is gone.

Debra is in shock.

Daniel looks into her eyes. "Debra, are you all right?"

She stares at him.

"Debra?"

Still no response. He decides to kiss her and she finally blinks. "What just happened?" She touches Daniel's chest. "I'm dreaming?"

Karl smiles once more. "Time to go home. We can discuss this over dinner tomorrow night—my treat."

"That's nice of you, Karl," says Daniel.

"That's very nice, Professor Anton," says Debra. "You've done so much for Daniel—taking him under your wing."

"That's a nice way of putting it," says Karl.

"I really feel it should be us taking you out," she says.

"Just consider it a pre-wedding celebration."

"Wedding?" Debra's eyes light up.

"Well, I haven't asked her yet, Karl." Daniel gives her a passionate kiss.

"I think you just did," says Debra. "And here's my answer." She kisses him back.

As they begin to exit the exhibit, Karl looks up. "Pardon me if I'm wrong, but I didn't see anything in the rules that I can't be a guardian angel for two people."

"Yes, of course you're invited."

18

ERNIE

It's Christmas—1964. A young man by the name of Thomas Riley obtains part-time employment at a small downtown jewellery store. His job is to assist Ernie, an odd little man who works in the damp basement of the establishment. Thomas will soon discover that Ernie is much more than he appears.

—

The city street and all the little shops along the way have been transformed into a winter wonderland of coloured lights and Christmas decor. The snow that fell the night before is being shovelled to the curb by the employees to ready themselves for early-morning shoppers, hustling their way through the stores to be the first to grab a bargain.

—

Warmly dressed in a wool overcoat and scarf, sixteen-year-old Thomas Riley gazes into a storefront window. Past Christmases would find him with his nose pressed against the cold glass with eyes filled with excitement and anticipation as he viewed every toy and thrilled at the slow and repetitive moving displays.

This year was different. He passed by the toy store without even a glance. He was sixteen and considered himself too mature to be affected by children's toys and fantasies. He headed straight to Alwyn's bookstore. Approaching the small display window his eyes zoned in on a large book standing on its own—*The Complete Works of Charles Dickens*. This was at the top of Thomas's Christmas list. The book was ajar just enough that he could cock his head to the side and view the penciled-in price. His enthusiasm and smile disappeared. It was far more than he could afford and far greater than any one gift his parents would allow. Sucking in a deep breath of cold air dispelling the steam from his nostrils, he continues down the street with his unzipped galoshes, flapping and slapping together, creating the most irreverent music.

—

He enters Stein's Jewellery Store where he has recently obtained seasonal employment—the job will provide him with a little financial independence, but now realizes that it would take him two Christmases to purchase the Dickens book.

He greets the friendly sales staff as they make ready for the influx of customers—arranging display cases and lightly dusting the shelves.

"Good morning, everyone!" says Thomas.

"Good morning, Thomas!" they reply.

"Ready for a busy day?" one employee asks.

"Let's hope so!" says Thomas.

Being his first job, he is glad the staff is so cheery. It may just be the Christmas spirit that evokes such joy, but for Thomas it adds to the pleasure of the job.

At the back of the store the watch repairman, Ivan, sits at his desk meticulously working a piece of jewellery. He wears an eyepiece strapped around his balding head with only a little turf around the ears that extends to the back of his cranium. To most people it would seem that Ivan is oblivious to everything around him, but he knows everything that goes on. While his eyes and hands are busily fixing watches, his ears are open for business —everyone's business.

"Good morning, Ivan!" says the bright-eyed Thomas.

Ivan stays completely focussed on his work, but always replies in his Polish accent. "Good morning to you, Mr. Thomas. What, we go for liver today, ya?"

"Liver sounds good, but I don't have enough money, Ivan."

"Ivan pay."

"I can't have you pay," says Thomas.

"No worry. You make company for Ivan. Twelve o'clock, we go."

Thomas smiles. "Okay, twelve o'clock."

Thomas then heads for the back of the store, where there is a large shipping door. Directly across from the door, a set of stairs leads down to the basement and alongside it a conveyor belt. As Thomas makes his way down the stairs, the basement is in direct contrast to the main floor. It's very dark and dingy with overhanging pipes and cold, damp walls—not a place for the clean, well-groomed sales staff above.

Reaching the last step he hears the slightly high-pitched voice of an older man, who seems to be talking to himself.

At the end of a long wooden workbench rests Ernie. He has an English accent and speaks as though he popped right out of *A Christmas Carol*. Sitting atop a high stool, his stature is evident—legs dangling in the air, while he leans over a small polishing machine, cleaning a ring. He has thin, white hair, slicked back on his head. Wire-rimmed glasses sit low on his prominent nose, well balanced by a protruding chin, mainly due to the fact that he has no teeth. They are available—resting in his pants pocket, where they would only be a part of his attire when upstairs, in public view. Thomas finds him endearing.

"Good morning, Ernie!"

Ernie looks up from his glasses. "Uh, good morning, Master Thomas! If you wouldn't mind finishing off this ring, I'll make us a spot of tea."

"And will you read my fortune again?"

Ernie climbs off the stool, looks at Thomas and points a finger in the air. "And what would a cup of tea be without a marvellous fortune inside."

"Precisely, Master Ernie!"

"Oh, listen to you now. Do I detect a little Sherlock Holmes there?"

"Perhaps, my good man," laughs Thomas.

—

Allen is the manager of the store. A dedicated company man, who embodies the corporate spirit. He's suitably dressed for the clientele in this blue-collar area of town with a red tie for the season and grey houndstooth sports jacket. He does have one three-piece suit that hangs in his bedroom closet, wrapped in plastic, waiting for the day when he can elevate his status by moving downtown to the head office.

He stands outside of his tiny office stretching his neck in search of Millie, one of the older members of the sales staff. His eyes zoom in on her as she sprays and wipes clean a glass countertop.

Everyone in the store knows that when Allen looms outside of his office, something is about to surface. The staff continue working but all eyes are now on Allen.

Slowly, but strategically, he begins to move his tanned, suede shoes in Millie's direction. The tension in the store builds, but at the same time there is almost an audible sigh of relief from each one as he passes them by.

Millie, who is pricing rings at a glass counter, is oblivious to the encroachment.

In his tactical, soft tone Allen drops the bomb. “Millie, would you please see me in my office when you’ve finished?”

Everyone knows those words and tone, including Millie.

“Okay, Allen. I’ll be right there.”

As soon as he turns to head to his office, Millie clutches her stomach.

—

Thomas and Ernie sit by the workbench finishing the last of their tea.

“That was great tea, Ernie, now how about those tea leaves?” he says, handing Ernie his cup.

“Let’s have a look, shall we.”

Ernie holds the cup in both hands as if it were the Holy Grail. He peers inside the cup coated with tea leaves.

“Not much going on in there, is there, Ernie?”

“Hmm, I would say quite the opposite, Master Thomas.”

Thomas’s eyes enlarge. “What is it, Ernie? What do you see?”

“I see something special happening to you—something ...magical.”

“Magical?”

Ernie looks above his glasses and pronounces, “It is Christmas, you know. Magical things always happen at Christmas.”

“You mean like Santa and flying reindeer, and crap like that?”

Ernie gently places the teacup on the table.

“Oh yes. I’ve forgotten.”

“Forgotten what?”

“Forgotten how old you are. It’s sad when one loses the ability to see beyond.”

“Beyond what?” asks Thomas.

Ernie gets down from the stool, collects the two cups and heads for the sink to clean them. “Beyond your nose; but whether you believe or not...” he turns back to Thomas with a smile and a twinkle in his eye, “The magic will happen.”

Millie walks into Allen's office. The door closes, but is left ajar. Ivan sits at his desk with his eyes on his work and his ears on the door.

"Millie, I'm sure you're aware that your sales are way down."

Ivan listens intently.

"I did mention in the past that you would have to bring them up by Christmas."

"I'll do better, I promise. Please don't let me go now. Not at Christmas."

"It would never be my intention to let you go, but that's not my decision. I have to send in my report to head office by the end of next week, and if they see that your performance hasn't changed..."

"Oh, but it will, Allen, I promise! My sales will be right up there!"

"Well, we'll see."

Millie walks out of the office and straight to the washroom with one hand over her mouth.

Allen steps out as Ivan begins to hum a tune. A tactic he uses to let Allen know that he doesn't agree with his handling of the situation. Allen eyeballs the back of Ivan's head, then clears his throat, straightens his tie and walks off.

—

Thomas and Ivan are enjoying each other's company, as they feed on liver and onions at the small restaurant across the street. Ivan likes the convenience of its location. It enables him to enjoy his full allotted lunch hour. The only drawback is when Allen has a rush repair and makes a beeline right to Ivan and disturbs his lunch—which he has demonstrated on occasion.

"...and the clockmaker said, and I was fixing my clock to the whistle of your factory."

Thomas laughs. "That's so funny. You have the funniest stories, Ivan."

Thomas shovels a full fork of food into his mouth. Ivan's face turns serious.

"Now, I have something not so funny."

Thomas slowly swallows. "What is it?"

Ivan takes a sip of coffee. "Millie."

"What's wrong with Millie? Is she sick?"

"They going to fire her."

"Fire her! But why? She's such a nice lady."

"They don't care about nice. They care about this." He rubs two fingers together.

"But what's money got to do with it?"

"Huh! Money is everything. All business is money. You don't make enough money for store—good-bye."

"Oh boy, what's she going to do?"

"Allen give Millie one week to do better. If no, she go."

"That's awful. I wish there was something we could do."

"Christmas always sad for people. People with money always good Christmas. People with no money...bad time. I remember Poland during war: People have nothing, no food, no hope, no Christmas—very bad."

Thomas replies in a soft, concerning tone. "Yeah...very bad."

—

Upstairs the staff is swamped with the first wave of customers. The conveyer belt is in full swing. Articles from the main floor are sent down to be gift wrapped. For Ernie, it's a great adrenaline rush. He loves this part of his job.

"Okay, my boy! Two coming down! Hand me the first one! You take care of the next one!"

There are two rolls of Christmas paper hooked side by side over top of the workbench. They each rip off enough for the size of the items. It becomes somewhat of a competition to see who finishes first, and does the best job.

"Now don't forget to pick a complementary bow," says Ernie.

Thomas looks at the box of bows and quickly decides on one.

"Oh, getting fancy are we?" says Ernie.

"Just trying to follow the master."

"Oh my, now that'll get you into trouble."

Thomas laughs, then thinks about all the sad stories of people like Millie and hopes he always has an Ernie to make the workday a good experience.

—

The store is closed—empty of customers and staff. For the last time today, Ernie mops the salt and water from the snow tracked in by customers. Thomas appears from the basement.

"All cleaned up and ready to go for next week!" says Thomas.

"And that's it for me too, Master Thomas. What say we have a nice spot of tea before we head out into that cold evening air?"

Thomas grabs the pail, and Ernie, the mop. Thomas tries his English accent again.

"Precisely my thoughts; an absolutely delightful idea, Master Ernie."

"Oh, that would have to be Dr. Watson?"

They are enjoying their tea and conversation when Thomas remembers Millie. He rests his cup on the workbench.

"Ernie? When I was at lunch today with Ivan, he told me something that really upset me."

"This sounds serious," says Ernie, putting his cup down.

"He told me that Allen wanted to see Millie in his office. He overheard Allen tell her that her sales weren't good and that if she didn't do better next week, he'd have to fire her. Right before Christmas! Ivan says, because it's all about money. Don't they care about people?"

Ernie has a quick flashback about saying good night to Millie, as she was the last to leave before he locked the door.

"I remember saying good night to Millie, and I told her to have a nice weekend. She said that she would try. I thought that was odd, but now it makes sense."

"I wish there was something we could do."

Ernie takes a sip of tea. "I think you just gave yourself the answer, Master Thomas."

"What do you mean? All I said was I wish—"

"That's it, wish."

"Wish?"

"Yes, wish. Wish that Millie will have a great week of sales!"

"I don't think that's going to do it."

"I told you, whether you believe it or not, Christmas is magic."

Thomas shakes his head. "Sure, if you're a little kid."

"The magic of Christmas is not restricted by age, only by heart. Let's try it. I'm sure we could create a little magic together.

"We wish Millie will have a great week of sales."

"Ah, that's silly. That won't work."

"Are you not that same gentleman that asked me to read his teacup?"

"Okay, you got me."

"Together now."

In unison they wish Millie will have a great week of sales.

"Now, all we have to do is wait and watch the magic."

—

Thomas shows up for work a little earlier. When he arrives in the basement, he sees Ernie wrapping a couple of items.

"Hi, Ernie!"

Ernie seems nervous and tries to hurry with the wrapping. Thomas takes note and before commenting, he sees that the Christmas paper Ernie is using is not the store paper. It is more for children with patterns of Santa and sorts.

"Oh! Good day, Master Thomas! You're a pinch early today."

He quickly takes the finished items and puts them to one side and stands in front of them.

"And how's my number one employee doing today?"

"Good. Isn't that different paper than what we use?"

"Different?" Ernie moves aside to show the wrapped items.

"Oh! Yes! It's uh...couple of gifts for my nephew. Wouldn't want to use the store's paper, that wouldn't be right, would it?"

"No, I guess not."

After a short uncomfortable pause...

"Well now!" says Ernie. "I was just about to make some tea. Would you be interested?" he says with a smile.

—

Upstairs Millie is so nervous about losing her job that every customer is a challenge.

"I think this is such a gorgeous ring. It's 14-karat gold. I love the brilliance and cut of the diamonds."

The woman customer leans forward to get a closer look. "Yes, it is. It's quite beautiful."

Millie bites down on her lower lip as she waits for the woman's decision.

"I think..."

Millie takes a deep breath and holds it.

"I think...I'll wait until after Christmas. You know how it is, you always put yourself last."

Millie tries to hide the disappointment on her face, but it still comes out in her tone. "Yes. I know."

"Well, have a Merry Christmas, and we'll probably see you in the New Year," says the woman.

"Oh, yes. Have a...Merry Christmas."

Millie's eyes follow her as she walks out of the store. You can just about read her mind—there goes my job.

—

Thomas is enjoying his tea break and Ernie's endless stories.

"...and then, the ghost disappeared back into the picture and never returned again."

"That was a good one! I hope someday I'll be a writer and write great stories like that."

Ernie looks over his glasses. "Remember, if you want it to happen, it's not hope; it's wish."

"Okay, wish. Speaking of wish, how is Millie doing?"

"I don't think she's doing very well yet. Magic never happens by your clock. That's what makes it magic. You never know how or when it's going to appear."

"Okay, gentlemen!" yells one of the sales staff from the top of the stairs. "We need these wrapped and ready to go in three minutes!—six coming down!"

The conveyor rolls. The six boxed articles quickly descend to the basement. Ernie and Thomas hustle over to the conveyor belt, grab the boxes and take them to the workbench to wrap. They look at each other with excited eyes.

"We wish to wrap these gifts in three minutes!" says Thomas.

"That's the spirit!"

—

Millie is not having any luck at all as she stands at the counter looking deflated. She sees all the staff with customers and decides she should at least look busy. She pulls a tray of rings from the glass case and begins to polish them. She hears someone clear their throat. She looks up to see a distinguished, elderly gentleman with a white beard standing before her.

"Oh, I'm sorry, sir. May I help you?" She puts the tray back in the case.

"You most certainly can."

With that, a beautiful, captivating, smile appears on his face. Millie is mesmerized— like a trance that she quickly shakes off.

"Is it a ring you're looking for?"

"A ring? Yes, a ring."

"And would this be for yourself or..."

"It would be for...my wife."

Millie finds it strange that he seems unsure of what he wants and who he wants it for, so she handles it with caution. At this time of the year there are more than Christmas spirits at play.

"Now, would she prefer white or yellow?"

"White or yellow?"

"Yes, white or yellow gold."

She now thinks this is maybe something he's not used to doing, so he may be a little nervous.

"Oh, yes. Hm. I would say white. White as new-fallen snow."

Millie reaches into the display case and remembers what she was taught. Always start at the top. Her hand reaches for an exquisite, high-end ring, but her self-confidence eludes her. She hesitates and moves to a lower-end ring.

"How about this one? It has three beautiful diamonds."

"Oh, well, that is quite beautiful."

He gives it a quick look then begins to scan the display case. His eyes rest on one ring.

He points. "And what about...that one?"

Millie realizes the ring he has chosen was the one she hesitated to show. Nervously, she confirms the choice by putting her finger on it. "This one?"

"Yes. May I see it, please?"

Millie tries to hold her composure. She has never sold anything so expensive. She reaches into the case and slowly pulls out the ring. Her hand slightly trembles. She hands it to him. He holds it up to admire it.

"Excellent." And without hesitation, "I'll take it."

Millie's knees buckle. She braces herself against the counter, thinking she should disclose the price before they are both disappointed.

"This ring is fairly expensive," she says, showing him the small price tag attached to the ring.

"Yes, indeed. And no need to wrap it, I'm quite proficient at doing that myself."

At this point Millie wants to scream.

"Yes, sir!"

"Oh! I'm sure you would like payment for that."

He reaches into his coat pocket and pulls out a letter-sized envelope and hands it to her.

"I think you'll find the appropriate amount inside."

Millie takes the envelope. She is still in shock.

"Yes. I'll be right back."

She heads to the cash register at the back of the store with the envelope and the ring.

The rest of the sales staff look on in bewilderment. The gentleman looks back at them and smiles, "Merry Christmas."

They just stare back nodding with open mouths.

Millie rushes back with the receipt. She places the ring into a small box, then places it and the receipt into a bag. Holding the bag with two hands, she presents it to the gentleman.

"Merry Christmas, sir!" she says with the broadest smile.

She remembers his change that she had put back into the envelope. She holds out the envelope. "Oh! Your change!" He ignores the envelope.

"And a very Merry Christmas to you...Millie."

He turns and walks out the door.

"But..."

Millie can't believe it. The envelope holds a hundred dollars. If that wasn't strange enough, she wonders how he knew her name. Then she realizes it was her name tag. She looks down at her lapel. There is no name tag. Reaching into her jacket pocket, she pulls out the tag.

—

Thomas is at the workbench watching Ernie wrapping an item.

"Well, my boy, tomorrow is Christmas Eve. So we have to—"

Ivan comes rushing down the stairs filled with excitement.

"This is good Christmas! Very good Christmas!"

"What is it, Ivan?"

Ivan puts his hands together. "Millie! She make big sale! She sell very expensive diamond ring! Allen say Millie do best! More than all sales peoples! She don't lose job now! Like magic!"

Ernie smiles and gives Thomas a look.

"Like magic, Master Thomas. What do you think of Christmas now?"

"I guess I would have to say...jolly good!"
"Indeed."

—

The store is closed. Ernie and Thomas are at the door wishing the staff a Merry Christmas with Millie being the last to leave.

"Well, this is going to be a great Christmas!" says Millie. "It's funny how your life can turn around so fast!"

"Well, it is Christmas. Anything can happen," says Thomas.

Ernie smiles.

"That's so true!" says Millie and gives them both a hug. "Merry Christmas to you both."

Ernie quickly locks the door behind her. He seems to have a little anxiety going on.

"Well, my boy, we're almost there! If you wouldn't mind mopping up, I'll go down and finish my work and meet you here when I'm done."

"Are sure you don't need my help?"

"No-no-no. You tend to the mopping. I'll be fine." Ernie moves his little legs as fast as they can go, looking more like a penguin.

Thomas becomes suspicious and thinks—something doesn't seem right. I don't recall anything that needed to be done in the basement. A moment goes by and then he decides to sneak his way to the back of the store. He peers down the stairs and sees Ernie building up a huge pile of presents by the conveyer belt. They're all wrapped in non-store Christmas paper, just like the ones Ernie said were for his nephew.

"Look at all those presents!" he says in a whisper. "They can't all be for his nephew."

He hears the sound of sleigh bells and high-pitched voices—like little children just outside the shipping door.

There's a knock. Thomas scrambles to hide behind Charlie's office door. Ernie climbs to the top of stairs and opens the door.

"Hi, Ernie! We miss you!"

"Shoo! I'm not alone. You'll have to move quickly and be very quiet!" says Ernie.

Thomas peeks out and just captures Ernie heading back down the stairs. He looks toward the door, but all he can see are small shadows that appear to be children. The conveyer starts up and the presents begin their journey up the belt. Thomas can see little hands and arms reach out to grasp the presents.

Finally, all the gifts are out of the store. Ernie returns to the top of the stairs.

"Thank you, Ernie!"

"Yes, that's a big help!"

"You should come back, at least for a visit!"

"Oh, I think I've been gone too long. I couldn't manage the cold weather up there anymore. Merry Christmas and say hello to the big fellow for me, and tell him thanks for Millie."

"We will! Have a Merry Christmas, Ernie! Bye till next year!" Thomas can't believe what he's just witnessed—"And thanks for Millie?" he whispers to himself.

He begins to tiptoe back to the front of the store and starts to mop as Ernie shuts and locks the door and now heads to the front.

"Well, how are we coming along up here?"

"Oh, pretty good."

"Pretty good? Looks like you need some Christmas magic to hurry you along. I'll grab the other mop or we'll be here till the New Year."

—

Ernie and Thomas are standing outside all bundled up as Ernie locks the door.

"Well, that does it. Another Christmas all set to go. Everyone at home and the children will soon be tucked into their beds and then the magic begins."

"Ernie, can I ask you something?"

"Why, of course."

"I heard a knock at the back door earlier, and when I went back to see what it was I heard voices and saw presents coming up the conveyer and going out the door."

"You did? Well...those were the presents I was telling you about for my nephew."

"Seemed like quite a lot of gifts for one nephew."

"Oh, did I say nephew, I meant nephews."

Thomas tilts his head to the side.

"And what about those voices?"

Ernie looks trapped.

"Voices?—Oh, voices. Family...my family came to pick up the presents."

"But they seemed like...little children."

Ernie shrugs his shoulders. "Small people, you know. It's the short gene—runs in the family."

"But then you mentioned—"

"My, it's getting quite cold standing here, Master Thomas. I suggest we begin to move. Now, are you walking my way?"

"Where do you live?"

He points to the right. Four blocks that way."

"You're on."

"Now, did I ever tell you the story of the ghost that haunted..."

—

The sky is black and filled with bright, twinkling stars. The streets are deserted. They are enjoying each other's company when Ernie comes to an abrupt halt in front of a large old rooming house. He looks up at Thomas with a childish grin.

"Well, Master Thomas, this is my humble abode. You've been a very good employee and a great friend."

"Thanks, Ernie."

"Perhaps we'll see you again next Christmas."

"I'm not sure about next year."

Ernie seems a little saddened to hear that.

"Well, a year is a long way off."

They start out with a handshake, but that doesn't seem to do it so they embrace.

"I'm going to miss my fortune being read."

"I've seen nothing but good things in that cup for you, my boy."

A tear forms in Ernie's eye. "Now, carry on before you get a chill."

Thomas's eyes are fixed on Ernie as he shuffles along the walkway to his house.

"Ernie!"

Ernie turns to Thomas. "I will be back next Christmas!"

There's a huge smile from Ernie. "Smashing! We'll see you then! And don't forget...wishful thinking, Master Thomas!"

Thomas waves. "I won't."

—

Christmas morning and Thomas and his parents are in the living room beside the Christmas tree, opening the last of the gifts. Thomas opens a present that contains a pair of leather winter boots.

"These are beautiful! No more one-man-band walking down the street! Thank you so much."

"You're welcome," says his mother. "Your dad, believe it or not, picked them out."

"Once in a while, I get it right. There's only one drawback. We won't be able to hear you coming up the street anymore."

Thomas looks around the tree.

"Well, I guess that's it, folks. I think I'll go in my room and rest up for that turkey."

"No such luck for me. Back to the kitchen to make that dressing," says his mother.

Thomas lies on his bed with his arms behind his head.

"Ah, this is nice."

He happens to glance at his dresser and notices a rather large present sitting on top.

"What the..."

He picks up the present, then sits on the edge of the bed and begins to unwrap it. His eyes bug out—*THE COMPLETE WORKS OF CHARLES DICKENS*. "I can't believe it!"

He opens it and there, on the inside page, is a handwritten note—"There is magic all around us. If we choose, we can see it every day. It appears more often at Christmas in the wishes of the young at heart—wishing you a Merry Christmas, Master Thomas." He looks up from the book and smiles.

"Ernie."

He settles on his bed and begins reading the book as snow falls gently outside his window.

—

Thomas went back to the store the following year. He never worked in the basement with Ernie again. He was promoted to sales staff. But he always managed time to go downstairs to sit and have a chat, listen to a ghost story and have his cup of tea with Ernie; and most of all, his fortune read and his wishes come true.

19

ROY CORBETT IN REEL TIME

The projection room is dimly lit as Roy Corbett sets up a 35 mm reel on the projector. He starts it up and watches it carefully feed through the old machine. He peers through a small window into the theatre where his eyes focus on the huge, white screen. The projector is stopped at the precise moment.

"There we go. All set," he says with pride.

He slowly manoeuvres his way down the rickety, wooden steps that lead to the theatre lobby. He pokes his head into the theatre. Two young ushers, Pete and Tom, are sweeping between the aisles' seats.

"How we doing, boys?"

"Just fine, Mr. Corbett!"

"We'll be done in five!"

"Good, because we open in ten."

Roy passes the snack bar, where another teenager, Michael, is preparing the popcorn.

"Michael. We have to fill that bin to the top. This film is a popular one. I'm expecting a good turnout tonight!"

"I'll have it bursting at the seams, Mr. Corbett!"

"That a boy!"

He remembers something and walks back. Leaning over the counter and in a soft voice...

"Michael."

"Yes, sir."

"I know you're sweet on that girl..."

"Rachel."

"Yes, Rachel. How does she feel about you?"

"I'm not sure."

"Well, maybe we could sweeten the pot a little. If she shows up tonight, don't charge her for the popcorn. That might sway her a little."

"Thanks, Mr. Corbett!"

Roy starts to walk away then turns back again.

"Oh, and uh, make sure it's the large size."

"Yes, sir, Mr. Corbett!"

Now on to the ticket booth. He pops his head in to see his wife, Beth, putting together the cash float. Even in her late sixties, she still holds her beauty.

"All set, Beth?"

She nods her head and smiles.

"My goodness Roy, after forty-eight years, you're still asking me if I'm ready."

He snuggles close to her ear.

"I wasn't talking about the cash float."

Her face turns pink.

"Roy Corbett, you stop that right now."

As he rubs his cheek against hers, he says, "Nice to see a little colour in your cheeks."

"Roy, you get out of here before I rest this cash float on your head."

"All right, all right." He peers out the window. "Looks like a nice line-up out there."

He rubs her shoulders.

"And they don't need to see any hanky panky going on in here."

"Oh, is that what you call it," says Roy. "Back in my day we called it romance."

"We called it roaming hands. Now get."

He smiles and kisses her on the cheek. "I'll see you after the show, sweetheart."

Roy stations himself at the lobby entrance. This is his favourite part of the job: greeting the patrons as they file in and hand their tickets to Roy. He rips each one in half, giving the customer their stub.

"Evening—Thanks for coming—Evening—enjoy the show..."

His old friends John and Liz make their way over.

"Well, my night wouldn't be complete," says Roy.

"And this time," says John, "I didn't come empty-handed."

"He thinks he has you with this one Roy," says Liz.

"You never know. Let's have it."

"The Marx Brothers—what was their first film and when was it made?"

"Is that the best you can do? *The Coconuts*—1929."

"You're too good, Roy."

"You should have asked me what Harpo's shoe size was."

"What was it?"

"I don't know. See, you would have had me."

They laugh.

"Enjoy the show and don't be stingy, John. Get your wife some popcorn."

"One kernel or two?"

Roy chuckles and moves on to other patrons.

The night was a success, as they usually are on Saturdays. Roy bids the last of the patrons adieu and locks the large glass entrance doors. Beth moves in behind him and hugs him close.

"Let me see now. Ethel?...Marjorie?...Ruth?"

"That cash float isn't far away, you know."

"Oh, Beth!"

He looks down at her hands wrapped around his waist.

"Are those the roaming hands you were telling me about?" he says, and then turns around to her.

She looks into his eyes. "No, but these are the lonely arms."

"You know, the only other place I've seen such a beautiful face is on that big screen in the other room."

"Oh, Roy."

She holds him tight.

"Now this is worth a year of Saturday night receipts," says Roy.

She closes her eyes. "Mmm."

"You know what else would be nice?" says Roy.

"I'm afraid to ask."

"Hot chocolate and a toasted Danish? How does that sound?"

"Sounds like foreplay to me."

Roy kisses her nose.

"Works every time."

They walk across the street to Dora's Diner. Over the years, Roy and Beth have enjoyed their time there. A simple place—nothing fancy, nothing complicated—like the theatre and the town, you get what you see.

They sit in their usual booth by the front window. They enjoy watching the many friends that pass by and give them a wave. Conversation is never a problem as they sip their hot chocolate.

"Another Danish, Beth?"

"One for each hip? No thanks. At my age I can't afford another one."

He holds her hand across the table. "You haven't gained an ounce in forty years."

"That's because I keep refusing that second Danish."

"Forty years. I don't know what I would have done without you, Beth. And I don't know how you've been able to put up with me all these years."

"Don't be silly. You've given me yourself and the movie theatre. I couldn't have asked for any more than that."

"But I never took you anywhere. Not a trip to an island, Europe, nowhere."

"Sit beside me, Roy."

He moves to her side.

"We've spent endless nights sitting in that theatre after everyone had gone, watching films that would take us to places all over the world—you, me and popcorn. We've watched all the changes: the fads, the technology, the history, like being in a time machine. The theatre has been a home to us. And what a great family we've raised."

"Family?"

"Sure, our audience—generations growing up right in that theatre, year after year."

She holds his hand.

"Let's go home, Roy."

"The theatre?"

She smiles. "Not tonight, Romeo."

—

The next morning Roy is at the theatre cleaning the entrance doors when a man taps on the window.

Roy opens one of the doors. "Yes sir, can I help you?"

"Mr. Corbett?"

"Yes," he extends his hand.

"Harold Moody, Silver Star Productions."

"Oh yes, the distributor, come in."

"Is there a place where we can talk?"

"Sure, my office. Right this way."

They walk past the the snack bar and into his small office.

Roy offers Moody a seat.

"Can I get you a coffee? It's not that great. It's from the machine in the lobby."

"No thanks, I'll pass. I've had enough of those over the years."

"So, what brings you here? Did a film go missing? I know the payments have always been on time."

"Never a problem there, Mr. Corbett."

"Some promotion for a new picture then?"

"No. We're in the digital age now, Mr. Corbett."

"We sure are. It's everywhere."

"Yes, including theatres."

"Well, no need to worry. I'm quite happy with the films and my projector."

"The worry isn't ours, Mr. Corbett, it's yours."

Roy becomes puzzled.

"What do you mean?"

"I mean, all the theatres are switching to digital projection. You'll have to switch over."

"Switch over. But why can't I stay with my projector?"

"Because, Mr. Corbett, there won't be any more films. It's all going to be on a hard drive. Digital is a fraction of the cost."

"How much cheaper would that be?"

"Right now it costs $1,500 to make a copy of a 35 mm film and ship it in those metal canisters, and only $150 for digital. Now if you were a distributor, which would you choose?"

"I see what you mean. So, no more films?"

"No more films. You'll have to have a digital projector."

"And who pays for that?"

"I'm afraid, that's your department. We did send you a letter in regards to this change a year ago. Did you get that letter?"

"Yes, but I thought it was just talk. Something down the road."

"Well, now we've come to the end of that road."

"And what's this going to cost me?"

"It will cost...$65,000. You have three months or...I'm afraid you'll have to close."

"Close!"

The terror shows on Roy's face.

—

Roy and Beth are back at Dora's.

"$65,000!" says Beth.

"That's what he said."

"And where are we supposed to get that kind of money?!"

"I don't know."

There's a moment of concentrated silence and then...

"My father built this theatre and its audience. The only real changes that he went through were black and white to colour, bigger screen, better sound and competition from TV, cable, VHS and DVD. But we survived it all, Beth. Now, we're going to lose the fight, not because we can't keep up with technology but because we can't afford to."

Beth gets a sparkle in her eye.

"Roy. Remember when that tornado passed through about ten years ago, and Jake lost his barn and livestock and the Dawson family half their house?"

Roy smiles. "Yeah, the whole town pulled together and fixed that problem lickety-split. Why, we even had a fundraiser at the theatre and the whole town showed up. We had to schedule two extra shows, remember that?"

"That's right. So why can't it happen for the theatre?"

"The theatre?"

"Sure! How many old films do we have in storage?"

"Well, my dad was quite a collector, I would say close to a hundred."

"We have three months, Roy! We could show a movie every night! And instead of a set price, we'll ask for donations! That way people will feel that they are really helping out!"

"I don't know. Ten years has changed everything. We lost the mill. A lot of people are out of work."

"The theatre is the heart of this community. It brings them together every week. They come with their families and friends and for two hours they get to leave their problems at home. You can see it in their faces when they leave: all smiling and stress-free. It's magical. No one wants to lose that. They didn't have a choice with the mill, but they do with the theatre."

"Beth, you're right! That's the answer! You're brilliant!"

They raise their coffee cups and make a toast.

"To the theatre," says Roy.

"And the community," adds Beth.

—

Roy, Beth and Michael are in the lobby finishing up with handwritten posters to distribute about town.

"Okay, hold that up, Michael, and let me see how it looks," says Roy.

He holds up the poster.

SAVE YOUR THEATRE
BRING YOUR DONATIONS
AND WATCH GREAT FILMS
EVERY EVENING

"That looks great," says Roy as he puts his arm around Beth.

"That should do it," says Beth. "It'll work, Roy. You'll see."

"They're here, Mr. Corbett!" says Michael.

Pete and Tom walk in.

"Perfect timing, boys!" says Roy. "Now we have seventy-five posters. If you each take twenty-five you'll have them done in no time."

"And remember, boys, put them in locations that can be easily seen."

"Don't you worry about that," says Pete. "We'll have the whole town covered!"

"Michael!" says Roy.

Michael turns back.

"How's that Rachel doing?"

He gives Roy the thumbs up.

Roy smiles. "Must have been the popcorn. Well, Beth, I guess all we can do now is wait."

"I think we should start off with a bang," says Beth. "Let's show *Gone with the Wind."*

"Excellent choice. I think I still have the original poster somewhere."

—

Roy sticks his head into the ticket booth. Beth is working overtime. "How we doing?"

"Out!"

"Yes ma'am."

Roy heads for the snack bar where all three boys are tending the crowd. He smiles and peeks into the theatre and sees that it's three-quarters full. Moving halfway up the stairs that lead to the projection room, he turns and waves to Michael until he gets his attention. Roy raises an open hand to let him know he'll start the film in five minutes. Michael's so busy all he can do is nod. Roy smiles as he takes in the sight of the large crowd at the snack bar.

"My God, Beth," he says to himself. "I do believe this is going to work."

A great night was had by all, especially on the financial end. Roy stands in the lobby with the biggest grin, thanking everyone and shaking hands.

"Now don't forget, folks! Tomorrow night is *The Petrified Forest!* You don't want to miss that one!"

He calls Michael over.

"Michael, can you go into the basement and grab the film *The Petrified Forest?"*

"Sure, Mr. Corbett."

"Roy!" Beth calls from the office. "I have a final count!"

"Be right there!" says Roy.

He finds Beth with a smile from ear to ear.

"Well sweetheart, by the look on your face I'd say we did pretty well. Should I ask for a drum roll?"

"Donations...$1,626."

"Yes!"

"Snack bar...$348.75, which comes to the grand total of $1,974.75!"

"Wahoo!"

"I told you it would work!" Beth says, and throws her arms around Roy.

"Yes you did, you little genius. Great start! At this rate we should have no problem reaching our goal!"

Michael shows up with two film canisters.

"Mr. Corbett. Here's the film, and I found this other one that doesn't have a label on it." He hands it to Roy.

"That's strange. I don't have a clue as to what this one would be. Thanks, Michael. I'll have a look at it later." He places the canister down on a chair.

"I'm curious to see what that is too," says Beth.

—

Breakfast is being served at Dora's. Roy and Beth occupy their regular table, but the mood is subdued as they reassess their expectations of knocking the donations out of the park.

"One month left," says Roy. "What are we looking at now?"

"Well, with the $418 from last night, it's now a total of $21,360."

"We won't make it, Beth. We've squeezed all we can out of this town."

"We put up a great fight, Roy, and have nothing to be ashamed of." She reaches across and holds his hand.

"It's not shame I feel, it's sadness. And I feel like an idiot by jumping the gun by calling that guy Moody and telling him we'll be buying one of those bloody machines shortly. Then he sends me a congratulations and complimentary film on a disc. What was the name of it?"

"*The Last Hurrah*," says Beth.

"How ironic is that; comedy, no doubt."

—

Beth is cleaning the glass doors when Roy walks up.

"Are you still curious about that mysterious film reel?" he asks.

"Of course."

"Okay, I'll go set it up and meet you in the theatre."

"This should be interesting."

"We'll see."

Beth is comfortably seated in the theatre chewing licorice as Roy joins her. She offers him a bite.

"No thanks. I'm good."

Empty scratched frames begin to pass the screen. A picture of a frail, old man sitting in what looks to be an older version of Roy's office appears on the screen.

"That's my dad!"

"Hello, son. I know you're surprised to see me again, but I felt it necessary. I want you to know how proud I am of you for taking over this theatre and understanding the importance it holds. I don't know what obstacles will befall you in the future. Keep the magic alive. I am leaving you with a little magic of my own. I can't explain what it is because I don't know how it will be of value to you. This, you will find out on your own. Hope it helps. Good-bye, son."

The film returns to empty, scratched frames.

"What was that all about?" asks Beth.

"I don't know. For some reason he thought I'd be in trouble and wanted to help."

"But what was he talking about, magic of his own?"

"I think as time went on, my dad became one with fantasy and less with reality."

—

Roy has gathered the boys into the lobby.

"Fellas, I've been around this theatre all my life and enjoyed every minute. I've had a great run. But I guess it's time to let go. We haven't been able to raise enough money. It's not anyone's fault. The town has given all it can. This will be our final weekend. And I want to tell you that you have been the best employees anyone could ever have, and you certainly don't deserve this."

"And you don't deserve it either, Mr. Corbett," says Michael. "We love this theatre too."

All three have tears in their eyes.

"Well, let's pull ourselves together now and go out there and give them a hell of a show!"

"Yes, Mr. Corbett."

"We'll give it our best."

Roy smiles. "Thanks, boys. Okay then, on with the show!"

Roy walks into his office and plunks himself into his chair. He opens up a desk drawer and pulls out the DVD that Moody had sent him.

"The Last Hurrah. I never would have imagined my life being ended by a little disc."

He sits silent for a moment.

"All right, let's get on with it."

Before walking out the door, he glances over at his dad's film canister resting on the chair and drops the DVD on top of it.

"Well," he says to himself, "there you have it: the past, the present and no future. Roy Corbett rides slowly into the sunset."

Beth sits quietly staring out the window of the ticket booth. Roy appears behind her and rests his hands on her shoulders.

"You all right, Beth?"

"I'm okay. How are the boys?"

"Well, they were upset, of course. But they're young and resilient, they'll bounce back. They're good boys."

"They are, Roy. We've been lucky to have them."

"Yeah...So what's the damage tonight?"

"Thirty-four people."

"Well, I guess I should start the film." He kisses her on the cheek. "We'll get through this, sweetheart."

"I know."

He walks slowly into the lobby with the posture of a defeated man. Passing the snack bar, Michael calls out to him.

"Mr. Corbett. We're almost out of cups."

"Okay, Michael, come into the office. I'll get you the keys for the storage room."

As Roy opens a drawer to get the keys, Michael notices the DVD. He picks it up and reads the title.

"The Last Hurrah! I saw the trailer. Looks like a great comedy!"

"You can have it if you want. No use to me."

"Gee, thanks, Mr. Corbett!"

Roy glances over at the canister.

"That's odd."

He moves closer. There is now a label on the canister—THE LAST HURRAH.

"What's this?"

He opens the canister and takes out the reel. He pulls down part of the film and holds it up to the light.

"H-o-l-y Christmas!"

He rushes from the office with the reel and heads to the projection room.

He takes off the reel that was intended to be shown and replaces it with his dad's reel. He starts to feed it into the projector. He moves to the small opening that peers into the theatre and looks to see if there have been any additions to the audience, but it looks true to Beth's calculation. He steps back and turns on the projector light, then switches on the film. He watches intently.

"It is! It's *The Last Hurrah!*"

He turns to go and tell Beth, but turns back for one more look.

"Yep! That's it all right!"

Rushing to the ticket booth he finds Beth removing the cash from the float.

"Beth! Beth!"

"What's happened? What's wrong?"

"Come with me!"

"But what about the float?"

Roy quickly grabs all the cash from the float and jams it into his pockets.

"Roy, what are you—"

"There. Let's go!"

Roy stops at the theatre doors.

"What movie are we showing?" asks Roy.

"The Guns of Navarone."

He partially opens one of the doors. Laughter pours out.

"Does that sound like the *Guns of Navarone* to you?"

"Roy, what's going on?"

"I put the DVD, *The Last Hurrah*, on top of the canister that has my dad's film inside. Beth, I think it turned the reel into that movie!"

"Oh Roy, don't play silly." Then she realizes he's serious. "You're not joking. But how could this happen?" She puts her hand over her mouth. "Your dad!"

"I don't know? Maybe, but it doesn't matter! My dad's magic, a miracle, fate, karma, whatever!" His face lights up. "If this is for real...it's a game changer! Beth, we may be back in business!"

"But Roy, how do we know it will happen again?"

"Well...just a minute."

He rushes to the snack bar.

"Michael, do you have that DVD handy?"

"Yes sir, it's right here."

He brings it out from behind the counter.

"Can I borrow that back for a few minutes?"

"Of course, Mr. Corbett."

They reach the office with the DVD. Roy finds a film canister labelled, *ABBOTT AND COSTELLO MEET FRANKENSTEIN.* He places the DVD on top of it.

"All right, we'll just give it a second...Okay, when I take away the DVD it should have a new label that reads, *THE LAST HURRAH."*

He lifts off the DVD to reveal...

"It's still Abbott and Costello!"

Beth hugs him. "It's okay, dear. It was a nice thought."

"So much for magic and miracles," says Roy, feeling totally deflated.

"Wait a minute!" says Beth. "We've got this wrong!"

"What do you mean?"

"It's your Dad's reel we need."

"Of course! How stupid of me! As soon as the movie's over we'll try it again."

"And maybe we should try using a different DVD."

"Right. Beth, get one of the boys to go down the street and buy a used DVD from that video store that's closing down. It doesn't matter what it is."

Roy waits in the projection room for the last few sprockets to click through the film. He pulls off the reel and places it into the canister and puts on the lid, then makes his way down the stairs and into the office where Beth anxiously awaits with another DVD.

"All right Beth, let's give it ago. What DVD did he pick up?"

"WHEN HARRY MET SALLY."

"Oh, that's a good one."

Beth rests the DVD on top of the canister.

They sit there staring until Beth whispers, "How long do you think we should wait?"

"I'm not sure. I'm a little nervous. But I guess if it's magic, it doesn't matter. Let's try it."

Beth takes away the DVD and there on the canister is a new label reading, *WHEN HARRY MET SALLY.*

"It worked!" says Beth.

"Not so fast," says Roy.

He opens the canister, takes out the reel, pulls down a strip of film, and holds it to the light, carefully examining it.

"What do you see, Roy?"
"I see... Beth, you have a look, my eyes aren't that good."
"Your eyes have always been good."
She takes a look. *"WHEN HARRY MET SALLY!"*
"Are you sure?" Roy says with a smile.
"You can't fool me. You knew all along."
"Like I said, we're back in business!"

—

The lobby and snack bar are overflowing with patrons once again. Roy sits in his office with his feet on the desk, talking on the phone to Moody.

"Moody. Corbett here...Yes, I did get that latest hard drive. You can send all the movies you want...Yes, my new system's working great. I've got it all covered. Works like magic!"

Roy places the hard drive on top of the old canister then lifts it off to reveal a new titled label.

"I think we'll be doing business for quite some time."

He hangs up and stands as proud as a peacock, then walks through the lobby shaking hands and mingling, as he melts into the crowd.

20

REHABILITATION CHAMBER

The eyes are closed. The face is etched with scars from years of battles that resemble a piece of relief art. Massive forearms taper down to huge, orange-tipped, sausage fingers that raise the rag-top cigarette to the dried, cracked lips. A long draw of smoke is sucked in and settles comfortably into rusted lungs. The eyelids separate. The calm, quiet mood is deceiving: Like an inactive volcano, it needs the slightest disturbance to open the gates of hell.

A nine by twelve cage keeps the beast at bay. It's been two years, seven months, nine days since its capture. Its name is Ray Manning—just a pup when it comes down to time spent on death row. Some wait years, decades with many dying of natural causes awaiting their special day. There are a few Ray-types here at the moment. Some remorseful, some in denial and then—there's Ray himself. No remorse, no denial, no guilt.

Today starts like every other day that melts away like drops from a candle—but Ray's life, or lack of it, is about to change. Something is brewing. It's coming down the pike like a huge ocean wave. You can hear it hit each cell as it moves toward that last wall in the south wing that houses Ray. He knows the sound, and the news is never good. The wave will soon arrive on his doorstep.

Some would say that Ray must have come from a troubled home. His father had to be a drunk or drug addict, and either abused him physically or emotionally—to the contrary, Ray came from a good family. His parents were model citizens of the community. His mother was an elementary school teacher who taught grades five and six for thirty-two years, and his father was a respected life insurance agent. No, Ray grew this tumor all on his own. He grew up in a quaint little town in Nebraska, just your average kid passing through the eighth grade. His mind was filled with sports and his buddies. When high school arrived he sprouted tall and slender, but not attractive enough for the girls, who outnumbered the boys almost two to one.

His parents were financially secure, and with Ray being their only child, money ran freely into his hands, which made him an easy target for some of the young ladies. Keeping them in food and entertainment presented him with certain popularity.

Even though he knew what the game was, Ray felt that at least he was getting some attention and always hoped there might be a chance things would go his way—especially in the physical sense. By the time eleventh grade came to a close, every male in school had their hormones bouncing off the walls, and Ray was no exception. But his attitude toward women took a sudden nosedive. He became tired of giving and not receiving, and resented the fact that most of his friends had girlfriends.

The designated smoking area was the place for that talk, leaving Ray on the outside. To avoid embarrassment or ridicule, he abandoned that daily ritual and became a recluse, finding himself at the far end of the schoolyard leaving him insecure, friendless, and sexless. Ray's anger was on slow boil.

At the end of the school year Ray called it quits, despite his parents' pleas to stay and at least finish high school. He went from one job to another. A week before his twenty-first birthday, he moved out of the house, leaving his parents to undergo years of worry and anguish. On this particular birthday, he celebrated by going to a strip bar with a couple of friends. Little did he know that this new road he was about to embark on—one of booze and women—would be a long and lasting one.

—

The sleazy establishment was on the edge of town for a reason, and for a twenty-one-year-old, it was the Disney World of the sordid. What made it popular was the fact that most of the patrons worked at a nearby factory and used their Friday nights to separate themselves from their jobs, their paychecks, and for some, their families. The place was full of hormonal energy.

The boys sat in front, not wanting to miss a moment of flesh. Once the first beers were dropped, it was like watching thoroughbreds out of the gate—they never looked back. The more the women danced and paraded their wares on and off stage, the thirstier Ray got, and it wasn't for beer. Then, it happened—the main attraction.

The bartender picked up the mic behind the bar and blurted out with feedback, "And now, for your pleasure, the luscious and scrumptious—the one and only, Cleo!"

She was true to her name and used her body in ways that might have Larry Flint raising an eyebrow. Ray was mesmerized. Why wouldn't he be? He had never witnessed the live pleasure of a woman's body. Magazines and videos had always been his right-hand man. When she was finished, Ray was just getting started. Besides his heart, there was another pounding to the same beat. Ray waited the rest of the night, one beer at a time.

Finally, she made her way out of the dressing room—said good night to the bartender and grabbed her coat. Ray knew she would slip out the back door, so he said farewell to his buddies and stumbled his way out a side door to intercept her in the back parking lot. When Ray arrived, she was already opening her car door. He was a little awkward in his approach, but she thought that he was cute and invited him over to her apartment—Ray was ecstatic.

In the apartment, her first move was the wrong one. She poured Scotch, and with Ray full of beer, it was sugar on a grease fire. After three generous drinks, Ray was all over her. The vintage bottle of pent-up rage had finally been uncorked. There was no gentle touch, no slow arousal—it was all about Ray. Her resistance was short-lived. Beaten senseless and beyond recognition—like being mauled by a grizzly—every damaging blow transformed her face. Blood from his fist sprayed over the wall like a Jackson Pollock painting. His powder-blue T-shirt drenched crimson. By the time Bob, the fifty-year-old neighbour, responded to her cries and burst through the door—she was playing the harp. An intense but brief struggle ensued, and Bob was shown the same courtesy.

So began the rapid decline of Ray the human being into Ray the animal—the gates of hell had swung open. Some people take to killing like others take to alcohol and drugs. Once they draw first blood it's like Bela Lugosi unchained.

For Ray, murdering a defenceless woman was part of the sexual experience. The stalking was the date—the beating, the intercourse and the murder, the climax. If the sex didn't happen while the victim was alive, Ray would have his way after her last breath. He would enjoy that too because he would have complete submission, then justify it in his distorted mind by thinking—if she didn't want me, she would have resisted.

Before his incarceration he made a modest living renovating houses. An excellent way of being inconspicuous while carrying out his after-hours activities. He learned early that his choice of victims would have to be prostitutes, for only their cohorts would be concerned if they turned up missing or dead. He would still be murdering and renovating if he hadn't changed his game plan. Ray became too cocky.

—

Madison was a university student that had just missed the bus and was going to be late for a final exam. She was now desperate and her better judgement took a back seat when Ray arrived in his pickup and she accepted his invitation for a ride. What Ray didn't know was that Madison wasn't just any student. Ray picked the cream of the crop, the top in her class in criminal law. She may not have had the upper hand in physical strength, but she did level out the playing field with her smarts. The second she stepped in, shut the door and heard the click of the lock—she knew. Her fear of Ray was briefly overruled by her anger at herself for being so stupid. Then the reality of the situation hit—like that experience you had when you were a kid and slammed your face on the side of a tree in full flight. That one brief blink of an eye, when you took your focus away and felt that nose-breaking crunch and the shock that rattled you to the core, along with the sick feeling that arrives a short time later when you see the blood and you know you've done some damage.

Ray began to engage her in simple conversation and then phased in some sexual content. She pretended to sound interested, but inside her head the wheels were spinning at the speed of light. Ray was getting excited. He reached over and began to rub the inside of her thigh. She knew better than to resist, and when she felt his hand move up her leg she quickly lowered the side window, explaining to him that he was making her hot. Ray had to change lanes, so he put his hand back on the steering wheel. Madison seized the opportunity and took her notebook from her bag, and when Ray took his eyes away and focussed on the road, she let the book drop out of the window.

She cried out for him to stop so she could retrieve it for her exam. Ray didn't want any evidence of the encounter to be left behind, so he pulled over and let her out. She ran as fast as her tight jeans would allow. Ray watched intently from his rearview mirror. She didn't stop. She scooped up the book in mid-stream and kept running, waving her arms frantically in the air at the next vehicle a short distance back.

Ray was furious that she had duped him. He launched the pickup into reverse, but it was too late. A car had already pulled over. Ray slipped it back into drive, and as he peeled away, Madison captured the license plate on her cell phone.

A woman had been murdered a few months earlier, so the local authorities were eager for any activity that could aid in the capture. It didn't take them long to put the pieces of Ray's whirlwind tour of destruction and DNA into a neat package for the courts.

—

The wave is now one cell away. Ray's eyes open wide. He cocks his head to the side to make sure. He's expecting the second worse news: someone being transferred to the penitentiary where they're fitted for the chair. The worst news—it would be him.

Finally the wave hits. JC, a slight-looking inmate from another block, shuffles the lunch cart up to Ray's door. He opens the slot to pass Ray his lunch tray featuring ground up fatty meat, a vegetable and the big treat of the day that resembles chocolate pudding. "They got some new machine," says JC as he pushes the tray through.

Ray grabs the tray and blows a cloud of smoke through the door into JC's face.

"What are you talking about?" Ray asks in his deep, monotone voice.

"A machine that gives you a choice—if you want to live or die."

Ray's short fuse ignites. "What the fuck are you saying?"

"If you decided to take this machine instead of the chair," says JC, "and you live, they let you out—you're free. But here's the kicker—they say that it could be so bad that you'd wish you had taken the chair." He acknowledges the guard standing by, staring at him. "There you are, Ray. Gotta go," he says and then carries on with his squeaky cart.

One of Ray's eyebrows lifts slightly as his brain sucks up this new bit of information. He takes a long, slow drag and pops out a large, thick smoke ring. "Gives you a choice, huh?"

He knows he'll be hearing more when he meets the other three death row inmates in the rec room. He places his food tray on the table, and then stretches out on his bed enjoying the last few draws on his cigarette as he ponders what just transpired. This could be my out, he thinks. A machine instead of the chair? What could be worse than the chair? What kind of machine lets you live, and then they let you out?

For the first time since occupying his cramped little box, Ray is excited. He just might have a future. There hasn't been a day that escape wasn't on his mind. He has read books, articles and watched every movie on prison breaks. He'd twirl all kinds of escape scenarios in his head with two or three other inmates or all by himself, preferring the latter.

"How crazy is that?" he says, "walking out the main gate a free man."

As the last spoonful of pudding makes its way down, Ray hears them coming for him—time for the rec room.

Art and another guard approach his cell. "Okay, Ray," announces Art. "Play time."

Ray gets up and turns his back to the door. He puts his arms back and through the slot. They cuff him, then open the door and lead him down a few hallways and through a few more doors. Even though his upper movement is restricted, he enjoys the freedom that the walk provides his legs.

—

When they arrive at the rec room, he's uncuffed and sent into the room like a child sent out for recess. Inside the room Marty, Greg, and Eddie are waiting at the card table. The mood is sombre—no one speaks. Ray takes his seat and he knows damn well they are all thinking what he's thinking. The cards are shuffled and dealt.

Finally, Marty steps up. "I guess you heard, huh?"

Ray looks at his cards. "I heard something."

They look at each other, somewhat surprised with his lack of interest.

"So, whatcha think, Ray?" says Eddie, the least likely to be on Ray's escape list.

Ray raises his head from the cards and looks Eddie straight in the eyes.

The apple in Eddie's throat takes the slow elevator up, then down.

Ray stares at him for a moment just to watch him squirm.

"What's wrong with you, asshole? I told you, I heard something—doesn't mean I know something."

Greg intervenes. "Come on, Ray, don't bullshit."

Ray chuckles, "So what do you want from me?"

"We want to know what you think," says Marty. "Do you believe it? Do you think it's true that we have a chance of getting out?"

Ray answers with a question of his own. "Would you rob a bank without knowing the setup? We don't know the setup. I want to know more. If you can get more, let me know. Then maybe I'll be interested."

—

The Warden is having a heated argument in his office with Helmut Friedman, the German scientist and inventor of the Rehabilitation Chamber.

"I know that the state has approved this contraption and wants us to begin using it," says the Warden. "But my question is this: Does it really work? I mean, I can't be letting murderers out of here just because some machine says they're cured."

"You're right," says Friedman. "I totally agree. The Rehabilitation Chamber is only the procedure and it does work perfectly, but whether certain individuals can be rehabilitated is another matter."

"Then what the hell's the point?"

"The point is this: They are then evaluated, and with careful analysis, it will be determined if the patient has benefited successfully to be released into society."

"And if it isn't successful?"

"Then, they would return for their original punishment."

"But if it is, we just let them walk out?"

"Yes," says Friedman, "if that's what the final analysis shows. Don't forget the financial benefit for the state, a savings of about one hundred thousand dollars a year. But there is another factor that must be considered."

There's a soft knock at the door. The Warden's assistant walks in. "Sorry to bother you, sir, but there's a skirmish going on in the cafeteria."

"Is that something I should be bothered with? Are there any weapons involved?"

"No, sir. They just wanted me to make you aware of it. They said something about a food fight."

"A food fight? Okay, you've told me."

"Yes, sir," she says and leaves the office.

"Sometimes I think I'm running a daycare. Now, where were we? Oh, yeah. So, I would just open the door, wish them all the best and have a limo waiting there to take them to some south sea island?"

"Like I had mentioned, there is one other item that will need to be addressed. We faced this problem in Germany. You must deal with the family and friends of the victims. Also the media and the death penalty advocates."

"I couldn't give a rat's ass about that!" says the Warden. "Those people will always be there. If the state wants this, then it's out of my hands, just like the death penalty—if they say kill 'em, I kill 'em. If you want to try and rehabilitate them with some machine, go ahead. Just don't come back on me if something goes wrong."

—

Ray hears the squeaky wheels of the lunch cart approaching. Another day, another meal as JC makes the rounds. Art stands looming in the background. Not a word has been spoken on the subject since the card game. Like a gator in calm waters it rests below the surface.

JC whispers, "Ray. I got somethin' for yuh."

"Prime rib?" asks Ray.

"It's a magazine."

"Skin?"

"No. It's a few months old."

"Well, that makes a difference. I'd sure like to read the latest news from a few months ago."

JC becomes anxious. He doesn't want Art to get suspicious. His job is just to feed the inmates. "No Ray, you don't understand. Quick, come and get your shit. I'll pass it to you."

Ray approaches the door. JC passes the tray with the magazine underneath.

"This better be good or you'll be eating that magazine next time you come round."

"Hey!" says Art. "You two want to talk romance, do it on your own time."

"For Christ's sake! Smoke some pot or somethin', will yuh? Just tryin to feed the guy," says JC, and then vanishes with the squeak of a wheel.

Ray places the tray on his bed and pulls out the magazine. It's folded to a specific page. He takes a close look. It's an article with a picture of Dr. Helmut Friedman.

THE REHABILITATION CHAMBER—Digital Technology catches up to Dr. Friedman's Dream Machine.

"Hmm," he says as he begins his read. "I may be closer to that prime rib than I thought."

—

A few reporters are gathered in a room with the Warden and Friedman. The Rehabilitation Chamber rests in the centre—a room within a room. The door is open for all to see—an ominous, intimidating, inner sanctum of digital hardware—like gazing into a space shuttle. In the middle of the chamber is a chair similar to a dentist's chair, but with straps for arms and legs. Each reporter takes a turn glimpsing in to view this new technology. One reporter comments, "This seems more sinister than the electric chair."

The Warden begins his introduction. "All I know, gentlemen, is what the state tells me, and sometimes that isn't much. So, I'm going to turn the floor over to Dr. Friedman, the inventor of the Rehabilitation Chamber, and he will be able to explain and answer all of your questions."

"Dr. Friedman," asks a reporter, "I understand that this chamber works on brain waves, could you elaborate on that?"

"Of course. First, I will explain how it works, and then what it does for the subject."

Another reporter pipes up. "You mean murderer, don't you?"

"If that is the case," says Friedman.

"Well what other case would there be that would need this type of procedure?" asks another.

"That's a very good question."

The reporter smiles—Friedman continues.

"The Rehabilitation Chamber is not geared for murderers alone, but for any antisocial criminal behaviour."

"Say, I'll bet the military would love to get their hands on this!" says a reporter. "It beats waterboarding!"

Friedman smiles. "They have already shown some interest."

"I should have known," says the reporter under his breath.

"Now," says Friedman, "getting back to your original question of how this extraordinary machine operates. The subject is seated in this chair and the headgear you see resting on the chair is equipped with sensors and placed over the subject's head. Then the computer generates a series of brain wave frequencies at specific levels and into the brain—these being gamma, beta, alpha, theta and finally, delta—where the brain goes into unconsciousness or a deep sleep. Once this is done, we begin to supply binaural beats to stimulate the episodic memory where more personal memories are stored, such as emotions and personal associations of a certain place or time. When we have that, we bring in the visual memory. The sensors pick up this information and send it back to the computer where we can visually see the patient's memory on the monitor."

"Now Dr. Friedman," says another, "how does all of this rehabilitate the murderer?"

The Professor glances at the Warden and notices that his mind seems to be elsewhere.

"This is the part that I think the Warden would be interested in hearing."

The Warden straightens up.

"If the prisoner is a murderer, we alter the visual picture and the episodic memory to allow that prisoner to take the place of the victim he perpetrated."

"What?" says a reporter.

"In other words, he will see the murder taking place from the victim's perspective. If the subject can handle the torture and killing they bestowed on their victim without trauma or remorse, they go back to prison. But, if a total acknowledgement of the crime is understood and empathy now becomes the driving force and the experience doesn't kill them or destroy them mentally, they will be rehabilitated and should, at that point, be released."

"That's incredible! So who will be the first guinea pig?"

"That will be decided by the Warden."

—

Ray sits on the edge of his bed pondering the possibilities of life on the street. There's a childlike twinkle in his eyes and a sideways grin on his face. "Rehabilitation Chamber, I do like the sound of that. And when I get out, there's going to be a hell of rehabilitation."

—

The Warden takes on the task at hand. Sitting at his desk he mulls through file folders of those on death row. He grabs another folder—it's Ray's. "There's a challenge for Friedman's machine."

In the rec room the boys are playing cards when Ray shows. His demeanor is unusual. He seems suspiciously upbeat.

"Ray, you want in?" asks Eddie.

"Sure, why not, I feel lucky today."

Just as he pulls up a chair the guard hollers, "Ray! Warden wants to see you!"

Greg decides to give him a jab. "Guess it ain't your lucky day, Ray."

Ray stands with a smile. "We'll see about that. Carry on, boys."

—

The Warden sits back in his chair with his hands behind his head awaiting Ray's arrival. There's a timid knock at the door. His assistant enters.

"Ray, sir."

Ray walks in with a guard. The Warden greets him with a very relaxed and unfamiliar smile.

"Ray! Have a seat."

Ray makes himself at home. The Warden motions the guard to leave. The secretary stands erect with her hands folded in front of her.

The Warden eyeballs her. “Is there something else?”

“No, sir,” she says and departs to the security of her desk.

Ray sits in a leather chair and rubs the armrests. “Nice upholstery. So, what is it today, Warden? I didn’t eat all my peas at lunch?”

“I have a proposition for you, Ray.”

“It uh...wouldn’t have anything to do with a certain machine, would it?”

“Well, it looks like you’re right on top of things.”

“That’s what the ladies used to say,” says Ray with a smile.

“So, how much do you know about this machine?”

“Enough to know that it could put me over the fence.”

“It could also be fatal.”

Ray spreads his arms out. “And this ain’t? You should have been a comedian, Warden.”

“So, are you interested?”

“Will it screw up my brain?”

“Now who's being the comedian? Dr. Friedman says that any altering in the brain would be done by the patient themselves —how they handle their own emotions. Do you have any, Ray?”

“Brains or emotions?”

“Guess we’ll find that out soon enough.”

—

Ray is back in the rec room shuffling cards when the other three inmates stroll in.

“Well boys,” says Ray with an ear-to-ear grin. “What’s the game today?”

“Look at the smile on that!”

“If I didn’t know any better, I’d think the Warden wined, dined, and proposed marriage to this boy.”

“And it looks like Ray accepted. How’s your asshole, Ray, still sore?”

They all have a laugh as they sit around the table.

“Okay, Ray,” says Marty. “What’s the real story?”

Ray continues with the cards. "The real story is this—I'll be wining and dining, but it won't be with the Warden, and it sure as hell won't be in this fucking place."

They look at each other puzzled.

"Boys, I'm going to be waltzing out of here with the Warden's blessing."

"What do you mean, you're walking out?" asks Greg.

Ray waves his arms in the air. "I'm being rehabilitated! Praise the Lord!" He lets loose with a booming, satanic laugh that raises the hair on their backs.

—

The Warden is enjoying his morning coffee when the secretary rushes in.

"Sir, Dr.—"

Friedman barges past her.

"Warden, I have to discuss the patient you've selected!"

"Well, this is a surprise. I've barely finished my first coffee of the day."

"You can't use the chamber on him!"

"Ray; and why not?"

"I've looked at his files. He is the ultimate psychopath! There is no rehabilitation here whatsoever. He has zero empathy! He's hollow! There is nothing inside this man!"

The Warden comes out swinging. "Look! You come here with claims about your machine, and now you say it won't work! What kind of shit are you trying to pull?"

"It works, but there has to be something going on in the brain that can offer hope. If you want to start a fire, you at least need a spark. There is no spark here, therefore, no fire. You'll have to choose someone else."

The Warden has had enough. He slams his hands on the desk and stands to confront him.

"Now you listen to me, Friedman! Ray's the worst guy we've got here! If you don't use him, there's going to be questions! They want to see this bloody machine work on this bastard that the system has no hope in hell of saving! If you can prove yourself with this guy, they'll believe in this Rehabilitation Chamber." He takes in a deep, slow breath to calm down. "All right, let me go in another direction. If you don't go ahead with this, your name won't be worth a dime. Respect for you and your machine will be kaput. Capisce? It's up to you. You choose."

Friedman's eyes shift from side to side as he mulls it over.

"Obviously, there is nothing to choose; it appears my back is up against the wall. All right, against my better judgement, we'll do it your way."

"Now you're talking!"

—

Ray is lying on his bed contemplating a bright, new future when the squeaky lunch cart wheels its way toward his cell.

"Lunch, Ray," says JC with some reserve.

Ray doesn't respond.

"Ray?"

"I hear you." Ray's up and JC hands him the tray through the opening.

"Good luck today, Ray. I hope you make it out."

"Thanks." Ray looks down at his meal. "Same shit as every other day." He yells to Art. "Hey! Don't I get a special meal today? Where's my prime rib?"

Art laughs. "You only get that when they roast yuh."

"Yeah, well that ain't going to happen."

"Now that's disappointing. I've already put in my request for a drumstick."

JC responds under his breath, "Bastard."

—

The Rehabilitation Chamber awaits its featured guest. Beside the chair stands Dr. Friedman and the Warden as Ray is escorted in by two guards.

"Hello, Ray. I'm Dr. Friedman."

Ray looks around. "What, no party balloons?"

"Please, sit down."

Ray sits in the chair. "A little off the top and leave the sideburns."

The Professor picks up the headgear. "Ray, I'm going to place this on your head. I want you to relax. Try to clear your mind. You will begin to hear soft, soothing music." He puts the headgear over Ray's head.

"I prefer Neil Young."

The music begins.

"Oh, that's sweet. Pass me my slippers, will yuh?"

The guards strap his legs and arms.

"Now," says Friedman. "I want you to close your eyes and just enjoy the music."

Ray closes his eyes. He begins to drift through darkness. Flashing images appear—his cell—the rec room—other inmates. It begins to scramble and distort. He sees the tunnel that some describe in their near-death experiences. He thinks he's been tricked and that they are actually executing him. But something is missing. There is no light at the end of this tunnel. He becomes uneasy and another thought occurs to him—if there's a tunnel and no light at the end of it, is he going to hell? Not that he thought he didn't deserve to—just never believed it existed.

The tunnel fades and he becomes one with the beautiful, tranquil music that he had earlier criticized. It is then replaced by loud, booming music. The volume intensifies to the point where there is no room in his mind for anything else.

An image of a crowded bar explodes on the visionary screen of his mind. This looks familiar, thinks Ray. Wait a minute, something's wrong here. I'm looking around the room, but I can't control where I'm looking.

The bartender looks right into his eyes. He smiles and says, "You looked good up there tonight, Amy. I love the new routine."

Amy? Is he talking to me? Who the hell is Amy? He hears a young woman's voice that seems to be coming from inside of him.

"Thanks, Mike. See you next week."

What is this shit? He finds himself walking out a door and into the street. I remember this place. He's startled as he sees himself walking toward Amy. Shit! That's me!

"Hey sweetheart, I saw your show tonight. You were great. I like the way you move."

Amy responds, "Thanks. I noticed you drooling."

"Yeah, me and fifty other guys."

I know this girl, Amy. Now I remember. I did her in.

"So, where you headed?"

"Just home."

"Need a little company? I've got a nice bottle of Jack Daniels in the car."

No! Don't do it! says Ray.

"My favourite," says Amy.

"So, where's your place?"

She nods, "Across the street, above that convenience store."

"Now that makes sense; convenience at a convenience store."

Brilliant line, asshole. Run, Amy! Get the hell out of there!

"Follow me, Big Boy."

Amy's apartment is small, but cozy. Furniture is sparse and outdated. Couch, coffee table, end table, and a kitchen table for two, pushed into a corner of the living room.

"Make yourself at home. I'll get glasses."

She heads for the bathroom before entering the kitchen. Her personal laundry is hand-washed and displayed over the shower pole. She pulls it down and throws it into the tub and shuts the curtain—checks the toilet and gives it a flush.

I didn't need to see that, thinks Ray.

The drinks are poured and the two settle in for an intimate encounter with different objectives: Ray's being physical—Amy's financial. She figured that with the amount he's consumed at the bar, a few extra shots of whisky should render him inoperable, and his Friday night wallet would be ripe for the picking.

Amy was never good at math and her adding up of the situation was a gross miscalculation. She forgot to add in Ray's physical presence and the fact that the night also included pizza and wings to slow the distribution of alcohol.

After twenty minutes a third of a bottle is all that remains. Ray decides that the end of small talk is way overdue. He makes his uncompromising move on Amy.

Being inside of Amy has now become terrifying for Ray. He's making out with himself. His tongue entering his own mouth —and fingers all over the map. He screams out! But it's Amy's voice he hears.

"Ray, stop it! You're hurting me!"

I can't take it! Get me out of here! Amy! Stop him! Stop him!

"Ray, stop it! You're being a jerk!" yells Amy.

"Shut up!" Ray is all over her like molasses on bread. He starts ripping off her clothes.

"Get the hell off me, Ray! Ray! This is fucking crazy! I can't take this shit!

Ray puts his hand over her mouth. She bites it. He goes into a rage and starts punching her hard in the face. Amy starts screaming! Ray starts screaming!

"Uhhh! Stop! You're killing me!"

He watches through Amy's blurred eyes, as Ray gets up and stumbles into the kitchen. Ray's back with a kitchen knife and straddles Amy. He raises the knife.

"No! Don't do it! You're killing me! Raaay!"

"You little bitch!" He plunges the knife deep into Amy's chest! Ray feels it all the way. The slicing flesh! The cracking of bone!

"Uhhh! Help me! Somebody help me!"

The stabbing continues. Blood splatters everywhere. Ray feels his mind exploding into fragmented bits of unrelated memory, then speeding back through the tunnel.

—

Ray is back in the chair screaming, crying and struggling to get out. He's drenched in sweat. The headgear and restraints are quickly removed.

Friedman anticipated this reaction and speaks to Ray in a calm voice. "It's all right, Ray. You're back now. Nothing can hurt you. You're safe."

Ray is going into shock. The guards place him on a gurney and once again strap him down.

The Warden looks concerned. "Shouldn't we give him something to calm him down?"

"No. He has to do this on his own," says Friedman. "Okay, take him back to his cell and don't let him out of your sight."

The Warden is stunned. "Holy shit! I've never seen anything like it! To witness a murder first hand is the most frightening thing I've ever seen. And to watch Ray just break down like that. He just blew his mind. Is he going to remember this?"

"Of course, that is the whole point; but will it be enough to change him?"

"Christ, it would me."

"But you're not Ray, and I'm not convinced yet. We have to observe him for a while."

—

For the next three days no one saw or heard anything of Ray. It was as if he had taken the chair. On the afternoon of the fourth day the boys were playing cards and discussing Ray's fate.

"I heard he freaked right out."

"I can't see that. Not Ray."

"Remember what they said, if you survive it, you'll wish you hadn't."

"Yeah, but this is Ray."

At that moment the rec room door opens and all eyes turn. It's Ray. His look is strangely tranquil, but not drugged.

He walks over to them and puts on a smile like they've never seen before—pleasantly eerie.

"Hey fellas, who's winning?" he asks in a calm tone.

They're not sure how to handle it. "Hey Ray. Did you want in?"

"Sure," says Ray. "What's the game?"

"Just straight poker, Ray."

"Good. I like simple."

—

The Warden and Friedman are discussing Ray's progress.

"But he looks good. He is different. You did it, Friedman."

"I still have some reservations."

"What's the problem?"

"The problem is this: It's true, he was in a state of shock. He was terrified. But was it for the horrific pain and suffering she was going through, or was it just for the pain he was enduring?"

"Ah, come on! What the hell does that matter? You saw him; he was like a little lamb. It was a success and now he gets to walk out the door, just like you wanted. He gets that second chance to change his life around. Friedman, you're a genius."

At this point Friedman is just as concerned with the Warden's attitude as he is with Ray's.

"I don't know if I can accept this."

"Friedman, don't do this to me!"

"To you? This isn't about you or me. It's about—"

"Now you listen to me!"

"No!" Friedman fires back. "You listen to me!"

The Warden backs off when he sees the anger in Friedman's eyes.

"I can't and won't approve of this without further observation! This isn't someone with the flu! This isn't just changing the life of one person, it's transforming a whole society! We have to be responsible! Can you not see that?"

The Warden changes his tactics. He speaks calmly, almost patronizing.

"Of course, I'm sorry. This is a game changer. Now, how much time do you think you would need?"

"Three weeks."

The Warden is taken aback. "Three! Okay, three weeks it is."

—

After the first week of observation, the Warden receives a call.

"Yes, Governor."

"What's the holdup over there? I've got everyone in the state interested in this machine. Did it work or not?"

"I think it did, Governor, but Dr. Friedman wants more time, another two weeks."

"We can't wait that long! Even the President's on my back! Do you know how much it costs us to keep these guys under lock and key?"

"Yes, sir, I sign the checks."

"How long have you been at that job now?"

"Twenty-three years, sir."

"You think your opinion counts?"

"I'd like to think so."

"Then that's good enough for me. Release that bastard so we can start saving some money around here and run it like the corporation it is!"

A smile widens on the Warden's face. "Yes, sir!"

—

The next morning Dr. Friedman makes his way down the corridor to the wing that holds Ray. A guard meets him at the door.

"You here for Ray?"

"Certainly."

"I'm afraid you're too late."

Friedman's face tightens. "What do you mean, too late?"

"The Warden released him about an hour ago."

The blood drains from his face. It's hard to imagine that anyone could extract the emotions of disbelief, fear and anger into one singular, distorted, facial expression and have it all squeeze out of his mouth like toothpaste—"F-I-C-K-E-N!"

Ray, now out of prison, is celebrating at Chuck's Roadhouse with friends.

"How's that prime rib, Ray?" asks Bob.

"Primo."

"I can't believe you're here. This must feel like a dream to you," says Frank.

"Yes, it does, Frank," he says in a calm voice.

"You sure have changed."

"Sometimes change is good, Bob."

Ray gets up from his chair. "Well, I'm going to leave you boys." He looks at his watch for the first time in three years. "I have a lovely lady waiting for me."

"That's nice, Ray. Have yourself a good time," says Frank.

Ray turns to leave...

"Yeah, you're a lot better now, Ray. You used to be such an asshole," says Chad.

They all freeze and look to Ray for a reaction. But there is none. Ray slowly turns back and approaches Chad with a smile.

"Well, Chad, sometimes you just don't want to disappoint your friends."

Ray grabs the steak knife from his plate and sticks it into Chad's hand, impaling it to the table. Chad lets out a painful holler.

"Have a good evening, gentlemen," says Ray, then turns once more and calmly walks out the door.

—

He arrives at his car, opens the door and hears a woman's voice.

"Hi, Ray."

He turns to see this beautiful young woman smiling at him.

Ray smiles back. "Well, hello."

She walks up to him. “How’s your new lot in life feel?’

“Feels great,” he says as he tries to figure out who she is. “I’m sorry, have we met before?”

“No, we’ve never met, but I know of you. My name’s Ruth. If you have some time tomorrow, we could get together for a drink.”

“Well that sounds great. How about meeting at Chuck’s about seven?”

“Sounds good, I’ll see then.” She turns and walks away.

As Ray gets into his car she turns back. “I’m Amy’s sister.”

Ray acknowledges with a wave. “Amy?” He turns the key in the ignition. “Amy!”

The car explodes into a blazing ball of fire! Ruth smiles and continues to walk away.

THE END

Dear Reader,
If you enjoyed this book, please tell your friends,
and write a review on GoodReads.com and Amazon.
Thank you, Neil

www.ingramcontent.com/pod-product-compliance
Lightning Source LLC
Chambersburg PA
CBHW070804180626
46818CB00001B/96
* 9 7 8 1 9 4 7 6 4 6 2 1 6 *